SKIES OVER CALEDONIA

THE HIGHLANDS SERIES

BOOK FOUR

SAMANTHA YOUNG

Skies Over Caledonia

A Highlands Series Novel

By Samantha Young
Copyright © 2024 Samantha Young

Cover Design By Hang Le
Couple Photography by Wander Aguiar
Edited by Jennifer Sommersby Young
Proofread by Julie Deaton

ALSO BY SAMANTHA YOUNG

Other Adult Contemporary Novels by Samantha Young

Play On

As Dust Dances

Black Tangled Heart

Hold On: A Play On Novella

Into the Deep

Out of the Shallows

Hero

Villain: A Hero Novella

One Day: A Valentine Novella

Fight or Flight

Much Ado About You

A Cosmic Kind of love

The Love Plot

October Kiss

On Dublin Street Series:

On Dublin Street

Down London Road

Before Jamaica Lane

Fall From India Place

Echoes of Scotland Street

Moonlight on Nightingale Way

Until Fountain Bridge (a novella)
Castle Hill (a novella)
Valentine (a novella)
One King's Way (a novella)
On Hart's Boardwalk (a novella)

Hart's Boardwalk Series:
The One Real Thing
Every Little Thing
Things We Never Said
The Truest Thing

The Adair Family Series:
Here With Me
There With You
Always You
Be With Me
Only You

The Highlands Series:
Beyond the Thistles
Among the Heather
Through the Glen
A Highland Christmas: A Novella
Skies Over Caledonia

Young Adult contemporary titles by Samantha Young
The Impossible Vastness of Us
The Fragile Ordinary

About the Author

Samantha is a *New York Times, USA Today,* and *Wall Street Journal* bestselling author and a Goodreads Choice Awards Nominee. Samantha has written over 55 books and is published in 31 countries. She writes emotional and angsty romance, often set where she resides—in her beloved home country Scotland. Samantha splits her time between her family, writing and chasing after two very mischievous cavapoos.

ACKNOWLEDGMENTS

First, a big thank you to my mum for just being the bestest friend a girl could ask for. Second, thank you to my buddy Catherine Cowles for reassuring me along the way that I was doing justice to Allegra and Jared's story. And for just being a fantastic friend and awesome human.

I have to thank my amazing editor Jennifer Sommersby Young for reminding me I can do this thing called writing. Even after all these years, that encouragement from people I admire is appreciated more than I can say.

Thank you to Julie Deaton for proofreading *Skies Over Caledonia* and catching all the things. I'm so glad you fell in love with Jared!

And thank you to my bestie and PA extraordinaire Ashleen Walker for helping to lighten the load and supporting me more than ever these past few years. I really couldn't do this without you.

The life of a writer doesn't stop with the book. Our job expands beyond the written word to marketing, advertising, graphic design, social media management, and more. Help from those in the know goes a long way. A huge thank-you to Nina Grinstead, Kim Cermak, Kelley Beckham and all the team at Valentine PR for your encouragement, support, insight and advice. You all are amazing!

A huge thank you to Sydney Thisdelle for doing all your techy ad magic to deliver my stories into the hands of new readers. You make my life infinitely easier and I'm so grateful!

Thank you to every single blogger, Instagrammer, and

book lover who has helped spread the word about my books. You all are appreciated so much! On that note, a massive thank-you to the fantastic readers in my private Facebook group, Samantha Young's Clan McBookish. You're truly special. You're a safe space of love and support on the internet and I couldn't be more grateful for you.

A massive thank-you to Hang Le for creating another stunning cover in this series. In fact, I can't remember the last time readers were this in love with a cover. You are a tremendous talent! And thank you to Wander Aguiar for the beautiful couple photography that brings Jared and Allegra to life.

As always, thank you to my agent Lauren Abramo for making it possible for readers all over the world to find my words. You're phenomenal, and I'm so lucky to have you.

A huge thank-you to my family and friends for always supporting and encouraging me.

Finally, to you, thank you for reading. It means more than I can ever say.

For Mum,
I'm so proud to be your daughter. Thank you for being my best friend, and for having my back no matter what. Love you always and forever.

AUTHOR NOTE

Dear Reader,

It's impossible to get married in Scotland on the spur of the moment. You need a minimum of twenty-nine days for the necessary applications to be processed. Please forgive any inaccuracies for the sake of fiction, but I was unable to wait twenty-nine days. It would have given Jared or Allegra (most likely Jared) too much time to change their mind about their scheme.

And well ... we couldn't have that now, could we?

PROLOGUE
ALLEGRA

Five years ago

Ardnoch, Scotland

I spotted him as soon as I strolled into the Gloaming. I froze, blocking the exit.

There were many appealing things about Scotland. Its beauty was a feast to my artist eyes. The musical brogue that changed from place to place. The fact that I could hang out legally in a bar at twenty years old if I wanted to. And the men.

At least the men here in the Highlands.

They were growing them damn nice here in the Highlands.

Like him. Sitting at the bar. Laughing with the pub's hot bartender and co-owner, Arran Adair, whom I'd already met.

A traditional old building in the middle of the Highland village of Ardnoch, the Gloaming was exactly what you imagined a Scottish pub to be. Low ceilings with dark wooden beams, a roaring hearth on one wall, booth seating covered in a smart tartan fabric skirting the edges, with a few cute tables and chairs here and there. The pub was attached to the rest of the hotel and restaurant, and from the look of the architecture, it was the oldest part of the building.

I loved its atmosphere. As an artist, I was more focused on glasswork, but I liked to paint too. Mostly landscapes. I was not a Renoir by any means, but moments like this almost made me want to pick up a paintbrush. The pub was busy, but not as crowded as I knew it could get during the summer.

A large dog laid out by the fire, soaking up the heat on this dreary September day. People were smiling and talking, all the while nursing their drinks as chart music drifted out of the speakers on low volume.

My attention returned to Arran and the delicious man he conversed with. Arran owned the Gloaming along with his brother Lachlan, who also owned a private members-only club for TV and film professionals. It was situated in his family's converted ancestral castle and estate on the outskirts of the village. My father, legendary film director Wesley Howard, was a club board member. We had a beach house on the estate, and my big sister Aria was the club's hospitality manager.

Whenever I could get away from school, I visited. With Aria here and, well, just Ardnoch's whole vibe ... this place felt way more like home than Malibu ever had. Even Rhode Island where I attended the School of Design didn't hold my heart like this place. I couldn't explain why it so appealed to me.

But views like the one at the bar certainly explained some of it.

He was broad-shouldered and I could see the ripple of his biceps straining against his dark T-shirt as he leaned into the bar. Laughter lit up his face, and I felt an answering swoop of attraction low in my belly. I aged him at between five and ten years older than me, with dark hair cut short at the sides and long on top. I watched him a few seconds longer as he scrubbed a hand over his dark, neatly trimmed beard before saying something that made Arran laugh in return.

The man's answering grin was so sexy, I swear my knees trembled.

Yes, please.

Although I had no time for a guy in my life right now. I'd had my fair share of trauma these last few years, I was unsettled in life, and unsure of where I was going. But that didn't mean I couldn't have fun occasionally, and the guy at the bar made me want to have a whole lot of fun. I was supposed to be meeting Aria and her friends here in a little while, but I could fit in flirting before that.

Crossing the room, I hopped up easily on to the bar stool next to the hot mystery man. Our eyes met and I sucked in a breath. The stranger had the most beautiful jade-green eyes I'd ever seen. I wanted to capture the cool, pure color in my art.

For a moment, I think I gaped until his eyes flared before warming. Shaking myself, my answering smile was flirtatious before I looked at the bartender. "Hey, Arran. Can I have a club soda, please?"

Arran nodded in greeting, a knowing twinkle in his eye. "Of course. How are you?"

"Good. You?"

"Aye, always." He winked at me. "Allegra, this is Jared. Jared, this is Allegra." The helpful Scotsman moved to the end of the bar to make my drink.

Feeling the mystery man's gaze, I turned to meet it. Wow. Those eyes. I just couldn't get over them. "Hey. Jared."

A smile quirked the corner of his gorgeous mouth as he held out a large hand to me. "Nice to meet you, Allegra." His voice was deep but smooth. His accent was a little more pronounced than Arran's, and I wondered if he was from another part of the country.

"You too." As my fingers slid against his, a shiver skated down my spine, awakening tingles around the curve of my breasts. Whoa. His hand closed suddenly around mine like he'd felt the spark.

"Allegra is an unusual name." He seemed reluctant to release my hand but slowly did.

At his questioning tone, I offered, "My mom is Italian." I didn't want to mention that he'd probably heard of Chiara Howard since she was a retired supermodel. When someone didn't recognize me or know who I was, I liked to keep that information to myself for a while. I wanted people to get to know me for me, not for who my famous parents were.

"Really? But you're American? Tourist or ..." His eyes narrowed, something like disappointment dimming his expression. "You're not a member of Ardnoch Estate?"

His obvious lack of enthusiasm over the idea made me even more reluctant to tell him who I was. I laughed instead. "Me? An actor? Um ... no. I'm an artist. Just visiting."

A club soda landed a little loudly in front of me and I raised my gaze from it to Arran. He wore a look of admonishment, like he knew what I was doing.

Mind your business, I directed silently.

He shrugged and moved away to serve a newcomer.

"A traveling artist," Jared presumed, raising an eyebrow. "You sell any of your work?"

"I do. I mostly make art from glass. A few galleries sell my stuff." That was the truth. But I didn't mention that in compromising with my family about my future, I was also a student back in the States.

"Impressive."

"What do you do?"

He smirked, took a slow sip of his beer, and wiped the foam off his lips. My eyes snagged on his mouth, my breath hitching a little at the thought of it pressed to mine. "I'm a farmer."

"No." The word shot out of my mouth in disbelief. "There's no way."

Jared raised an eyebrow.

"No, I don't mean that how it came out. I just ... you just ... well, you don't look like a farmer."

"What's a farmer supposed to look like?"

Wincing, I groaned. "I'm being offensive, aren't I?"

He snorted, those stunning eyes twinkling. "It takes a lot more than that to offend me."

"You have the most beautiful eyes," I blurted out.

His expression warmed again as his gaze danced over my face. "So do you."

My large dark eyes were my favorite feature, but his were something else. "I'd love to capture the colors."

"Forever the artist?"

"Maybe." I leaned toward him. "So ... farming? Were you born into it? You had to be. You can't be more than ... twenty-five?" I guessed.

He nodded slowly. "Spot on."

"Well? Born into it?"

Something sad flickered in his gaze and he looked down into his beer. "Aye, something like that."

Without thinking, I reached over to place a hand on his arm. It was warm and strong beneath my palm. "I'm sorry if I said something to upset you."

His attention drifted to my lips. The air charged between us, and I found myself leaning in closer. I couldn't explain the pull. I didn't know him. All I knew was that I was physically attracted to him on a level I'd never experienced before.

And I wanted to have sex with him.

There.

That was being honest with myself.

After my last relationship, it took a year of therapy before I finally started dating again, but I'd kept it casual. No relationships. Just hookups. My therapist, Gail, said that was normal and healthy for now, especially for someone my age.

At that moment, I wanted to get naked and casual with Jared. For the good of my mental health. Ha!

When our eyes met, I knew he saw the wicked thoughts in them.

We now *both* leaned toward each other, and my breathing grew shallow. "You fancy getting out of here?" he asked gruffly.

Straight to the point. I liked it.

I nodded, forgetting the purpose of my being in the Gloaming in the first place.

Reading the heated triumph on his face, we both moved to slide off our stools when my sister's voice sounded behind me. "Oh, good, you've met Jared."

I whipped around as my feet hit the floor and looked up at my big sister. Aria stood by the bar, her arm around her fiancé North. There was a tightness in her eyes, despite her warm smile as she glanced between us. "It looks like we're first to arrive. Walker and Sloane are grabbing a booth." She gestured across the bar where, sure enough, her friends were seated, watching us.

Just then, the pub door opened, and Sarah McCulloch and Theo Cavendish walked in. Theo was a famous screenwriter and club member. Sarah was a local who'd worked at Ardnoch as a housekeeper. She quit last year to pursue a successful career as a crime writer and was now in a relationship with Theo.

Familiarity hit me. I glanced from Sarah to Aria to Jared.

I *knew* him.

He was Sarah's cousin. I'd witnessed the awful moment he'd told Sarah that their grandfather had died. Their grandfather ... the farmer.

From whom Jared had inherited the farm.

Oh my God.

"Jared, this is my little sister, Allegra. She's only twenty and in college in the States," Aria added pointedly.

My head whipped around as I glowered at my sister. At her not-so-subtle warning.

But as Sarah and Theo approached and everyone greeted one another, I let my gaze wander to Jared. Whatever warmth had been in his expression was gone, replaced by a guarded look when our eyes met.

That wariness hurt more than it should, considering we barely knew each other, so as a whole group of us huddled around a booth, I did my best to be friendly to everyone. To engage. But my body was still wound up from the anticipation of sex and the disappointment of it not happening. I couldn't help the way my attention drifted back to Jared as he sat directly opposite me. I wanted that warmth back. I wanted him to reveal his obvious attraction from earlier. He wouldn't.

So I pestered him with questions about the farm, showing him my interest had not waned upon the discovery that our family members were friends.

But *his* interest had waned.

Jared made that perfectly obvious when he excused himself from our table and began flirting with some woman at the bar. She was attractive and definitely older than me.

They left together.

And I told myself the crushing feeling in my chest was an overreaction, and I should probably talk to my therapist about why.

Yet I think I knew why.

Some people I met, when they discovered who my family

was, just wanted to hang around me to be near the spotlight and success and fame. Others assumed negative things about me, that I was spoiled and pampered and didn't know a damn thing about real life. My own family thought that, so why not him?

Or—my rational mind fought through my insecurities—maybe he realized it was too complicated to hook up with someone in his friendship circle.

It doesn't matter, anyway, I told myself as I left the bar with my sister and her fiancé. I didn't want to hook up with a guy who could so easily trade in sex with me for someone else on the same night. That was a turnoff. I didn't want to be interchangeable.

Even if it was just sex ... I wanted to feel wanted for *me* in that moment, not just a body.

I had more important things to worry about than a stupid attraction to Jared McCulloch.

Like where I was going to live when college finished next year. What I was going to do. How I was going to build my business as an artist. How I could find a way to be close to Aria, who was the one person in the world who made me feel safe.

So much to think about.

When you're a kid, no one talks about how overwhelming being an adult will be. One minute, there's structure and safety and rules to guide you ... and the next you're flung out into the big wide world and expected to fly with wings you've never used before.

It didn't help when those wings were a little broken.

But I had to figure out how to use mine. And fast.

ONE

ALLEGRA

Present day

Edinburgh Airport, Scotland

Sudden nerves filled my belly as I watched the frown deepen on the customs attendant's face. This was taking longer than it usually did, and I should know. Since graduating from art school four years ago, I'd been flying back and forth to Scotland. Legally, I could only stay for six months on a visitor's visa, so I'd fly wherever the wind blew me for a few months and then fly back to Scotland for another six months.

Suddenly, she looked up, expression blank. "You'll need to come with me, Ms. Howard."

My heart thudded in my chest. "Why?"

"Come with me, please," she insisted sharply.

Okay. Yeah. Don't argue with customs officials, Allegra!

Feeling like I was being led to jail, I followed the short, scary woman beyond the customs desks, ignoring the curious gazes of the other passengers behind me. She held open a door for me, gesturing me inside a small room.

Thankfully, I didn't have a ton of luggage because I'd slowly brought everything I needed over here these last few years. But I was going to miss my connecting flight to Inverness if whatever this was didn't end soon. I said as much to the attendant and she ignored me, gesturing toward a standard table with a chair on either side. To my frazzled, jet-lagged brain, it looked like an interrogation room.

I let go of my small carry-on roller bag and slumped into the chair. "What's going on?"

She waited until she was seated opposite me. "Ms. Howard, we'd just like to ask you a few questions regarding the reason for your visit to Scotland today."

I leaned toward the iPad she had in front of her. "Didn't I put that on my forms?"

"Yes. But considering you've spent an accumulated forty-two months in Scotland in the last four years, that suggests to Immigration that you're permanently living in the UK without the correct visa."

Oh shit.

I gaped at her, not sure how to respond because she was kind of right.

"Two of my colleagues are on their way to ask you a few questions about this. Hopefully, it won't be too long and we can sort this out."

"My sister lives here," I said hurriedly. "I'm only visiting my sister. I promise."

"Like I said, my colleagues will discuss that with you."

An overwhelming panic filled me at the thought of being sent back to the States. The kind that made my breathing turn shallow and my cheeks tingle. As the woman left the room, I closed my eyes and focused on the breathing exercises I'd learned while studying mindfulness.

It will be okay, I promised myself, trying to shove out the fear.

———

Somewhere between Inverness and Ardnoch
Eight hours later

We were barely twenty minutes into the hour drive to Ardnoch when my cab driver started making disapproving sounds that soon turned into a jumble of Scottish I didn't understand. Except for the curse words. Those I understood.

"What's wrong?" I asked from the back seat of the old taxi.

"Warning light's on. Sorry, doll, I'll need to find somewhere to pull over."

I slumped back in the seat, cursing myself for getting in a car that looked like it was older than me. But the guy had been the only taxi left outside the airport.

It was early June. Tourists were crawling all over the Highlands, taking all the cabs with them.

Sure enough, he slowed the car and pulled it up onto the grass at the side of the road. I'd visited enough times, spent hours and days exploring the Highlands, to know that the tranquil water gleaming in the late-afternoon sun on our left was an inlet of the Cromarty Firth.

We were still a good forty minutes from home.

Home.

If I didn't do something soon and fast, my home would be taken from me.

I threw the thought away because it tightened my chest. Leaning forward, I asked, "Can I call someone for you?"

"On it." The cabbie waved his cell at me and then proceeded to contact someone called "Bowbeh." I assumed his name was actually Bobby. Scottish people. You gotta love those accents.

I did love those accents.

Pressing my nose almost to the passenger window, I sighed heavily. I loved the landscape. I loved the dichotomy of the soft, the gentle, against the rugged wildness. Most of the Scots I'd met were earthy and real in a way I hadn't always experienced growing up as a child of a famous director and supermodel. Scots had a strong sense of self, of country, had a great sense of humor and were not easily offended, which was refreshing in a world where everyone was offended by everything.

Except for Ardnoch during the summer when tourists descended, the Highlands felt like it was part of another universe entirely. It sounded kind of crazy since I was only twenty-five years old, but I'd found peace here. This beautiful, largely untouched place filled my soul and calmed the voices of a past that still haunted me.

And this place had one hold on my heart that no other had.

Aria was here.

My big sister.

My safe place.

Tears threatened at the thought of not being near her anymore. To returning to long-distance phone calls and daily texts. It just wasn't the same.

June wasn't overly hot in this part of the country, but the sun was beating through the window and with the car engine off, there was no AC.

The driver hung up. "Sorry, lass. My mate is coming to

tow me to Inverness. We'll sort you out with a taxi when we get back."

Shit.

I was jet-lagged, worried, and I just wanted to be in Ardnoch already. Nodding numbly, I mumbled, "I'm going to step out for some air."

"Be careful of that road. It's a sixty."

I knew that from the way cars flew past us, making the vehicle shudder. "I'll stick to the grass," I promised.

I stepped out of the car, my sneakers hitting the lush green blades. My legs trembled a little as I straightened. Shutting the car door behind me, I stared out at the inlet. Across the way, a patchwork of fields in varying shades of green, dotted with trees here and there, swept upward. Peeking behind them were hills I'd seen covered in snow only a few short months ago.

The sky above was blue, enjoying a reprieve from the clouds that were now floating into the distance. The sun warmed my face even as a gentle breeze swept up from the glassy surface of the firth. The musky, sweet smell of a nearby cluster of purple thistles mingled in the air with the salty scent of sea and the earthy odor of the surrounding fields.

Home.

I dragged a shaking hand through my hair, trying to quiet the rising panic. Sucking in a gulp of air, I began to pace along the grassy roadside. *Think, think.* So Immigration told me this was my last visit to Scotland for a while. I was not getting in if I returned in another six months because they'd assume I was trying to live here without a visa. I could fix this. Aria would help me fix this. I'd already been looking into business expansion visas, so maybe I just needed to move my ass on that.

A car horn startled me, and I glanced away from the water to see an old Range Rover Defender pulling up behind the taxi. My first thought was that the cabbie's friend had arrived, but then I caught sight of the face behind the wheel.

I stumbled to a stop, my heartbeat skipping so it felt like a throb in my throat.

As soon as the road was clear, Jared McCulloch jumped out of the Defender. At the same time, my cab driver got out to see why.

"We're all right, mate," the cabbie called. "Got a tow coming."

Jared lifted his chin but gestured to me. "I know her."

"Ah, good stuff." The driver grinned at me. "He can give you a lift, then."

Butterflies erupted in my belly at the thought. But Jared, expressionless, just nodded. "Of course. You got luggage?"

In answer, the driver opened the trunk and pulled out my carry-on. Jared took it. "Thanks, mate." Then he looked at me and jerked his head toward the passenger side. "Get in."

I bristled a little at the order. And the handling of the situation by these two men. No one asked me if I wanted Jared McCulloch to give me a ride home!

Facial muscles straining against a frown, I gave the driver a tight-lipped smile before I grabbed my other bag out of the back seat. With a muttered thanks, I traipsed over to the Defender and reluctantly hauled myself up into it.

My skin prickled with awareness as Jared got in. The Defender smelled of his cologne. He was a farmer. Wasn't he supposed to smell like a farm? It was so unfair. I felt all of thirteen again, on my first date with Colton Gold. We went to the movies and I barely breathed the entire time in case he thought I breathed too loudly. Every single tiny movement he made I was aware of, and I still, to this day, cannot remember what movie we saw.

That's how it was with Jared.

How it always was and had been for the last five years.

It was worse being stuck in a car with him.

He didn't say anything until he'd pulled the vehicle back onto the road. "You all right?" he asked for some reason.

"Fine. You?" He stared straight ahead, and I studied him as I tried to ignore the flutter of attraction I felt simply looking at him.

Usually, there was some warmth to Jared, even if he'd never flirted with me again once he discovered who I was. I wasn't sure if that was because his cousin Sarah was married to Theo Cavendish who was best friends with North, my sister's husband, or if it was because I was Wesley and Chiara Howard's daughter.

Anyway, there had been zero acknowledgment of the heady attraction between us that first meeting, and ever since, Jared had acted like I was a sexless relative. We'd been forced into socializing over the years because of the familial connection. Last year, we'd even shared Christmas dinner.

But he at least treated me with a distant friendliness. And he was warm and funny in a gruff sort of way with everyone else around him.

Today, there was a brittle aloofness in his manner. "Fine."

"Are you sure?" He didn't seem fine. "I'm sorry if I'm putting you out."

"You're not putting me out," he replied tonelessly. "I was on my way back from Inverness, anyway."

My gaze flickered to his hand resting on the curve of the drive stick. He had strong hands, long-fingered but big-knuckled. The nails were blunt and surprisingly clean. The flash of an image, those knuckles caressing my bare stomach, heated my cheeks and I blinked the thought away.

The truth was that I was used to sexual attention. Since I was fourteen years old, I'd been chased by people, young and old. Sexualized before I was ready for it. I could blame genetics for that. Mamma made her money from being beautiful, and everyone said I looked a lot like her. I grew up in a world obsessed with that kind of beauty, around people's selfish desire to have it for themselves. So I'd always sought out sexual partners who saw beauty in things that other people didn't. Guys who didn't make me feel like they just wanted to fuck me for bragging rights.

Jared was the first man I'd ever met who I just wanted to jump because I was attracted to him on a level I couldn't explain. I didn't know him or what his thoughts were on the world. I just wanted him.

And for a few exhilarating moments, he'd wanted me too.

The fact that he didn't anymore because of who I was hurt in a different way to all those who had wanted me because I was Chiara Howard's daughter.

We drove in silence, but it wasn't an easy, comfortable silence. I was too aware of him and wondering constantly if he was really that immune to me or hiding his awareness.

While Jared wasn't a big talker, this monosyllabic version of him didn't seem right either.

Worry pricked me. "Are you sure everything's all right? You seem ..."

He flicked me a quick look. "I seem ...?"

"Preoccupied," I decided.

Jared replied with a grunt.

Just a grunt. Nothing else.

I didn't know why that hurt. We barely knew each other, really. In five years, he hadn't made an effort to get to know me. We were simply cordial whenever we were thrown together.

Turning away, I kept my gaze on the countryside outside the passenger window.

No more words passed between us until we reached Ardnoch.

"You're staying on the estate, right?"

"Yeah."

So Jared silently drove me outside the village, down the tree-lined road toward the security gates that led not to the castle that hosted the main club, but to the private gate for residents.

The guards recognized me and let Jared drive in. I directed him down the winding road because it branched off toward other properties.

My parents owned a beach house on the estate. It sat on the cliffs that dropped dramatically toward the dunes and the North Sea beyond. Aria and North bought the beach house next door when a famous studio head had put it up for sale five years ago.

"That one." I pointed to the New England–style home with its wraparound porch.

Jared made a sound in the back of his throat, drawing my sharp gaze.

"What?"

"Nothing," he muttered. He shut off the engine and threw open his door, jumping out.

With a heavy sigh, I got out and was just closing the door behind me when he rounded the Defender with my luggage.

"Thanks." I took it.

"You're welcome." Those stunning green eyes barely met mine before he turned on his heel and rounded the back of the car.

I stood there, watching as he got in and drove away without another look or word.

"What the fuck was that?" I huffed at the empty space he left behind.

Two

Jared

I'd just pulled up to the farmhouse when my phone rang again. A glance at the screen said it was Sorcha. Guilt niggled at me as I ignored it and jumped out of the Defender.

Georgie, the only farmhand I had left, was waiting by his car outside the house. Dread settled in my gut, hoping he didn't bring me more bad news.

"Did you get Sorcha sorted?" he asked, pushing away from his vehicle.

Sorcha Penman was the woman I was casually seeing. After years of one-night stands, I'd started dating Sorcha because she knew the score. It wasn't serious. We both knew I would never commit. She promised she didn't want commitment and I had to hope she meant it. I liked Sorcha, but I'd never love her. I wasn't even sure I was capable of romantic love.

What we had was convenient for both of us, but it was starting to interfere with the farm. I'd gotten a hysterical call from her a few hours ago because her dog, Brechin, had eaten a bar of chocolate. I was fond of the wee thing, so when she'd asked me to come be with her at the vet in Inverness, I'd gone. Brechin would be fine.

But Sorcha had clung to me like I was her adoring boyfriend, and it made me seriously uncomfortable. Maybe it wasn't so convenient anymore.

Georgie read my expression. "I know that look. I take it you ended things."

I shook my head. "Not yet. I'm not such a bastard I'd dump her the day her dog almost died. How was today?" I hated that I'd left Georgie to the farm when things were shit.

The farming industry was more stressful than ever. Dependent upon the mood of the weather, every year was always a possible struggle. But these last few years had been devastating. The turnover was so bad, I had to let my other farmhand (and friend) Enzo go.

He'd since moved down south to work on a farm in Kent.

Last winter, there was so much rain we hadn't gotten our winter barley into the ground fast enough. The barley needed to be cultivated, sprayed, cultivated again, and then drilled. All within two weeks. Nearly five hundred acres needed to be done in those fourteen days. But it rained and rained last September, and we weren't fast enough. The yield dropped off, along with the profits.

Only the April before, my rapeseed crops were destroyed by the flea beetle. They destroyed the lot of it. Thousands and thousands of pounds' worth of loss.

Enzo had been my shepherd, and as much as Georgie and I tried, we couldn't look after the fields, the cattle, and the sheep. So I'd sold my flock. But the problem with that was, not only did we lose money in lambing season, we lost money on our crops. The Department for Environment, Food & Rural Affairs gave me money to *not* grow crops. I had wildflower meadows that made money by simply existing, but I had to mow those fields—and my flock of sheep had done that for me.

Everything was connected on the farm. Start to break it apart and failure seemed inevitable.

The thought of failing my grandfather, for being the one responsible for the end of the McCulloch Farm, was a knife in my gut.

"The rapeseed is looking good this year." Georgie clapped me on the shoulder, giving me a reassuring smile.

I relaxed marginally and blew out a breath. "Good."

My friend sighed.

Oh fuck. "What happened?"

"I had to get Ennis out."

Ennis was the local farm and equine vet. "Why?"

"One of the cows had a sore on her leg. Ennis looked at her and says she's just injured herself, nothing to worry about. But ..." He shrugged apologetically.

"More money." Ennis wasn't cheap. "It's fine. You did the right thing." I felt a familiar tightness in my chest and suddenly I desperately needed to be alone. "Head home. I'll finish up."

"Everything's done that can be done today." Georgie frowned. "Go get some sleep."

It was like he knew I hadn't been sleeping. It had felt like weeks of tossing and turning, worrying about the farm. How to fix it. How to make it work before it was too late.

A few minutes later, I was alone in the house I'd lived in for the past nine years. I'd visited my grandparents' home before then, during summers as a kid. But it had truly been my home from the moment my grandfather took in a scared-shit-less twenty-one-year old. He'd taught me to farm, and it had become a way of life for me. When he passed away almost six years ago, there was no question in my mind that I would take over the family business.

My cousin Sarah had lived with our grandparents since she was a young teen. She'd gone on to become a best-selling crime writer, to marry the man who turned her book series into a globally successful television show, and they spent half their year in London and the other half here. Sarah had already gifted the farm a new tractor and a few other bits and pieces. If she knew the farm was in trouble, she'd offer to help in a heartbeat.

But that would make me feel like an even bigger failure.

Granddad wouldn't want me to take money from Sarah to turn the farm around. He'd want me to find the solution myself.

I was trying. Fuck, I was trying. For him. For me. That tightness compressed my chest and I squeezed my eyes closed against the panic.

What a day. What a fucking day.

First Sorcha dragged me away from the farm (though it wasn't like she knew it was in trouble), and then giving Allegra Howard, of all people, a lift home.

Her perfect features flashed in my mind and I groaned, scrubbing a hand down my face.

Allegra was one of those women a man couldn't believe was real. The first time I saw her, I thought I might be hallucinating. Ardnoch, because of the club, had seen its fair share of beautiful people, but Allegra ... She was the kind of beautiful that stopped traffic. The kind of beautiful that surely was only meant for the television screen or a perfume ad.

Yet she wasn't an actor or a model. She was an artist.

But she was also the daughter of Hollywood director Wesley Howard, and you didn't have to be into movies to know who the hell he was. Her mum was Chiara Howard. I'd known guys who kept posters of her in nothing but her underwear in their mechanics garage back in Glasgow.

Aye, Allegra was from another world. Not for me. She'd

been too young when we met, which made it easier to avoid temptation. But she was twenty-five now ... and still she looked at me like *I* was fascinating. That was hard to resist.

But I would.

I should've driven past her today, but the sight of her pacing along the side of the road with a troubled expression on her stunning face ... I had to stop. Had to make sure she was all right. Then I'd been a sullen bastard because I didn't know how to act around her.

Guilt pricked me.

"Enough. Fuck." I pushed up off the couch, shoving thoughts of the American out. I had far bigger things to worry about than Allegra Howard.

I'd realize just how true that was a few hours later when I got out of the shower to find a missed call on my phone and a voicemail waiting for me.

Sitting down on the bed that Sarah had bought as a gift when I took over my grandparents' old bedroom, I switched the phone on speaker as I listened to the message.

My blood chilled at the familiar voice echoing into the room. "Jar, long time, pal. But your auld man needs to talk to you. It's important. Call me back on 08798256825. And don't make me wait, pal, awright." The last was a threat.

Fuck.

What the fucking hell did my waste-of-space dad want now after all these years?

THREE
ALLEGRA

Aria blinked rapidly, like she was trying to process her feelings on my proposal without giving away her immediate thoughts. That's exactly what she was doing. I knew her too well.

She stood, leaning against her desk, her arms crossed over her ample bust. Aria always made me feel like I'd just rolled out of bed, even if I'd taken my time getting ready for the day. She was one of those women who always looked put together and gorgeous. In fact, my big sister had no idea how beautiful she was and all because she was curvier than Mamma or me, and Mamma never let her forget it.

Sometimes, I disliked Chiara Howard. Not a nice thing to say about one's own mother, but it was true.

Aria had been born without that innate selfishness both of our parents had. Worse, I worried I was selfish to my core too. That it was genetics, and I couldn't fight nature. Aria knew some of our parents' faults, but not all of them, and I'd like to keep it that way. She saw the best in people. That was a good thing because I needed her to see the best in me.

I needed someone to believe in me.

"Well?" I knew my eyes were wide with pleading, but I couldn't help it. She felt like my last hope. For not the first time. Poor Aria. She really got stuck with me.

My sister sighed. Heavily. She smoothed a hand over her hair, her engagement ring winking in the light next to her wedding band. "I don't think you've thought this through."

After years of Aria running Ardnoch Estate as the hospitality manager, Lachlan promoted her to managing director. Lachlan, alongside his very famous brother Brodan, also owned a whisky distillery outside of Ardnoch, which they opened just six months ago. Lachlan wanted to put his energy into making it a success and needed Aria to take the reins at the estate. She pretty much ran the entire show. The promotion brought with it the benefit of hiring a PA, and Aria's PA had just given notice. I'd suggested *I* become her new PA so I could get a work visa. A work visa would keep me here for three years, giving me plenty of time to build my business and apply for a business expansion visa. The government might even grant me indefinite leave to remain.

"Of course I have. It's a great solution." My heart started to race because I hadn't expected my sister to object. "If you're worried about me not being able to do the job, I can. I am very capable. You know I've run galleries before. And I'm a quick learner."

Aria waved a hand. "I'm not worried about you not being able to do the job. You're more than capable. But working as my PA for the next three years will completely derail your business as an artist."

"No, I'll do it simultaneously."

She huffed. "Which tells me that you completely underestimate what the job of my PA entails. Ally, before my promotion I was drowning here. The club membership grows almost every year and I work very hard. So does my PA."

Dread roiled in my stomach. "I know that. I can make it

work. I'll work with you Monday through Friday and do my art in the evenings and weekends."

She shook her head again. "Sometimes I need my PA to do overtime. Why do you think Sandra is leaving? She can't keep up with the pace."

I frowned. "*You* have a life. You make time for North when he's home. I can have a life too."

"It's not about having a personal life on top of this job. You're talking about having a full-time job on top of this very demanding full-time job, all the while trying to grow a business. You'll have no personal life because what you're trying to do is impossible."

Desperation turned to anger. "Aria, I need this. Didn't you hear what I told you? Yesterday, Immigration warned me that they wouldn't let me back into Scotland next time I try to visit."

She pushed off the desk, expression sympathetic. "We'll figure something out. But I'm not giving you a job when all it will do is derail your future. You are too talented an artist not to strive for the career you actually want."

"Can't we figure something out?" I asked bitterly, hurt mingling with the anger. "Don't you care that we won't see each other when Immigration boots me out of the country?"

Aria scowled. "Of course I care."

"No, you don't!" Resentment suddenly burst out of me. "You have your life here. You have North. It doesn't matter if you don't see me."

"Allegra—"

"You just up and moved here without even caring that you were leaving me!"

There it was. Those words that had lived in me for years suddenly hung between us in her grand office in this grand old castle that she'd chosen over her little sister.

"Ally, that's not how it was. Or is." She took a step forward but I retreated.

Tears burned my eyes as all the feelings I'd kept inside bubbled to the surface. "I know you were desperate to leave, and you felt obligated to stay for me. I get that it's selfish to wish that you'd stayed ... but you didn't even blink. As soon as Mamma decided she wanted to stick around, you were out of there, like somehow it meant that I didn't need you anymore."

Aria sucked in a breath. "That isn't fair. I didn't leave you. I just went after what I wanted in life."

"I know that!" I cried, the tears rolling down my cheeks. "But why did you have to go somewhere I couldn't follow? Do you know what that feels like? When the only person you've ever truly trusted and ever needed in this life goes where you can't follow?" I sobbed the last word and whirled, fumbling for the door.

My sister called my name, but I kept going, rushing out of the office. I ignored her pained shouts as I shot down the hall. Staff and club members gaped at me as I ran past, but I darted by them, following the familiar halls away from the public spaces and into the staff quarters.

The cool summer air hit me as I burst outside, running toward the Range Rover my sister always let me borrow from the estate fleet when I visited.

As I tore out of there, guilt cut through my hurt.

Everything I'd said to Aria was true. It *was* how I felt. But that didn't make it right. Aria had looked after me in a way no one had ever looked after her. So she'd wanted a life for herself. So what? I was going to make her feel guilty for that because that life didn't include me?

See? Selfish.

Selfish to my core.

Sometimes I really hated myself.

It had been a year since I felt like I needed a check-in with my therapist. Gail always advised that regular check-ins were a good thing, but I'd honestly not needed to process my feelings of late. However, I considered maybe it was time to talk to her. Something this disruptive was obviously going to affect me emotionally. However, I wanted to believe that I could handle life's little shake-ups better than I used to.

I didn't know where I was going, but it was no surprise I ended up in the village, parking the Range Rover outside the Gloaming. My heart did a little jump when I recognized the Defender I'd parked next to.

Jared was here.

I wiped at my cheeks, checking my reflection in the rearview mirror. Thankfully, I hardly ever wore makeup unless I was going out to dinner or an event, so there was no messed-up mascara to fix. Quiet panic rode my shoulders as I hopped out of the vehicle and strolled into the pub. I didn't know what I was going to do. I had to figure out a way to stay in Scotland. I suppose I could ask around the village, see if anyone else was hiring.

Maybe Jared needed a new farmhand.

I snorted at the thought because, even though I wasn't opposed to getting my hands dirty, I'd probably be useless. The only thing I'd ever been truly good at was making art.

The pub was fairly quiet at this time of day and the sight of Jared on a stool at the bar, with his head in his hands, caused a spark of concern to cut through my self-involved despair.

What was Jared doing here at this time? I knew from Sarah that farm life was hard work. I'd only ever seen Jared here in the late evenings.

The bartender, an older woman I didn't know, greeted me as I approached the bar. "Afternoon. What can I get you?"

"Uh, whatever NA beer you have." I slid onto the stool next to Jared as he reluctantly lifted his head from his hands.

The Gloaming was one of my favorite places. I just loved the cozy atmosphere. But a pub was a strange place to call a favorite when you didn't drink. When I was fifteen, something happened that sent me on a downward spiral of partying, drugs, and alcohol. By the time I was seventeen, I got caught up with the wrong guy and while I was high, I got myself into a nasty situation. If it weren't for Sloane Ironside, a friend who, as luck would have it, also moved to Ardnoch and married a Scot, I might not be here. Or I might be living with even worse emotional scars than I had now. Sloane got me out of that situation, and Aria and my parents got me into rehab and therapy.

I've never referred to myself as sober because my stint with drugs and alcohol was short-lived and I didn't feel I'd earned the right to say I'd been sober for eight years. Instead, I just told people I was teetotal. Plus, it was nobody's goddamn business.

Shrugging off memories, I met Jared's gaze and frowned at the bleariness in his eyes.

He was Drunk with a capital D. I'd never seen him drunk. Not even at Christmas.

"Hey, you, what's going on?" I asked quietly.

He fumbled for his beer and shakily raised the pint glass to me. "Shrinking."

I gathered he meant drinking.

Oh boy. "Jared ... what's going on?" I repeated.

The man frowned as if confused by my question and it was ridiculous that he was kind of adorable. How a man that sexy could be adorable, I wasn't sure, but right then, he was both. "Ale." He tapped his pint. "I am having."

My lips twitched, my argument with Aria fading into the background. "I can see that. But why are you having ale at one o'clock in the afternoon? What about the farm?"

Jared's handsome features slackened with anguish, and my heart squeezed painfully in my chest. "The farm. The farm." He scrubbed a hand over his face and then just leaned his forehead into his palm. "That bashstard will take it."

"What bashtard?" I teased, trying to lighten his mood.

Those green eyes met mine and hardened. "I'm failin'."

Realizing something was seriously wrong, I shimmied my stool closer to his as the bartender set my drink down. I thanked her absentmindedly as I leaned in close to Jared. He reeked of alcohol. Had he been here since the pub opened? "Jared, what's going on?"

"The farm," he whispered, pain in the words. "I'm goin' tae lose it. Everythin' Granddad worked for. Gone."

"What?"

"Too many disashters. Losht money. Cannae seem to get back on track. Gonnae need to shell it."

"Sell it?"

He nodded grimly.

"Why can't you ask Sarah for the money?" His cousin was wealthy. I knew that from Aria.

Jared shook his head, glaring at me through narrowed eyes. "No gonna dae that." His accent had thickened with his drunkenness. "Ma dad did that. Abandoned everybody and ashed everybody to bail him oot. No gonna dae that. Ma problem to sholve."

Suddenly his phone rang, drawing my attention to it on the bar counter. Jared ignored it, so I leaned over to squint at the screen. Someone named Georgie was calling.

"Not going to get that?"

He grunted and took another pull of his ale.

When the phone stopped ringing, I pulled it toward me

and saw there were thirteen missed calls from Georgie. The name was familiar, and I suddenly remembered he worked on the farm with Jared.

I picked up his phone before he could protest and tapped on Georgie's name.

"What are you doin'?" Jared grumbled but didn't make an effort to stop me.

"Jar, where the fuck are you?" a man's voice bit out angrily down the phone.

"Um, this isn't Jared. This is Allegra Howard. I'm at the Gloaming and Jared is here. He's ... he can't drive home in his current condition. Can you come get him?"

I heard him let out a beleaguered breath. "Aye. I'll be there soon."

I made small talk with a sleepy Jared for fifteen minutes or so until a man who couldn't be much older than him strode into the pub, dressed much the same in a long T-shirt, jeans, and work boots. He thanked me for calling and helped a belligerent Jared out of the pub.

Just before they left, Jared looked back over his shoulder at me. He looked so lost. So young. As if all the years had melted away and he was just a kid again.

I knew the feeling.

A sense of kinship filled me as I gave him a sad little wave.

Then, as he disappeared out the door, the idea hit like a lightning bolt.

I gasped, anticipation and hope filling me.

It could work.

It could really work.

I'd just need Jared McCulloch to agree to it.

FOUR
ALLEGRA

Call it shame mixed with guilt mixed with hurt. Call it cowardice. But I did not return to my parents' beach house that day or night. Aria lived next door, and I knew she'd be waiting for me.

Instead, I turned to Sloane.

Sloane Ironside, despite the incredible wealth she'd inherited from her father, lived in a humble bungalow in a quiet residential area of the village. It was her husband Walker Ironside's home, and when they got together, Sloane and her daughter Callie were only too happy to move in with him. Sloane used her inheritance to set up a bakery in Ardnoch. A very successful bakery that only opened a few days a week, much to the dismay of the locals.

Sloane (also born in Los Angeles) and I met when I was off the rails and dating her skeezy and dangerous ex-boyfriend Nathan Andros. Sloane had gotten pregnant by Nathan when she was sixteen years old. He was a thug, working his way up the hierarchy of a gang that traded in drugs and chopped cars. After a few years of his abuse, Sloane took Callie and got out from under him. Kind of.

Then at seventeen, I was unwittingly swept up in his world, seeking a wildness to distract me from my despair, taken in by his good looks, thrilled by the danger. Until one night he locked me in a room with two men, intending to share me with them, when Sloane turned up. I later learned she was desperate for money for her and Callie, and she'd come to Nathan for help. Instead, she ended up saving me. My personal avenging angel.

I was stupid and combative, and Nathan started whaling on me. Sloane jumped in to help and I managed to grapple Nathan's gun off him, but I accidentally shot Sloane in the arm.

Nathan lost it. He beat the living daylights out of me and he would have killed me.

But Sloane shot *him* and got me out of there.

Somehow we ran through the neighborhoods with me fighting unconsciousness the whole time. Before the lights went out, I told her who to call. My dad. He took care of everything. Nathan went to jail. I wouldn't tell my family what drove me to drugs, drinking, and the thug, but I was scared shitless enough to go to rehab and tell a therapist.

In thanks to Sloane for saving my life at great risk to hers and Callie's, Aria, who had just accepted a job at Ardnoch Estate, offered Sloane a job there. She moved to Scotland with Callie to work as a housekeeper. It was there she fell in love with Walker Ironside, a security officer on the estate. He'd once been a bodyguard to the stars, and when Nathan got out of prison and started making trouble for Sloane again, Walker stepped in to protect her. It turned out Sloane's stepmother had put Nathan up to the business of killing Sloane for her inheritance. Really. You can't make this shit up.

Anyway, both Sloane's stepmother and Nathan will rot in prison. Nathan will never breathe free air again.

Through it all, Walker and Sloane fell in love, got married,

Walker adopted Callie as his own, and nearly four years ago, Sloane gave birth to their little boy Harry.

It was a full house but, despite the friends I'd made in Ardnoch, Sloane was the person I felt closest to after Aria. We'd been born into the same world and we'd experienced the same feelings of neglect from our parents, and we'd both been driven off the rails of a privileged life. She got me in a way most people, including my sister, didn't.

I felt safe to run to her, and she never turned me away whenever I did.

"You're sure I'm not putting you out?" I asked quietly that night as Sloane led me into Callie's bedroom.

She shook her head, handing me a pair of clean pajamas. "Callie is sleeping over at a friend's house." She smirked, although there was worry in her eyes. "Or that's what she tells me."

I frowned because Callie and Sloane had the kind of mother-daughter friendship dreams were made of. Callie even spent a lot of her free time at the bakery, learning from her mom, and had plans to work alongside her once she graduated. "Callie wouldn't lie to you."

Sloane glanced over her shoulder as if to make sure Walker wasn't in hearing distance. When she turned back to me, she whispered, "Callie Ironside would lie to the angels if it meant getting to spend time with Lewis Adair."

My lips twitched. Ah, young love. I wondered what that was like. "You think she's with Lewis?"

Her brown eyes filled with worry. "I hope not. I love my girl, but I do not want her to follow in her momma's footsteps. If she comes home pregnant at sixteen, Walker will kill Lewis. And though I do not want a pregnant teenage daughter, I love Lewis. I'm grateful my kid fell in love with a boy like him, and I really don't want Walker to end him."

I nodded. They'd moved to Ardnoch when Callie was ten

years old. She was almost seventeen now. Lewis Adair, Lachlan's brother Thane's son, had been in Callie's class and they'd become fast friends. Over the years, that friendship had blossomed into more. Since she was thirteen years old, Callie had told me openly and often that she wanted Lewis to be her boyfriend. Lewis had taken a little longer to catch up. When Callie went on a date with another boy, he'd finally cottoned on. They'd been seeing each other for over a year, the epitome of teen love.

"They'll be smart," I whispered, trying to assuage her concerns. Even though the thought of little Callie Ironside having sex made me feel old at twenty-five.

Sloane had not appeared entirely convinced as she bid me good night. "And text your sister back or I will," she warned before she closed the door.

She referred to the fact that I had a bunch of missed calls and texts from Aria. Not wanting my sister to worry, I did in fact text back.

> I'm OK. I'm safe. I'm really sorry for what I said. But I don't want to talk yet. xx

I sent the text, feeling like shit all over again. Aria deserved better than me, that was for sure. For some reason, however, that feeling of not being wanted—a feeling I was familiar with regarding my parents—was excruciating when it came to Aria.

Later, after tossing and turning as I went over and over the plan plotting in my mind, I must have finally fallen asleep from sheer exhaustion.

I didn't know how many hours of sleep I got, but I was awoken by arms snaking around me. At first I thought I was dreaming and then when it started to register that I wasn't, my eyes flew open. I blinked against the soft light pouring through the curtains as I tried to orient myself.

"I didn't mean to wake you, Aunt Ally," a familiar voice whispered.

Callie.

Tension melted from my body as I turned around to find a pretty young thing lying next to me. She grimaced comically, her blond hair splayed across the pillow. A soft laugh of relief escaped me. "I'm in your bed," I whispered back, "so it's kind of okay."

Even in the dimness of the room, her eyes were a striking light blue. "What are you doing here? Are you okay?"

Callie had a Scottish accent. The American accent she'd been born with disappeared over the years. Sloane told me she'd read that kids learned their accents from their peers at school, not their parents. Even so, now and then I'd hear just a touch of an American twang from the sixteen-year-old.

"I'm okay," I promised. "I'll tell you about it later. What are you doing home so early? Your mom said you were at a sleepover."

Callie blanched as she snuggled closer to me. "Can you keep a secret?"

Oh boy. "Is it going to be one I'll regret keeping?"

"Only if you're happy for my dad to kill Lewis," she replied wryly.

"You were with Lewis," I surmised. Her mom had guessed correctly.

She bit her lip against a dopey smile. "We spent the night in his parents' annex, but we thought I better leave early because Mr. Adair gets up at the crack arse of dawn. Lewis and I rode back here on our bikes. He rode all the way here with me to make sure I got home okay."

Though it wasn't my place to be imparting advice on how to behave as a teenager, I had to ask, "Were you safe?"

"We didn't have sex," she promised hurriedly. "I mean ... we did *stuff*—"

"Don't need to know the details," I interrupted.

She giggled quietly.

"You will be safe, though, right? When the time comes."

Callie nodded, expression serious. "We love each other, but we're not stupid."

"And Lewis isn't putting pressure on you?"

"No way." Callie squeezed my arm in reassurance. "Aunt Ally, it's *Lewis*. If anyone's making the moves here, it's me."

I chuckled, shaking my head. "Please stop talking."

She laughed again, her expression filled with such joy I felt a pang of envy. Callie Ironside wasn't even seventeen years old and she was in love in a way I had never experienced. It was written all over her. She exuded happiness. Feeling a well of affection push out the envy, I pulled her close, tucking her into my side. She wound her slim arms around me and I felt her relax, readying for sleep.

But before she drifted off, I warned, "Your mom already guessed you were with Lewis last night."

Callie tensed. "She did?"

"Mmm-hmm."

"She didn't tell Dad, did she?"

I snorted. "No. She doesn't want Lewis to die an untimely death either."

Her giggle vibrated against me and I squeezed her closer. I wanted to protect her happiness. I wanted to make Lewis Adair promise me that he'd never break her heart. Because I didn't want Callie to ever feel like I felt right now. Desperate and lonely, and ready to do absolutely anything to stay with the only people who brought me contentment.

FIVE

JARED

That morning I'd woken up to a pounding sore head. I'd clearly passed out midday, and I had the vague memory of Georgie taking me home and putting me to bed. But I gathered I was dehydrated more than hungover. After a shower, I forced down eggs on toast and as much water as I could. By the time Georgie arrived to pick me up so I could collect my Defender, I felt somewhat human again.

But I was mentally kicking my own arse. Yesterday's actions would have shamed my grandfather. I'd acted more like my parents. Drowning my sorrows and feeling sorry for myself. A good sleep and a hangover was enough to give me a quick kick up the behind.

That morning, I'd already started thinking on a plan instead of wallowing. It would take capital, but there were a few business owners in town who might be interested in investing.

You see, what the farm did have in spades was land. And we lived in a tourist trap, thanks to Ardnoch Estate.

I could put holiday lets up on the land. Maybe something quirky like those glamping pod things that had become all the rage. In fact, if I went down that road, it might not take as much capital as lodges would. Research would be required to see if it was worth the expenditure. If it would generate enough income to help float the farm during bad years.

Georgie thought it was worth looking into. As he dropped me off at the car park outside the Gloaming, I was so lost in my thoughts that I didn't see him. As I was getting into my Defender, his familiar voice cut through me. "Well, well, this saves me a trip out to the farm."

Dread sank in my stomach like a weight pulling me down. Expression shuttering, I turned around, holding the vehicle door open for escape.

Sure enough.

There he stood.

My waste-of-space father.

Hamish McCulloch.

I sneered inwardly. He didn't deserve to bear the McCulloch name.

Eyes the same shade as my own glared at me. "Forgotten how to return a phone call, boy?"

Anger rushed through me, but I didn't let him see. Calmly, I replied, "I'm not a boy."

He huffed. "What? You think you're a man now, eh?"

"I'm the opposite of what you are ... so, aye. I'd say so."

Hamish's eyes flashed with fury. "You jumped-up wee shit. I see my da did a good job of turning you into him."

"Let's hope so."

He curled his lip. "I say good riddance to the auld bastard."

My blood turned hot in an instant as I took a step toward him. Unlike his father, he'd inherited his height from my grandmother's side of the family. I'd inherited it from him too. We weren't short, but we weren't tall. However, I did have youth and muscle on my side as I stopped inches from his face.

"Collum McCulloch was a thousand times the father you ever were. Say one more derogatory thing about him, Hamish, and I'll put your teeth through the back of your fucking skull."

The man, this stranger who'd donated his seed for my existence, blinked in surprise at my calm threat. A flush of red coated his neck and face. He took a step back. "I didn't come here to argue, son."

"Don't call me son." I pointed toward the road that led out of Ardnoch. "Now I suggest you crawl back into the hole you came out of."

"Now, now, no need to be like that." He straightened the lapels of his coat like I'd grabbed him by them. "I came to talk to you about the farm. About what I'm due."

If I'd been hot with anger before, I suddenly turned icy with rage. "Excuse me?"

He jerked his thumb toward the Defender as if it exemplified the farm. "That farm was my da's. Kenny got himself killed for it." He referred to Sarah's father Kenneth. My uncle. He'd died in a farming accident before I was born. "So that leaves me as the rightful heir."

"Heir? You? Are you fucking kidding me?"

Hamish's expression darkened, eyes cold and empty. "Naw, I'm not. That farm is mine."

I prowled toward him and he puffed up his chest like the hard man he thought he was. "Grandad left the farm to me in his will over five years ago. To me and Sarah. She signed it over to me."

"Aye, aye. But that doesn't mean anything. I'm just here to let you know that I've enlisted the help of a solicitor in Inverness. I'm contesting the will."

I laughed at his stupidity. He'd waited this long to contest an ironclad will? Fucking moron. "I see you're still pissing your money away."

His answering grin caused unease to shift through me.

"Well, it'll piss away your money too. Word has it that things haven't been easy lately. You canna afford to waste that kind of money. So ... why not just give me what I'm owed, and I'll give up contesting the will?"

"You're blackmailing me?"

"Nah, nah. Just getting what I'm owed. You could sell a bit of the land to pay me off."

Now I grabbed him by the collar. He shoved at my hands but his efforts were pathetic. "Come after me or the farm and you'll wish you were dead by the time I'm done with you, Hamish."

The vicious smirk on his face made me want to kill him then and there. "Naw. By the time *I'm* done with *you*, lad." Hamish shoved my hands away again and I released my hold. "You'll be hearing from my solicitor. But you might see me around the farm, checking over what is mine."

"I'll have you arrested for trespassing."

"Fuck. Took you for not much, son, but I didn't take you for a grass."

"You don't know me, Hamish. You have no idea what I'm capable of. Come near my farm and you'll regret it for the rest of your pathetic life."

Wiping his nose with a humorless laugh, he nodded. "I'll stay off the farm. For now. The day I walk back on it is the day it's mine. And on that day, a big fucking for sale sign goes on that land and I will rake in the millions you're too much of a pussy to make."

I scoffed in disgust and strode back to the Defender. Less than a minute later, I swung it out of the parking spot outside the Gloaming, refusing to acknowledge Hamish as I sped away.

His brand of nuisance was the last goddamn thing I needed right now, but his appearance made me even more determined to save my grandfather's farm. I'd die before I let Hamish anywhere near it.

Tonight I'd start my research on the holiday lets. If it was worth pursuing, I'd talk to Lachlan Adair and see if he was interested in investing. I'd turn things around. There was no other option.

Six
Allegra

I only returned to the beach house when I knew my sister would be at work. Even then it was for a quick shower and a change of clothes. I packed a few things in a duffel bag in case my plan went according to ... well ... plan.

Aria had responded to my text with a forlorn one of her own.

> Please come home. We need to talk about this. xx

Home.

Didn't she realize it wouldn't be that for me anymore if I didn't do something to stop being kicked out of the country? I felt like she didn't understand my urgency, my desperation.

Before I could talk myself out of it, I jumped back into the rental SUV and drove off the estate, heading out of Ardnoch toward the McCulloch farm. I'd never been to Jared's farmhouse, but I knew it was signposted.

A narrow country road only wide enough for one vehicle at a time cut through lush green fields up toward the farmhouse. It appeared among a ramshackle collection of buildings that housed what I assumed were farm vehicles and equipment. The farmhouse itself was an attractive two-story sandstone brick home with slate roof tiles. Dormer windows suggested the attic space had been turned into a room or two as well.

The yard around the house was mostly a gravel drive. It was muddy and unkempt compared to the house and exactly what a person might expect on a farm.

Jared's Defender, however, was nowhere in sight.

Damn it.

I wanted to do this before I lost my nerve.

Turning around, I drove back down to the main road and made my way slowly (much to the aggravation of any traffic that found me) along it, searching the fields on my left. Another unmarked road appeared and I took it on the off chance it led me to Jared.

Sure enough, a minute later I spotted his Defender parked beside a gate to a field. Jared waited at the gate as a tractor, driven by Georgie, I assumed, worked the land.

At the sound of my engine, Jared turned and stiffened.

Butterflies erupted in a riot inside my belly. I considered myself a pretty confident person. Yes, I got nervous about things that mattered to me or situations that were out of my comfort zone, but I tended to march into them head-on. In fact, I kind of got off on the fluttery nerves of anticipation.

This was different. I felt like I might upchuck.

It's a good plan, a voice inside insisted. *Get out of the car.*

With trembling limbs, I pushed open the car door and jumped out. Jared crossed the space between us to meet me. I was a jumbled mess of "Oh my God, I can't believe what I'm about to propose to this guy" and "Maybe proposing to a guy this hot is a bad idea."

And he was hot.

So freaking hot.

Even in a dirty long-sleeved tee, old jeans, and mud-splattered work boots.

The sun glinted in those startling jade-green eyes. I could drown in them.

This is a bad idea.

A frown marred Jared's brow as we stopped before each other. He wasn't overly tall, about five eleven. But he was so broad of shoulder it gave him the sense of being taller. I hadn't inherited my mother's height, but I was five foot eight, which wasn't exactly short.

Somehow I felt dainty standing before Jared, looking into that handsome, scowling face.

"You all right?" he demanded. "What's happened?"

Those butterflies suddenly swarmed up into my throat, making my pulse throb. I squeezed my hands against the nerves. Whoa, I couldn't remember the last time I'd felt like this.

Jared ducked his head slightly to look me directly in the eyes. "Allegra? What's going on?"

At the note of genuine concern in his voice, I shrugged my shoulders back and took a deep breath and slow exhale.

Jared straightened as he watched me, his gaze unreadable.

"I have a proposal to make to you. About the farm."

Something about my words put him visibly on the defense. Jared crossed his arms over his broad chest and widened his stance. "What do you want with the farm?"

Prickly, prickly. So far this was not going well and I'd barely said a word. The tractor growled in the distance, distracting me. "Can we go somewhere to talk?"

He gestured around us impatiently. "This is as private as it gets."

"Right." I licked my lips nervously, and Jared's gaze dipped to my mouth.

His expression tightened, a muscle in his jaw flexing as he looked away.

What happened at the airport with Immigration abruptly spilled out of me. Jared studied me with that same unreadable expression as I told him about my fight with Aria too. "So you see, when I leave Scotland, they're not going to let me back in. For who knows how long." I shrugged helplessly, hating that I was here, putting my fate in the hands of a mere acquaintance, being vulnerable with him, but doing it, anyway. "This is my home now, Jared. I ... if I'm forced back to the US ... I was never happy there. I'm afraid what will happen to me if I go back there permanently. Anyway, I need time to figure out how to get a business visa. More time than I currently have. And you ..." I gestured to him and then the surrounding land. "You need someone to invest in this place."

Jared shook his head slowly. "Where are you going with this, Allegra?"

I ignored the thrill that coursed through my body at the sound of his voice wrapped around my name. "I came into my trust fund when I turned twenty-one. There is more than enough money to invest whatever you need into the farm. And ..." I drew myself up, shrugging on a confidence I did not feel. "As my husband, I would grant you access to those funds."

The words hung between us for what felt like forever. Then Jared blinked a few times and shook his head almost comically. "Wait a minute ... Are you ... What the fuck?"

My lips twitched with nervous amusement. "I am proposing a marriage of convenience. As your wife, I get to stay in Scotland. As my husband, you get the capital you need to turn the farm around. To turn your grandfather's farm around. I know how important it is to you. And I know you want to do it yourself, but this is a solution, Jared. To both our problems."

He turned away, scrubbing his palms down his face before blowing out a loud whoosh of air.

I fidgeted nervously behind him.

"I think you've seen too many of your dad's movies," he scoffed.

"My dad doesn't make rom-coms."

"You know what I mean." He stared at me incredulously. "A marriage of convenience?"

"Y-yes."

"What does that even look like?" he asked, then scowled. "Fuck! Why am I asking? Clearly this is insane."

"No, it's not." I took a few steps toward him and he retreated like I might bite or something. Grimacing, I stopped moving. "Jared, this would solve our problems. I'm not suggesting a real marriage. Of course, it has to look like a real marriage or I think there are fraud implications—"

"You think? You do realize you *are* asking me to do something illegal?"

"No one else will know that, though. We'll get married, I'll move into the farmhouse, and for a while, we'll make it look real but, obviously, we'll just be roommates. I'm not suggesting anything sexy here." *Though I wouldn't be opposed to it.*

"Our friends and family will know the truth."

"Yeah, but they won't tell anyone."

"Allegra," Jared growled, pinching the bridge of his nose in frustration.

I took heart in this overwrought response.

It meant he was contemplating it!

"Just marry me and stay married to me for eighteen months. No matter if I get my gallery up and running, I will grant you a divorce in eighteen months."

He glowered for what felt like forever. Then, "And am I expected to remain a monk for eighteen months?"

A sharp stab of something I didn't want to call rejection panged in my chest. "No. Men cheat." I shrugged.

Jared's nostrils flared. "So, I'm to look like the arsehole who married a wealthy Hollywooder to secure his farm and then cheated on her?"

"Well, I'm not going to be a nun, so they'll think we're both assholes. I think we can both agree to not have sex with other people for two months to sell the lie. Then whatever happens after that, happens."

Something flickered in his eyes before he looked away. He watched Georgie move the tractor up the field before turning back to me. "How much money are we talking about here, Allegra?"

Triumph started to course through me and I struggled to hold back a smile. "Millions."

His expression tightened. "For eighteen months of marriage?"

"Yes."

"And we'll have to live together?"

"To make it believable, yeah. And we'll have to, you know, get to know each other. I'm sure Immigration might have questions."

"So, I'll have to commit fraud and lie?"

I swallowed hard. "In exchange for whatever you need to get the farm back on track, yes."

"They'll know we're lying."

"No, they won't. I've been staying here for years, Jared. On and off. We could have been secretly seeing each other all that time. You're hot, I'm hot, shit happens."

"That shit won't be happening just because we'll be living together."

I tried to focus on the fact that it sounded like he was giving into the idea, and not on his continued rejection of me. It stung too much, considering Jared McCulloch was a flirtatious manwhore with a reputation. Why I was the only woman alive he didn't want to touch was something I didn't want to contemplate.

Shrugging nonchalantly, I replied, "Of course not. Like I said earlier, we can both see to our needs elsewhere after two months. Can you go without sex that long?"

He narrowed his eyes. "I'm not a fucking sex fiend."

"All evidence to the contrary."

"What does that mean?"

"It means you have a reputation. And the sex thing was the first thing you asked about."

"Then perhaps you shouldn't marry me," he bit out.

"I'll be marrying you, Jared, not sleeping with you."

Jared's eyes darkened as they dropped to my lips for a second too long.

My breath caught as awareness quivered through me. Needing to break the electric moment, I infused boredom into my tone. "Look, do we have a deal or not?"

After a beat or two, he huffed, "I must be out of my goddamn mind."

SEVEN
ALLEGRA

I'd visited Inverness many, many times. In fact, I was in the process of showing my glasswork at the finest art gallery in the city. Michelle, the owner, had been selling a piece here and there for the last few years, and last year she finally talked me into doing an entire show. The big event was just a month away.

In being fairly familiar with the capital of the Highlands, I'd somehow assumed that the registry office we'd marry in (goodness, just thinking that thought knocked the breath out of me) would be in an older building within the city center.

Instead, Jared had brought our long (it was only an hour but it felt like forever) and tense car journey to a halt *outside* the city center. We'd traveled down a road along the River Ness, passing a football field and a skate park before stopping in front of a building of contemporary design.

We'd called ahead yesterday to book an appointment to get married.

Now here we were, standing next to each other as a kind-faced registrar married us and two staff members acted as witnesses. The registrar eyed me with concern and I tried to smooth the nervousness off my face. Jared didn't look nervous. Nor did he look ecstatic or excited.

So far, we were not doing a very good job of pretending.

I kept thinking about the wedding party that departed the room before us. The bride wore a beautiful white gown, the groom a gray kilt, and they had bridesmaids and groomsmen. They had guests. And more importantly, they looked so happy together.

The weather agreed with the previous couples' mood, the sun shining brightly through the large windows of the ceremony room. I'd dressed in an off-white summer dress with a simple silhouette and thin straps and I'd worn my long hair down in its usual beachy waves. Bright pink platform Mary Jane shoes completed my attempt to look somewhat nice for my wedding.

Sweat slicked my palms as I held the small bouquet Jared had surprised me with that morning. They were wildflowers he'd picked from his own fields and bound in twine. Little did he know how perfect they were for me. I was not the fancy flower type.

I'd spent the night at his place because I didn't want Sloane or Aria to discover what I was up to. Jared let me sleep in Sarah's old room. It had been weird and tense between us at the farmhouse and a prelude, I imagined, to how it was going to be living together.

Jared showing up in his living room that morning in his three-piece suit did make me question all my life choices. My bridegroom was hot. Jared looking like a movie star instead of a farmer in his sexy suit was actually of great concern. I did not need to lust any harder for my fake husband. Thank God he hadn't worn a kilt.

"Jared, please repeat after me," the registrar said. "I do

solemnly declare that I know not of any lawful impediment why I, Jared McCulloch, may not be joined in matrimony to Allegra Emma Howard."

I tensed beside him, looking up at his handsome profile as he easily repeated the words I'd already forgotten. Shit, what if I couldn't remember what I was supposed to repeat?

Concentrate, girl, concentrate!

"Allegra." The registrar zeroed in on me and I nodded, wide-eyed, trying to focus. Her eyes glinted at my expression, but she continued, "Please repeat after me. I do solemnly declare that I know not of any lawful impediment why I, Allegra Emma Howard, may not be joined in matrimony to Jared McCulloch."

Nope.

Did not hear a damn word.

I cleared my throat, my voice a little shaky as I replied, "I'm sorry, can you repeat that?"

She nodded kindly and just as she opened her mouth to do so, strong fingers slid between mine, grasping my hand and squeezing gently. Surprised, I looked up at Jared and found him gazing down at me in concern. Even though we didn't know each other that well, I somehow knew what his eyes were saying.

We don't have to do this if you're having second thoughts.

For the first time since he'd strolled into the living room that morning, I didn't feel alone. I remembered we were in this together.

It centered me.

I squeezed his hand back, enjoying (too much) the feel of his calloused palm against mine.

When the registrar asked me to repeat the words, Jared kept holding my hand and I repeated the words without a hitch.

"Now, turn to each other, please."

We did so and I reached for Jared's other hand so we held them between us. I gave him a mischievous smile that lightened his expression for a brief second.

"Jared, repeat after me ..." She declared the words for Jared to repeat.

His big hands tightened around mine, and I found myself staring at his mouth as he said in that rumbly delicious voice of his, "I call upon these persons, here present, to witness that I, Jared McCulloch, do take thee, Allegra Emma Howard, to be my lawful wedded wife." His fingers squeezed harder around mine upon the word *wife*. I dragged my gaze off his lips to meet his and there was something intense in his eyes I couldn't quite decipher. A shiver skated down my spine.

A few seconds later, I found myself repeating, "I call upon these persons, here present, to witness that I, Allegra Emma Howard, do take thee, Jared McCulloch, to be my lawful wedded husband."

Husband.

This man was seconds from becoming my husband.

Holy shit.

My stomach flip-flopped so aggressively, it stole my breath.

The registrar offered us the rings. I took the gold wedding band I knew had been Jared's grandfather's and tried not to get emotional about it for him. When he'd presented them to me last night, he'd told me the rings belonged to his grandparents and that they'd suffice for the ruse. I'd asked him if he was okay with that, and he'd just shrugged and said aye. I wasn't so sure, but we didn't have any other options.

I trembled as Jared slipped his grandmother's simple gold band onto my finger. And a possessiveness I knew I had no right to feel swelled in my chest as I slid his grandfather's gold band onto his. Both of the rings were a little big for us, but it didn't stop the weird primal urge to jump him at the sight of the symbol of our marriage.

"I now pronounce you husband and wife. You may kiss your bride, Mr. McCulloch."

Oh shit.

Yeah, I forgot about this part.

He gave me a questioning look and I returned it with a barely perceptible nod.

Then he kissed me.

And I mean, he KISSED me.

He released my hands to wrap one of his around my nape, yanking me none-too-gently against his hard body before pressing his lips over mine.

I gasped in surprise at the move, allowing his tongue to lick over mine.

Desire flooded me, my skin burning hot, my fingers curling into his suit jacket as I returned his voracious kiss. Jared McCulloch kissed like it would be his last. It was the kind of kiss that made you want to fuck.

His hand tightened on my neck seconds before he pulled back, gentling the embrace, and he released me with a shivery brush of his mouth over mine.

My lips felt swollen and I was pretty sure the strapless bra I wore just barely concealed my pebbled nipples.

Holy fuck.

Had I ever reacted to a kiss like that in my life?

Nope.

No.

In fact, kissing had always been low on my pleasure score-board when it came to sex. I'd always preferred the main event.

Until now!

Oh no.

This was a big, big mistake.

My hands rested on my lap as we drove back to Ardnoch, and I couldn't stop staring at the gold band on my finger.

After we'd signed all the necessary documents, we'd bid the registrar and the strangers who'd acted as our witnesses goodbye. Their names were Carol and Susan. Susan had given me a hug and whispered in my ear, "You know, for a moment there, I was worried you were being blackmailed into the marriage. Until that kiss. Woo!" She'd waved a hand over her rosy cheeks with a chuckle.

I'd laughed, flushing at the memory of Jared's mouth hungrily taking mine. Of the tickle of his short beard against my skin. I wanted to feel it between my thighs.

My fingers curled against the fabric of my dress as I threw that image out of my mind. We'd already decided there would be no funny business between us. In fact, I should be pretty pissed at him for that kiss.

Why did he have to kiss me like that?

The question suddenly blurted out of me.

Out of my periphery, I saw Jared's hand flex around the wheel. Then he replied gruffly, "The registrar looked suspicious. If by some chance Immigration interviews her, I wanted to leave her with a lasting impression that helped to not betray us."

So he'd kissed me like he wanted to fuck me and it was as fake as our marriage?

Stupid disappointment filled me. "Right. That makes sense."

"Sorry if ... sorry if it made you uncomfortable."

"No. Nope. It was fine."

At his silence, I turned to find him glowering out at the road ahead of us.

"You regret this, don't you?"

He glanced sharply at me. "Do you?"

"No." And I actually didn't. "I get to stay now."

Jared nodded. "Look ... I've been thinking and I know you're not going to like this because I don't like it, but I think we need to lie to *everyone*."

"Everyone?"

"Sarah, Aria ... your parents. Everyone."

No. It wasn't possible. "They'll know we're lying."

"Even if they do, if we don't tell them the truth, it protects them legally. It might hurt us to lie to them and for them to know we're lying to them, but once it's all over, we can explain."

Shit.

"Shit, shit, shit." I pressed my head back against the car seat and heaved a sick-feeling sigh.

"I take it that means you agree?"

"Yes, unfortunately, that means I agree." And it meant I was about to make my relationship with Aria worse than it already was.

"Fuck."

Jared chuckled, but it wasn't a happy sound. "You've got a mouth on you."

"Well, you would know," I quipped.

He flashed me a dark look before returning his gaze to the road. Noting the white of his knuckles, I apologized.

"It's fine. I just ... hope you know that kiss was all for show."

Anger was better than the hurt I felt at his continued need to prove he didn't want me. Keeping my tone light, I replied, "I know you find me repugnant, Jared, so don't you worry your pretty little head that I'm going to catch feelings here."

A muscle ticked in his jaw, but he didn't deny it.

And I racked my brain wondering what it was that I had done that had turned him off so much. Then I reminded myself that whatever it was wasn't my fault, that Jared was merely a tool to get what I wanted, and it didn't matter what he thought of me otherwise.

It did matter what Aria thought of me.

Dread filled me the closer we drew to Ardnoch.

EIGHT

ALLEGRA

I t seemed right to me, especially because I'd been avoiding
her since our argument, that I should tell Aria about the
marriage myself. However, Jared pointed out that a real
couple would do it together. So we decided we would tell Aria
and Sarah as a couple.

I'd texted my sister to let her know I'd visit that evening. I
had to collect my stuff from my parents' beach house and take
it to the farmhouse. Sarah's old room was now mine. We'd
entered Jared's home, awkward tension hanging over us, as if
we'd both just realized the immensity of what we'd done.

As a kid, I'd gotten it into my head I wanted to act, so my
parents enrolled me in a prestigious after-school acting class.
They'd thrown us into improv a lot. I'd left behind the acting
for art, but apparently not the improv. This would be the
biggest role I'd ever attempted.

Jared and I hadn't discussed how this would really work.
We'd made the decision and as if afraid one of us would back
out, we'd booked the registry office and hightailed it down
there the next day.

Now we were stuck together with no real plan.

And the fact that Jared had the power to affect my feelings meant I'd chosen the wrong man for this job. I thought so even as I laid the flowers he'd given me gently down on the dresser in Sarah's room, already planning to preserve them in an art piece.

As regretful as I was that I'd picked him, I was grateful for Jared's quiet, solid presence as we pulled up to my sister and her husband's beach house. I was about to lie to the only person in my life who really cared about me. The only thing that soothed my guilt was the knowledge that it wouldn't be the first time I'd lied to protect her.

The door to the house opened and Aria stepped out onto the porch in her work clothes. She always looked so chic and put together. Even with worry etched into her beautiful face. A pang of remorse over our last conversation burned in my chest.

"Are you ready?" Jared asked.

I met his gaze, ignoring, as always, the flutter in my belly. It happened every time he looked at me. Fuck my life.

"As ready as I'll ever be."

Aria straightened at the sight of Jared getting out of the car with me. Her eyes bounced between us and widened as I reached for his hand.

He squeezed it in reassurance just like he'd done earlier that day, and it bolstered me.

"What is going on?" my sister asked as we reached the wraparound deck.

"Can we come in?"

Her green eyes narrowed on where my hand was enfolded in Jared's. I'd always envied her those eyes. They were a different shade of green to Jared's. A mossy green with flecks of gold in them. Warmer than Jared's cool jade. Usually. Today they were a little chilly with suspicion.

"I guess you better." She stepped back into the house and

held the door for us before strolling ahead into the open-plan living space. Her shoulders were stretched taut, her spine stiff. I tightened my grip on Jared.

To my surprise, North was lounging on the couch in the swanky space. Their beach house was more contemporary than my parents', with one wall of glass facing the North Sea and the beach below.

"I didn't know you'd be here," I said as my brother-in-law got to his feet at the sight of us.

"Apparently, we're all surprised this evening," he answered quietly as he took in Jared. North was a tall blond with clear gray eyes and a swimmer's physique. He was also unbelievably gorgeous and one of the finest actors of his generation. The first time I saw Ari and North interact, they were bickering like an old married couple, and I swear to God I could feel the sexual tension crackling in the air.

Despite their protests, I sensed there was something electric between them. So I'd acted a little immaturely, a little impulsively, to get them together, but it had all worked out. They were madly in love, and I was so thrilled for my sister that she'd found a partner who was so devoted to making her happy.

At Aria's wary expression, North slipped a comforting arm around her waist. "I got a few days off set to come home to be with my wife."

It was time to put on the show. I sidled close to Jared. His hard heat felt a little too nice. "That's good. It means Aria doesn't have to tell you. I can. Jared and I got married."

Jared's fingers flexed against mine as silence fell over the room like a heavy, suffocating blanket of doom.

Then ...

"You did what?" Aria yelled.

Aria hardly ever raised her voice. At least not at me.

Panicked, I blurted out, "We've secretly been seeing each

other for over a year and we're in love and we decided to get married and we're sorry for keeping it from you, but we only just realized how we were feeling and we didn't want to wait any longer to do something about it."

My sister scoffed in disbelief as she stepped toward us. "Or you found out you might not get back into the country, so you wrangled poor Jared into marrying you for a visa!"

Damn. She knew me too well.

"What's this about a visa?" Jared frowned with surprising authenticity. If I didn't know better, I'd believe his confusion.

"Oh, please." My sister apparently did not.

"Aye, please do tell me this is a joke." North glowered at Jared. "Because marrying someone so they can stay in the country is illegal."

"We're not doing that. God! We're"—I gestured between us—"like, in love."

Aria turned back to North. "And that is why she is a way better artist than actress."

"It's *actor*." Yes, I know, a pathetic response. "And I'm not acting. This is real between Jared and me."

"Really?" Aria crossed her arms over her chest. "So, what's his favorite movie?"

"He doesn't watch movies," I lied.

"You don't watch movies?" my sister asked incredulously.

Jared shrugged nonchalantly. He was very good at remaining calm. I was kind of envious of his cool attitude.

"Favorite color?"

"Green," I guessed, probably incorrectly.

"Favorite meal?"

Wanting to put an end to this line of questioning, I threw her a wicked smile and replied, "Me."

Jared made a small choking sound, and I glanced up. His lips twitched as he struggled against laughter.

The sight of him amused for the first time today filled me with unexpected pleasure.

"And it doesn't matter to you that you aren't the only meal he's been partaking in?" North asked with a blandness that belied the anger in his eyes. "He's fucking some woman from Inverness."

I tried not to stiffen as Jared narrowed his eyes. "And what the hell do you know about it?"

"Her name is Sorcha, and you've been shagging her for six months." He grinned, but it was all teeth and more menace than I'd ever seen on my brother-in-law's face. "Theo likes to gossip more than social media."

"Fucking Theo," Jared muttered while I tried not to betray my surprise at this new information.

It wasn't like I didn't know Jared slept around, but I hadn't known he was seeing someone monogamously for six months.

"Allegra and I agreed to see other people because we didn't ... we thought it was just going to remain casual between us. So I was seeing Sorcha too," Jared explained. And even though he owed me nothing, I had to fight the urge to remove my hand from his. He hadn't told me about Sorcha when we agreed to do this. "When Allegra told me how she felt about me, that was it. End of me and Sorcha."

"Well, Allegra does come with more money than a high school maths teacher," North sneered.

Hurt flared across my chest. I knew we were lying to my sister and North and I hated it ... but the insinuation that Jared might only want me for my money hit a little too close to home. My family name and wealth were the only things people ever saw when they looked at me. I expected it from most people. I had not expected it from North who had fought so hard to prove to Aria that she was more than that too.

I tried to tug my hand out of Jared's but he held tight.

"I don't give a fuck that you just insulted me," Jared responded in a low, dangerous voice. "I do give a fuck that you just insulted my wife. I don't care who you are. You watch your mouth when it comes to Allegra."

My pulse raced at the way *my wife* sounded on Jared's lips.

As if realizing what he'd just said, North turned to Aria. Her wounded look said it all. His expression tightened at his mistake, and he gave her a tender grimace of apology before turning it on me. "I did not mean that the way it sounded. Of course, anyone would want you for all that you are, not who you come from. I'm just concerned that it was a nice *bonus* for McCulloch who runs a farm. And we all know that keeping a profitable farm is not easy."

Jared cut me a dark look. "I'm going to kill Theo."

I felt the need to call Sarah so she could warn her husband he was in deep shit.

"Jared is managing fine. It's nothing to do with the farm," I hurried to say. "And for your information, I knew about Sorcha. I had *relationships* as well, you know."

"Taka Aikawa?" Aria queried curiously, seeming to forget for a moment the bomb I'd just dropped.

How did she know about Taka?

"The actor?" North eyed me curiously.

Taka Aikawa was a Japanese American actor who'd become a member of Ardnoch a few years ago. We might have hooked up a time or ten after being introduced three years ago at an Ardnoch Estate New Year's Eve party. His dad was a famous director, too, and I always liked that Taka just saw me as an attractive female and not as Wesley Howard's daughter.

"How did you know about that?"

Aria shrugged. "I have my ways."

"Security better not have reported it to you."

"Maybe you shouldn't make out with men in public places on the estate, then."

I opened my mouth to argue that a few kisses in the estate gym was not making out when Jared squeezed my hand. "Taka?"

There was something unexpected in his eyes. Not jealousy. Concern, perhaps. Oh. Did he think I'd given up a serious relationship for our marriage?

"So, you knew about Sorcha but Jared didn't know about Taka?" North's tone was that of a shit-stirrer. I never knew he was such a stirrer of the shit until this moment.

"He didn't know because it wasn't serious," I promised my new fake husband. "We just hooked up a few times."

Jared gave me a sharp nod of acceptance.

"And that doesn't bother you?" My brother-in-law narrowed his eyes. "Because if Aria had been screwing someone else while we were in our 'no-strings' phase, I'd have probably killed him."

"Not true," my sister threw over her shoulder.

"I'd have at least hit him," North argued. "And eviscerated him in my mind over and over again."

Aria's eyes glinted with amusement as she met my gaze. "That I do believe."

Her simple warm look gave me hope that maybe she might get on board with this marriage after all.

Until Jared ruined it with, "I guess I'm just more secure. After all, Allegra didn't marry Taka, did she?"

Why was his arrogance so goddamn hot?

North coughed into his fist. "Arsehole."

Aria rolled her eyes.

"Hey!" I frowned. "Before I walked in the door and told you we got married, you and Jared were friends."

"Aye, until he went behind everyone's back and married my wee sister."

That North thought of me as his sister warmed me to my soul. "North ..." I released Jared's hand to cross the distance between me and my brother-in-law. When I wrapped my arms around him, tucking my head against his chest, he couldn't resist. The big softie hugged me tight. "I'm just worried about you," he murmured in my ear. "So is your sister."

I pulled back, gave him a reassuring pat on the shoulder, and released him to reach for Aria. I hugged her and her arms banded around me.

"I'm going to be okay," I whispered. "I promise."

Discomfortingly, I wasn't sure if I'd just lied to her again or not.

NINE
JARED

Even when we weren't in the same room, I could feel Allegra. Just knowing she was in the farmhouse made me aware of her every second. It chafed. I was used to being able to go about my business without thinking or worrying about anyone else.

After the visit to her sister's, we'd gone to her parents' beach house and I tried not to overanalyze the sheer level of wealth Allegra was used to. I mean, I'd married her for it. But actually seeing the houses on the Ardnoch Estate, witnessing the quality of the goods inside, I felt less than. I didn't want to touch anything. Felt like it wasn't my place. And I didn't do well with feeling like I didn't belong somewhere.

All of that, along with the reminder that I'd married a woman for her money, sat heavily in my gut as we drove back to the farmhouse. What the fuck was I doing? Even knowing Allegra was gaining something from our marriage, too, didn't make me feel any less of a dishonorable bastard. When North had called me out for it, I'd felt like scum.

Now seeing with my own eyes the world Allegra came from, discomfort and embarrassment rode my shoulders when

I brought her back to the farmhouse. That just pissed me off because my family had built this place with their own hands, and there was nothing to be ashamed of here. It wasn't my fault my fake wife was used to finer things. Or dating men like Taka Aikawa.

I'd googled him when I was alone in my room.

He was a good-looking fucker and according to Wikipedia, he came from money before his acting career took off. Taka was definitely more in Allegra's league.

Yet here she was. Married to a Scottish farmer who'd once run around with criminals.

Not that she knew that last part.

Our plan was to tell Sarah in the morning about the marriage. I knew Aria and North didn't believe us, and I had a sneaking suspicion Sarah wouldn't either. It didn't matter as long as they could claim ignorance to our scheming in case it went tits up.

I was awake before Allegra to meet Georgie out in the fields at five thirty. Years ago, when Grandad was still alive, I used to run regularly. I'd get up before he needed me on the farm and run for miles down the beach. Since taking over, I rarely had time for running. I missed it. But the farm came first. And we had a fault in the irrigation system to fix. They were forecasting a pretty dry summer, so we'd need it up and running.

"Every year this fucking thing needs fixed," Georgie grumbled as we got to work. "How old is the system?"

"Too old." I stopped what I was doing to look at my friend and farmhand. "It doesn't matter, anyway. This fix is temporary. I'm going to invest in an irrigation boom."

He snorted. "Aye, and how are you affording that, mate?"

"Allegra Howard and I married yesterday. Her money is now my money."

Georgie's head snapped up at my blunt declaration.

"What?"

"You heard me."

"Is this a weird joke?"

"It's not a joke."

He sat up, wiping mud from his hands onto his jeans. "Allegra Howard, as in Wesley Howard's daughter? Allegra Howard is your wife?"

"Aye." My heart thudded a wee bit faster.

Eyes roaming my face, he shook his head. "What the fuck did you do? What is she getting out of it?"

"We married because we wanted to marry," I lied. "The money is just a bonus. She wants to help."

He huffed in disbelief. "You think for one second I'm going to believe you've been shagging Sorcha all the while you've had Allegra Howard in your bed? Do you think I'm daft? You did this for money, and she's getting something out of it too."

Expression hard, I replied, "Georgie, all you know is that I married Allegra and that I've been secretly seeing her for a year. Do you understand me?"

He opened his mouth to argue.

"Georgie. That's all you know. Right?"

Understanding finally donned. "Fuck," he muttered. "Aye, that's all I know. But I hope you know what you've done here, Jar. And I hope this farm is bloody worth it."

"It is." To protect this land from my arsehole of a father, I would have done much worse than marry a woman who was practically a stranger. "Now that we've got money coming in, I'm going to buy some sheep, hire a shepherd. But I've got bigger plans than that."

Georgie studied me hard for a wee bit longer, then shook his head with a wry grin. "What are you thinking?"

"Caledonia Sky." I referred to one of my fields that had far-reaching views of the North Sea. It was currently a meadow.

"What about it?"

"Have you heard of glamping pods?"

A slow smile lit Georgie's face.

———

A few hours later, I returned to the farmhouse, annoyed about the nervous churning in my gut as I strode in through the mudroom. As I took off my boots, I couldn't hear anything. A glance out the front window as I headed upstairs told me Allegra's rental car was still here. Passing what was Sarah's room, I heard the low murmur of Allegra's voice as if she was on the phone to someone. Hurrying by, I strode into my bedroom and closed the door behind me.

The room had once belonged to my grandparents. While Granddad was alive, I'd roomed in the attic conversion, but it was sweltering hot up there during the summers. When Granddad died, Sarah had surprised me by having his old room redecorated for me. New furniture and all. It had been bittersweet to take over the room, but I'd gotten used to it in the last five years.

I'd left Georgie out in the field because Allegra and I had a video call appointment with Sarah. We'd asked Aria and North not to tell Theo or my cousin before we had the chance to.

Last night had been pretty shitty lying to Allegra's sister, but I suddenly understood how she must have felt about it. I hated lying to Sarah. My cousin might be older than me, but she'd always feel like a younger sister. She was the kindest person I'd ever known, and I wanted to protect her from anything that might hurt her. Even me.

After a quick shower, I changed into a clean shirt and jeans. Then I stared down at my grandfather's wedding ring where it laid on my bedside table. I hadn't put it on this morning because jewelry and farm work were a terrible idea. Now, however, I reached out and slipped the cold metal onto my finger. It was a wee bit big, but my knuckle stopped it from slipping off.

I didn't know how to feel about the sight of it on my hand. It was a claiming, after all, and I'd spent my whole adult life avoiding any woman's attempts to claim me.

Shouldn't I feel trapped? Suffocated?

I didn't.

Probably because I knew it wasn't real.

Stepping out into the hall, I came face-to-face with Allegra.

"Oh!" She startled at the sight of me as she closed her door. "I didn't know you were back."

I tried not to look at her too long as I strode by. "Aye. Just needed a shower."

At the sound of her following me downstairs, I tried not to tense.

Repugnant.

The word hit me again, not for the first time, since she'd said it yesterday.

This woman actually thought I found her repugnant.

It was baffling. But I hadn't corrected her. If she knew how much I'd wanted to turn that phenomenal kiss yesterday into multiple rounds of energetic fucking, it would complicate this thing between us. She was better off thinking I didn't want her.

She was out of my league, but I'd fucked women who had more money or higher social status than me. It wasn't about that. The fact was that she made me feel something more than attraction. I couldn't explain it. Had never been able to figure out that spark between us from the moment she sat down next to me in the pub five years ago.

I didn't want to figure it out. I wanted to run from it.

Instead, I'd bloody married her.

So, aye, it was best I kept my distance, in whatever way I could.

"Ready to do this?" Allegra asked, following me into the kitchen where my laptop sat on the table. I pulled out a chair for her and gestured for her to sit.

"Ready as I'll ever be," I replied gruffly, sliding into the seat next to her to open the laptop to call Sarah.

Allegra rested her hand on my arm and I stiffened.

She immediately withdrew it.

"Sorry," I muttered.

"It's fine." She wouldn't meet my eyes. I was such a prick. "I just wanted to say that I know how crappy it is lying to someone you love. But we're doing it for their sake, so they don't get in trouble."

"I know." I nodded at her in thanks. "Let's do this."

———

"Right." I stood up not long later, grabbing my car keys off the hook on the wall leading into the mudroom. "I'm off."

I had no time to process the conversation with Sarah, her reaction, or the fact that she'd announced she was now coming to Ardnoch earlier than planned. She didn't believe us and she wanted to talk to me alone. That meant I had to double down on my lie. Something I was not looking forward to. For now, I had one more person I needed to speak with before I could allow myself to think about the magnitude of my and Allegra's actions.

"Oh. You're heading out onto the farm again? I wanted to talk to you about ... well ... the financial situation."

I glanced at Allegra as I stuffed my wallet into the back pocket of my jeans. Yesterday, she'd looked stunning in a simple dress and sexy fucking shoes. Today her dark hair flopped around the top of her head in a messy bun. She wore a faded Kaleo T-shirt that slipped off one shoulder. Tight jeans and bare feet completed the outfit, proving the woman not only had great taste in music but that she looked gorgeous no matter what she wore.

It was surreal seeing her in my kitchen, barefoot, like she lived here.

Well, she did live here.

Heat coursed toward my dick, but I doused it with willpower. Like I had done since the first night she slept here.

I brushed past her. "We'll talk about it when I get back. I've got some investment ideas to run by you that would make me more comfortable with the whole money side of this bargain. But I have something to do first."

"Oh?" At my sharp look, she flushed. "Sorry, I didn't mean to sound like a nosy wife."

Wife.

I shoved the way that word made me feel to the back of my mind. Deep, deep to the very back where it might hopefully one day disappear. Still, we were supposed to be in this together. "I, uh, have one more person I need to tell face-to-face." At her curious silence, I continued, "Sorcha."

Allegra's expression didn't change at Sorcha's name, and her tone was calm, neutral as she inquired, "Why didn't you tell me about her? I didn't mean to mess things up there."

"Do you really think if I was serious about a woman, I'd have married you?"

She studied me thoughtfully and then replied in that quiet, soft voice I liked too much, "Fair."

I sighed. "But she deserves to hear it from me directly. I'll be back in a couple of hours. We can talk then."

"Great." She looked around the kitchen. "I might go grocery shopping, if that's cool? Buy some things I like to eat."

"Of course," I answered gruffly. "This is your home for the

next eighteen months. You should buy whatever you need to be comfortable. I'll see you."

"See you."

Fifteen minutes later, I was out of Ardnoch and on my way to Inverness. On the drive, I focused on plans for the farm and for the holiday rental business so I didn't have to think about my impromptu marriage, Allegra, or how fucking shit it felt to lie to people I cared about.

All to keep my scumbag father's hands off the farm.

It didn't say much about me that I didn't really think about Sorcha until I reached the city and was closing in on her flat. Sorcha's one-bedroom apartment was on a touristy, Victorian street close to the city center. A lot of the flats and homes around here were holiday rentals. Hers was in a Victorian end of terrace house that had been converted into two flats.

Sorcha knew I was coming because I'd texted her last night to ask if I could drop by. She'd replied in a flirty way that suggested she thought I was visiting for sex. I felt bad about breaking things off with her, but I'd been planning to beforehand, so the marriage was the perfect excuse. I didn't feel awkward about it because we'd both known the score from the moment we'd started sleeping together.

I parked across her driveway because I wasn't intending to stay long. As I neared the door, it opened, and she stood in the tiny entrance at the bottom of the stairs that led up to her place. Brechin came bounding past her legs to jump on me.

Grinning, I rubbed the labradoodle's ears. "Hiya, boy. Nice to see you too."

Glancing up from him as he slobbered all over my hands, I kept my expression blank as I met Sorcha's pretty blue eyes. "We need to talk."

Her expression fell and she stood back, opening the door wider for me. "It's like that, is it? Well, I suppose you better come in."

TEN
JARED

Sorcha's flat was small but comfortable. If I was being honest, it reminded me a bit of my mum's place growing up. Sorcha's taste in furniture and all that shit was old-fashioned, but she was a modern woman otherwise.

She'd married and divorced a fellow high school teacher in her twenties. Reading between the lines, it had been a harrowing time for her and she was dead set against marriage or any sort of relationship. Thirty-seven, smart, sexy, independent, and completely uninterested in commitment, Sorcha had been the perfect kind of temporary for me.

Lately, I'd felt like she was angling for more, which didn't make sense.

But her attitude now relieved me. She sensed what was coming and appeared to be okay.

I'd accepted her offer of a coffee because it was polite and I needed the caffeine. As I took the mug from her, her gaze caught on the ring on my finger. Her eyes widened. "What is going on?"

I took a gulp of the dark brown liquid and then looked her

straight in the eyes. "I wish I'd had a chance to talk to you first, to end things right, so for that I apologize."

"You're married?" Sorcha gaped. "Married? You? Jared McCulloch?"

"I am."

She threw her hands up. "To whom? When? What?"

"You and I never agreed to be monogamous."

Scowling, she huffed, "I know that! Do you think you're the only man I've slept with in the last six months?"

I had actually, but was relieved to hear I wasn't. "Of course not."

"But marriage ... you said ... you made it clear that a relationship wasn't even on the table, never mind marriage."

I saw it then. What I really hadn't wanted to see. A flicker of hurt. "I didn't think that was what you wanted either."

"I ... I ..."

Not wanting her to admit to feeling more for me than just attraction because I didn't want to cause her pain, I hurried on, "Allegra and I have known each other for five years. She's American, so she just visited when she could." Swallowing past the discomfort of lying, I continued, "I've always had feelings for her but didn't think she'd want to stay here. It turns out she feels the same way and ... we got married yesterday."

Silence settled between us as Sorcha processed this. Leaning her curvy arse against the kitchen counter, she crossed her arms over her ample chest. "She must be something."

"She is," I answered truthfully.

"Ouch." Sorcha winced.

"You're something too. You and I are just not ... that."

She nodded, staring at the floor. "Can ... Do you have a picture of her?"

Panic flitted through me. I had no pictures of Allegra. No selfies. Surely a couple who were married would have a shit ton of pictures of each other. It was something I'd need to discuss with Allegra when I returned home. "Why do you want to see a photo of her?"

"Curiosity."

"You can google her." She'd find out, anyway. I sighed heavily. "Allegra is Wesley Howard's daughter."

She stared at me blankly for a second and then realization dawned. "The film director? Is she from that swanky estate in your village? Is that how you met?"

I nodded.

Sorcha let out a huff of amusement as she pulled her phone from her back pocket. Her fingers flew over the keypad and after a second, she whistled. "Okay. Aye. Well. How does a mere mortal compete with that?" She looked up at me, a wistful expression on her face. "She's stunning, Jared."

I shifted uncomfortably because the truth was, to me, Allegra was the most beautiful fucking woman I'd ever seen in my life and no one would ever compare in that respect. Guilt was an unwelcome emotion. "You know you're gorgeous too."

Her lips curled up at the corners. "Don't let your wife hear you say that. Bloody hell. Your *wife*." She stuffed her phone back into her pocket. "Does she know about me?"

I nodded. "She and I were casual too. Until ..."

"Until you weren't."

"Aye."

Brushing her blond hair off her face, she gave me a breezy grin. "Can't say I won't miss our time together."

"Aye, it was fun."

"It was. But I also liked just having you in my life. Can we still be friends?"

"Of course." I bridged the distance between us and pulled her into a hug. "You're a good person, Sorcha. Thanks for everything. I wish you nothing but happiness, you know."

She hugged me tight. "You too." Pulling back from her embrace, she surprised me with a quick kiss. "Goodbye, Jar."

Eleven
Allegra

I assured myself that Jared hadn't been gone long enough to have had one last round of sex with this Sorcha person. It was a two-hour round trip to Inverness, and he was back in two hours thirty.

Thirty minutes was *so* long enough for a quickie. Damn, a minute was long enough for a quickie.

He wouldn't have done that, though. He'd promised me monogamy for two months so we could sell the lie.

I was desperate to ask about her, and I couldn't ignore the niggle of jealousy I experienced over this woman who Jared McCulloch had wanted long enough to be with for six months.

When he returned, he was brooding, which worried me. Did he have real feelings for Sorcha? Had I fucked up something important for him by offering him a chance to save his farm? Had I inadvertently forced him to choose between the farm and Sorcha? Instead of sticking around to talk like he'd suggested, he changed back into his work clothes and went out to find Georgie.

He didn't come home for the dinner I'd made. It was

nothing special. I'd just boiled some pasta and made a sauce. I'd also burnt the garlic bread in his oven because I wasn't used to it yet.

When it hit nine o'clock and he still hadn't returned, I knew he was avoiding me. Sarah had told me a while ago that Jared kept early hours as much as he could. Early to bed, early to rise.

Not wanting to sit there like a little wife waiting on her husband to come home, I'd covered his plate with foil and left a note for him that the food was there if he wanted to heat it up. Retiring to my room that still didn't feel like mine, I'd set my alarm for four thirty because I was determined to discuss important things with Jared. He would not avoid me tomorrow.

As soon as my head hit the pillow, thankfully, emotionally exhausted, I fell asleep. But my last thoughts before I drifted off were about my fake husband and where he was tonight and if he intended to sleep in his own bed like he'd promised.

———

Walking into the kitchen early the next morning, I found Jared braced against the counter, sipping from a mug of coffee. Light streamed in through the kitchen window. During summer here, the days were long; it started to get dark around eleven at night and light just after three in the morning. I slept with a sleep mask.

It was five o'clock and the sun was already shining, casting a halo around the back of Jared's head. Until I moved farther into the room, I couldn't read his expression.

His eyebrows rose at the sight of me. "You're up early."

"We have a lot to discuss today ... so I thought you could give me a tour of the farm while we talk. You can tell me about your plans, and I can help make them happen."

He appeared surprised. "You want to tour the farm?"

"Of course."

"Won't you be bored?"

I puckered my brow. "What do you think I do all day, Jared? Spend my daddy's cash and laze around?"

He frowned at the bite in my tone. "Of course not."

"Good. I might have a trust fund, but I also have my own money. I'm a successful artist and I get my inspiration from nature. I love walking and hiking and all the things. So ... show me around."

"Okay." He nodded agreeably. "You want a coffee?"

I moved to the cupboard beside him, ignoring the way my skin prickled as my arm brushed his. "Yesterday, I bought some of this heather tea I've fallen in love with since moving here."

"You don't drink coffee?"

"Not anymore."

I glanced into his mug as I passed him to boil the kettle for my tea. "You're a black coffee guy?"

"Aye."

"Good to know."

He cleared his throat as he turned to me. "I ... uh ... I'm sorry about last night. I didn't realize you were making me dinner."

"It's fine," I said, more blasé than I felt. "Did you manage to heat it up?"

"I'd already eaten. Georgie and I went to the Gloaming for dinner and a few pints."

Irritation niggled at me and I couldn't look at him as I poured the hot water into my mug. "It's not really a great look ... you disappearing all evening the night after you're married. People expect newlyweds to be all over each other."

At his silence, I gathered the courage to look at him.

Jared scowled, then bit out a curse as he rubbed a hand over his beard. "You're right. I didn't think."

And I didn't want to think about the fact that after dumping his casual girlfriend, he hadn't wanted to spend the evening with me. "It's fine. I'm ...you know ... I'm sorry if I'm cramping your style here." I gestured around me, indicating the house. "I could stick to my room if that helps."

"No." He grimaced. "Fuck, Allegra, I'm sorry. I don't want you to feel uncomfortable here. Yesterday was just ... it was a lot. I'm not a man who lies to people. In fact, I'm known for being brutally honest. So ... it fucked me up a bit and I just needed ... I don't know."

"I get it," I promised. "Believe me, I get it."

He seemed to accept that and relaxed. "I did have a thought yesterday."

"Oh?" I sipped at my tea, trying not to stare too hard at his handsome face.

"We don't have any photos together. No selfies. Nothing."

Damn. I hadn't thought about that. "Well, if it comes up, we can just say we were keeping our relationship quiet so we deliberately didn't take any. Now that we're married, maybe we should try to take at least one a day. Just so we have them. We could take a selfie while we're out on the farm today."

"All right." He nodded gruffly and glanced down at my feet. "Do you have wellies?"

"I have hiking boots."

"Those will do. Breakfast first." He pulled open the refrigerator and removed eggs. "Eggs on toast work for you?"

"You're cooking me breakfast?" The thought caused a little kernel of warmth in my chest.

Jared shot me a too-sexy smirk. "I'm cooking myself breakfast like I have done for years. It's only polite to ask if you'd like some too."

I rolled my eyes. "Fine. I'd like eggs on toast too."

"Sunny side up or over easy?"

"Over easy, please."

He smiled at the pan as he placed a knob of butter in it. "Guess we can tell people we have one thing in common—we like our eggs the same way."

I grinned as I pulled the bread out of the larder to make the toast. "Imagine that."

———

Jared would never be a big conversationalist. I got the impression he was more of a listener. But at least at breakfast he wasn't as coolly distant with me as he had been. I peppered him with questions about the farm before we departed, and he told me how many acres he had across eight fields. Each field had a name and a purpose.

Our first stop was the henhouse, right behind the farmhouse. I'd heard the hens clucking around and, of course, the rooster, nature's own alarm clock. Jared explained he had one rooster to twelve hens.

After we'd eaten and cleaned away our dishes (Jared was very tidy, which I'd already guessed from the state of the farmhouse), he'd pulled a bag of what he called layer pellets out of a large cupboard in the mudroom. While he handed me the bag along with a bag of mixed corn, he grabbed a bucket and filled it with water from an outside tap.

"The chickens need food and water daily, but the food has to be removed at night to discourage pests. Their bedding needs changed once a week, and the henhouse requires disinfection every four months," he told me as we strolled over to it.

The house was twice as big as any I'd seen, as was the attached chicken run. At the sight of Jared, the chickens came running toward him, squawking eagerly.

I smiled at their excitement and studied what Jared was

doing as he poured water into a trough-like dish the chickens could access from inside the run. Next to it was an even longer trough.

He reached for the pellets and corn, but I kept my grip on them and walked over to the trough. "Do I just pour them both in, like a mix?"

At his silence, I squinted back against the early-morning sun. I'd need to return to the house for my sunglasses before we left to explore the rest of the farm.

"Well?"

Jared frowned but nodded. "Aye, just pour it in."

"Until the bags are empty?"

"Aye."

I nodded and poured it all in, laughing at the way the chickens ran at it, pecking at the pellets and corn before I'd even finished. "Hungry, huh? Is that yummy? Mmm, it sure looks yummy." I murmured some compliments to the ladies as the laid-back rooster suddenly squeezed in between them. "Oh, here he is. The man of the hour. This is the life, huh? All these ladies to yourself."

The rooster cocked his head at me as if to say, "Well, yeah" and I giggled, turning to Jared.

The soft expression on his face made my smile falter.

He'd never looked at me like that before.

As if realizing it himself, he strolled abruptly past and opened a box next to the henhouse. Inside were egg cartons. Weirdly excited about fresh eggs, I hurried to his side and watched as he opened a part of the home that housed the chickens.

He revealed beds of wood shavings inside, and they were dotted with fresh eggs.

"Oh my God." I clapped my hands together. "Freaking eggs!"

Jared chuckled as he glanced at me before carefully

collecting them. "You're acting like you've never seen an egg before, but we just ate them, remember."

"Yeah, but I've never seen them fresh from the source." I peered into the carton as Jared filled two. A dozen eggs. "Do they lay this many every day?"

"Almost every day. I keep some for myself and I sell the rest to Morag who runs the grocery store and deli. When Sarah lived here, she looked after the chickens and dropped the eggs off with Morag every morning before her shift at Ardnoch. Now I do it."

"I could do this," I told him as we walked back to the house.

"Do what?"

"I could feed and water the chickens. Look after them. It would take one more chore off your plate."

Jared shook his head. "You'd need to be up at this time every morning to do it so I could run them to Morag's in time."

"I could do that too. Take them to Morag's. I know Morag, you know. I've practically been living here for four years."

"It's fine, Hollywood. I don't expect you to help out on the farm."

Hollywood? I scowled at the nickname. "I think it would sell our story better if I did help in some way. I'm not lazy. I'm not used to sitting around doing nothing, and early mornings don't bother me. I don't sleep a lot, anyway." It was true. When inspiration struck me, I'd often forget to sleep while I worked on a project.

"I didn't say you were lazy, just that you don't need to help out. You're not used to this kind of life, Allegra."

What did that mean? "Well, I think it would look good if I was the one to take the eggs to Morag," I insisted stubbornly.

Jared stepped into the mudroom, holding the door open

for me. I held his gaze, wondering what thoughts were hiding behind his. "You want to look after the chickens?"

"Yes. I am capable of looking after another living creature."

"I never said you weren't. Are you always this defensive?"

Irritation flushed through me. "When I feel like I'm being judged, yeah."

With an aggravated sigh of his own, Jared grabbed his car keys off the hook by the door. "I'm not judging you. You've just never experienced work like this. On a farm. It's constant and tiring and as far from the world you're used to as it gets. Farm life isn't glamorous. It's not art and art shows and galleries and all that champagne stuff. I just don't want you feeling pressured into changing your life any more than this scheme already has."

Thinking of his night at the pub last night, I wondered if he didn't want me feeling pressured or if *he* didn't want to feel pressured? And I was getting kind of tired of him making assumptions about me based on what he thought he knew about me. Was this why I was so unattractive to him? Because he thought I was a spoiled, Hollywood princess who la-la-la-ed her way through life with art and art shows and galleries and *champagne stuff.*

I stepped into Jared's path as he moved back toward the door. "I know we don't know each other very well, Jared, but I'm going to tell you a few things that might stop you second-guessing me in the future." I leaned into him a little, his cologne tickling my senses. "One: I never do anything I don't want to do. Two: I'm not some Hollywood princess whose been protected in bubble wrap her whole life. I've almost died, I've shot someone, and I've been to rehab. And that all happened before I was eighteen years old."

His nostrils flared in surprise at my confession.

"Life is hard, Jared. And painful. Not even money can

protect you from that. I'm not who you think I am, and I'd like it, if going forward, you could just treat me … as a person and not as Chiara and Wesley Howard's daughter." I tried to keep the bitterness out of those last words, but I wasn't sure I succeeded.

For the first time since we met, Jared looked at me. Really looked at me. Those spectacular eyes roamed my face as if he hadn't seen me until just then. My heart rate escalated as the silence between us stretched.

"Okay," he said on a heavy exhale.

I deflated with something like disappointment, but I wasn't sure why. What had I expected Mr. Monosyllabic to say?

"Okay." I nodded and turned on my heels. "Let's go sell some eggs."

TWELVE

ALLEGRA

There were no words between us as we drove into Ardnoch. Jared parked his Defender behind the buildings on Castle Street, the main thoroughfare of the village. Morag met us at the back door of her grocery store, her eyes widening at the sight of me.

"Allegra, what brings you here this morning?" Morag asked, friendly and warm as always. Every other month she changed the color of the rinse in her hair. Today it was purple.

A familiar knot tightened in my stomach as I prepared to tell her about our marriage. I really had underestimated how much it would suck lying to this community of people who had become my home. It was especially horrible with Morag because she was the first person to hear the news and be delighted by it.

"That's wonderful!" she exclaimed, pulling me into a tight hug.

Stupid tears pricked my eyes, and I blinked rapidly to stop them falling. My gaze caught Jared's and he looked as torn up as I felt.

He quickly pasted on a small smile as Morag turned to

him. "And you! Och, I knew you'd eventually find someone who'd knock you on your well-formed arse, Jared McCulloch."

I giggled at that as Jared easily took her embrace and hugged her in return. The affectionate look on his face made me feel a little envious of the older woman.

"And of course it would be Allegra," Morag said as she released Jared. She reached out to touch my cheek affectionately. "This one is very special. I hope you both know how lucky you are."

Those tears burned again. "Morag ..." I gave her hand a squeeze in thanks. My guilt sickened me.

In fact, I was never so thankful to get back in the Defender and drive away from her kindness.

"That sucked," I finally broke the silence between us as Jared drove back toward the farm.

"Aye. It did. I suppose we'd better get used to the feeling."

"I didn't think about this part when I proposed marriage. I didn't think about how hard it would be to lie to *everyone*."

"I know."

"Do you regret it already, Jared?"

He shot me a hard look. "Do you?"

I turned away, watching the village pass by, watching it turn into trees and then fields and mountains and sea. I would never be able to explain why this was the place my soul felt at peace. The truth was, I didn't care why it was. Just that I'd found it. Minutes disappeared between us before I finally answered, "I'd do anything to stay here. So no. I don't regret it."

"I'd do anything to keep the farm," Jared replied gruffly. "So I don't regret it either."

———

> Have you told Mom and Dad yet? xx

The text from Aria arrived an hour after our trip to Morag's. My heart leapt at the question and I quickly texted back:

> Not yet. Please let me tell them. xx

Less than a minute later, my cell pinged again.

> Okay. But you need to tell them. And I would like to have lunch. Just the two of us. So we can talk. xx

> Sure. I'm getting settled on the farm for now but I'll call you. xx

My phone pinged again but I ignored it, focusing on the tour. Jared officially introduced me to Georgie, whom I'd briefly met when he collected Jared from the Gloaming the night he was drunk. He was around Jared's age, shared a similar broad-shouldered build, but had a thick crop of red hair and an even thicker dark brown beard. While Jared was tan from working outside year round, Georgie had pale skin and freckles.

His blue eyes twinkled with mischief upon our introduction, and I knew without asking that *he* knew this was all a ruse. I could only hope Jared had warned him to keep quiet about it.

Our first stop was the cow shed in the first field next to the farmhouse. Shed was an inaccurate description for the huge structure that housed the cattle. Inside it were two injured cows. The rest were out in the fields. Jared showed me their setup for milking, how the fresh milk was collected and then transported to a processing plant to kill the bacteria, before being sold on to major dairy brands.

The rest of the morning, we drove all over the farm. He showed me his rapeseed crops, the barley fields, and the meadows where he intended to put sheep.

"That's one of the first things I want to do. Buy sheep, hire a shepherd again," Jared told me as we drove onto a meadow field with the most spectacular far-reaching views toward the sea. "Equipment needs replaced too. I'll make a list of the costs so you know exactly what's happening financially."

"You don't need to do that," I assured him. "Just buy what you need. My financial guy is going to transfer the money to your business account."

Jared gave me a hard, penetrating look. "I want you to know exactly where the money is going."

"Okay," I agreed.

I could tell by the slight ticking of muscle in his jaw that Jared was frustrated. My gut told me he hated his part of the bargain—taking money from me. The farm was worth the hit to his pride, though. And I understood that.

"This field is different." He gestured for me to follow him out of the vehicle. He opened the gate and I breathed in the sweet-smelling air as we traversed the wildflower-strewn ground.

There was barely a cloud in the sky and the sun was warm on my bare arms. It was like we stood in a mammoth great hall with a sky-blue ceiling above, and lush green, purple, and white carpet beneath our feet. Beyond the fields were trees that hid the main road in the distance, so all a person could see was the glinting sparkle of the North Sea.

"This is so beautiful," I whispered.

Jared heard me. "Which is why I think it would be perfect for a holiday rental opportunity."

I turned to him. "You mean houses? Build houses here?"

He shook his head. "Have you heard of glamping pods?"

"Yeah. I've stayed in a few." Excitement thrummed

through me as I realized what he was planning. "Jared, that's a fantastic idea." I shaded my eyes as I gazed up toward the top of the sloping field where the land leveled out. "Up there?"

"Aye." He jerked his head for me to follow him, and we strode uphill until we reached a large, flattened area. Jared gestured to his left. "A costly part will be putting a road in that brings guests right to the top. But I think it'll be necessary."

"Agreed."

"I reckon we'd get six glamping pods on here. I've looked into it, and if we make them high spec, we can charge about a hundred a night in high season, sixty per night low season."

My brain whirred. "You know I've seen some really successful social media accounts for holiday rentals in Scotland. They have so many followers, they're booked out eighteen months in advance. That's three grand a month in the high season per pod. That's a gross income of eighteen thousand a month."

Jared nodded, expression serious, thoughtful. "Aye, if you can make it work on social media. I don't have any social media."

"I do. For my art." I shrugged nonchalantly. "I have a different artist's name. Lucy Stella. No one really knows it's me because I never post my face. I have almost four hundred thousand followers."

Jared's expression softened with admiration. "That's amazing."

I shrugged again, my cheeks a little flushed. "I'm creative. The whole social media thing comes naturally to me. So I could help with that. I'm not bad with a camera. I could take the perfect shots." Pulling my phone out of my pocket, I tapped on a social media icon. "Here, let me show you what I'm thinking."

Jared bridged the distance between us and I ignored the way my heart jumped at the feel of his hard shoulder touching me. My skin prickled as his head ducked beside mine to look at the screen. "Here." I tapped on a particular account of a holiday rental on Skye. "They've captured the kind of luxury hygge lifestyle perfectly. People eat it up and want to experience what they're selling."

He appeared thoughtful for a second. Then he glanced down at my feet. "You up for a small hike?"

"Um ... sure. Why?"

"This way." He started through the clearing that would house the pods and into the woodland behind it. I hurried to follow, keeping all my questions to myself. After a few minutes walking through a dense woodland that was cool and shaded, we began going downhill.

It was kind of steep, and Jared kept glancing back to make sure I was okay. My legs, however, were strong from all the hiking I'd done since moving here.

Then suddenly beyond us, something sparkled through the trees. Anticipation filled me, and I was not disappointed as the ground leveled out and the trees opened up. Jared stopped and turned to me, eyes alight with pride as we stood on the banks of a small inland loch.

There was room enough for two more glamping pods here.

"This ... Jared, this is stunning."

"Do you think you could do with this what those people have done on social media with theirs? There's a rough road over the hill at the back there." He pointed toward the east. "It would be more money, but we could bring it close enough so guests don't need to hike to get here. What do you think? Could you make this place look amazing on social media?"

I nodded, meeting his inquiring gaze and trying not to drop mine to his mouth. "Absolutely."

"Great. We could split the profits."

"So it'll also feel like an investment for me?" I asked pointedly, knowing it was important to him that it didn't feel like I was just giving him my money.

"Aye, aye, definitely. Plus you'd be helping me make it work, right? You should get paid for your time." The first real smile I'd seen from him in ages flashed across his face, and it made me want to kiss the hell out of him. "We could make this happen."

"We could." I grinned. "It's exciting." I stepped toward the water. It was still as glass and almost green from the reflection of the surrounding trees. In fact, it was reminiscent of the famous green loch, An Lochan Uaine. I'd driven south to the Cairngorms last summer and walked the forty-five minutes to get to it.

At the time, I'd thought what a wonderful place that loch would be to have an artist's studio. I'd been searching for the perfect spot for so long. My chest ached as I gazed around at Jared's own green loch. I realized the ache was envy. This place *would* be perfect. I could see myself here with a studio that had at least two walls made entirely of glass. Surrounded by natural beauty and inspiration as I disappeared into my creations.

"Is something wrong?"

I yanked myself out of the thought and met Jared's concerned gaze. "Oh. Um. Nothing."

His brows drew together so tightly he appeared almost angry. "Tell me. Are you having second thoughts?"

"No." My smile was reassuring. "I'm ... just ... honestly, I'm a little jealous of your future guests. This place would be ideal for an artist's studio."

His brow cleared. "Oh." He glanced around, taking in the surroundings. "Aye, I suppose it would. Do you not have a studio?"

"A temporary one. In the village. It's a garage attached to the converted blacksmiths. The owners rent it out to me."

"That doesn't sound very inspiring."

I chuckled dryly. "It's not. But it'll do for now." I pulled my cell from my pocket. "We should take that selfie."

"And then head back to the house for some lunch so we can talk about the financials?"

"Sure." Trying not to make a big deal out of it, I moved into his space, pressing my back to his hard chest as I tapped my screen to camera. In selfie mode, I lifted the phone above us and attempted not to react as Jared settled his hand on my waist and leaned down so our faces were level.

"Say cheese," I joked before smiling brightly into the camera.

Jared's lips softened so he was almost but not quite smiling, and I took the shot.

He immediately released me and stepped away.

I will not take offense to that, I lied to myself.

"It's cute." I glanced quickly at the photo, not wanting to be caught lingering over it, even though I planned to stare at it as soon as I was alone.

Jared cleared his throat. "Good. Let's head back."

After our quiet hike uphill, I asked him a few more questions about the farm as we returned to his Defender. Jared replied with one-word answers.

When we reached the farmhouse, Jared made us mammoth sandwiches I couldn't finish so he ate all his and my leftovers, and we talked money.

However, that emotional wall he liked to erect between us was back in place, shutting me out.

He was Mr. Coolly Distant again.

THIRTEEN
JARED

For the first time in five years, I sat in my grandfather's old office at the back of the house without feeling a familiar churning in my gut. Three days ago, after providing Allegra with an estimate of what the farm needed, as well as a very rough estimate of cost for the glamping pods, the funds she'd promised had cleared the farm's bank account.

I wasn't going to lose the farm, and the figures that stared back at me from spreadsheets on the computer screen no longer scared the shit out of me. For the last hour, I'd been on the phone to different contacts, ordering equipment or booking appointments to go look at equipment I was interested in purchasing.

Two minutes ago, I'd gotten off the phone with a recommended company who designed and built glamping pods. We had a meeting in a few days. If I liked them, they'd draw up plans for six pods so we could submit them to the council for planning permission.

A flicker of movement outside the window drew my attention from the computer screen. The flash of dark hair in the back garden made me stand to get a better look.

Allegra stood between the house and the chicken run, her phone pressed to her ear. Whoever she was talking to made her laugh loudly. My skin prickled with sudden warmth at the sight.

It had been a week since I'd taken her to Caledonia Sky and then the inland loch in the woodlands beyond. Something about her excitement over partnering with me in the glamping pod business had caused some panic. Just because we were teaming up to make this work didn't mean we were a *team*. This whole fake marriage thing meant lines had to be clearly drawn between us. This was nothing more than a business deal. We were not friends.

So why hadn't I told the pod architects I needed plans drawn up for two lochside pods as well? Why couldn't I get the fucking yearning on Allegra's face out of my mind as she'd told me it was the perfect spot for her studio?

She nodded vehemently as she talked to the other person on the end of the line and pulled her dark hair off her neck. My gut tightened at the way it made her back arch, her T-shirt stretching over tits that would fill my palms perfectly.

For over a week, Allegra Howard had been on the other side of my bedroom wall. Testing my willpower and determination to stay away from her.

"Your wife does make quite the view."

"Fuck!" I hissed, startled as I whipped my head to the left. Sarah stood at my side.

She grinned mischievously. "You were somewhere else entirely, Jared. A stampede of elephants could have run right through the house and you wouldn't have heard them."

Confused, I blinked stupidly at my cousin for a second or two. "What—"

"But I can see why." Sarah gestured to the window, a thoughtful expression on her face. "I've always thought Ally was lovely. In every way. I'd like to think the way you were looking at her means I'm wrong and this isn't a sham of a marriage?"

At her quirked eyebrow, I evaded her silent questions by pulling her into a hug. "You're home early."

Sarah returned the embrace. "I told you Theo and I were leaving London." She stepped out of my hold but only to take my bearded face in her hands. Her green eyes, the same shade as my own, filled with concern. "What have you done, Jar?"

I gently extricated myself from her hold. "Where's your husband? I'd like to talk to him about gossiping and how it's bad for his balls."

Sarah snorted. "Theo stayed at the club. I told him I wanted to see you alone first. Also, you're going nowhere near my husband's balls. I'm quite protective of them."

I grimaced. "You know you sound more like Theo every day."

She laughed again. "He tends to rub off on a person."

"Or rub them the wrong way."

"Och, you love him really. Right?"

Leaning against my desk, I crossed my arms over my chest. "I would like it if he wouldn't spread my business around. He told North about Sorcha. And that he thought the farm might be in trouble."

Nibbling on her lip, she nodded. "I understand why you're upset. But please know Theo isn't running around telling everyone your business. He told North. Whom he trusts not to gossip. And anyway, Theo is as worried about you as I am." She gestured toward Allegra, who'd hung up the phone and was now over chatting to the chickens. As good as her word, she'd taken over their care and was growing attached to them.

"You married Allegra Howard, Jared. You. Mr. 'I Will

Never Marry Ever, Ever, Ever.' You're not seriously going to stand there and repeat the nonsense you spewed last week on the video call? I talked to Aria. She said Allegra was warned she wouldn't be allowed back into the country next time she visited. And you ... well, you've denied it, but I can tell you've been worried about the farm." Her expression was full of knowing. "You two made a deal, didn't you? You marry her so she can stay in the country, and you'll benefit from her wealth as her husband."

Feeling like an enormous prick, I lied. "No."

"Jared—"

"We married because we wanted to. End of story."

"And what about Sorcha?"

I scowled. "What about her?"

"Wasn't she upset?"

"Why do you care? You never met her."

"I care if you're going around breaking hearts, Jared."

"Oh, for fuck's sake, Sarah, I'm not some twenty-year-old sowing my wild oats anymore. Sorcha knew the score. No one got hurt. We're still friends." I shrugged. "We texted last night."

"You're still friends with the woman you were sleeping with only last month? Does Allegra know?"

Discomfort thrummed through me. "Why would she care? There's nothing going on between me and Sorcha. There never will be again."

"Your wife would care." Sarah narrowed her eyes. "Unless she's a wife in name only."

"Och, sweetheart, let's not go over this again." I gave her a hard look. "Allegra and I are married because we want to be married to each other. Nothing you say will change my response. Do you understand?"

My cousin exhaled slowly and heavily. Then, "I do understand. I wish ... I wish you hadn't done it this way, but I understand. Just ..." She stared out the window, and I followed Sarah's gaze to find Allegra heading back to the house. Her slender, gently curved hips swayed from side to side. The woman's sensuality exuded from every inch of her without her even trying. "Don't hurt her, Jared."

My head snapped back to Sarah. "How could I hurt her?"

"Because no matter what is really going on between you, I've watched Allegra Howard watch *you* from the sidelines for five years. You most definitely have the power to hurt her."

Stunned, I stared after Sarah as she left the office to greet Allegra. I knew there had been a mutual attraction between me and Allegra when we first met. We'd been ready to leave the pub for a hookup until I found out who she was. But I'd assumed that attraction had dissipated on her side. That I was a fleeting flirtation for her.

Sarah couldn't be right.

Allegra could have anyone.

And she was too smart and savvy to marry a man she had a crush on for a business deal.

"Nah," I muttered, shaking off Sarah's suspicions. Allegra had said herself that after two months of marriage, she would start seeing other people.

We were on the same page. This was just an arrangement. No real feelings were involved.

No one was going to get hurt.

———

"So what did your parents say about the marriage?" Sarah asked Allegra as we ate lunch in the kitchen together fifteen minutes later.

Allegra tucked a strand of dark hair behind her ear,

showing off the row of piercings. I'd noted she had four piercings on her left and three on her right, but she wore tiny studs
that you only really noticed when they winked in the light.
"Um ..." She shot me a quick look before lowering her gaze to
her sandwich. "I haven't told them yet."

Irritation niggled in my gut, but I ignored it.

Sarah, however, put my thoughts into blunt words. "Has
this got something to do with the ridiculous story you told
Aria? That you were hiding your relationship for a year
because you didn't think your parents would approve of you
dating a farmer? Whose idea was that?"

Over the last few years, my cousin had gained confidence.
She'd always been fiery beneath that shy exterior, but now she
took no shit from no one. Being married to someone as blunt
as Theo was definitely rubbing off on her. I was proud to see
her come into her own like she had.

But I wanted to defend Allegra against the accusatory glare
in Sarah's eyes. It was me who'd come up with the idea to tell
everyone that we kept our relationship a secret because we
didn't think her parents would approve. Unfortunately, that
meant it had to look like Allegra agreed with me. I hadn't
really considered that she might *actually* suspect her parents
wouldn't approve, though.

I suppose it made sense. If *I* knew I was out of her league,
of course her parents would too.

Allegra lifted her gaze to meet Sarah's and flinched. She
shifted in agitation. "Look, I am not ashamed of Jared. Of
course I'm not. But Aria has a very different relationship with
our parents than I do. I'm not close to them. I don't ..." She
looked away, pain etching itself in her features. "I don't really
tell them much about my life at all anymore."

At the hollowness in her eyes, I had a sudden urge to pull
her into my arms. To protect her from whatever was causing

that awful expression. I remembered her words from last week. About how she'd nearly died, shot someone, and been to rehab before she was eighteen.

It had taken all my self-control not to ask her every single day since what she'd been talking about. I'd even googled it. But there was nothing online about a traumatic past, so whatever happened to Allegra hadn't been leaked to the press.

Did it have something to do with her parents?

"I don't want them to think that by telling them right away, I'm interested in their opinion about our marriage. Because I'm not."

"Do you think they would contest it?" Sarah asked quietly, seeming to sense the same grief that shrouded Allegra when she talked about Chiara and Wesley Howard.

"Dad? No." Allegra shrugged, a cynical smirk on her face that didn't suit her. "He likes to think he's down with the working people. Mamma ... Mamma knows she isn't and likes it that way. I'm twenty-five. My trust fund is mine, no take-backsies, and I have my own money from my art even if they could, by some miracle, take my inheritance from me. Which they can't. My financial advisor has assured me of it. There was no stipulation on the trust fund. I can marry who I like. I married Jared." Her eyes flickered to me before returning to meet Sarah's. "They can like it or lump it, as Mrs. Hutchinson likes to say." She referred to the head housekeeper at Ardnoch Estate, Sarah's old boss.

Sarah's answering smile was half-hearted. "I still think you should tell your parents. I mean ... you want people to believe this marriage is real, right?"

"Sarah—"

"You know." Allegra suddenly stood. "I have a final piece I need to finish for my art show at the end of the month and, uh, I don't mean to be rude, but this interrogation is kind of messing with my head. So, um, I'm going to my studio." She didn't look at me as she threw in my direction, "I might be home late."

Surprised by the uncharacteristic coldness and the abrupt way it had come over her, I sat in silence with my cousin until we heard the front door slam shut behind Allegra.

Sarah bit her lip, a slight flush on her cheeks. "I'm sorry if I was pushing. I didn't know her relationship with her parents was so bad. I mean, I know Aria has some issues with her mum, but they still talk. And she's close to her dad. North said Wesley was a mess when Aria was kidnapped all those years ago. She never ... she never said Allegra had a difficult relationship with them."

I rubbed a hand over my beard, trying to piece together the bits of information she'd given me. "I have a feeling Aria doesn't know."

"A feeling?" Sarah let out another beleaguered sigh. "You're her husband, Jar. You should know if your wife has a difficult relationship with her parents."

At her pointed look, I turned away. "It's been nice catching up, but I need to get back to work."

"Okay." She stood, not at all put out by my abruptness. Instead she reached over to squeeze my arm. "Be careful. I don't want you to get into trouble."

"Marriage is trouble?" I joked half-heartedly, trying to maintain the lie.

My cousin saw right through me. "It is if you married for the wrong reasons."

———

Hours later, Allegra hadn't come home. I distracted myself with dinner and cleaning the house. I'd brought down a load of laundry from my room to do, only to discover Allegra had left dirty clothes in the machine, and a pile of clean laundry on top of it. Shoving my things in with hers, I'd set the machine and then considered the clothing in the basket I'd laid down on the floor. Allegra had folded the clothes that were clean and dry and piled her clean underwear on top of that.

I tried not to look too hard at the mix of lace, cotton, and silk as I lifted the basket to take to her room.

It was strange stepping inside what had been Sarah's room. She and Theo still stayed in here at Christmas. Now they'd be relegated to the attic. I felt almost like I was trespassing in my own home as I entered the bedroom. Allegra's scent hit my nose as I wandered slowly inside.

She hadn't changed it much. There were scatter cushions on the bed I didn't recognize and the duvet was different. Her things cluttered Sarah's old dressing table. Settling the basket of laundry on the bed, I wandered over to the table. A perfume bottle shaped like a glass grenade caught my attention. Lifting it up, I noted the word *Flowerbomb* on it and sniffed.

My gut tightened with need as Allegra's scent filled my senses. It wasn't a sweet, light perfume. It was floral but earthy. Confident, assured. Sexy as fuck. Just like the woman who wore it.

Jewelry glinted on the table's wooden surface, and I lowered the bottle. There was a pile of rings and earrings scattered across the dresser. I'd noted Allegra switched up her jewelry regularly, but she had a specific style and taste. The rings looked handcrafted, some hammered metal, some not quite smooth and perfect like they would be if they were machine-made. All of them were fairly unusual, either unadorned metal or with small stones. Not outlandish. But unique.

Kind of like their owner.

Near the jewelry was a picture frame. It also looked hand-crafted and held within it a photo of Allegra with Aria. Aria was in her wedding gown and Allegra in a soft silver blue bridesmaid dress. I'd attended the wedding with a date. Allegra had gone alone. I could admit to myself my eyes had wandered to her more than once at the wedding. The dress she wore was made of silk and had clung to her body in all the right places. She was fucking breathtaking on a normal day, but that day it almost hurt to look at her.

Sighing, I shook myself from the memory and strode back to the bed to take her laundry out of the basket.

Lifting out the pile, I laid it on her duvet but the under-wear started to fall. When I reached to stop it, my fingers caught on a pair of barely there lace knickers. Hot blood flooded southward as I swallowed hard and I lifted the pants up with both hands.

Holy fuck.

Allegra was wandering around my house wearing shit like this?

The wife who was legally mine and yet I could not touch was walking around the house we shared with this under her clothes?

The image of peeling the lacy knickers down her toned thighs made me instantly hard.

Fuuuuuck.

I dropped the knickers like they burned, my eyes alighting on a bra in the same material. Lifting it up, I took in the matching bra with a hard swallow. The sheer cups were edged in the same soft pink lace.

Her nipples must be visible through this thing.

Suddenly too hot and feeling like a pervy bastard, I dropped Allegra's underwear and hurried out of the bedroom with the emptied basket.

"This is fucking torture," I muttered aloud as I practically threw the basket back in the utility room. Images raced through my mind that I couldn't stop until I was restless and agitated and in desperate need of release. If I stayed in this state when Allegra came home, I knew my willpower would break. I knew I'd initiate something we'd both regret.

I needed a shower.

A cold, very, very cold shower.

Marching back upstairs, I glowered at Allegra's bedroom door as I passed and then undressed in my own room. My movements were hurried and furious.

And when I got in the shower, I let those images run riot in my mind. Where they were safe. Where I was allowed to fantasize about my wife in her sexy knickers and bras ... and I did it with my hand wrapped around my cock.

———

Later that night, I lay in bed, body still thrumming with restlessness. Turning my head on the pillow, I reached out for my phone on the nightstand and pressed the side button. The screen lit up.

Two twenty-three in the morning.

Allegra hadn't returned to the farm yet.

She'd said she was out at her studio and that she might be late ... but this late?

"Bloody hell." I huffed and slammed the phone down. Worry churned in my gut.

This was not supposed to be part of the arrangement. I did not sign up for lying in bed, wondering where the fuck my fake wife was, and feeling rising panic at her absence.

What if she'd run off the road in the dark? The roads to the farm were winding, and arseholes were always driving them too fast.

Or ... what if she was fucking someone?

We'd agreed to two months of abstinence to sell our lie ... but Allegra had been acting strange when she left. She was upset.

The thought of her in another man's bed caused me to flush hot from the tips of my toes to the top of my head. I *hated* the idea. It filled me with an indignant rage I attempted to ignore. But it was writhing in my blood as I tossed and turned.

The sound of gravel kicking under tires had me sitting up, straining to hear. My heart thudded hard as I listened for the sound of the front door opening.

It did.

Her quiet, light footsteps caused the stairs to creak as she ascended. She apparently paused when she reached the top because it was a second or two before I heard her bedroom door open and close. Her floorboards creaked as she crossed the room and then I heard water running from her bathroom. Not long later there was more movement as she presumably readied for bed.

The entire time I had to force myself to stay in my own room.

To not confront her.

If I faced her, she'd see the truth.

She'd see my worry and my jealousy, and it would fuck everything up.

How dare she make me worry about her? How dare she make me jealous?

I had to be up in a few hours. I didn't need this kind of shit keeping me awake. Slumping back onto my bed, exhausted, I decided I'd avoid her like the plague tomorrow to reduce the probability of confronting her. After all, I had no right to.

She wasn't really my wife. She could do as she pleased.

Though we did have an agreement and she might have broken that agreement tonight.

I flinched at the image that appeared behind my eyes. Of some faceless bastard crawling over Allegra's naked body. Possessive fury exploded through me as my eyes flew open.

I was so absolutely fucked.

FOURTEEN
ALLEGRA

I f Jared McCulloch grunted at me one more time, I was going to scream. He'd gone from politely distant to downright rude this morning. It was a miracle I'd managed to get out of bed considering I'd only had a few hours' sleep, but I didn't want to let Jared down with the chickens. I promised him I'd take care of them, and I meant it. Just because I'd lost track of time last night working on a final piece for my show didn't mean I could shirk my responsibilities within our new arrangement.

Jared had appeared surprised to see me up and about too. He looked a little haggard, and anytime I asked him a question he just grunted at me. Suspicion grew as he abruptly stood up to clean his breakfast plates. I could tell he was going to walk out of the house without another word. Head heavy with tiredness, I didn't want to argue with him, but why was he treating me like I was an annoying gnat in his kitchen? Did I keep him awake last night, waiting for me to come home?

Had I inconvenienced him?

At the tense lines of his broad back, I suddenly remembered how I'd felt the night he'd gone to the Gloaming instead of coming home. I'd worried he was with someone, breaking the terms of our deal already.

Would he ... could Jared be concerned that I was with someone last night? Not jealous ... but irritated I might have broken my word? Or ... yeah, jealous?

Stupid hope blossomed in my chest. Stupid, stupid hope. It wasn't like there was ever going to be a real future between us. Yet, it might be nice to know that Jared did like me and find me attractive, after all. If only to soothe my wounded pride.

I pushed up from the table, fumbling for my phone as I approached him at the sink. "I'm sorry I was so late last night. I hope I didn't keep you awake."

He grunted.

Caveman.

Attempting to clear the scowl from my face, I leaned into him, and he stopped cleaning his plate (which was already clean) and straightened. If he was tense before, his body was now rigid with *move away from me* vibes. I didn't. I tapped on my phone screen and held up the photo before his face. "What do you think?"

Jared scowled at it. "What am I looking at?"

"I got so inspired last night that I abandoned the final piece I'd originally intended to use for my show." I traced the image with my finger. Instead of paintings on canvas, I made art with glass. I infused the glass with flowers, gemstones, real liquid gold, copper, and silver ... the glasswork I showed Jared was a large piece that I'd painted in a mix of greens, blues, and golds. I'd taken some of the wildflowers from the wedding bouquet Jared gifted me and pressed them in around the edges. In the middle was a small cascade of aquamarine and peridot gems to represent the water. Faint streaks of gold shimmered through the center like the sun dapple over the surface. "It's the loch behind Caledonia Sky."

Jared took my phone to study the glass art. "This is yours?"

"Yeah."

"I've never seen your art before." He glanced up from the phone. "It's beautiful."

A flush of pride filled me. "Thank you."

Jared handed the phone back.

My fingers caressed his as I took it, and his eyes flashed to mine. "I was at my studio all night," I explained pointedly. "When I get inspired like that, time just slips away. I'll try to be better about that."

He searched my face and nodded slowly. "Why don't you go back to bed? I can look after the chickens."

"I'll see to the chickens. I made a promise, Jared. I *never* break my word."

Understanding dawned in his expression. He nodded carefully. "Me neither. I know what people say about me, but if I promise a person I'm going to do something or *not* do something, I always keep my word."

The tension I'd been carrying since he'd visited Sorcha in Inverness eased.

"I've spent the last week filling out forms for change of address, change of name, and uploading all my documents for my citizenship. My art has kind of fallen by the wayside in all of that so, I just ... yeah, I got lost in it. Which is good because I have my show in a few weeks." I gave him a small smile. "Would you ... I know it might not be your thing, but I'd love it if you could attend it with me."

That familiar frown wrinkled his brow. "I ... that kind of thing isn't really ... You're right. It's not my thing."

Hurt sliced through me, but I kept my smile in place. "Oh. I just ... I thought maybe it might look good to the outside world if you showed up for me."

Jared moved away from the sink, giving me his back as he

wandered into the mudroom. "Aye, but they also know me and know I'm not really a cultured kind of bloke."

Right.

Except this wasn't really about him. I huffed bitterly to myself. Truthfully, I shouldn't be surprised at this point. Jared wandered back into the kitchen, boots on, keys in hand. Expression blank of all emotion.

I breezed past him. "I'm going to feed the chickens."

I could sense him watching me as I shoved my feet into my boots and grabbed what I needed. As I strode outside into the sunny but cool morning, I told myself not to be wounded by Jared's rejection. No one in my family, except Aria, had ever been interested in my artwork. My parents liked to brag that I'd graduated from RISD, but they'd never attended any of my shows. They'd always had some work commitment. While they liked to brag about my success as an artist, I doubted they'd ever contemplated owning a piece of my work.

Aria had. She'd bought pieces for her own home and for Ardnoch Estate. And I knew it was because she genuinely appreciated my work if she was buying them for Ardnoch. Was it any wonder I put too much pressure on her to be every-thing for me? She was. She was the only person who'd ever really given a shit.

It should not surprise me in the least that my fake husband wasn't interested. Hell, I bet a real one wouldn't have been. It was weird ... I'd had men become infatuated with me. Most of them, except for one, couldn't see past my face and body. Their infatuation meant nothing. It was shallow and physical, and they didn't care who I really was. I seemed to lack the ability to interest people enough for them to get to know me and to develop real feelings.

That thought, Jared's complete disinterest in me, floated above my head like the only dark cloud in the sky as I drove into Ardnoch that morning with the eggs for Morag. I considered calling Gail, my therapist, to arrange a session.

Morag sensed my preoccupation and didn't keep me long. But as I was walking back to my car, I heard a familiar voice call my name.

I turned and found Sloane waving at me from the back door of her bakery.

Sloane.

Seeing her pulled me out of my gloom. Because *Sloane* cared about me. I knew she did. Which was why I'd been avoiding her since I'd married Jared. I dreaded telling her. Mentally scolding myself for the wallowing self-pity that had overcome me, I forced myself to walk toward her.

Guilt was already building up from my feet with each step, and it only sharpened when Callie suddenly appeared at her mom's side.

Ah, hell.

Lying to them pained me.

As soon as I reached them, Sloane grabbed my left hand and pulled the ring up to her face. She gaped at it and then at me. "I wasn't sure I quite believed everyone until this very moment. You've been avoiding me, Allegra Howard. Or should I say Allegra McCulloch?"

My gaze darted between her and Callie's identical expressions of indignation. "I ... we've just ... We felt bad about lying for so long. I guess, I just didn't know what to say." There. That was pretty much the truth.

While Sloane studied me with a deep line between her brows, Callie suddenly beamed. "Aunt Ally, all anyone can talk about is how you got Jared McCulloch to settle down. No one's surprised it was you, though."

I scoffed, my self-doubts still lingering. "Why?"

Callie frowned now too. "Because you're, like, one of the sickest people ever. You're an amazing artist, you've traveled, you're tougher than anyone knows, you treat everyone the same, even though you grew up in a mansion in Malibu, and you follow your own path. You and Mum are totally my heroes, Aunt Ally."

Her sweet words hit and soothed every sore spot on my heart.

Before I could stop myself, I burst into tears.

"*Okay.*" Sloane's eyes widened a second before she hauled me into the bakery kitchen.

"Did I say something wrong?" I heard Callie ask worriedly as I covered my face with my hands and sobbed.

I shook my head, trying to calm myself.

Sloane rubbed my back, leaning into me. "Allegra, talk to me. What's going on?"

Grabbing tight to my emotions, my crying slowed, and I wiped at my tears. "I'm sorry. I didn't sleep last night because of work, and it's just been a really emotional few weeks." I reached out to cup Callie's face tenderly. "You just ... what you said means a lot to me, sweetie. That's all."

Callie nodded, though she still appeared troubled.

"Right. I've decided." Sloane squeezed my hand. "You and Jared are coming to dinner on Saturday so I can make sure you're all right. There's no saying no. You don't show and I'll send Walker to come and collect you both."

I laughed tearfully at her warning. "Okay. We'll be there. Just text me the details." Jared would have to show up, whether he wanted to or not.

"Oh, and, Ally?"

I met Sloane's suddenly reproachful gaze. "Go talk to your sister. She's worried about you. Now I am too."

Guilt slashed through me. "I'm fine."

"That may be ... but I'd feel better if you'd stop avoiding Aria."

"She told *you* I'm avoiding her?"

Sloane nodded. "She's really upset."

I was such a shit sister. "I'll go talk to her now. I promise."

———

The security guards at the main entrance of the estate recognized me and opened the gates. I'd made the drive onto the grounds many times, but it never got old. Ardnoch Castle was magical. The long driveway led through a stretch of woodlands before the trees disappeared to reveal grass for miles around the large castle. Flags were situated throughout the rolling plains of the estate—a golf course. It was still early in the morning, but there were a few figures in the distance, playing.

The castle was a rambling, castellated mansion, six stories tall and about two hundred years old. It was the club's main building, but there were several buildings throughout the mammoth estate, including permanent residences that belonged to members like my parents and North and Aria. The estate sat on the coast and offered pine forests, rolling plains, heather moors, inland lochs, and golden beaches. A private beach was just a ten-minute walk from the castle.

As I approached, the familiar details of the building grew clearer—the turrets, the flag of the St. Andrew's Cross flying from one of the parapets. Columns supported a mini-crenellated roof over an elaborate portico that housed double iron doors. They opened as I drew to a stop and a valet appeared to take my keys so he could park my vehicle in the mews around back.

Stepping inside the castle, I drank it in with a soft smile, despite my nerves over seeing Aria. I stood in the entrance of the great hall. This was where Lachlan and my sister hosted ceilidhs and their Christmas and New Year's parties. Aria had also added an end-of-summer party to the annual agenda since the estate was busiest at this time of year.

The great hall was a spectacular room for an event.

It had polished parquet flooring. The décor was traditional, slightly Gothic, with more than a hint of Scotland and luxury. A grand, wide staircase descended into the room, fitted with a red-and-gray tartan wool runner. It led to a landing where three floor-to-ceiling stained glass windows spilled colorful light. Then it branched off at either side, twin staircases leading to the floor above, which you could partially see from the galleried balconies at either end of the reception hall. A pennant flag hung from either balcony with the Adair family coat of arms on it, bearing the words *Loyal Au Mort*. It was the Adair clan motto. Aria told me it meant *Faithful unto Death*.

I thought that pretty fitting considering they were a family who'd clearly do anything for one another. Plus, I'd never seen men and women more devoted to their spouses. Other than North and Aria. And surprisingly, Theo and Sarah—the surprising part being Theo, not Sarah. The handsome Englishman turned into an entirely different person around Jared's shy but strong cousin. His adoration for her was clear for all to see. It made me kind of envious. All of them did.

I stared at those words on the flag for a moment, trying not to overanalyze my sudden misery.

Then a crack brought my attention to the fire. It burned in the huge hearth on the wall adjacent to the entrance and opposite the staircase. Tiffany lamps sat scattered throughout on end tables to cast a warm glow over the dark, wood-paneled walls and ceilings. Usually the smell of burning wood and flickering flames in the hearth made Ardnoch's great hall a bit cozier.

But it would grow hot out soon, so I saw no reason for the fire to be lit today. Aria must've requested it for some reason.

Maybe it had something to do with the member who sat opposite the fire in one of the two matching suede-and-fabric buttoned sofas. There was a coffee table in between where her laptop sat while she tapped away on her phone.

More light spilled into the hall from large openings that led to other rooms on this floor. I could hear the rise and fall of conversation in the distance beyond just as the head butler, Wakefield, appeared. He was dressed like the underbutlers and footmen in black tailcoat and white gloves. His waistcoat, as well as the maître d'hôtel's, was dark green instead of white to differentiate them from the rest of the staff.

"Mrs. McCulloch," Wakefield greeted me with a deferential nod, and I tried not to show my surprise that he knew of my change of circumstances. "Are you here to visit with Mrs. Hunter?"

"Yeah. Is she available?"

"I will inquire. May I offer you a refreshment while you wait?"

My mouth quirked at the corner. I just loved the old-fashioned manners here. "I'm all right. Thanks, Wakefield."

"Very good, Mrs. McCulloch. I will return shortly."

I nodded, flushing a little because every time he called me Mrs. McCulloch, I experienced a fluttering in my belly. *Not going to analyze that either.*

A few minutes later, Wakefield ushered me into Aria's office.

The room was a smaller version of the estate library. Wall-to-wall dark oak bookshelves, an impressive open fireplace, and two comfortable armchairs situated in front of a captain's pedestal desk. A floor-to-ceiling window adjacent to the desk let in light so it didn't feel too dark. Tiffany lamps aided in chasing off the gloom too. Luxurious velvet curtains at the window pooled on the wooden floors, most of which were covered in expensive carpets.

Aria leaned against her large desk. "So she finally appears."

I blanched. "I'm sorry."

She crossed her arms over her chest and sighed heavily. "You know you used to say that a lot when you were younger. I thought we were past all the apologizing."

Tears burned in my eyes. "I need you to know that no matter the stupid shit I spewed a few weeks ago that I would never intentionally hurt you."

She remained unmoved, and I didn't blame her. I'd acted impulsively in the past, said and done things I didn't mean, and I thought I'd grown up since then. But what I'd said to her ... "I know you love me. That you would have done anything for me. I had no right to make you feel guilty about going off into the world and finding what made *you* happy."

She grimaced, wincing as if in pain. "But you were right that I didn't have to go this far away. Where ..." Her mouth trembled as her eyes turned glassy. "Where you couldn't follow me."

I hurried to her, gripping her hands as my tears spilled free. "I am not your responsibility. You get to go wherever you want. To make a life where you want. I do not get to make you feel bad about that and ... that's why I've been avoiding you. Because I'm ashamed. I'm ashamed that I'm so selfish, Ari."

"It's not selfish to need someone."

I sobbed for the second time that day. "I'm sorry for putting that on you."

"Allegra." She tugged me closer, dipping her head to meet my eyes. "Since you were fifteen years old, I have been plagued with worry that something happened I don't know about. I thought ... I thought it was something outside our family, but the last few years ..." Her grip was almost painful. "You seem so bitter toward our parents."

The question hung between us, and panic tightened my chest. "They ... they just ... they've never been there for me,

Ari. Not like you." I pulled out of her embrace, hating the lies that sat between us but knowing they were necessary. "You know they've never been to one of my shows. I doubt they've even seen my artwork outside of what you have here on the estate."

"Well, that's not true. About the artwork, I mean. Dad just asked me the other week if you had any pieces for sale. He wants something for the New York apartment. Though why he can't just call *you* and ask, I don't know. Maybe because you never answer his calls."

"What calls?" I scoffed, backing away. "The only time Dad and I ever see each other is on the forced family video calls."

"Forced?" She scowled.

I shrugged, turning away so she couldn't see my resentment. "Anyway, you and I are good now, right? Because that's all that matters to me."

"You know what matters to me? You. Your happiness. I'm worried about this situation with you and Jared. I know you're a grown-up, but—"

"Ari," I cut her off, my expression falling. "I don't want to lie to you, so please don't make me."

Fear darkened her gaze. "This could get you into so much trouble."

I was optimistically starting to believe she was wrong. "It won't. I've filled out all the forms for citizenship and uploaded all necessary documents. I have an appointment in Aberdeen next week to do all the biometric stuff. And that's it. They'll give me a decision within six months. It's all going to be fine."

"I'm not talking about *that* ... Ally ... I see the way you look at him. How you've always looked at him."

Anxiety knotted my gut. "Ari—"

"I don't want him to hurt you when this is ... when it's done."

It took a great deal of acting, but I managed an insouciant

shrug. "The key is to never give anyone too much power over you. Not even my husband. Jared can't hurt me."

My sister winced. "No matter how your marriage came about, I assure you, the one person in the world who has the power to hurt you more than anyone is your husband. That's why your choice of husband was always going to be one of the most important choices you'd ever make."

FIFTEEN
JARED

My fields were grateful for the break in the weather. It had rained for two days straight, and the skies were dark and overcast as I drove Allegra to Sloane and Walker Ironside's home. I knew the couple fairly well as I'd been drawn into a friendship with them through Sarah. It was hard to believe the cousin who'd been so shy she barely had any friends was now in a book club with the wives of the family who owned most of Ardnoch.

None of the Adairs would be at this dinner tonight. Sloane had assured Allegra that it was just us.

A tense silence existed between Allegra and me as we pulled up outside the bungalow in the quiet cul-de-sac. Everyone knew, because it had been all over the news at the time, that Sloane Ironside had inherited a fortune from her dad. It made the news because her stepmum had hired Sloane's ex-boyfriend to kill her so she'd inherit instead.

Yet, she'd moved into Walker's unremarkable bungalow when they married. It wasn't so unremarkable inside, but still, I liked her choice. She knew what really mattered in life, despite her privileged upbringing. The thought made me glance at Allegra as we got out of the car. Allegra didn't seem to be missing the luxury of her family's beach house, but I wouldn't know for certain. We'd barely spoken in days.

My doing.

After the way I'd reacted to her coming home late, I knew I needed to put even more distance between us. To make matters worse, my father had called me, but I hung up at the sound of his voice. He sent a text before I could block him.

> Heard u married money. That wont stop me frm takin whats mine.

I'd blocked the bastard, knowing he was just trying to mess with my head. He knew now I could best him in court if he took it that far, but he didn't have the cash flow. It was a bluff. Didn't mean it didn't fuck with me, the reminder that I was the son of a piece of shit.

Locked in my head, I barely said a word to Allegra for the rest of the week.

And she'd finally stopped trying to get to know me. The questions about my life before the farm, about why I loved the farm, what I wanted for the future ... I didn't respond to them, and she stopped asking.

It was a bit twisted, but I hated the cool silence she treated me to now.

I hated the sadness I caught on her face when she thought I wasn't looking. I just didn't know how to fix it without complicating things we had no business complicating.

"Ready?" I asked as we approached the house.

"Sure," she replied tonelessly, refusing to meet my gaze.

She hadn't looked at me in days, and it made me realize that I liked the way she looked at me. Allegra always gave you her full attention and seemed to find me genuinely interesting. Funny how I'd unconsciously taken that for granted.

A burn flared across my chest, and I ignored the sensation as I knocked on the door. It flew open as if Sloane had been waiting for us. The blond was a few years older than me but looked about the same age as Allegra. As the women embraced, Sloane's sunny blond prettiness only highlighted Allegra's dark beauty. My wife took my fucking breath away just standing there. Possessiveness curled in my gut.

Sloane turned to me. "And here's the husband."

Allegra allowed her smile to drop while Sloane's attention was elsewhere. She walked away as I embraced Sloane, and I fought the urge to go after her. To tell her I was sorry for being such a prick. For years, I'd watched my mum let men treat her like shit. Whether they shouted at her constantly, bullied her ... or ignored her. I'd vowed never to treat a woman like that. And I never had. Until her. Until my wife.

Covering up my gloomy thoughts of self-reproach, I gave Sloane a tight smile as she led me into the dining room.

Where I discovered Allegra hugging her sister and greeting everyone else.

As in more than just me and her and Walker and Sloane.

Sarah and Theo and North and Aria were also in attendance.

"Regan and Thane are babysitting Harry." Sloane referred to Regan and Thane Adair. "And Callie's staying at a friend's house tonight, so it's just us adults."

"If it's just us adults, why is Jared here?" Theo drawled in his posh English accent.

Walker tried not to smirk at my cousin-in-law's dig as he greeted me with a hard pat to my back. "Take care of her, eh." It wasn't a statement. It was a warning.

I nodded and then grit my teeth as North and Aria came to greet me too.

Soon we settled in the sitting room with drinks with Walker or Sloane or both getting up now and then to check on dinner. Allegra sat beside me on the couch, and I tried not to notice the abject difference between our body language and the other couples in the room.

Walker didn't sit but hovered at Sloane's chair, his hand on her shoulder as she conversed. North sat as close to Aria as he could, his hand resting possessively on her knee. And Theo never could seem to keep his hands off my cousin, even five years down the line. He sat on an armchair and had pulled Sarah down onto his lap like they were teenagers.

There was at least five inches of distance between me and Allegra.

"So ... no honeymoon, then?" Theo suddenly asked us. There was a gleam of mischief in his eyes I knew well. My cousin-in-law was a total shit-stirrer.

Allegra didn't look my way or answer, so I shrugged. "Things are busy on the farm right now."

Theo gasped in mock outrage. "Too busy for a honeymoon? I thought all that animal husbandry would have taught you a little something about ... well ... *animal husbandry*."

Sarah elbowed him, trying not to laugh. North didn't even bother covering his. Usually, I'd laugh, too, but my sense of humor had withered in the coldness of Allegra's aloofness.

"We'll do a honeymoon sometime later," Allegra said before taking a sip of the soda Sloane had offered. Again, she didn't look at me. My eyes trailed the curve of her soft profile as she swallowed. There was a tightness in her jaw.

"Oh? Where are you thinking of going?" Sloane asked.

"Maybe a beach somewhere." I shrugged because there wouldn't be a honeymoon.

"Ally's not really a beach person," Aria informed me with a quirked eyebrow. "She prefers city breaks where she can be a real tourist and go to art museums. That kind of thing."

Right.

That did make sense. I didn't know why I'd immediately thought beach. Maybe because she grew up in Malibu.

At least I knew that much about her.

"I had mentioned the idea of a beach, actually," Allegra jumped in with the lie. "Well, really a resort. Laze by the pool kind of vacation."

"Oh."

Awkward silence fell between us for a few seconds.

"Did Ally ever tell you about the time she yelled at everyone in the Sistine Chapel?"

"Oh, Ari, no." Allegra slapped a hand over her face with the first giggle I'd heard out of her in days. I couldn't take my eyes off her. "Please don't."

"Please do," Sarah insisted.

"Well, when Ally was ten years old, our mom, who's Italian, decided to take us on a grand summer tour of her home country. She almost immediately got called to some far-off place for a job, and I was left to take Ally around." Allegra shot her sister a sad, knowing smile as Aria continued. "It was better this way because with Mamma, we'd have to do everything after hours so she could have privacy. This way, we got to do all the tourist stuff like regular people."

"Who have private security," Allegra teased.

"Fair, fair. We did have private security. Anyway, in Rome, we did a tour of the Vatican. And talking is prohibited in the Sistine Chapel. But there were so many people, and no one would shut up. Ally, this cute little ten-year-old, wanted to experience the Sistine Chapel the way it was supposed to be experienced—in utter silence. And all these tourists were being noisy. I could see Ally getting more and more agitated. I did not, however, expect her to suddenly stop and yell, 'Don't any of you know the meaning of quiet!'"

I chuckled at the imagery and Allegra shot me a surprised look.

"We were asked to leave," Aria finished the story with a snort.

"Like I was the rude one." Allegra huffed.

"Jared, have you ever been to Italy?" Sloane asked.

Discomfort cut through my amusement. "I've never been out of the UK. Travel's not really my thing."

"Oh?" North quirked an eyebrow. "Your wife loves to travel."

Allegra narrowed her eyes on her brother-in-law. "Actually, I love Scotland more than I love to travel."

As the conversation continued from the sitting room to when we were seated around the dining table, I grew more uncomfortable. The couples asked us questions and it became clear to everyone in the room that Allegra and I knew very little about each other.

It was my fault.

She'd tried to make conversation with me. To ask me questions. I always had some excuse to be elsewhere so I could keep my distance. When Allegra had shared that she thought we might not even have to do an interview for her visa, I'd grown even more distant with her.

But as I avoided the concerned glances of the people who cared about us, that guilt I'd felt earlier formed into a hard knot in my gut. I was desperate to get back to the house, to escape the feeling, but Sloane had insisted on after-dinner coffee. I'd excused myself to use the bathroom, but it was really to get a reprieve from them and from my own self-flagellating.

What I didn't need was to step out of the bathroom and almost walk right into my cousin-in-law.

Theo nodded silently toward a back room that was set up as an office. With an irritated sigh, I followed him.

"What a fucking mess you're making of this, old boy," Theo opined in a low voice.

I scowled. "Why do you care?"

"Because Sarah cares." He crossed his arms over his chest. "I don't like when she's worried about you. It detracts her attention from me."

Liar. He just didn't like when she was worried, period. Sarah had him tied tightly around her wee pinky finger. "Well, it's none of your business."

Theo's expression was grim. "If you want people to buy that you married Mrs. McCulloch for love—and by people, I mean the appropriate authorities—you are going to need to stop treating your wife with the indifference of a stranger."

That guilt swelled almost painfully inside me. "I don't do that."

"Yes, you do. You might not want her—though I don't bloody well know why not—but you could at least treat her with a modicum of interest. At least encourage friendship."

"You're giving me relationship advice?" I scoffed.

Theo closed the distance between us. "Everyone thinks I'm a cold bastard who doesn't care about anyone but Sarah. They can think what they want. Frankly, she tops a very small list, so they're not wrong. But when I married her, you became family, whether either of us wanted that or not."

"Gee, thanks," I muttered.

"I treated Sarah badly once," Theo admitted hollowly.

His tone surprised me, the irritation slipping from my face.

"Worst I've ever felt. I still think about it, and even after all these years, it still makes me feel like scum." His voice lowered again. "Everyone Allegra cares about ... she's lying to them. You have absolutely no idea what that girl has been through in her life. I don't either. But it doesn't take a genius to know she's been through *something*. My guess? You married her to save the farm and she married you for a visa—don't worry, I won't repeat that—which means the only person she's not lying to, and has as a confidant right now, is *you*.

"That's the bargain you made when you married her. And you'd be an epic sort of prick if you left her to feel alone in this scheme of yours. No one's asking you to love her, Jared." He patted my arm. "But you could at least treat her with something more than indifference. For her sake. And for yours. Because I know you. If you hurt her, you'll start to hate yourself for it."

I nodded grimly at him.

Allegra had already changed because of my callous attitude. And I was starting to hate myself for that alone.

Sixteen

Jared

Our respective family members and friends exchanged more concerned glances as we left the Ironside home. They weren't exactly subtle about it. Theo's surprising words of wisdom and my own fears of turning into someone I didn't like forced me to reexamine the way I played out this marriage.

Was I really not strong enough to forge a friendship with Allegra without it turning into something more?

On reflection, I refused to believe I had such little self-control as that.

As Allegra sat in stony silence on the drive back to the house, I considered all the reasons I'd put up this barrier between us. And if I was honest with myself, it was mostly self-protection. Not just from her and the way she made me feel, but from letting her know me. Really know me. To know where I came from and the bad shit I'd done in my life before my grandfather gave me a chance to be better.

The security lights on the house cast a warm glow over Allegra's soft features as she waited for me to let her in. When

I didn't move, she finally looked at me. There was that sensation again. Like I'd just been punched in the gut.

I was determined not to let it scare me off.

"I don't work tomorrow," I told her as we stood in the cool night air. Sundays were my one day off. Georgie worked Sundays, and he took Mondays off. "I don't need to get up early."

A slight wrinkle marred her brow. "Okay ..."

"Would you ..." I cleared the gruffness from my voice. "Would you sit with me a while? We could ... talk."

Surprise glittered in her eyes.

I waited for her to reject me. To punish me for being such a bastard. I wouldn't blame her. Instead, she surprised me right back.

She exhaled slowly. "I'd like that."

Relieved, I let us into the house and locked the door behind us. "Drink?"

"Tea. I'll make it."

"I'll get it," I assured her as we kicked off our shoes and then wandered through the living room. Gesturing to the sofa, I said, "Get comfy. I'll bring it ben."

"You'll bring it what?"

Stopping, I glanced back at her. "Four years you've lived here, and you've never heard someone say *ben*?"

She shook her head in amusement, before curling up at the end of the couch. "Never."

I chuckled at that, scrubbing a hand over my face. "Maybe it's more of a Lowland thing, I'm not sure. Granddad and Sarah always knew what I meant. It just means 'I'll bring it through.' You could say, 'I'm coming ben.' Or 'I'll bring it ben to you,' or 'Bring it ben to the kitchen, living room, etc.'"

Her gorgeous smile widened. "I've never heard that. I wonder if North says it."

"You learn something new every day." I shrugged and left to fetch the tea and a decaf coffee for myself.

"Why don't you have a dog?" Allegra suddenly called from the living room.

Amused and bemused by the question, I called back, "Why would I?"

"Don't all farmers have dogs?"

"I didn't need one. My shepherd brought his."

"You should have a dog."

Chuckling, I grabbed the mugs and sauntered back into the living room. "And why is that?"

Allegra took hers from me, and I settled down on the other end of the couch. She turned, knees drawn to her chest so she could face me. "This house needs a dog running to greet you."

"Did you have family pets growing up?"

She considered me, as if still taken aback I was asking personal questions. "Mamma didn't want pet hair in the house. Even though she was rarely in it herself."

At the tinge of bitterness, I said, "I didn't realize things were rubbish between you and your parents."

Lowering her gaze, she shrugged. "It is what it is."

There was a coolness in her response, a distance.

She didn't trust me with the whys and hows. And why should she? I had made it clear I wasn't interested in being her friend.

I had to make the first move.

And the only way I was going to get over the fear that she'd judge me for who I really was—and maybe even end this ruse between us because of it—was just to tell her.

The words stuck in my throat. I didn't tell my story often. In fact, I hadn't really told my story to anyone but Granddad and Sarah. Georgie knew bits and pieces. I was rusty at trusting people with that part of me. That kid seemed like a world away from who I was now.

"I'm not close to my parents."

As soon as the words left my mouth, I had Allegra's focused attention.

I gave her a joyless smirk. "My grandfather was my dad's dad. Unlike Sarah's dad, mine decided that life in a wee Highland village on a farm was beneath him. He left Ardnoch as soon as he could. Moved to Glasgow. Got mixed up with drugs and crime. Knocked my mum up. She grew up in foster care, so she had no one. And my dad bailed on us when I was four. My dad had previously asked my grandparents for money, so they knew about me. I'd met them. They tried to help when they could, but my mum was too proud to ask for it. She'd send me here for the summers, but she wouldn't take anything from them. My granddad used to slip cash into my bag before I went home, told me to hide it and use it if I needed it.

"Sometimes we *really* needed it. Mum tried. She did. She worked hard, but it meant leaving me alone a lot. And she went through men like ..." I shook my head. "Looking back, I can see it for what it was. She was just desperate to find someone to take care of her. But she also let them treat her like shit. Let them treat me like shit. I can't tell you how many punches I took so she wouldn't."

Emotion gleamed in Allegra's eyes. "I'm so sorry, Jared."

"Don't be." I huffed a wee bit shakily. It was only then I realized my heart was *pounding* with this trip down memory lane. "I was a wee prick too. Angry at my dad, angry at her, angry at life. I started knocking around with the wrong lads. It was easy to find trouble. We jacked cars. We sold drugs. Broke into homes and took things from people who barely had anything." I sneered at that past self. "I was scum. And it took my mates almost beating one of our own boys to death before

I woke up. I didn't want to be *that*. I wanted to be better than my dad. I wanted to just be better."

"Is that how you ended up here?"

She didn't look horrified.

Only sad. Sympathetic.

My heart slowed a little and I nodded, remembering vividly that night after I'd dropped Welsh off at the hospital. The pure self-loathing I'd felt after dumping him at the entrance and driving off to save myself from being charged. I was twenty-one. Living in a shithole with a mate I didn't particularly like, surrounded by stuff we'd stolen. Leaving a guy who was supposed to be my pal alone to possibly die, all because he'd shagged the wrong girl. Thankfully, he'd lived. And I'd called my granddad and told him I needed help. That I needed to get away. Far enough away the guys I ran around with wouldn't follow.

"My grandmother had died a few years before, and a few years before that when Sarah was about twelve, they'd taken her in. After her dad died, her mum took her away and she'd had a similar childhood to me. She was smart enough to ask for help earlier than I did.

"My grandfather didn't hesitate. He told me there was a place here if I was willing to work hard, and so I jumped on a train the next morning and never looked back. My mum is still in Glasgow. She sends a Christmas card each year, but we haven't spoken in over a decade. It's sad, but I don't miss her like I should. She always felt more like a roommate than a mum. And Granddad ... he was how I always thought a dad should be. He could be a belligerent auld bastard." I chuckled, grief burning in my throat. "But he loved me and Sarah. He gave us a second chance at life. I'll never be able to repay him for that."

"Your grandfather sounds like he was a really special person."

I smiled, thinking how he would have blustered about being called special. "Aye, he was."

"And your dad? Did you ever hear from him again?"

Expression grim, I nodded. "He was in and out of my life while I lived in Glasgow. Usually when he needed money. And I heard from him a few days ago. In fact, just before you came to me with the marriage proposal, he approached me for the first time in years." I took a chug of the coffee and then placed the cup down on the side table. "He's one of the reasons I said yes to you. He threatened to contest my grandfather's will and take the farm off me with plans of selling all the land."

"That asshole," she snapped, her dark eyes sparkling with fury. On my behalf. "Let him try. I have access to the best freaking lawyers on the planet. We'll destroy him."

Tenderness and guilt mingled at her fierce declaration.

I'd told her the worst of me ... and yet she offered me this ... a kind of blind loyalty.

Suddenly, I wanted nothing more than to kiss her. To press her down into the couch and cover every inch of her with me. My taste, my scent, my heat ... I wanted her to drown in it and I wanted to drown in hers.

Her breath caught, her gaze dipping to my mouth as if she could feel my sudden hunger.

"Jared?" she whispered.

There was desire in her eyes but confusion in her tone. It was enough to snap me out of the dangerous spell she'd put me under. I yanked my gaze from her and cleared my throat. What had we been saying?

My dad.

Right.

"He, uh, he texted me a few days ago and he knows about us. So he knows that he's fucked financially. He's just trying to mess with my head."

I felt a touch on my hand and turned to find her slim fingers covering mine.

When our eyes met, she offered sympathetically, "I'm sorry." Her touch was brief. I wanted to snatch her hand back to me.

Attempting to orient myself, to get us back on track, I asked bluntly, "Why don't you get along with your parents?"

She drew her knees even tighter to her chest. "I ... um ... it's not ... it's hard to explain."

Tamping down my frustration, I pushed, "You don't have to tell me anything, Allegra. But you can trust me. What I told you ... I've only ever told my grandfather and Sarah."

"Really?"

"Aye, really. I'm not exactly a fountain of information, if you hadn't noticed."

She chuckled at my droll self-deprecation and tucked a strand of hair behind her ear. I followed the movement, swallowing the urge to bridge the distance between us on the couch.

"I haven't told *anyone*."

That's when I saw it. What Theo had mentioned. A hollow sadness in Allegra's eyes. It was always there, I realized. I'd seen it before. I'd tried not to wonder at it and told myself it was none of my business. She was good at covering it up with smiles and optimism.

"Not even Aria?"

She shook her head. "Especially not Aria." Her exhale this time was long and shaky.

"You don't have to tell me anything you don't want to," I promised her.

Allegra considered this. "Whatever happened tonight ... I know you are making an effort to get to know me. Right?"

"Right."

"Why?"

"Because ... we're alone in this bargain. Just you and me. And I didn't want you to be lonely. Just because this is a business deal doesn't mean we can't be friends. Right?"

Nibbling on her bottom lip, she took a moment before nodding. "I am lonely."

Fuck.

"Allegra ... I'm sorry."

"It's not your fault." She blinked away tears. "I've been lonely for a really long time."

That killed. That killed way more than it should for someone I wasn't supposed to care that deeply for. "Why?" My voice was gruff with the feeling.

"I was ... I've been forced to keep secrets. To protect myself. To protect Aria ... Only my therapist knows and it's not the same. She's paid to keep my secrets, you know. I just ... I feel like everyone sees me as Chiara and Wesley Howard's daughter. A Malibu princess. And then I feel like the people who actually know me see me as a grand fuck-up. The one who Sloane Ironside had to save from a psycho when she was seventeen years old, after which her family forced her into rehab." She shook her head. "That's not who I feel like I am inside. I was just really angry and messed up and I had reason ... and I can't tell anyone. I can't tell the one person who matters more to me than anyone the real reason. So now I will always be the selfish sister. The one with impulse control issues." She gestured between us, laughing bitterly. "I guess marrying a guy for a visa doesn't exactly prove otherwise."

"Tell me," I implored. "Tell me what you can't tell Aria. I promise it will never leave this room."

SEVENTEEN
ALLEGRA

As I contemplated confiding in Jared the way he'd confided in me, sweat gathered under my arms. Only one person knew my story, and she didn't count because she was a mental health professional. I'd told no one, not a single friend or lover, about what happened to drive me completely off the rails. The truth was, I wasn't proud of that person for so many reasons, but now that I was older, I ached for that kid. I'd put so much on myself that I shouldn't have. Yet, there was still a part of me that feared censure from anyone I cared about.

Staring into Jared's eyes, I thought about the man who had vacillated between casual friendliness and outright cold indifference. Could I trust someone like that? An hour ago, I'd have said unequivocally not. Even with all the evidence I'd witnessed of his kindness and care toward Sarah and his friends over the years, I could only have said no because of the way he'd treated me these last few weeks.

But then he'd gone and told me a story that I knew, from the shaky way he'd confessed it, he really had only told very few people. He'd offered me his trust.

And maybe I was just desperate enough to unburden myself for the first time in ten years. I was so tired of being the only one who carried the truth. "You have to promise me that what I tell you ... you never tell Aria. No matter what."

Jared's brows drew together in curiosity, but he nodded. "I promise."

Sick nerves awakened in my gut as the words hovered at the base of my throat. *Just do it.* "Everyone thinks my parents' relationship is the stuff of dreams. Even Aria. Even my mother. She's deluded herself into it." I kept Jared's gaze because it anchored me, and I began to calm more as I spoke. "When I was fifteen, I got angry at Mamma because she'd promised me a spa weekend before school started. Like always, she bailed for a last-minute job. It wasn't about the spa. It was about time with her. Time she never seemed to have. My dad was busy a lot too, and he would text me every day if he wasn't at home. At that point, he was filming in San Francisco, and I was mad at Mamma. So I got it in my head to just go surprise Dad for the weekend." Blood whooshed in my ears with my thundering heartbeat, remembering how it felt ... "Dad grew up in San Francisco. He had just bought an apartment in the city, and he told us it was because he missed it, and he wanted to spend more time there. I'd come to realize there was a specific reason he wanted to spend time there."

Jared frowned. "What happened?"

"We had an apartment in Brooklyn and we always kept a key in a hidden lockbox, in case of emergencies. I assumed Dad would have set things up the same way in San Francisco. He had. Same code for the lockbox. So I let myself into the place and I walked in on my dad fucking another woman." I still felt sick at the memories. "He was so angry at me. Like, I've never seen my father that angry. I fled. By the time I got back to Malibu, Dad had alerted Mamma to my spontaneous little trip, and she'd flown home. I told her what I'd walked in on." Tears filled my eyes. "She slapped me."

"Fuck." Jared reached across the sofa for my hand and squeezed it. "I'm sorry."

"She told me I didn't know what I was talking about and that if I repeated it, she'd make me sorry. It was like both my parents became totally different people that day. I ... I've done some investigating since, and this woman is not just some person Dad randomly fucked. It's a long-term affair. They're still seeing each other. She was his high school sweetheart. She's an anonymous widowed nurse." Pain for my mother, despite how she'd treated me, flared across my chest. "I think he loves them both. Her and Mamma. He just didn't want to choose. And Mamma loves him so much that she pretends it's not happening. I mean, she's never raised a hand to me or Aria in her life, but she hit me that day. And she looked at me with such hatred and fear, like I was about to rip everything away from her."

"Fucking hell, Allegra ... that's so much for a kid to carry."

I wiped at tears now leaking freely down my cheeks. "That's not the half of it." Taking a shuddering breath, I continued, "I knew I couldn't tell Aria. Mamma messed my sister up good just by constantly nitpicking at her appearance and making her feel like shit because she wasn't a size 2. Dad was Aria's safe place. He still is. I can't take that away from her." I gave him a hard look. "And I never will, so this stays between us. There's no need for her to know. What good would it do? For so long she thought men cheated. Dad was her beacon of hope, and I think knowing how much he loved Mamma was what allowed her to give North a chance too. I don't want to take that from her. And I don't want it to fuck things up for her and North."

He squeezed the hand I hadn't realized he still held. "I promise I will never tell her."

Nodding, I leaned back against the sofa. "I was pissed, Jared. I was so pissed at them for lying to the world and then making me feel like I was the bad guy. They both avoided me for weeks, and I was a kid who'd just found out her dad was cheating on her mom." I turned my head on the cushion toward him. "Do you know my mother was named the Sexiest Woman in the World four times?"

He shook his head.

"Four times. Sexiest Woman in the World. I grew up in a place that rewards good looks, and I think it kind of warped my perspective. If my mother could get cheated on, anyone could. And if my father could cheat, then anyone could. Growing up, I really only had Aria. Mamma 'retired' and returned home when I was a teen, but she still wasn't *there* there. And so, I'd tell myself that it was fine because when you grew up, you fell in love, anyway, and that person became your safe place. But seeing Dad do that to Mamma ... Love suddenly didn't feel safe at all, you know.

"Anyway, I got angry and started looking for an escape. I approached a kid at our school who I knew partied a little harder than the rest of us. I fell in with his group of friends and we went clubbing, partied, drank, did drugs. One night we went to this club in the city that turned a blind eye to our fake IDs because we all had money to spend ..." Grief burned in my throat. "That's where I met Ashton." I pulled my hand from Jared's. "He was eighteen. He grew up in Chino, but when he was thirteen, his mom had married this bigshot defense attorney and they'd moved into his mansion in the Hollywood Hills. Ashton hated his stepfather. So he partied hard.

"I ... I just wanted to disappear. To not feel so angry. To not have to hide from Aria why I was so angry. And I started dating Ashton. No one knew. I kept up appearances at school, kept my grades up, stayed on the honor roll. But all the while, he and I were texting and emailing constantly." A sad smile curled my mouth. "Ashton loved to write. He wrote short stories. And he liked to write me these long emails. I still have them.

"Anyway ... I'd head into the city almost every weekend to see him, and we'd hook up and we'd take whatever drugs he could get his hands on that day. We'd drink until neither of us could think. I doubt either of us remembered half the times we hooked up because we were so drunk or high. For me ..." I finally looked at Jared again and hoped that tender sympathy in his expression didn't disappear once I'd finished my story. "It was just an escape. I cared about him as much as I could, considering my parents had broken my belief in love. But he wrote me love letters in those emails. He told me he loved me all the time. And he started getting moodier, more depressed. He was always talking about running away together. Then ..."

Tears flooded my eyes again. "And then he emailed me one night. He needed to tell me something because he was afraid if he didn't tell someone, he'd lose his mind. He told me ... he told me his stepfather had been abusing him since he was fourteen. That he was so fucked up and angry that he was afraid he might kill his stepfather."

Jared let out a haggard breath. "Allegra ..."

"I was just a kid," I pleaded with him to understand. "And I was scared. I didn't know how to deal with something that big, that messed up. My first thought was to tell my parents, but I didn't trust them anymore and I was afraid they'd have Ashton arrested since he'd been sleeping with a minor. I didn't even think about what they'd do about his threat to kill his stepfather. So ... I emailed him back telling him I was sorry but that we had to break up." My gaze did not want to lift to Jared, to see his expression, but I had to know.

Honestly, I couldn't tell what the hard look in his eyes meant. So I pulled my knees in tighter to my chest and continued hollowly. "Ashton killed himself a few days after I broke up with him."

"Oh Jesus ... fuck, Allegra, you know that wasn't your fault. Right?" Jared moved across the couch, his touch gentle on my chin as he forced me to look at him. His expression was grim, eyes gleaming with sadness. For me. "You were just a kid."

I licked my suddenly dry lips. "I know that. I mean ... I'll always wish that I'd been better. That I'd been stronger. Not so afraid. That I'd gone to him and begged him to tell an adult the truth. Instead, I felt crushed by this responsibility being placed on my shoulders. Too selfish, too scared to think rationally. Maybe if I'd had time, I would have done the right thing. But it was too late, and I'll always feel guilty about that. If there's true blame, however, it lies with his stepfather."

The tears blurring my vision rolled down my cheeks. "You know he's the state attorney general now. Andrew Gray. He also has a special focus on suicide prevention in memory of his beloved stepson. The fucker. He ... he's a monster."

"I'm sorry."

"I've thought often about sending those emails to the media or the police. But I don't want to do that to Ashton. Have something so painfully private splattered all over the news. And that just makes me feel like shit all over again because what if Gray is hurting someone new? What if Ashton's story could help? Yet it's not my place, right?" I begged Jared to understand. "If I did that, I'd be sharing a story that he didn't give me permission to share. I've had private investigators on Andrew Gray since I came into my trust fund, trying to dig up something else we can bury him with, but they said his shit is locked down. So much so that they're almost positive he's into something bad."

"That is so messed up." Jared exhaled heavily and rested against the sofa. "That's so messed up for a teenager to deal with. It's fucked up for you now to have that hanging over you."

"Yeah, well, I handle it better now than I did back then. I'd been on a rocky path before that, and after, I veered right off a cliff." Feeling a little more at ease now that he hadn't condemned me, I told him, "Before Ashton died, I was keeping up with school and my grades ... but by the time I was seventeen, I was self-destructing on every level. The guilt over Ashton's death was eating me alive. So I looked for escape in the worst places possible. Like Nathan Andros. Sloane's ex-boyfriend. Callie's birth father."

"You mentioned you shot someone ..."

"Yeah." I nodded, blanching at the memory. "I shot Sloane. By accident."

Jared was stunned.

"I think I honestly thought it would be fine if I died. That maybe I deserved it. So I put myself in stupid, dangerous situations, and Nathan was one of those. He was a criminal. Hung around a bunch of thugs who thought they were big men. One night at a house party, he took me into a room with these guys, and I realized quickly that he was intending to let them use me."

Jared snapped up so fast from the couch I was surprised he didn't get whiplash. "Please tell me they didn't ..."

I shook my head in reassurance, eyes wide at his visceral reaction. "They didn't. Thanks to Sloane. She showed up there, ballsy as hell, desperate for money because she was about to be evicted. Pretty soon it was just us three in the room. Nathan locked the door. I ... I stupidly mouthed off and he ... I think he was going to rape me in front of her."

Rage filled Jared's eyes and he slowly lowered himself beside me again.

"She ... she stopped him. And I knew then that I didn't want to go out like that. I didn't want to experience what

Ashton had, and I didn't want to die. So we all got into a tussle and I grabbed his gun and I shot at him, but it hit her in the arm instead. He ..." I could still recall the evil in Nathan's eyes as he turned on me. "I was just a little rich girl he got off on corrupting. Sloane was different. His kid's mom. And he thought of her as his possession. He was enraged that I'd shot her. I can ... I can still feel his fists. I thought it was never going to stop. But then, it did. With a bang." I unconsciously eased closer to Jared, lowering my knees from my chest. "Sloane shot him."

Jared's eyebrows rose now. "I can't even picture that."

"Picture it." I grinned unhappily. "Sloane is a badass. She got us both out. I don't know how she managed it because I could barely walk and she was shot, but we got back to her place and I ... I told her to call my dad because, despite the past, I knew he'd fix everything."

"Is that how Sloane ended up here?"

I nodded. "Yeah. My family was so grateful to her that Aria got her a job on the estate to get her away from Andros. And my parents ... my dad assumed that the reason for me going off the rails was because of what I knew. About his other woman. I mean, it partly was, so I let him think it. He begged me to go to rehab. I would have gone, anyway. The whole thing with Nathan and Sloane was a huge wake-up call. Aria was so worried about me. I'd never seen her like that. Even my parents were visibly shaken, you know. As angry as I was at them, as much as I wished they were better parents, I knew they loved me in their way. I didn't want to put them through that, so I went to rehab." I shrugged.

"And then I just got on with life. I'm not close to my parents because Mamma knows I know she's living in denial about Dad. And Dad ... I think he's terrified that one day I'll tell Aria. She's a daddy's girl through and through. His first kid, his baby. It would kill him if she saw him in a negative light. And I think he's just waiting for the ax to fall. If he'd take two seconds to be in a room with me, I could promise him that for her sake, not his, that will never happen."

Silence fell between us as Jared sat forward, elbows on his knees, and stared at the floor. My heart raced as I pondered what he was thinking.

Finally, he turned to me. "You've been carrying all of that by yourself since you were fifteen?"

I nodded.

"I'm sorry, Allegra."

"People have been through worse. Aria was kidnapped by a stalker. Sloane was almost killed by her ex. Worse things have happened to people."

"Aye. But they all had folks around them to share that with. You've kept these secrets because you either wanted to protect Aria or protect Ashton. But who ..." He snatched up my hand, his grip tight. "Who was protecting you?"

I sucked in a teary breath, my vision blurring. "Jared ..."

"I don't know if what I say means anything, but I want you to know that none of it was your fault. As someone who did really awful, stupid shit as an angry kid, I know what it feels like. But I had my grandfather. He knew everything about my past. And having him carry that for me made all the difference. I know our marriage is just a business deal, but our friendship can be as real as you want it to be. I promise you now that you'll always have it. And I'll carry this for you. I don't want you to be alone in it anymore."

Overwhelming awe and gratitude flooded me and before I could second-guess myself, I leaned in and slid my arms around him, resting my cheek on one of his strong shoulders. Jared didn't hesitate. He twisted to face me, my cheek shifting onto his chest instead and he returned my embrace.

I don't know how long we sat there, holding each other, but I wished it could have lasted forever. His body was strong and hard and warm, and being held by him felt wonderful. Because for the first time in a long time, I didn't feel alone. I never wanted that feeling to fade.

Yet I knew come morning, there was a huge chance it would.

So I didn't make a move to leave his arms. I held on as long as I could.

EIGHTEEN
ALLEGRA

The next morning I woke with a pounding head and a dry mouth. It almost felt like a hangover, though I hadn't had one of those since I was seventeen. As the memory of last night came crashing down on me, my legs shook as I got out of bed. In fact, all of me felt a bit shaky while I showered. There was a strange sense of relief and calm that came with finally telling my truth. But I also felt naked. Vulnerable. Like I'd given Jared the power to hurt me.

With that thought in mind, I apprehensively entered the kitchen.

Jared stood at the stove grilling what smelled like bacon and eggs. At my entrance, he glanced over his shoulder. His smile was soft, his gaze searching. "Good morning."

I found myself relaxing a bit. "Morning."

"You hungry?" He switched off the stove and gestured to the buttered bread rolls he'd placed on the counter. "I'm making egg and bacon rolls."

My stomach growled in answer.

Jared grinned. "I'll take that as a yes."

As we settled at the table, I thanked him for the food, and

he gestured impatiently for me to dig in. I could feel him watching me as I ate.

"What?"

Jared followed suit, swallowing the large bite he'd taken. "Do you fancy spending the day on the farm with me? The sheep are arriving, as is Anna, the shepherd. Thought you might like to be there to see them introduced to their new home."

Surprised by his offer, I asked, "Are you sure?"

"Only if you want to. I know it's not glamorous, but I'm starting to realize you don't care about all that stuff. Do you?"

Pleased that he finally saw that, I shook my head. "No. I don't. And I would really like to spend the day with you on the farm."

Something unreadable crossed his face, and I thought he might reveal whatever it was. But instead, he nodded abruptly. "Good."

———

It turned out Anna was a woman in her late forties who had her own sheep and hired her shepherding services out to a few farmers along the NC 500 (the North Coast 500). She used to work with Jared until he'd sold his flock last year. Anna was friendly but had a no-nonsense attitude, and she came with a beautiful border collie named Jess.

I asked Anna questions about her life as we waited for the sheep to be delivered. She was married to a woman named Rachel who worked with the Forestry Commission and knew Arrochar Adair. Arro was the only sister of the Adair brothers and we'd socialized, though weren't especially close, but the connection seemed to make Anna warm up to me more. She was surprised to learn I was Jared's wife yet took the revelation in stride.

Soon a large truck appeared on the road leading to the field and the sounds of bleating sheep accompanied it. I stepped back to allow Jared and Anna to take control. I watched, entertained, as the sheep fled the truck and into the field. They followed one another, seeming happy to be out of the vehicle.

A few hurried back toward the gate just as Jared closed it. They were surprisingly cute. Why had I never noticed what adorable faces sheep had? They stuck said faces through the gates at me and I reached out to stroke one. "Hey, it's okay," I promised.

"I'm going in to get acquainted with them," Anna said, slipping through the gate with Jess in tow.

I pointed to a particularly adorable sheep that had black patches around both its eyes. "We should call that one Zorro."

Jared settled a hand on my lower back. A brief touch. But it made my breath catch. He gave me a softly chiding look. "Don't name them. I made that mistake when I first started working with my grandfather." He chuckled, but it wasn't a happy sound. "I threw up my breakfast the first time he made me drive a sick ewe to the abattoir."

Oh. God. Right.

"Do you ... don't you feel bad?"

"It's a part of life." He gave me the side-eye as he teased. "Did you feel bad eating that bacon this morning?"

I shoved him, guilty as charged. "Okay, I get your point."

Butterflies fluttered in my belly at his deep, masculine chuckle.

Attempting to ignore my reaction to him, that unbearable awareness that had heightened since our confessions last night, I leaned on the fence. "What now?"

"They'll settle in. Anna will come by to move them from field to field when we need her to."

"So what are you doing for the rest of the day?"

"I'm cutting hay for market." He turned, his jade eyes glistening like pale green pools of water in the morning sunlight. "Do you want to ride on the tractor with me?"

"Really?" I beamed. "Because I have to tell you I've been wanting you to ask me that since we got married."

Jared laughed again. "Apologies for the late invite. C'mon."

———

Jared's tractor had a small passenger seat because it was an instructional tractor. He didn't need an instructional tractor apparently, but he'd gotten a deal on the mammoth vehicle. It meant I could ride along with him in my own seat without getting in his way. Kind of. Because it was still pretty cozy in that cab.

The sun beamed through the glass, and we were both more than sweaty by the time Jared was finished cutting the hay with the haybine in the field he called Little Ardshave. I marveled at how much he knew about the land, as if every piece of information his grandfather had ever shared had cemented itself in Jared's brain.

It took hours. I chatted about everything and nothing, pestering Jared about his favorite movies, color (it was blue!), food, books, subjects at school. He answered every time and reciprocated the questions. However, he mostly just nodded and wore a small smile on his lips as I talked his ears off.

Once he'd finished cutting the hay, we headed in for a late lunch. Jared drove the tractor back to its barn.

"Wait there." He jumped out of the cab first and then reached for me. His palms felt dry and attractively rough compared to my clammy ones as he pulled me toward the door. Then he gripped my waist, lifting me easily out of the cab as if I weighed nothing. Not expecting the maneuver, I fumbled for purchase and ended up falling into him like a heroine in a bad movie.

"Oof." I face-planted inelegantly against his chest. He smelled of heat, grass, and that spicy cologne that made me want to lick his neck.

Jared's grip on my hips tightened, almost bruising. "Fuck, you all right?"

Extremely conscious of how sweaty I was and how that might have translated to smelly, I pushed against his muscled chest and stumbled back, righting myself. My cheeks felt scalding hot as I smoothed my hair down with an embarrassed smile. "Yeah, sorry."

Jared's gaze dropped to my chest, the top of his cheeks slightly flushed as he quickly looked away with a clearing of his throat. "Let's grab something to eat."

A quick glance down told me that my tank had slipped to reveal the top of my athletic bra. There was nothing remotely sexy about that bra. Shrugging, I pulled the neckline up and followed Jared out of the mammoth shed and toward his Defender.

We were barely in the vehicle two seconds when he announced abruptly, "I was thinking I should come to your art gallery showing after all."

I blinked at his randomness. "Oh?"

A bead of sweat rolled down his temple and he wiped at it with his forearm in the midst of a three-point turn. "Fuck, it's hot today."

Desire clenched deep in my belly, and I pressed my thighs together. While I was worried *I* was a mess, I thought sweaty Jared, all damp with perspiration and biceps flexing, was the hottest thing I'd ever seen. "Yeah. Hot."

He shot me a quizzical look and I realized I'd practically purred the words at him.

Oh God. *Get a grip, Allegra!* I cleared my throat. "Uh, so, art show?"

"Aye." He drove the Defender onto the farm road that would lead us toward the house. "You were right. I should be there. And you know ..." He cut me a seriously sexy smirk. "I'd like to see your work."

"Really?" A flush of pleasure suffused me.

"Aye, really."

"Okay. I'd really like for you to be there."

"Good. That's settled." His hands squeezed around the wheel for a few seconds ... then, "Did you enjoy your morning on the farm?"

"I did," I told him honestly. *I'd enjoy anything as long as I was with you.* The thought popped into my head and I blanched, turning away. *Do not catch feelings, Allegra.* "You seem to really love it. The farm, I mean."

"I do. It saved my life."

Studying his handsome profile, I nodded. "I know it did. I love it too just for that."

Those words probably revealed more than they should, but I couldn't help myself.

"Thanks," Jared replied, voice rough.

We fell into silence, this time a comfortable one, until we pulled up outside the farmhouse. I glanced at the Range Rover I'd borrowed from Ardnoch. "I really need to return that and get my own."

"We can go car shopping whenever you want," he offered as he got out.

"You'll come with me?" I followed him.

Jared frowned. "Of course. Salesmen will just try to rip the piss out of you if you go alone."

I laughed. "Isn't that a little old-fashioned?"

"It's prehistoric. But a fact."

"Okay. We could go this weekend."

"Done. I'll get Georgie to look after the farm." He let us

into the house, and I was just enjoying the way his T-shirt clung to his broad back when my cell blared from my rear pocket.

The screen told me it was Aria. "I gotta take this."

Jared shrugged. "I'll get lunch ready."

"Hey!" I answered my phone, stepping out into the front yard. "How are you?"

"Well, you sound chipper," my sister said with a smile in her voice.

"It's been a good day. I helped Jared welcome in our new sheep and then I got to ride in his tractor while he cut hay in the fields."

She chuckled. "Who would have thought my little sister would like the farm life?"

"I gotta admit, it's charming me more than I could have imagined." All of it. Mostly its owner. Damn it.

Aria muttered. "Shit."

"Shit? What?" I scowled.

"I just hate that I'm calling to tell you this when you're in a good mood. And even more so because I was worried about you last night after dinner, but you sound like things are good and—"

"Aria, why are you rambling? You never ramble." Unease shifted through me.

"Ally, I'm sorry. I got a call from a journalist contact that keeps me informed of any news that might break about the estate members."

"And?"

"The media have found out about you and Jared. There's a story running online tomorrow from a major tabloid."

Oh fuck.

"You ... it's time to tell Mom and Dad."

"Yeah." I squeezed my eyes closed. Things were finally good with me and Jared and now this. "I guess so."

NINETEEN
ALLEGRA

Before my relationship with my father crumbled upon learning his secret, Aria and I used to attend a lot of his film premieres. We stood on the red carpet in fancy gowns beside our glamorous parents while paparazzi shouted at them to "Look this way" all the while blinding us with their camera flashes.

Footage of us had more than once been discussed by a group of famous women who hosted a panel show where they conversed about social and pop culture. They'd argued over if my clothing was suitable attire for a girl my age, and how proud Aria should be for touting society ideals about body type. Like it was Aria's choice to be a curvy goddess and not Mother Nature's. And like it was any of their fucking business what she looked like or what I wore.

I remember being followed by a pap when I was fourteen and on a date with Dax Reynolds, the actor Moira Reynolds's son. Dax was two years older than me, but we attended the same high school, and everyone was so jealous he'd asked me out. At the time I'd just been excited to be dating him, but once the photos of us were published, people online started talking about how he was too old for me. Dax got weirded out by the attention and dumped me.

Lately, I'd made peace with the images of me and Jared that were splashed all over the internet with headlines like "The Farmer's Wife," a supposedly cute reference to my father's movie of the same title. I should have known they'd go there. Jared and I had avoided being seen in the village together, not wanting to give them fodder for their newspapers. The great thing about living in Ardnoch was that the villagers were protective of the tourism brought in by the estate's celebrity members, and thus protective of the celebrities. Paps were not welcome. So, they got bored after a few days and left. Jared took it all in remarkably good stride.

Long ramble short, I was used to being the focus of attention in certain situations. However, the one place I'd never gotten used to it was at my own art shows. I'd had quite a few over the years, the worst being at art school where the purpose was to be judged and graded. There was no way I'd ever get used to someone scrutinizing something I'd created. Something that was born from a deep, personal place inside me. Standing in a room filled with people looking at it was almost as bad as standing there completely naked. In fact, I'd probably deal with public nudity better than this.

"Are you okay?" Jared's warm breath tickled my ear and I had to force off a shiver of want.

The last few weeks, since our heart-to-heart, things between us had been different. Better. And also worse. Jared was warmer and more open with me, but that also meant it was easier for me to catch feelings. I was trying very, very hard *not* to catch feelings. Unfortunately, the physical desire train had left the station long ago. Tonight he was my support. But also my temptation, because as "husband and wife," this was the first time Jared was *really* playing his part since the wedding.

And apparently it involved keeping a possessive palm pressed to my back or taking my hand in his whenever he could. Touching! It involved touching. I was already nervous for the show but with Jared's hands on my body, I was over-stimulated.

I glanced up at him from under my lashes. "I always get nervous at these things."

"You've no need," he replied sincerely. "Seriously, Allegra ... I'm no expert, but I think your work is phenomenal."

I leaned against him. "Thank you."

Together we'd survived the world finding out about our marriage and the explosiveness of revealing it to my parents. Well, the explosiveness of *my mother* discovering the truth. My dad was, as I'd guessed he would be, congratulatory and intro-spective about the whole thing. Mamma was not. Mamma was incensed that not only had I married behind everyone's back, thus depriving her of a wedding, I'd married a Scotsman, just like my sister. *Why did we want to be so far away from her?* she'd demanded. Then, of course, she didn't disappoint with "And a farmer! A farmer, Allegra!"

Jared had left the room at that point and my protective instincts kicked in. I had intended to be cool and calm while my mother ranted. However, hearing her insult Jared flipped a switch in me. While she yelled at me in Italian, I yelled back in good old-fashioned English.

Dad attempted to calm Mamma down, but she stormed off in a melodramatic wail of tears. I'd have felt bad if I believed for a second any of her concerns truly had to do with my well-being. Don't get me wrong. I knew my mother loved me. But her first thought would always be for herself, and how it looked that Chiara Howard's daughter had married an anonymous farmer.

"We're coming to Scotland at the end of the summer

before filming on my new movie starts," Dad had replied with an unsure smile. "We'll meet your young man then."

"Yeah. Okay."

"Congratulations, angel."

Aching regret had plagued me at the sadness in his eyes. My feelings for my dad were so complicated, and I wished things were easier between us. "Thanks."

We'd ended the call and I'd gone to find Jared to apologize for my mother's appalling behavior. Thankfully, he didn't put up walls between us again and we'd found a rhythm in our marriage these last few weeks.

Other than the fact that we weren't having the sex my body so desperately wanted, we lived like a real husband and wife. I took over some morning chores at the farm, including helping to keep the house clean, then I went about my day, whether it was at the studio or exploring for inspiration. Or catching up with Aria and/or Sloane for lunch. Sarah and Theo had left for their place in Gairloch with an open invitation for us to visit. In the evenings, I'd come home and Jared and I would take turns making dinner, sometimes cooking together. We'd catch each other up on our days, and then we'd settle in the living room to watch TV before bed.

It wasn't glamorous.

It was a simple life.

And if it had also involved banging my hot husband every night, it would have been a perfect life.

A life I'd always dreamed of.

Which made it infinitely dangerous to me.

"I'll show you my favorite," Jared suddenly said, tugging on my hand.

He pulled me through the crowd, most of them turning to peer at us curiously as we passed. Then he stopped me in front of one of my larger pieces. It was a landscape, inspired by the northern lights. I'd visited Shetland in February. It was my first time on the island and the couple who ran the B&B I'd stayed at couldn't have been kinder. They pretty much adopted me on that trip, and they'd taken me to see the northern lights. It was one of the most wondrous moments of my life.

I'd painted the greens and yellows and pinks as if they'd been misted by rain, some lines splattered with a thickness to create texture. Shards of thinly sliced opal mingled with the paint, reflecting light and shimmer against flecks of metallic glitter. Darker shadows created the mountains at night. And through the paint I'd sprinkled tiny garnets over the mountains to emulate garnets that were found on the rocks on Shetland. A line of copper paint represented the sunset the evening I'd seen them, haloing the dark mountains.

This was one of *my* favorite pieces I'd ever done. "This is *your* favorite?" I asked in awe.

Jared nodded, studying it with genuine appreciation in his eyes. "I think it's stunning. It's the northern lights, right?"

I bit my lip to stop the cheesy grin. The art was titled *Shetland*, so the fact that he understood what I'd attempted to capture was huge. "It is." I turned to him, and Jared faced me. "It's so weird ... this is one of my favorite pieces ever. Michelle really had to talk me into selling it."

"Aye?" He frowned. "Don't sell it, then. If you want to keep it, you should. *You're* allowed to enjoy the art you create."

Studying the glass, I realized he was right. I'd let Michelle convince me to sell this one because I thought as an artist, I was supposed to share everything I created. But ... why couldn't I keep this one for me?

"It would look great above the fireplace instead of that old mirror we have now," Jared murmured thoughtfully.

He wanted to put my art in the farmhouse?

My heart skipped a freaking beat.

"Let me just find Michelle and tell her to stick a SOLD sign on it."

Jared grinned. "You do that."

Michelle's gallery in Inverness was not a huge space. This was my second time showing at her gallery, and the place was more packed than it had been the first time. Aria had been set to attend until I learned this weekend was the only chance she had to see North while he was shooting on location in Paris. Otherwise, she wouldn't see him for another few weeks. I'd told her to go visit her husband. I had mine to keep me company.

As for the rest of our friends, I hadn't told them about the show. It was easier to be vulnerable with strangers about my work than with those who knew and cared about me.

Approaching Michelle, I commented on how busy the gallery was.

"I told you people are loving your work. I've been sending pieces all over the country." Michelle gave my shoulders a squeeze. "You're one of my top artists, Allegra. You should be so proud of yourself."

I did feel a swell of pride. Grinning, I replied, "Speaking of, I want you to put a SOLD sign on *Shetland*."

"Ooh." Her blue eyes rounded with excitement. "Did someone else offer on it?"

"Else?"

"Yes, it's already been bought. I was just about to put a sticker on it."

"Well, unsell it. I'm keeping it."

Her expression fell. "That's one of your most expensive pieces."

Now I squeezed her shoulder. "You'll still get your commission, but it's too special to me. I'm sorry. I can't sell it."

She nodded with a sigh of understanding. "Okay. But you have to talk to Paul Gunner. He wanted to buy it, and he's been angling for an introduction all evening. I didn't want to interrupt your wee tête-à-tête with your husband, but now that you're here, you can do me a favor and smooth over the fact that he won't be getting *Shetland*."

"Introduce away."

Paul Gunner turned out to be a good-looking blond in what I'd guess to be his early forties. He was dressed sharp in a custom three-piece suit, and I clocked the twenty-thousand-dollar Tag Heuer watch on his wrist. The dude had money. No wonder Michelle wanted me to take time to meet with him. As soon as she disappeared to place a SOLD sign on *Shetland*, however, Mr. Gunner stepped a little too far into my personal space.

I recognized that glint in his dark eyes. Unfortunately, I'd had that look directed at me before it ever should've been. Taking a small step back, I brushed my hair from my face with my left hand, flashing my wedding band.

His gaze darted to it, but his expression didn't falter. "I've been eager to meet you since I bought my first piece," he said with an accent that could be either Scottish or English. It was difficult to tell. "I'm originally from Inverness but live in London now." Ah, that made sense. "I'm a bit of a collector."

"Really. That's great." I kept my smile polite. "Which piece are you most interested in tonight?"

"I'm looking at her," he replied boldly, his hungry expression leaving no doubt to his meaning.

My inner yuck alert system blared, but I didn't let my distaste show on my face. This was not the first time a fan of my art wanted to sleep with me. I chided gently, "Not sure how I feel about being referred to as a piece, but—"

"Oh, I meant no offense. Really. You're just … you are even lovelier than your art. I don't think I've ever met a more beautiful woman."

"That's very kind, but I'm married." I flashed my wedding

ring again. "Several of my works displayed this evening, however, are available."

"I've already told Michelle which pieces I want, and I've been very generous. Now I want to get to know the sexy woman behind them. I'm sure, considering my donation to your work"—he smiled with all the confidence of a wealthy man used to getting what he wanted—"you can indulge me with the pleasure of your company. I'm sure you've heard of me. Paul Gunner of Gunner Industries." He reached out to tuck a strand of hair behind my ear and I flinched back.

All pretense was gone. "You could be the richest man in the world, Mr. Gunner, and I still wouldn't be for sale."

"Allegra—"

"Lucy," I corrected him harshly. "Have you been looking into me?"

"I told you, I'm a fan." Paul's possessive gaze grew hard with determination. "It makes no mind to me you're Allegra Howard. I'm not interested in your parentage."

"It's Allegra McCulloch now."

He huffed in amusement. "One dinner. Just a dinner. That's all I ask. I'm sure it'll be enough time to change your mind." He then proceeded to trail the back of his fingers down my bare arm. I flinched from him again, unnerved by his persistence.

Then heat hit my back, a hard, familiar chest pressing against me as strong arms encircled my waist. Jared's scent, his presence, relieved me as he brushed a gentle kiss over my temple. I glanced up at him, his tender expression morphing into absolute menace as he turned to Paul Gunner.

"I'm the husband," he bit out coolly. "I don't know who you are, but touch my wife again and I'll break your fucking hand."

A thrill coursed through me at his possessive, protective words. And longing. For them to be real.

Gunner looked at Jared with a mix of fear and disgust. He flicked me a look that told me I'd gone down a million miles in his estimation. "I see your artist talents don't translate to taste. I think I'll let Michelle know I won't be buying anything this evening."

Jared tensed behind me, but I patted a palm over his hand in reassurance as I looked Gunner straight in the eye. "You do that. After all, money can't buy class."

He narrowed his eyes at me before storming off.

"Fuck." Jared turned into me, his expression apologetic. "I didn't mean to fuck up a sale. I just saw the way you were reacting to him and lost my shit a wee bit."

I grinned, having enjoyed every second of him losing his shit "a wee bit." "Don't apologize. Watching him almost pee his pants was worth losing the sale. Trust me."

"What did he say to you?" Jared stared over his shoulder as Gunner strode quickly out of the gallery. A shared glance with Michelle told me she wasn't happy. But I didn't care.

"He wanted to sleep with me," I replied bluntly. "Apparently, he thought buying a lot of my art would make it hard for me to say no."

"What the fuck?" Jared replied a little too loudly.

I hushed him, smoothing another reassuring hand across his chest. It was totally an excuse to feel him up. "It's not unusual. I've had a few wealthy fans, male and female, who have propositioned me for sex. Some are just creepier and more entitled than others." I gestured to the door where Gunner left. "That asshole decided he wanted something from me and thought his money could get it for him. He thought wrong."

"I should have knocked his teeth out," Jared muttered angrily, looking like he was considering chasing after Gunner to do just that.

"Allegra." Michelle was suddenly upon us, amusement

and disappointment mingling in her eyes. "Your possessive hubby might have to stay home at the next showing."

I flushed with pleasure at the words. "It's not Jared's fault. Gunner suggested I should have sex with him in return for all the money he was spending tonight."

Her face fell. "Oh. Oh dear. Oh, that's terribly disappointing. He'd picked out five pieces. Including the *Shetland* piece."

I shuddered at the thought of an asshole like him owning that particular work. "Well, no one is getting that piece."

"Is this your doing?" Michelle teased Jared. "Are you encouraging her to keep her art to herself?"

Jared slid his arm around my waist, pulling me tight into his side. "I'm encouraging her to keep the things that make her happy."

My breath caught.

Oh, Jared, please don't tempt me ... because I'm kind of scared one of those things just might be you.

———

We were both tired by the time we returned to the farmhouse, but a tension zipped between us. A tension we'd both been able to ignore thus far. Until that moment with Gunner where real feelings might have popped up to the surface.

"I'm sorry again about losing you the sales," Jared apologized, even though he really didn't have to.

We'd stopped at the top of the stairs before each of our bedrooms. I patted his shoulder in reassurance. "Don't be. Seriously. The thought of that asshole having my work displayed in his house makes me kind of sick, so you did me a huge favor."

"Okay. Good." He shifted a little awkwardly on his feet. "I, uh, it's late and I'm up early so ..."

"Jared." I stopped him as he moved to walk past. "Thank you. For coming tonight."

Despite the experience with Gunner, it had been a successful evening. A few people at the show had been a little pretentious, and I knew Jared was bored by some of the conversation. But he stood by my side all night.

Out of the twenty pieces on display, we sold ten, which was unbelievable. Michelle would put the remaining pieces up in her gallery and online.

"Of course." Jared bent his head to brush a feather-soft kiss against my cheek and this time I couldn't suppress my shiver.

His breath caught and he lingered a second in my personal space before seeming to jerk back as if I'd bitten him.

"Night," he said gruffly without looking at me.

Then he strode into his room.

I hurried into mine, pressing against the door, willing my pulse to slow and my skin to cool.

A few seconds later, I heard his bedroom door open again and I froze like a statue.

Please knock on my door, please knock on my door.

The floor creaked beyond my bedroom as if Jared had stopped right outside it. I held my breath, knowing if he did knock, my self-control would shatter. I'd welcome him into my room and into my body in a heartbeat.

Crushing disappointment filled me at the sound of him walking downstairs instead. Frustrated, I pulled off the sparkly flapper-style dress I'd donned for my show. As I readied for bed, I heard Jared returning to his room. Determinedly, I attempted to put him from my mind.

Ready for bed, makeup off, skin care regimen done, I crossed the room as quietly as possible, intending to head downstairs for a glass of water.

Uncontrollably drawn to my husband, however, I couldn't help but glance at his doorway as I stepped out of mine.

To my surprise, his door was slightly ajar, the lights still on. I tiptoed toward it, intending to shut it for him when I heard the shower running in his en suite.

Jared was in the shower.

Naked.

It was easy at that moment to fantasize walking into his room, pulling off the thin nightie I wore because of the hot summer night, and then stepping into his bathroom naked. To imagine that Jared would take one look at me through the steamy glass of his shower door, slide it open, and haul me inside.

How he'd press me up against the damp tiles and take my nipple in his—

The sound of a door closing wrenched me from my fantasy, and I realized in mortification that Jared's shower had stopped. That he was walking into view.

Naked.

Totally, absolutely, phenomenally naked.

My lips parted as heat pooled in my belly at the sight of him.

He rubbed his wet hair with a towel as he wandered over to his bed, checking his phone absentmindedly. Completely unaware he was being ogled.

There was a lot to ogle.

Rivulets of water trailed down between his hard pecs, following a light fur of hair that disappeared to reveal smooth, sculpted abdominal muscles. He wasn't crazy defined like Taka, who worked out constantly because he was usually half-naked at some point in one of his TV shows, but Jared was naturally muscular and hard from constant physical work.

When my gaze finally made it to his semi-hard cock protruding between muscular thighs, I had to hold in a gasp.

Jared was big. Above-average length. And thick.

The girth ...

Wet heat flooded between my thighs.

I itched to throw open the door and throw myself on him.

But Jared turned, thankfully with his back to me. Thankfully because not only did it provide me with an excellent view of his muscular ass, but it meant he didn't see me as he headed out of sight toward the bathroom.

What the hell are you doing? I shrieked at myself, backing up as quietly and as slowly as possible. This was wrong. This was so wrong.

I'd perved on Jared.

Forgetting about the glass of water, I scurried back into my room, barely able to hear over the rushing of blood in my ears.

Scrambling into bed, I reached over to switch off the lamp on the bedside table, plunging the room into somewhat darkness, considering the sky was still navy outside.

I tried to slow my breathing, to calm myself enough to sleep.

But every time I closed my eyes I saw naked Jared.

Naked Jared.

My naked husband.

"Ugh," I groaned. How unfair was it that he was technically mine ... and I couldn't have him.

As I tossed and turned, trying to sleep, unable to for the flush across my skin, I eventually decided that I could at least have him in my fantasies. So I held the image of him in my head as I touched myself and smothered the sounds of my orgasm in my pillow.

Finally, eventually, I drifted to sleep.

TWENTY
JARED

I couldn't remember the last time I'd had balls this blue.

When Allegra proposed we refrain from seeing other people for the first two months of our marriage, I didn't think anything of it. Contrary to popular belief, I had gone more than a week without sex. After my grandfather died, in fact, I'd gone six months without sex because I couldn't bear to be close to anyone, even in just a physical capacity. The only person I hadn't put my guard up with was Sarah because she was the only other person who was in as much pain as I was.

So I could go without sex.

The problem was that I'd promised to go without sex while married to and living with the sexiest fucking woman in existence.

Everything Allegra did turned me on.

One night, she brought all this girly shit downstairs so she could paint her nails while we watched a movie. When she'd stretched out a leg and bent over to paint her toenails, it might as well have been a striptease for how my body reacted.

I'd imagined knocking the nail crap out of the way, taking her gorgeous legs in hand, and hooking them over my shoulders so I could go down on her. Thankfully, she was preoccupied with her nails so she barely noticed me excusing myself to go stand in the open door of the goddamn freezer.

Last night, playing her husband was easy and difficult at the same time. I'd never wanted to be anyone's husband, but I couldn't deny the possessiveness I felt around Allegra. How much I'd wanted to knock that rich arsehole through the wall when I'd spotted him across the room reaching out to tuck a strand of my wife's hair behind her ear.

How many times had I wanted to do the same thing? To follow the move by trailing my fingers down her silky throat, to feel her pulse beneath my touch, to feel it race as I moved lower.

Being allowed to put my hands on her, in fact being "forced" to for the sake of our ruse, had stretched my willpower to its breaking point. If I didn't rein in this bloody need for Allegra, I was going to do something we'd inevitably regret. Even if it felt fucking amazing in the moment.

Weirdly, I didn't want our deal to end badly. When this was all over, I still wanted to be in Allegra's life. I still wanted to be her friend. I needed her to know that she had one person in her life who knew her truth and saw her for who she really was: a good person who would do anything to protect those she loved. Selfishly, I wanted her to remain my friend too. To have someone other than Sarah who knew my worst secrets and still saw good in me.

I smiled to myself as I watched her baby-talking to one of the hens she'd called Ginger after a character in the movie *Chicken Run*. She'd turned the chickens into pets. Ginger, to be fair, *had* taken a shine to Allegra. She ran like an excited kid toward her anytime Allegra was in the vicinity of the pen. My wife had announced after only one day of taking care of the chickens that she would never eat chicken again. We hadn't since.

Something the hen did made Allegra tip her head back in laughter, and my traitorous eyes shifted down her gorgeous body. Hunger like I'd never experienced in my life tightened deep in my gut and in my balls.

Fuck.

If I didn't get out of here now, I might just give into temptation.

I pushed open the kitchen window and called, "I'm heading out. I'll catch you later!"

Allegra turned toward me, eyes wide, lips parted as if to say something, but I turned on my heel and hurried through the farmhouse before she could come after me.

"Fucking coward," I muttered to myself as I drove the Defender away from the house.

———

"I was just about to call you," Georgie said, striding toward my vehicle as I pulled up at the field called North Creich.

His grim countenance had me jumping out of the Defender. "What happened?"

Georgie shook his head, a muscle ticking in his jaw. "Someone killed a ewe."

My chin jerked back in surprise. "*Someone*? What the hell do you mean?" I gestured for him to show me.

His voice was a wee bit shaky as he opened the gate. "I mean her fucking throat has been slashed."

Rage and confusion flooded me as I followed him up the field. The sheep were gathered all together on the hillside while Georgie led me away from them. If Georgie hadn't alerted me to a problem, the loud bleating from the sheep would have given it away. They were scared. "I don't understand."

Georgie led me right over to the fence that ran through North Creich and Little Ardshave. There was a dip in the land just before the fence and as we grew closer, I saw the body of the animal partially hidden because of it.

"Fuck," I muttered, approaching the ewe slowly. Rounding her, I crouched to examine her neck and to my horror saw Georgie was correct.

This was no injury or attack from another member of the flock. The cut across her throat was too precise. A wound on her abdomen suggested she'd been stabbed there first to subdue her.

Sorrow stung my eyes.

"What kind of sick fuck does this to an animal?" I seethed hoarsely.

"I don't know." Georgie was visibly distressed too. "We need to call the police, though, Jar."

Knowing he was right, I waited as Georgie called. He strode off to meet them at the gate, while I went over to make sure the rest of our flock was okay. They were nervous and frightened, and a male ran at me in warning to back off, protecting the rest of the sheep.

I called Anna to let her know what had happened and asked if she could come to move them out of the field. Considering the circumstances, she agreed to as soon as possible.

As for me, I returned to stand guard over the felled ewe, my mind racing with the possibilities. Because this was a deliberate, vindictive assault on an animal. On one of *my* animals.

My thoughts kept returning to one person.

Dear old Dad.

I said as much to the police when they arrived and explained my father's threats. I even forwarded on his text messages to the constables. Anna arrived to take care of the flock while Georgie and I loaded up the ewe so he could take her to the abattoir.

And all I wanted, after running away from her this morning, was to see Allegra's face. To take comfort in her presence.

So I followed that instinct and returned to the house, grateful to find her car still parked in the driveway. We'd gone car shopping a few weeks back and I was pleasantly surprised by her taste in vehicles. She'd ended up purchasing a Wrangler. Though she'd gone for a flashy bright yellow that made me chuckle every time I saw it.

Except for today.

I was in no mood for laughs today.

Allegra wasn't inside the house. I quickly washed up, changed my clothes, and then headed outside. I found my wife in the back garden. She'd dragged two kitchen chairs out, one to sit on and one for her legs. Her knees were bent as she sketched on a pad that rested on her thighs. A frown of concentration marred her brow, and as I grew closer, I realized she was sketching the farm. It wasn't the type of work I was used to seeing from her.

"It looks good," I murmured.

She jumped, startled, those big eyes wide with surprise. "What are you doing back so soon?"

Whatever she saw on my face caused her to take her feet off the other chair and offer it to me. I sat, our knees brushing we were so close. Then I told her about the ewe.

Hanging my head as worries coursed through me, I sighed at the feel of her fingers stroking over my head. I knew I shouldn't, but I leaned into her touch.

"I'm so sorry, Jared. I'm so sorry." Her fingernails lightly scratched over my nape and I reached for her, my hands light on the outside of her thighs as she continued to caress me. Soothe me.

Fucking comfort me.

It felt better than it should.

"I'm going to kill whoever did this," she vowed vehemently. "And we'll figure out together who was behind it. I promise."

Unbelievably, a smile tugged at my mouth. I lifted my head to look at her and the urge to kiss her was so bloody overwhelming, I knew my control had slipped. I felt myself moving toward her—

My ringtone screamed from my arse pocket. It was like a lasso around my torso, yanking me back from Allegra and into reality. Shit. I'd almost kissed her.

"Sorry. Might be the police." I stood abruptly to pull out my phone. Sorcha's name and photo was on the screen. Beneath it were several texts from her I hadn't opened.

Not really in the mood to talk to anyone but seeing it as an opportunity to avoid fucking things up with Allegra, I answered.

"Oh my God, Jared, thank God," Sorcha's frantic voice cut down the line.

My first thought was that something had happened to Brechin again. "Everything all right?"

"No, no. I've just gotten back from a hair appointment and my door was ajar. The wood is splintered and Brechin won't stop barking. I'm afraid to go inside. I think someone broke in."

What the ... could this day get any worse? "Did you call the police?"

"Aye, they're on their way. I just ... I'm scared. Would you come? Please."

"Sorcha, it'll take me an hour to get there ..." I sensed Allegra standing behind me.

"Please, Jared. Please." I heard sniffling and stiffened. I'd never heard Sorcha cry.

"Okay. I'll be there. But wait outside. Do not go in until the police get there."

What a bloody day. After I hung up, I turned to Allegra with an exasperated sigh. "Did you hear that?"

Her expression was unreadable. "Something wrong with Sorcha?"

"She thinks someone broke in. The police are on their way, but she's shaken up. I'm going to check it out."

She nibbled on her bottom lip and then gestured to my phone. "Doesn't she have anyone else she can call? I mean, you're having an awful day yourself, Jared."

"I'll be quick." I patted my pocket for my keys and realized I'd left them in the kitchen.

"Why—" Allegra slammed her mouth shut and sat down on the chair.

"Why what?"

"Why are you the person she called?"

She wouldn't meet my eyes as I stared down at her. I wondered if she was put out about this. "We're friends."

"Oh."

"Just friends," I offered. "I'll be back soon."

"Okay." She wouldn't look at me. Instead, she picked up her sketch pad and proceeded to ignore me.

Unease churned in my gut.

Fuck.

This was all I needed.

———

Sorcha's place was wrecked. Whoever had broken in had locked Brechin in the bathroom (thankfully hadn't harmed the wee man), and not only stolen anything of any value but the arseholes had trashed the place. The police had already been and gone by the time I arrived, and I found Sorcha crying on her sofa surrounded by the mess.

"I'm sorry, Sorch." I sat down beside her, clapping an upset Brechin with one hand and putting my other arm around Sorcha. "It's going to be okay."

"Is it?" Sorcha wiped at her nose as she looked at me. Her pupils were huge with shock. "Jared, I live alone. On a teacher's salary. I can't afford this emotionally or financially."

"You have insurance, though, right?"

Her jaw slackened. "Insurance?"

"Insurance." I rubbed soothing circles on her back.

Some of her tension eased. "Jared, insurance. Of course, I have insurance. I completely forgot about that. Oh, that's something." She leaned into me, resting her head on my shoulder. "I'm going to be too scared to go to sleep tonight."

"Is someone coming to fix the door?" The doorjamb had been busted open.

"Later this afternoon." She lifted her head, expression pleading. "But maybe you could stay tonight."

I stiffened. "You know that can't happen. Why don't you stay with Donna?" I referred to one of her closest friends.

Hurt flashed across her face. "I keep forgetting you're married. I just ... I miss you."

Discomfort shifted through me as I removed my hand from her back and stood.

Sorcha grimaced at the sudden physical distance. "Sorry, I didn't mean to be weird and awkward. It's just this ..." She gestured to the flat. "Most of the time I'm pretty happy on my own. Truly. But then something like this happens, and it makes me feel lonely."

Shit. Compassion filled me, but I forced myself not to embrace her. I didn't want to give her the wrong idea. "I get it. I'm sorry."

She studied me thoughtfully. "Do you really love her, then?"

I lowered my gaze, staring at Brechin who was giving me the same big puppy dog eyes as his owner. "Sorcha ..."

"I'm happy for you. She must be really understanding, letting you come out here to help. Letting you talk to me."

"Letting me?" I frowned. "You and I are just friends now. Allegra knows that."

Sorcha scoffed. "Jared, we're friends who used to fuck. If your wife says she's okay with our friendship, she's absolutely lying."

"No. Allegra's not like that." Especially because our marriage wasn't real.

"Oh. So if you found out she was still talking every week to a guy she used to fuck on the regular, you'd be fine with that?"

The thought of Allegra with any man filled me with a fury I didn't want to examine too closely.

"I'll take that murderous expression as a no." Sorcha chuckled humorlessly and stood. "I'm sorry for dragging you down here, Jar. I'm sorry for holding out hope that your marriage would fall apart, and you and I could go back to what we had."

My eyebrows rose in surprise at that confession.

"It's clear that you and she are solid, and I shouldn't be calling a married man to come and bloody rescue me." Sorcha scrubbed a hand down her face. "I'm so sorry."

"Sorch, it's fine."

"It's not." Her expression was apologetic. "Go home to your wife, Jared. I'll call Donna."

I shifted uneasily. "I can wait for her to arrive."

"No." She gave me a sad smile. "You're not mine to rely on. You never really were, were you?"

Guilt shafted through me. "I'm sorry."

"Don't be. We can't help who we love."

I felt heavy with the exchange after I said goodbye to her and Brechin and got back in my car. Instead of leaving immediately, I decided I'd wait until I saw Donna pull up in her Toyota. When I searched for my phone to text Allegra I'd be back soon, I discovered I'd left the bloody thing on the kitchen table when I'd snatched up my car keys.

While I was sure Sorcha was wrong about Allegra, considering our marriage was fake, I couldn't help but think how my wife wouldn't meet my eyes before I left. Just seconds before that, she'd been touching me, offering me solace and fierce loyalty. The combination was a massive turn-on. But she'd switched it off, turned from me at the mention of Sorcha.

Fuck.

Maybe Sorch was right.

I was relieved on multiple levels when Donna showed up. Relieved for Sorcha that she had company and relieved that I could get back to Allegra before any of this looked suspicious. Not that I technically owed her anything. But I did. I'd promised her fidelity for two months.

I needed her to trust that I'd keep my word.

I just needed her to trust me.

TWENTY-ONE
ALLEGRA

Around forty minutes after Jared ran off to comfort his ex, I heard his phone ringing in the kitchen. Seeing Georgie's name on the screen, knowing from Jared how worried the farmhand was about the animal someone had cruelly killed, I'd picked up. I'd told him where Jared had gone, and Georgie had sounded surprised. And a little pissed off.

I was right there with him.

I asked Georgie if I could help with what he needed, but he told me to just get Jared to call him when he returned from running to the rescue of his ex-girlfriend. Or fuck buddy or whatever she was.

Friend.

That's what he said.

So he was still in contact with Sorcha. This whole time.

I was such an idiot.

Hurt and jealousy and anger roiled in my gut, and I hated Jared for that. I'd never been a jealous girl. Honestly. Never. Not to sound like an arrogant asshole, but it was usually the other way around. I'd had a few boyfriends get all jealous and possessive, and guess what? It was a huge turnoff. So I would not be that person.

No way.

Not me.

I'd just seethe in my quiet fury.

A little over an hour after Jared left, his phone buzzed again, and thinking it might be an impatient Georgie, I'd picked it up. It was a text so the screen remained locked, but I could see enough of it.

Sorcha

Thnx for cmin. Srry if I crossed the li...

I couldn't see the rest of the text, but hot indignation rushed through me as I dumped the phone on the coffee table in the sitting room. What the hell? Did the rest of the text say "crossed the line"? And what did she mean by that?

Furious, I cleaned the house. A huge part of me wanted to jump in my car and disappear to my studio. But the rational part of me knew that Jared had been through a lot today. Someone deliberately killed one of his flock, and his ex-fuck buddy/girlfriend/current friend had her apartment broken into.

I needed to be cool.

A good friend to him.

After all, he wasn't my husband for real. He didn't owe me fidelity.

It was another hot day, so I'd shoved open the windows and changed into shorts and a tank to scrub the house from top to bottom. We'd had housekeepers growing up, but as soon as I moved out, I'd discovered I enjoyed cleaning. In the same way I loved the way my canvas transformed over time with layers of material, I liked the opposite process of returning a physical space to order.

The only room I didn't go in was Jared's. By the time I heard the front door open, I'd just started scrubbing the kitchen.

"Allegra!" Jared called.

My heart pounded in my chest as I snapped off the rubber gloves and threw them into the sink. "In here!"

"I left my phone"—his voice traveled with him as he strode into the room—"so I couldn't call you."

"I know." I shoved dishes into the sink because Jared didn't have a dishwasher. It gave me an excuse not to look at him so he wouldn't see the turmoil I wasn't allowed to feel. "Georgie called. Because of what happened I picked up. He asked that you call him back."

"Okay ... what's going on?"

"Sorcha texted too. I didn't mean to look. I just thought it was Georgie calling."

Jared sighed heavily. "Where's my phone?"

"In the living room."

"Is there a reason you won't look at me?"

I glanced over my shoulder at him. He leaned against the kitchen doorframe, frowning at me. All sexy and handsome. He looked unruffled, his clothes in place, his hair untouched. Only a few hours ago, my fingers had been in his hair. But had hers been in his hair today too? The thought made me wrathful.

I turned back to the sink. "Is she okay?"

"Sorcha is shaken up, but she'll be fine. I left her with her friend."

Honestly, what I said next I was fully intending *not* to say. But it was like someone else possessed me as I whirled on him. "Have you still been fucking her this whole time?"

Jared's eyebrows rose as his jaw clenched with anger. He pushed off the doorjamb and took a step closer. "Excuse me?"

I flushed with embarrassment and scrambled to sound

cooler and unaffected now that I'd blurted out my fear. "It's just—it looks kind of bad. We agreed to two months fidelity to sell the lie."

"Aye." His voice was gruff as his eyes hardened. "We did. Are you telling me you think I broke my promise?"

Perhaps I should have been more careful, considering he was clearly angered by my questioning, but I pushed, "I just think it's odd that of all the people your supposed ex could call, she called you to come running to her rescue."

"We're friends," he bit out.

Friends. Right. Something like crushing disappointment cut through my hurt. Why would I think Jared was any different from any other man? Of course he couldn't keep it in his pants. "Look, you're a grown-ass adult, you can do what you want. But while we're in this together"—I gestured between us—"a heads-up would be nice, that's all."

"A heads-up?"

"That you're fucking other women!" I spat it out with the hurt and fury I felt, and immediately cursed myself for the lack of control.

Jared froze, his expression blanking. "Fucking other women?" he asked so calmly, I probably should have heeded it as a warning.

I shrugged, crossing my arms over my chest as if I didn't care either way.

"Fucking other women!" he yelled suddenly and I startled, my arms dropping to my sides as Jared glowered at me. "When would I be fucking other women, Allegra? We had an agreement." He took a step toward me. "No fucking anyone for two months, right? So no, I didn't fuck Sorcha. I haven't fucked her since we made our deal! I haven't wanted to fuck her or any woman since we married because all I can think about is how much I want to fuck my wife!"

I sucked in a breath at his angry confession, my chest heaving, mirroring his own sudden breathlessness.

My skin flushed hot at the dark, hungry look he threw my way. No one had ever stared at me with such abject longing and desire.

I whispered his name.

His nostrils flared. "Fuck it," he snarled as he charged me. He hauled me against his body as his lips crashed down over mine.

Gasping in shock, already aroused by our anger, I returned his hungry, biting kiss. I moaned into Jared's mouth, licking at his tongue. One hand squeezed my hip, while his other tightened around my nape as he groaned with a need that rumbled down my throat and hardened my nipples. Then we were moving until the kitchen table hit my ass.

He kissed me so hard, so deep, I was panting for breath by the time he released me. The expression on his face wasn't soft or tender. Every feature was taut with need and he looked almost menacing with it. My clit throbbed in reaction as he grabbed the hem of my tank and yanked it up and over my head. Then my bra was unclipped and off, thrown over his shoulder. Jared's green eyes turned molten as he took my breasts in his big, calloused palms and caressed me.

"Jared," I moaned, arching into his touch.

He released me but only to lift me with ease onto the kitchen table.

"Jared?"

Eyes holding mine, he tugged down my shorts and underwear in one sweep. I gasped at the sensation of the wooden table beneath my naked ass as Jared gripped my thighs, spread them, and hooked my legs over his shoulders. "Jared!"

His head disappeared between my thighs.

His beard bristled deliciously against my skin as his tongue touched me.

"Oh my God!"

Jared lifted his head just enough to growl, "The first night you sat at this table with me, this is what I wanted to do. You're going to come on my tongue, Mrs. McCulloch. Then you're going to come around my cock."

My belly flooded with lust, the wet rushing between my legs. "Yes, yes." I nodded frantically, wanting all of that.

Triumph hardened Jared's features before he bowed his head again. As he licked his way up to my clit, I groaned as sensation spiked down all four limbs. Arousal tightened in exquisite need low in my belly and my heart pounded in my ears. "Don't stop," I pleaded.

His fingers dug into my thighs as he licked and sucked at my clit. Then he tortured me by leaving the bundle of nerves to scatter tickly kisses along my inner thigh. Just when I was about to scream for mercy, he pushed his tongue inside me, fucking me with it.

"Jared, Jared," I panted, my chest heaving as the tension spiraled tight inside of me. "Please!"

He stopped tormenting me long enough to return to where I needed him at my throbbing clit. My body tightened, my thighs closing in on him, my chest heaving and shuddering as the tension spiraled tighter and tighter toward explosion. Until the asshole stopped and playfully kissed my thighs again.

"No!" I reached for his head, my fingers threading through his silky, thick hair and curling tight. He growled at the tug and sucked my clit into his mouth at the same time he thrust his fingers inside me. That was it. The tension shattered and I screamed as the most explosive orgasm of my life rippled through me in shuddering waves.

Jared drank up every goddamn drop.

Tension bristled through him as he stood and drew a thumb over his lips. I lay splayed on the kitchen table, tremors still shaking through me from my climax.

His ravenous gaze touched every inch of me as he whipped off his T-shirt and threw it behind him. As he unzipped his jeans, his gaze returned to mine. "I've never wanted anyone the way I want you."

I sucked in a breath as I nodded. "Me too."

He reached into his back pocket, yanking a condom out of his wallet, before throwing the wallet to the floor. I shook with need as he tore the wrapper off the condom and shoved his jeans and boxer briefs down. Rolling the condom on his impressive cock, he warned, "This won't be gentle."

I shivered, my nipples peaking into tight pebbles. "I don't want it gentle." I reached for him, fisting him with a hard tug that elicited a deep, masculine groan. "Fuck me, Jared. Fuck me how you've wanted to fuck me since the night we first met."

Chest heaving, he gripped my wrist and pulled my hand from his. "Brace your hands behind you on the table."

Anticipation sizzled in my belly as I did as he asked.

Jared gripped my ass to lift me just long enough to spread my thighs until they were tight to his hips. Eyes locked to mine, he took his cock in hand and guided it until he nudged hot against me. Then he surged into me with a fierce grunt, teeth gritted with the sensation.

I wondered if it was as overwhelming for him as it was for me. My back bowed as I cried out at the unbelievable thickness. It was such an encompassing feeling, it was like he was inside every inch of me.

Jared rested his cheek against my temple, his breathing shallow, tight. "Are you ... are you ready?"

I nodded with a whimper of need.

"You feel so fucking good," he muttered in my ear. "Never felt better."

Then he pulled back and powered into me.

"Ahh!" I braced my hands behind me, arching into his

thrusts. Jared's lips pressed tight together as his fiery eyes roved over my body.

"You want this?" he gritted out.

"I do. Hard!" I panted, my head falling back as the table screeched against the floor with his powerful drives. My pleasured cries filled the kitchen, probably the whole freaking house, and I could tell it was spurring him on.

His lips parted and he began to groan with every thrust.

My thighs trembled against his hips as the tension coiled and coiled inside. I wasn't thinking about anything, if this was a good idea, a bad idea. All I cared about was the indescribable pleasure scoring through my entire being at the drag and thrust of him inside me and how I wanted it to last forever.

"Are you close?" Jared asked hoarsely.

"Yes, yes!"

"Thank fuck." His hips snapped faster, harder, his own deep sounds of pleasure mingling with mine. "Come, come, baby, come around my cock."

My orgasm exploded through me. White lightning licked up my spine and flared behind my eyelids. The shock of the intensity had my eyes flying open in surprise. My inner muscles clamped down hard on Jared, throbbing around him in voluptuous tugs that caused his own expression to falter with shock.

"F-fuck. Allegra!" he roared my name as his hips suddenly juddered, and he pulsed and released inside me. Jared's head fell to my shoulder and I wrapped my arms and legs around him as he continued to shake against me.

Finally, his climax eased and I couldn't help but smile in smugness at how goddamn hard he'd just come.

"Ah." I trembled around him. "Jared."

He lifted his head, our eyes meeting as he stared as if he'd never seen me before.

I tensed, feeling something like dread.

This was the part where he told me it was a mistake.

Jared reached up to cup my cheek, his thumb brushing my lower lip. "We'll talk about this later ... for now ... I want more."

I relaxed, tightening my thighs around him. "More?"

"More," he growled and then kissed me with just as much hunger as when we'd started.

TWENTY-TWO

JARED

My grandfather used to say that a farmer who couldn't accept the temperamental nature of Highland weather should find somewhere else to farm, or not farm at all.

"You can't rely on her heart to stay the same from season to season," Granddad had said one autumn when constant rain had destroyed any chance of us cultivating the land long enough to plant barley.

"Her?"

"Mother Nature." Granddad gave me a grin I knew he didn't feel. "Just when you think you know her, her heart will change." He'd gestured to the flooded fields. "And we have to be able to change with her or the stress will swallow us whole."

The memory of his wise words hit me as I stared up at my bedroom ceiling, skin damp with sweat, heart racing and my limbs relaxed with utter repletion. Turning my head on the pillow, my gut clenched at the sight of the beautiful naked woman in my bed.

Her hands were curled by her head, her breasts trembling as her breathing slowly eased.

Miraculously, I wanted her again.

Even though I'd just had her four times.

On the table, on the bed, on her hands and knees, and then her riding me.

Just looking at her caused a stirring in my cock, despite the last few hours of fucking.

Allegra sensed my stare and turned her head on the pillow. Her expression tightened and I saw questions and worries in those gorgeous, dark eyes. She didn't make me guess her thoughts, though. That was something I liked about her. A lot. "Is this the part you tell me it was a mistake?"

It was never a conscious decision to remain single all these years. I'd just enjoyed my autonomy. Why be in a relationship when I could have the best of both worlds? Sex when I wanted without the commitment. Honestly, I'd started to believe as time wore on that I wasn't made to be in a committed relationship.

But the thought of something that casual with Allegra caused an immediate agitation to edge through me. Because one primal thought had pounded through my head as I thrust into her, a thought I'd had to grit back from blurting out like a fucking caveman.

Mine.

I liked sharing space with this woman. I looked forward to coming home to her. Life was empty and cold without her. So I had a choice. I could remain steadfast in my belief that I preferred to be single and probably end up a miserable, lonely bastard for the rest of my life. Or I could accept that the wind blew in change whenever it felt like it and you either adjusted or fought against it to your ruin.

"I don't want it to be a mistake," I admitted, my voice sounding rough like I hadn't used it in a while.

Her eyes widened slightly as she pushed up onto her elbows. "What does that mean?"

"It means ..." I rolled over onto her, taking her left hand and pressing it deep into the pillow so our wedding rings touched. "We're married. I'm your husband and you're my wife. And we have eighteen months to decide if we want to stay that way."

A smile teased the corners of her lush mouth, and she bit her lower lip as if to stop it. My cock stirred between her thighs at the sight. "Really?"

I released her hand to smooth her hair back from her face as I whispered across her lips. "There's something here. Isn't there?"

This time she released the full blast of her smile as she looked up at me with tenderness and affection. "There is. I've thought that for five years."

My chest suddenly felt too full as I stared into her eyes.

Because how the fuck did I get so lucky? I didn't know what a woman like Allegra Howard McCulloch saw in me, but I was too smart to question it. Instead, I took her mouth in a slow, easy kiss. Savoring her now that the urgent fervor from earlier had cooled. Somewhat.

Remembering what had driven me to fuck my wife on the kitchen table, I lifted my head. I frowned. "I don't cheat." I knew she was messed up about fidelity because of her dad, but I'd never do that to her.

Remorse crossed her face as she reached up to smooth her fingers over my short beard. "I know. I just ... we weren't *together* together, and I thought maybe ..."

"I've never felt this way about Sorcha," I confessed gruffly. "About anyone. I wasn't lying when I said I hadn't thought about touching another woman since you moved into the house. It's been torture lying in this bed with you on the other side of the wall, unable to fucking touch you."

Allegra suddenly grinned, a twinkle of mischief in her eyes as she wrapped her arms and thighs around me. Fuck, she felt so good. I didn't understand why she felt so much better than any woman ever had, but I wasn't going to question that either. "I saw you naked last night."

Amusement filled me. "Aye?"

"Aye," she teased. "I stepped out of my bedroom to get a glass of water and your door was open. You came out of the shower."

"And you were spying on me?" I pretended to be affronted.

Allegra giggled, her breasts shaking against me. I reached down to stroke her, my thumb strumming over her nipple. Her breath caught. "I ... I went back to bed and touched myself."

I froze, hot blood rushing toward my cock. "What?"

"I touched myself, thinking of you, naked."

"Last night you were on the other side of my wall touching yourself?" My hips thrust with a mind of their own, nudging against the hot heat between her legs.

"Oh, that wasn't the first time."

The imagery made me mindless with want. I was going to take her again. "Condom," I bit out, and reached for the string of packets on the bedside table.

It seemed to take forever to get it on even though it was probably only a few seconds.

Relief flooded me as I pushed inside her tight heat. I took her mouth, groaning into her as I kept my thrusts slow and easy. She wrapped her arms and legs around me as before and held on as we just enjoyed the sensation.

When she came, her eyes holding mine, it wasn't just the feel of her coming that made me climax. It was watching Allegra come. It was knowing that *I* did that. That *I* took her there.

As I shuddered through my own orgasm, pressing kisses

across her cheek and down her throat, I realized that I'd just made love to my wife.

I'd never made love in my life before.

A slice of panic cut through the happiness buzzing between us. But I didn't want fear to fuck this up, so I pushed it back down as I rolled off her and pulled her into my arms.

TWENTY-THREE
JARED

"You two are shagging, aren't you?"

Scowling, I turned to Georgie. My mate smirked at me knowingly. I glanced at the men who stood congregated on the land that would house the glamping pods. Planning permission had been granted and the company I'd hired were out making final deliberations. The pods would be built at their factory in Aberdeen and then driven in pieces to the plot where they'd go up in a matter of days.

"Good thing *they* can't hear you." I huffed.

"Oh, come on. Tell me. I'm right, aren't I?"

How the hell did he know? I narrowed my eyes.

Georgie snorted. "Jar, despite the fact the police haven't found who killed our ewe, you've joked and laughed more this past week than I've seen in years. Plus, Gordon saw you snogging your wife in the car park behind Sloane's and now everybody knows about it."

Gordon was a retired businessman who used to own a lot of property here. He was also a gossiping auld bastard. I shook my head. "Fucking villagers." It was true, though. I had kissed Allegra when we dropped off the eggs at

Morag's. I was apparently incapable of being near her and not touching her. The last week had been a haze of sex and laughter and just feeling right for the first time in forever.

A call from the police informing me that my father had denied killing the ewe was the only dark spot. Without evidence, there was nothing the police could do. I just had to hope my father wasn't lying and it had been a random attack by a fucked-up tourist passing through.

"At first I thought it might have been for show, you two snogging, but you're acting very much like a man who is getting well and truly laid every night and laid well, my friend."

I cut him a warning look. I'd never been one to kiss and tell, anyway, but it was different with Allegra. No one was allowed to talk about her in that context. Not even Georgie, who I knew was harmless. "Shut it."

He raised his palms defensively. "Oh, we are territorial, eh? Aye, I suppose I would be too if Allegra Howard was my wife."

"McCulloch," I bit out. "Allegra McCulloch. And, Georgie, we are together. We're seeing how it goes. But you and I are not going to talk about my wife like that."

His grin took up half his face. "I'll be damned. Jared McCulloch finally fell."

"Fuck off."

"Look at you calling her 'my wife.' You like it. You fucking love calling her 'my wife.'"

"I'm going to fucking love running the tractor over you if you don't shut up."

"Do you make her say 'my husband'?" he continued.

"Fuck off, Georgie." I started walking toward the crew.

"Where is your *wife* this morning?" he called after me.

"Telling your wife to divorce you for someone with a

bigger dick!" I yelled back, making the men burst into surprised laughter.

"I'll have you know my dick is perfectly in proportion to my glorious physique!"

I grinned as the men laughed harder. "Sorry about that, gents. How's it looking here? Are we ready to roll?"

"It's looking good."

"And what about the other project?" I gestured toward the woods behind us.

"Aye." Craig, the project manager, nodded. "Let's head down there and go over the plans."

———

Apparently, we couldn't even watch a sex scene on a TV show without it turning us on. We made the mistake of watching a popular historical romance show. I was bored by it, but Allegra seemed into it, so we watched a few episodes after dinner. Then suddenly the TV show took a turn and there was a lot of sex. Like, a shit ton.

Next thing my wife looked at me with sharp desire in her expression and *our* clothes were coming off. I stretched out, back on the couch, while Allegra rode me. Watching her take what she needed was so fucking hot. Watching her shudder through an orgasm always made me come.

Afterward, she snuggled in my arms as we laid on the couch. The TV had long been switched off and a quiet silence existed between us as I trailed my fingertips down the silk of her naked back.

"I was thinking," Allegra spoke softly, "that we should get a health check and if we're good to go, we could stop using condoms. I'm on the pill."

Last time I had sex without a condom was my first time.

The thought of sliding bare into Allegra made my cock twitch. "Aye, that sounds like a plan."

I felt her smile against my chest. "Okay. Let's do that, then."

We'd already talked about our day over dinner, so I was happy to just lie there in relaxed silence together, but Allegra had other thoughts on her mind.

"Has sex never really been more for you? More than just sex, I mean? It's never been ... I don't know ... romantic?"

I didn't know why the question was important, but I didn't mind answering honestly. "Until you, aye. It's always just been for release. I was thirteen the first time and it was with a sixteen-year-old girl who lived in the same tenement. There was nothing romantic about it. Believe me. And we were lucky she didn't get pregnant."

"She was sixteen?" Allegra raised her head, expression horrified. "What was she doing having sex with a thirteen-year-old?"

I chuckled at her horror. "I looked older. Acted older. We all did, growing up in a place like that." I stroked her soft cheek. "It was different for you than us. I'm glad for it. I know you grew up too fast, too, but not like that."

Her eyes lowered and I felt her body tense against mine.

Worry coursed through me. "Allegra?" An unpleasant understanding dawned. "What ... what age were you the first time you had sex?"

She sighed, the movement pushing her breasts into my chest. Finally, she looked at me. My gut knotted at the sadness I saw there. "I was fourteen."

It might sound hypocritical considering I'd been a year younger, but I was shocked. I looked at kids now and realized how fucking young I was at thirteen. Just a child doing grown-up things no child should be doing. "Fourteen is young," I offered gruffly, waiting for her to say more.

She lazily traced circles on my chest. "As soon as I got breasts, I started to notice that boys ... and *men*"—her lip curled in disgust—"treated me differently. Boys at school. People who worked with my parents. They talked about how beautiful I was and how I was just like my mom. Looking me over, staring at my body in a way they shouldn't."

Anger burned hot through me and my grip on her back tightened. "I'm sorry."

Allegra met my gaze. "Nothing really bad happened, but it scared me. Suddenly, I wasn't being treated like a kid anymore, but I *was* still a kid. I was so scared of it all, but none of my friends seemed to be. They talked about sex like they were grown-ups. Looking back, I know now they were all bluster and trying to be cool. But back then, I thought there was something wrong with me because I wasn't ready to feel that way about my body yet. I decided that the only way to not be afraid was to face my fear. That summer, Dad invited me to be on set of his movie. There were a few younger actors. One of them was seventeen and he was very attentive. So I had sex with him."

I'd never have touched a fourteen-year-old when I was seventeen. In fact, I'd never even when *I* was fourteen. Despite my own young age, the girls I'd had sex with at that time had all been older. "Creep," I snarled.

"Yeah, turned out he really was. And, of course, I didn't get over my fear of being sexual, being seen as sexual. I just felt ... used." With a heavy sigh, Allegra rested her cheek on my chest again and I held her fast. I hated that for her. I hated that her entire teenage years had been such a fucking mess in general.

"The next time was with Dax. He's Moira Reynolds's son and he was my first real boyfriend. He dumped me when the paparazzi started following us. I thought I cared about him. I probably did as much as fourteen-year-old me could. Then

Ashton. I did care about him." Her voice shook a little as she spoke about him, and I knew no matter how much therapy or how much confiding she did, Allegra would always carry guilt over the boy.

"But he was the last person I had any real feelings for until you. Sex has just been sex ... until you." She rested her palm over my heart. "It used to drive me crazy that I wanted you so badly and you didn't seem to want me back. People only see me as a pretty face, and I used to tell myself that it was okay, because at least they found something worthy about me, even if it was the way I looked, which I couldn't take credit for. But you didn't seem to want me for any reason ... and I used to wonder what it was about me that you found so off-putting." She chuckled, but I heard the hurt there. Even after the last week of me worshipping every inch of her, she was still hurt I'd kept my distance for five years.

A pang of regret scored across my chest. I touched her chin, forcing her to look at me. For her, I would be honest, even if it cost me something. "I stayed away because I knew that once with you would never be enough ... and that I'd spend the rest of my life wanting someone I couldn't have."

Tears cast a wet sheen over her eyes. "Jared ..."

"You are the most beautiful woman I've ever known ... but you're so much more than that. You walk into a room and you light it up. People gravitate toward you. And it's not just because you're easy on the eyes, baby. It's because they feel your goodness and it makes them feel good too. You don't judge. You're always kind. You defend people you care about no matter what it costs. You're a fierce, fierce sister and friend. And you're so fucking talented, it blows my mind. And people see that in you, Allegra. *I* see that in you. I always have."

"Jared." She suddenly reached for me, her kiss hungry and desperate and it instantly ignited my own need.

I held on to her as I launched up off the couch. This time

it was my turn and I wanted her in my bed so I could take her as hard and as deep as we both needed. Because I could feel this thing between us buzzing through our veins like electricity. Overwhelming. Too much.

It was too much.

It was possible devastation.

But I couldn't have stopped myself from being with Allegra if the world depended upon it.

As we crashed down onto my bed, I powered into her, her now familiar cries of pleasure causing a hot zing through my blood.

"Mine," I growled against her lips as I fucked her.

Her fingernails bit into my back as she arched into me and gasped, "Yours."

"Yours." The word was guttural but freely given back to her.

Joy suffused the physical pleasure on her face and her thighs tightened around my hips. "Mine."

TWENTY-FOUR
ALLEGRA

For not the first time since I'd started sleeping in Jared's room, the alarm was an unwelcome noise waking us both from dreaming. I didn't mind getting up before the crack of dawn, but this past week ... it was almost a physical pain being dragged from the warmth of Jared's embrace.

He rolled over and the arm that had been slung over my waist, holding me close, disappeared to switch off the alarm. Then he was back, smoothing a hand down my hip as he brushed a tender kiss across my naked shoulder. "Why don't you sleep in this morning?" he offered, his voice raspy with sleep. "I'll take care of the chickens."

It was sweet of him, considering we'd only had a few hours' sleep because of sex, but I wanted to pull my weight. No one was ever going to accuse me of being a spoiled, pampered princess. I turned my head to catch his jaw with a kiss, his beard tickling my lips. "No, I'm getting up." At least during the summer it was warm. I could only imagine how much harder it was going to be to get out of bed in the height of a Highland winter.

We conserved time and water by showering together.

Though we couldn't linger, I still enjoyed smoothing shower wash over Jared's pecs and abs. When my hand dipped lower, he laughed and grabbed my wrist.

"If you keep touching me, I'm going to be late to meet Georgie."

Granting him mercy, I chuckled and stopped feeling up my husband. It was only serving to get me hot and bothered too. Once we were dressed and out of the shower, however, Jared decided *he* wanted to play the tormentor. Making breakfast together in the kitchen, he kept pressing his body to mine and trailing his fingertips across the bare skin between my tank and shorts.

"Stop!" I laughed as he leaned into me to watch me butter toast. His cock was hard against my ass.

Instead of stopping, Jared gripped my hips and nuzzled my neck. "I'm thinking I should be late for Georgie after all."

I gasped as he nudged into me. That's all it took for the fire of want to ignite. "I think so too." Pushing the plate of toast away, I fumbled for the button on my jean shorts. Within seconds I'd pushed them and my underwear down.

Jared hissed, cupping my bare ass in his large hands. "You excite the hell out of me." His fingers slipped down and pushed inside, testing me. "Fuck." I heard him fumble with his clothing, heard the condom wrapper crinkle as my fingernails bit into the kitchen counter with anticipation.

He nudged my ankles apart as far as they would go with my shorts and underwear wrapped around them, gripped my hip with one hand, and then turned my head up to the side. Jared crushed my lips beneath his, his beard tickling and rasping against my skin, as he surged into me. I gasped into his mouth at the overwhelming fullness. Our kiss broke as this insatiable thing between us exploded beyond our control. Suddenly, Jared spun me, pushing me belly down over the kitchen table. He took my hips in both hands and began fucking me.

I became nothing but my body and how he made me feel. Hot and needy and desperate. I had to push up onto my palms to take the powerful thrust of his cock. "Yes!" I kept crying over and over again in my mindless want.

"Look at you," Jared's voice rumbled at my back. "Look at you take me." His hands cupped the globes of my ass and squeezed. "So fucking perfect. So fucking ..." He growled suddenly, his hips snapping faster against me. "Come. Baby, come."

He was losing it. And the evidence that I turned him on that much was enough to send me over the edge. I screamed my release, my arms giving out as I slumped against the table, the wood cool against my cheek.

"Allegra!" Jared bellowed seconds before he shuddered over me, his cock throbbing inside me as he came.

Suddenly, I imagined what we must look like right now and I began to laugh quietly.

I heard Jared's amused grunt. "Should I take offense?"

I laughed harder, the sound only broken by a gasp of sensation as Jared pulled out. Pushing up off the table, I turned to him, getting tangled in my shorts. He disposed of the used condom as I pulled my clothes back up.

"I'm just laughing at our inability to get through an hour without jumping each other."

He grinned as he crossed the room, fixing his own clothes before he reached me. Sliding his arms around my waist, he tugged me against him until my palms rested on his broad chest. "I can't help it with you."

Looking up into his eyes, seeing the tenderness in them, made my heart pound. Sometimes I couldn't believe that Jared had agreed to give our marriage a real shot. Sex with no strings? Yes, I could absolutely see him agreeing to that. But with me, he wanted more. What he said last night were the most beautiful things anyone had ever said to me. He was the first man to make me feel like I was so much more than the face and body I owed to genetics and nothing else.

Whatever he saw in my eyes made him bend his head to press a soft, sweet kiss to my mouth. Soon it turned into more, our tongues touching, licking. With an agitated sigh against my mouth, Jared pulled back.

"I know." I smoothed a soothing hand over his chest. "We need to get to work."

"I wish we could stay here all day."

"I know," I promised him. "Me too. But we need to adult now. In a different way to how we just adulted on the kitchen table."

Laughing, he let me go with one last squeeze of my hip. "Let's get to it."

Since we'd already lingered too long this morning, we shoveled down our breakfast and I left Jared in the mudroom to go feed and water the chickens.

I knew almost immediately something was wrong because the chickens and I had become best buddies over the last few weeks. I knew their habits well, in particular, a hen I now called Ginger. She was my bird soul mate. She and her best buddy, Babs, adored me and would come running as soon as they heard the mudroom door open. I'd chat away and they'd preen as I cooed compliments at them. They were more interested in following me as I walked around the henhouse than even the food and water I brought them. They'd sit and watch me for hours whenever I decided to sketch in the backyard.

This morning, however, there was no running. No clucking with excitement. In fact, now that I thought about it … the rooster, Cogburn, hadn't made a sound this morning either.

"Jared!" I called, panic suffusing his name as I hurried

toward the henhouse. The sight of two hens lying motionless inside the run had me screaming, "Jared!"

As I opened the main door to the henhouse, I heard Jared shouting my name in return, his footsteps pounding toward me. "Fuck." I heard him curse, having clearly seen the chickens.

The sight that greeted me inside the house made me burst into tears.

They were all motionless, lying among one another. Stiff and unmoving. Ginger, Babs, Cogburn, all of them.

I reeled backward and turned, smacking into Jared. While he checked out the house, I stumbled away, unable to stop the tears streaming down my face.

Jared straightened. His face was pale and taut with anger. Whatever he was feeling, however, he put on hold. Bridging the distance between us, he pulled me into his arms and I clung to him, sobbing.

"I'm sorry, baby," he whispered, his own voice cracking with emotion.

"W-what ... w-hat h-h-happened?" I stuttered through my tears.

"I don't know." His arms tightened around me. "I don't know."

———

The two police constables were pissing me off.

After Jared called the vet out, she examined the birds and said she'd need to do a postmortem on one to be sure, but they displayed symptoms of cyanide poisoning. We found traces of food in their troughs that we hadn't put there.

"You think the food was poisoned?"

Jared had nodded grimly. "We'll bag it up, get it tested."

That had made me cry all over again because who would

want to hurt my chickens? The image of them lying dead together in the henhouse haunted me and I kept having to bite back tears. I was a farmer's wife, for goodness' sake. Shouldn't I be better at dealing with this? I wasn't, though.

My chest ached.

And right now, it also burned with fiery anger at the blasé way the cops were treating the situation.

"I mean, it's possible someone just left out some food that's bad for them, right?" The younger of the two police officers shrugged, looking so bored I wanted to slap the expression off his face.

"No, it's not," Jared snapped, clearly sick of their attitude too.

"Well ..." The older constable sighed heavily. "I don't really know what we can do here. This doesn't seem like a crime but an accident."

"Aye." The other broke a smile. "And it seems only fair since I can't count the times I've had chicken poisoning."

He did not just say that.

"Hey!" I took a step toward the young officer. "Show some respect. Those chickens were important to us. To me. And someone killed them. Do you honestly think it's a coincidence that all our chickens were poisoned within a week or so of one of our ewes having her throat slashed?"

The younger officer blanched as he glanced guiltily at the older police officer. The older PC cleared his throat in embarrassment. "Uh, well, we weren't aware of that."

Jared threw up his hands in agitation. "Fucking great. Absolutely useless."

"There's no need to be rude."

I quirked an eyebrow. "Says the police officer who laughed at the mass execution of farm animals."

"I think you're being a bit melodramatic. Typical American." He snort-huffed.

"Don't"—Jared took a menacing step toward him—"talk to my wife like that."

"And don't try to intimidate a police officer." The older man glared angrily at my husband.

"Get off my farm." Jared gestured to the front of the house. "And heads-up, I'll be filing a complaint against you both. I'm good friends with Chief Inspector Jim Rowley at Inverness. I'll be sure to let him know how utterly useless and disrespectful you've both been."

The younger paled even further while the other PC just sneered and stormed off. His partner followed him with another glance of worry over his shoulder.

I moved to Jared, sliding my arm around his waist. He immediately curled me into his chest as we watched the officers get in their patrol car and drive off.

"What now?"

"I wasn't lying. Jim Rowley used to be a PC at Tain. He and Granddad were good friends their whole lives. Jim worked his way up to chief inspector. I didn't want to call him about the ewe because I wasn't sure it was something. But now with this, I think we need his help. And he needs to know he has two arseholes among his ranks. He's a good man. He won't stand for it."

Worry knotted in my gut. "Who could be doing this, Jared?"

"I'm pretty sure it's my father."

I squeezed my eyes closed, hating that so much for him.

"I'm sorry." The sorrow and guilt in his voice had me lifting my head to look at him.

"Why are you sorry?"

"I know you loved them." He gave me a sad smile. "'Specially Ginger."

My eyes flooded with tears. "It's not your fault. None of this is your fault." My fingers gripped his shirt, desperate for him to hear me. "And I need to get better at dealing with things like this. My husband is a farmer. I need to toughen up."

"No." His voice was sharp as he cupped my cheek. Expression fierce, he insisted, "Don't ever change. It isn't weak to care. And nothing should have happened to those birds. Nothing." Jared glanced sharply back at the house. "Whoever did it was on our land while we were in the house and we didn't hear a thing."

Too busy caught up in each other, that's why.

Guilt flashed through me.

"My grandfather never installed a security system. He has a rifle cabinet. We *were* the security." He looked down at me, and I saw the thoughts whirring behind his eyes. "But we need to install a system that includes a few cameras. If it was just me ... but I won't chance anything happening with you in the house."

Fear flickered through me. "Do you think it could go that far?"

"No." He gripped my shoulders. "Hamish doesn't have it in him to physically hurt us. He's just messing with me. But still, I won't take a chance with you in the house. Plus"—fury glittered in his pale jade eyes—"I want to catch the bastard in the act."

TWENTY-FIVE
ALLEGRA

As much as I hated worrying people, it was nice to know that they cared enough to be concerned. Jared had contacted his friend, the chief inspector, and he'd sent out his own men to question us about the chickens and the ewe. He promised Jared he'd have someone bring his father in for a thorough interview. Then he asked us if there were any other possible culprits. We couldn't think of any.

From there Jared returned to work because he had to. And just because I had Jared now didn't mean I didn't need my sister. I'd gone to her, shaken up, and she'd taken the afternoon off work. Despite the circumstances, it was nice to catch up with Aria. I'd also subtly made it clear to her that Jared and I were really making a go at our marriage.

That caused her even more concern. I understood. Ardnoch had been quiet for five years, but for a while there, it was a magnet for danger, and not one of our friends had escaped unscathed. To be fair, Aria's danger had caught up with her in LA, but it had made her wary. People surprised you. Sometimes in awful ways.

"Honestly, we're pretty sure it's Jared's father behind all of this," I repeated what I'd told Aria to Sloane Ironside and Monroe Adair a few days later.

We sat in Flora's, the popular local café. Flora had given Sloane her big break with her baking, buying cakes and treats to sell to her customers. Once everyone knew where Flora was getting them, Sloane's baking business took off. When she discovered her wealthy father had left her all his money, she was able to purchase a property across the street and open her bakery.

Life was so good, she could afford to run it part time. The limited opportunity to buy goodies from Callie's Wee Cakery only added to her success. Sloane had tourists flocking to Ardnoch just for her baked goods and she had a waiting list for her wedding cakes.

Monroe Adair was married to retired Hollywood actor Brodan Adair, the third-eldest Adair sibling. He'd been a huge movie star, and I met him before I moved here because he'd starred in one of my dad's movies. However, when he returned to take a break at home, he discovered his old childhood best friend Monroe had moved back to Ardnoch. I didn't know the ins and outs of their romance, but apparently they kind of hated each other for something that happened between them when they were barely out of high school. They hadn't spoken in eighteen years. I thought it was so romantic that even with eighteen years between them, they'd fallen so in love, they got married within months of reuniting. Their son Lennox (Nox), now six, came along pretty fast too. Brodan co-owned the whisky distillery outside of town with his eldest brother Lachlan.

Monroe, despite her husband's wealth, hadn't given up her career as a primary school teacher. I admired the heck out of her for that because teaching was one of the hardest jobs on the planet.

"Poor Jared," Sloane grimaced. "It's beyond shitty when

our parents disappoint us on levels that are soap opera–worthy."

Monroe tucked a strand of her gorgeous red hair behind her ear and sighed. "Yep."

I wondered what the story with her parents was but decided it was too nosy a question to ask. "So ... no need to worry." I patted Sloane's hand. "We're all good."

"I'm glad." Sloane covered my hand, her brown eyes warm with affection. "We worked too hard to keep you safe for something to happen now."

I smiled, glad we could allude to that night all those years ago without either of us breaking down over it. "Yeah. Plus, I have Jared. He'll never let anything happen to me." I believed it.

Her eyes danced. "It would appear things have improved between you since our dinner."

"Dinner?" Monroe queried.

With a sheepish shrug, I explained, "Sloane invited us to dinner with her, Jared's cousin Sarah and her husband, and my sister and North. Jared was ... monosyllabic that evening."

"Diplomatic," Sloane praised with a snort.

"Okay. He was kind of an ass. But we're good." I gave her a pointed, wicked smirk. "Very, very good."

My friend laughed. "Oh, so it's like that."

"I tell you, these Ardnoch men ..." Monroe wore a secret smile that informed me Brodan Adair made sure she was very, very good too. It did not surprise me in the least. As for Sloane, she'd shared a while ago that Walker liked to tie her up when they had sex. The thought sent a shiver coursing through me. Maybe Jared and I needed to try a bit of that.

"In all seriousness." Sloane leaned forward, voice lowering. The café was packed with mostly tourists because it was summer, so I had to strain forward to hear her. "The village has been rampant with gossip about the sheep and the chickens. Everyone is worried about you two."

"We don't want to worry anyone. We're okay. I'm ... I can't believe how attached I got to my chickens, though." An aching sadness at the loss of Ginger, Babs, and the rest of my birds still throbbed in my chest. "Jared would usually just buy more chickens so we could keep supplying Morag, but he told me that we'll do it when I'm ready. I feel like I should buck up and just go get more now, but I keep seeing them ..."

"Hey." Monroe ducked her head to meet my eyes. "Just take your time. You're grieving them. They were living creatures with personalities. If a person is allowed to grieve their dog or cat, you're allowed to grieve your birds."

Grateful, I whispered, "Thanks."

"So, it's true, then," a voice cut through our little moment.

Glancing up, I squinted at the two women who stood over the table. Recognition hit and I tensed. One of them was Sadie Dunmoor. She was an attractive woman in her forties who, up until a few years ago, had been a single mom. She married some guy in Golspie and moved her kid there. But her hair salon was still in Ardnoch. The reason I knew so much about her wasn't because she did my hair (I was lucky enough to have access to the salon on the estate), but because she used to be Jared's fuck buddy. I didn't recognize the blond at her side.

"Excuse me?" I asked cautiously.

Sadie grinned, big and genuine. Gesturing to the wedding band on my finger, she said, "That Jared got married. I never thought I'd see the day."

"Oh." I covered my ring and sat back in my chair. "Yeah."

"Well, congratulations. And will you tell him I said congrats?"

Relieved that she was being cool, I nodded. "Of course."

The blond at her side, however, snorted. "You must be very confident."

Sadie shot her a quelling look while I narrowed my eyes. "What does that mean?"

"It means, Jared shagged every eligible woman in Ardnoch." She huffed, eyeing Sloane and Monroe. "Am I right, ladies?"

Monroe quirked an eyebrow. "I don't believe he ever touched you with a barge pole, Ursula."

Ursula? Why wasn't I familiar with her?

The blond grimaced. "Well, I'm married."

Sadie sighed heavily and gave me an apologetic smile. "Sorry, I just wanted to stop and offer congrats. Really. He's a good man. He deserves happiness."

"I appreciate that."

"After finding happiness between the legs of a million women," Ursula cracked.

"Urs!" Sadie hissed. "There are children in here."

"Och, I'm only joking."

"No." Monroe pinned her with a hard look. "You're being rude to my friend and pushing the feminist movement back fifty years. I don't know why you're so obviously jealous of Allegra, a woman you don't even know, Ursula Rankin, but you're letting the side down with the cattiness. So quit it."

Clearly, Monroe knew this Ursula person, so I guessed she was a local I hadn't been aware of until now. Obviously, *she* was aware of me. Honestly, it wasn't the first time I'd been treated with rudeness by strangers. People saw the wealth and the fame and the pretty face, and they resented me for things they wanted for themselves, without seeing me as a person with my own shit and trauma.

"God, Monroe, you always were a drama queen. I'm not being catty." Ursula looked at me now. "I'm just saying ... Jared even tried to shag Regan and Eredine Adair before the brothers slapped a ring on them. It's just shocking that he's finally settled down. Guess the allure of that Howard money was just too much to resist. Everyone knew his farm was in trouble."

The fact that Ursula was correct about why Jared married me stung. Because as much as our marriage was turning into something real, he probably never would have married me otherwise. But that she would say so to my face was despicable.

"Oh my God." Sadie glowered at her friend. "What is wrong with you?" She blanched, turning to me. "I'm so sorry. I really did just want to offer my sincere best wishes. We'll be going now."

"I appreciate it. I'll tell Jared." I gave her a reassuring smile before turning to Ursula. "And Jared didn't marry me for the money. He married me because the sex is mind-blowing."

Sadie, proving how cool she really was, burst into laughter and shot her friend a "so there" look.

"Whatever." Ursula rolled her eyes.

Sadie gave me an apologetic wave and nudged her friend toward the exit. We could hear her berating her under her breath the whole way to the door. Once outside, they stopped, and we heard their muffled yelling before Sadie marched off in anger.

"Wow."

"Ursula Rankin was always a petty woman. I never understood why Sadie was friends with her," Monroe opined.

"I think Sadie's wondering that too." Sloane gave a huff of disbelieving laughter.

"Why do women do that?" I asked. "It just lives up to the cliché that we're all catty cows in competition with one another all the time. And it's not true. Look at us! Look at Sadie! She's the one who had a reason to potentially be jealous and she was super nice to me."

Sloane, Aria, Sarah, and all the Adair women were as close as any group of women could be. They'd lay down their lives for their friends and family and wanted only happiness for each other. Women like Ursula were few and far between, but they were enough to keep feeding the cliché.

"I don't think it's only women, if that makes you feel better," Sloane said with a shrug. "I think men can be petty and jealous over things and people others have that they don't."

I nodded. "You're right."

But as the conversation turned to a different topic, I couldn't help but feel that sinking sensation of fear and alarm settle deep in my gut. Because Ursula had, unfortunately, hit a nerve. I hadn't thought it mattered that our marriage had started out fake as long as it was real now.

Yet, maybe it did matter.

Even if Jared and I had come together in another way and started dating ... would he have ever really committed to me in such a permanent way as marriage? And if he wouldn't have, what did that really mean for our future? We'd decided to give ourselves the eighteen months to decide if we wanted to stay married.

What if Jared couldn't make it eighteen months after all?

What if ... what if he grew bored of me by then?

The awful thought made my stomach churn, but I tried to block out my old insecurities. I focused instead on the wonderful things Jared had said to me, the way he looked at me. He'd never felt this way about anyone. He'd said so. And I had to believe that it was true, and that Jared knew his own mind.

I had to believe.

Otherwise, I was setting myself up for the biggest heart-break I'd ever faced.

Twenty-Six

Jared

The clouds above my head turned heavy and dark so quickly the automatic headlights on my Defender suddenly illuminated the road. I glanced up out of the windshield and saw the heavy, mauve bellies of the clouds straining.

A raindrop hit my windshield, then another and another.

"Well, at least something went right today," I murmured, relieved at the sight of rain.

It had been dry and sunny for days, and while I had invested in an irrigation boom to water the fields during the summer, it wasn't the same as nature's version. Everything was connected, so even if the soil was wet, it still wasn't the same when the trees and leaves surrounding the fields were dry and crisp from too much sun. The countryside was thirsty, and it needed the rain.

I drove toward the house, already anticipating seeing Allegra after hours of not being with her. She'd been a bit quiet these last few days because of what happened to the chickens. I wasn't going to push her to invest in more birds until she was ready. And I wasn't going to mock or judge her for developing emotions for the wee creatures. The way she'd looked after them and loved them was one of the many reasons she'd made it so hard to resist her.

Allegra had spent the day with her friends in town, so I knew she was all right. But I still needed to see her for myself, and, truthfully, I didn't like her being at the house on her own. The security company was coming tomorrow to fit the cameras and alarm system. Jim's police officers had found my father and pulled him in for a proper questioning. The bastard had tried to call me afterward from a new number and then texted me to back off and let him get on with his life. I'd blocked him. Again. The officers told me that my father had an alibi. He was in London the night the chickens were poisoned, and he had proof.

That didn't convince me that he wasn't behind it. He could have paid some arsehole to do his dirty work. And my father grew up on the farm. He'd know the easily accessible items that could poison a chicken or any animal, for that matter.

For now, however, there was nothing more the police could do. The officers had told me to contact them personally if anything else happened.

Relief flooded me as I drove up to the house. I could imagine in the winter it would be lit up, a warm, beckoning glow in the darkness. For five years I'd returned every night in the winter to no lights. To no one.

I thought that hadn't bothered me.

Apparently, I was wrong.

Striding toward the house, I glanced down at my T-shirt that was smeared with mud and damp with sweat. I should really head upstairs for a shower first, but my priority was to check in on Allegra. Rounding the house, I headed toward the mudroom. The sound of music hit my ears before I even opened the door. A song blared in the kitchen and my first feeling was agitation. Anyone could catch my wife unaware when she was listening to music that loudly.

I stifled the irritation because tomorrow it wouldn't be an issue. We'd have the security system in place, and I was going to insist she arm it when she was home alone. Just until this whole strange mess had blown over.

Toeing off my boots, I cocked my head as I realized she was listening to what sounded like jazz. It wasn't her usual thing. We shared a taste for a decent amount of the same bands. As I walked through the mudroom, Allegra came into view at the kitchen counter. She was washing dishes, her perfect heart-shaped arse swaying in exaggeration as she crooned along with the woman singing out of her phone. Instead of her usual tee and shorts, she wore a short summer dress. A strappy wee number that was sexier than I think she probably realized. Allegra had gorgeous fucking legs that went on for days. The hem of her dress fluttered with her movements, dangerously close to flashing her knickers.

The song was a jazz version of "Creep" by Radiohead.

Leaning on the doorframe with my arms crossed over my chest, I let my gaze roam over my wife as she sang, with not a bad voice, actually, along with the woman. I was relieved to see her enjoying life amid the madness. Yet I also sensed that familiar hunger no amount of sex with her seemed to satiate.

"I'm a weirdo!" Allegra yell-sang turning on the balls of her feet, hair flying. "Whahhh!" Her hand flew to her chest as she caught sight of me.

I chuckled as she shot me an embarrassed glare that immediately turned into laughter.

"How long have you been there?"

Walking over to her phone, I tapped the screen to switch off the song. "That's something you'd know if you could hear anything."

"I thought I was alone." She huffed, turning back to the sink.

With a gentle touch on her arm, I stopped her from turning away from me. I kept my tone soft. "Exactly. I just want you to be safe until we know who is behind the animal attacks."

Her eyes shone as she nodded. "I get it."

Brushing a soft kiss across her cheek, I stepped past her to wash my hands at the sink. Amusement bubbled on my lips. "So, apparently, sex with me is mind-blowing."

There was silence at my back for a second, so I glanced over my shoulder.

Allegra gaped at me comically. "Who told you?"

Shoulders shaking with laughter, I turned to lean against the counter. "When are you going to realize that you can't say shit like that in public here and have it not get around the entire village by the end of the day?"

"Seriously?"

I nodded, grinning. "So ...?"

She threw her hands up, a faint flush of red on the crests of her cheeks. "Okay, so, Sadie ... such a cool person and I can totally see why you went there. But her friend Ursula. Ugh. You should have heard what she said to me. I am not one of those catty women, getting into bitch fights. I avoided mean girls at school like the plague, but she was *rude*." Allegra gestured dramatically. "Like, so rude."

Annoyance cut through my amusement. I'd never liked Ursula. She was married and had come on to me multiple times behind her husband's and Sadie's backs.

Sadie was a different story. I'd first slept with her maybe a year after moving to Ardnoch. She was ten years older than me, a single mum, and she'd made it clear she didn't mind a hookup. I didn't want her getting the wrong idea, so I'd never gone back for thirds. We'd remained friends, though.

Then five years ago, on the night I met Allegra, I went home with Sadie. I'd done it to prove to myself I just needed to get laid, that whatever spark I felt with Allegra was nothing but lust. All I'd proven was that I was an arsehole for using one woman to forget another. I never slept with Sadie again, and she was cool with it. Ursula, however, had acted pissed ever since, like she somehow had anything to do with it. "What did she say?"

That Allegra wouldn't meet my eyes was cause for concern. "Just what I already knew. That you'd been around. I didn't ... I didn't know you were interested in Regan *and* Eredine, though."

Fucking Ursula. This fucking village. I huffed. "I flirted with them. Years and years ago, before either of them got with their husbands. What the hell is Urs doing bringing that shit up?"

She finally met my eyes and some of the tension drained out of me at the warmth in them. "She ... she's jealous. Of me. Maybe even of Sadie."

I grimaced. "Aye, she might have made her interest in me clear in the past. But I don't sleep with married women, and even if she weren't married, I wouldn't touch Ursula if my life depended on it. She's always been one of these people who covets what others have and is really fucking angry about everything."

"Well, maybe she took your rejection out on me because she certainly wanted to bring me down a peg. Apparently, you only married me for my money." She smirked, but I noted a hint of uncertainty there.

Fuck.

Fucking Ursula.

Reaching out, I took hold of Allegra by the waist and pulled her into me until her palms rested on my chest. "But I stayed married to you because the alternative sounds like the shittiest fucking fate I can think of."

Her expression softened, her whole body relaxing into me. How did she not know that by now? "Yeah, I made sure she knew she was wrong."

"And that sex with me is mind-blowing."

"Actually that sex with *me* is mind-blowing," she teased. "Are you saying it isn't?"

Desire throbbed hot and thick between us in an instant. "Of course it is. Best sex of my life. I can't get enough." I'd never needed a woman the way I needed Allegra, and I knew, just like I'd learned the night we met, that no one could be a substitute. It was her or it was nobody.

Allegra's hands slipped beneath my shirt, smoothing up my stomach with intent.

I groaned, my dick hardening against her. "I ... I need to shower."

"Don't." One hand slipped downward, pushing past my jeans. "I want you like this."

I grunted as she rubbed me through my boxers. "Fuck ... I'm sweaty."

"I know." She leaned on her tiptoes to lick my neck. "I want you just like this."

My hands slipped down her waist, slowly tugging up the hem of her dress so I could slip inside her knickers and cup her bare arse. Her breath shook against my throat. "You sure?" I kneaded her arse, pressing her against my erection.

"We can shower afterward." Her voice was hardly above a whisper.

My wife barely had to do anything to turn me into a sex-crazed teenager. It would be embarrassing if it wasn't so exciting and utterly satisfying. I gripped her arse in my hands and hauled her up my body as I stumbled toward the wall. Allegra hopped up, wrapping her legs around my waist just as her back met the space between the doorway and the kitchen cupboards.

Her head fell back on a gasp of pleasure as I rolled my hips between her thighs.

My lips sought her skin, skimming her jaw until I reached her ear. "You're on my mind all the time. You're all I can think about. Your smile, your laugh, your body. I want to fuck you hard every minute of every day so you know who you belong to and who belongs to you."

Her fingernails bit into my shoulders as her strong thighs tightened around me. "I feel the same. You're in my head. All day. Every day. I want you, Jared. I want you so badly, all the time."

Triumphant possessiveness heated my blood to the boiling point. "Lower your legs," I demanded.

Allegra released me, lowering to the floor so I had to bend to reach for her mouth. I loved the taste of her, the feel, the way she kissed like she fucked, hungry and assertive.

Needing deep inside her, I pushed her dress up to her waist and curled my fingers around the fabric of her knickers. I yanked, and the sound of them tearing from her body made me impossibly harder.

"Jared!" Allegra gaped at me in shock ... and pure horniness. She liked that. Good to know. She proved it by grabbing my head and crushing my lips over hers.

We bit and licked and nipped at each other as we both reached for the closure on my jeans. Allegra shoved them and my boxers down to my ankles, freeing me. She took my cock in her small hand and I watched her beneath my lashes as she pumped with a tight, hard grip that I loved.

I curled my hand over hers, enjoying it for a few more seconds before I released her hold. "Wait." I bent down to get my wallet out of my back pocket to pull out a condom. My dick was in a serious state of pleasure pain as I rolled it on.

Unable to wait any longer, I commanded, "Up."

Allegra hopped with ease and eagerness, legs around my hips, hands on my shoulders. I pressed her into the wall as I gripped her thighs, spread them, and thrust up into her. I groaned as sensation zinged down my spine and to my balls.

Being inside her tight, wet heat was perfection. Looking into her gorgeous, sweet face, watching her lips part and eyes glaze with pleasure was even better.

"Jared!" she cried out, arching into the feel of me. I let her adjust, sensing she was ready when her fingernails no longer bit so hard into my shoulders.

Then I took my wife.

Hard.

Her pants of excitement filled my ears as I pounded us into the wall, gliding in and out of her tightness, the wet slap of flesh against flesh spurring us toward climax.

It was always fast and explosive when we fucked like this. The need beyond our control. I was going to blow soon and I wanted Allegra to come first. My hand slipped between us, and I allowed myself the pleasure of feeling where I entered her before my thumb found her clit.

"Jared!" Allegra's hand slid around my nape, fingernails scratching across my skin. "Yes, yes!"

I circled her clit as I continued to fuck her and within seconds I felt her stiffen, then—

Allegra cried out as she came, her inner muscles pulsing around my dick in hard, awesome tugs.

"Allegra!" My spine stiffened as I peaked, my balls drawing up and then the release exploding through me. My dick throbbed as I shuddered against her, coming into the condom with such intensity it was a wonder the bloody thing didn't come off inside her. "Jesus." I trembled, resting my forehead on her shoulder as I continued to shake through the aftershocks of release.

The sound of us both trying to catch our breath and the scent of sex made me want to do it all over again.

See? Never enough.

"Mind-blowing," I murmured hoarsely, thinking of her words to Ursula.

She giggled. A tender ache speared across my chest.

"Hey, Jared."

"Mmm-hmm?" I brushed a kiss across her throat, loath to leave her body.

"How would you feel about tying me up to fuck me?"

I froze, not certain I'd heard her correctly. Lifting my gaze, I searched her face. She was flushed but her expression was serious. "Say that again?"

"I thought we could try you tying me to the bed. It might be nice."

It might be *nice*?

"I think you might be the most perfect woman in the world."

Her gorgeous face split into a wide smile. "I'll take that as a yes."

TWENTY-SEVEN
JARED

After years of living in Ardnoch, I was used to the vast differences of life in the village depending on the season. While tourists visited all year round, they were fewer during the winter months. Tables in the cafés and pub opened up, and Castle Street was quieter in the evenings.

However, in the height of summer, I still couldn't get parked on the main thoroughfare at seven thirty p.m. My visits to the Gloaming had been rare since marriage, and I glanced into the mottled front window to find it packed inside. Georgie might even be in there with a few locals we used to share a weekly pint with. To my surprise, I didn't feel the urge to go in and be with my mates.

Instead, I carried on my way, turning down the cobbled lane between the jail museum and the Chinese restaurant. Once the nights got darker, the lane would be lit by the Victorian-style lampposts, but this evening they weren't as the sun still hadn't set. My destination was William's Wine Cellar. It sold a wide selection of alcohol, and as Allegra had just told me, a fairly good selection of nonalcoholic wine. She liked a particular brand that William's sold. She'd mentioned offhand she fancied a glass, and I didn't mind a quick trip to the village to retrieve it.

Now that the security system was installed, I felt safer about leaving Allegra alone in the house.

Pushing the glass doors open, I came to an abrupt halt at the sight of Aria standing at the counter, chatting to William. I hadn't been alone with Allegra's sister ... well ... ever.

She glanced at me, her eyebrows rising. "Jared."

"All right?" I approached her reluctantly.

"Yeah." She gestured to the two bottles on the counter. "Just grabbing some wine." Pain I didn't understand flashed across her face. "'Cause I can drink it."

"Okay." Looking to William, I nodded in greeting. "You got any Binnie's NA red?"

William pushed away from the counter. "How many bottles?"

"Eh, make it two."

"So, Ally sent you on an NA run, huh?" Aria gave me a small smile, even as she searched my face. I didn't know what she was looking for, but I felt under inspection. Since I'd married my wife, I'd only seen Aria twice, and yet each time it was clear I was being judged. And I didn't like it.

"I offered."

Awkward silence fell between us as I pretended to study the whisky bottles behind William's counter.

"So ... how are you both?"

"Good."

"How is Ally really doing? You know, after the chickens? She was pretty upset."

"She's getting there. Even talking about getting more chickens."

"Oh, that's good. How are you?"

I frowned and repeated, "Good."

Aria snorted. "You're not big on the talking, huh?"

I shrugged, not sure what she wanted me to say.

She leaned in. "I just want Ally to be happy. To settle down. To stop ... to stop doing impulsive stuff."

"Impulsive stuff?" I bit out.

"Look, you don't know Allegra's history. But this is not the first time she's done something insane and paid for it. I don't want her getting hurt again." Concern etched Aria's features. "I'm worried that she's just built to self-destruct. I don't want that to be true ... so I really hope that whatever is going on between you works out. For both of you."

Agitation thrummed through me. It was seriously difficult to keep my tongue in check. Because Allegra was right. As much as her sister might love her, she didn't know her. Aye, she didn't know the real reason Allegra went off the rails in high school, but it was clear she'd started to believe Allegra was just a fuck-up.

And fuck that.

I scoffed. "You don't need to worry about Allegra self-destructing. The mere fact that you are tells me that in less than two months, I know and understand Allegra more than you ever tried to in twenty-five years."

Aria's jaw dropped just as William returned to the counter.

"How much?" I asked abruptly.

William frowned at my tone and told me.

I swiped my card over the payment terminal, feeling Aria's eyes on me but refusing to look at her. Thanking William gruffly, I grabbed the bag with the bottles of NA and strode out of the shop.

A few seconds passed and I heard her heels on the cobbles behind me. "Jared, wait!"

Anger still thrummed hotly in my blood, but I stopped. Aria rounded me. The woman was taller than me in her sky-high shoes. Indignation snapped in her green eyes. I'd always found her a bit too cold and aloof for my tastes, but right then, she was as fiery as her sister as she growled, "What the hell does that mean?"

I shrugged. "Just what I said."

"No one knows Ally better than me."

I gave a bark of incredulous laughter and I moved to pass her. "You know fuck all about Allegra."

Aria gripped my biceps. "What don't I know?"

Shrugging out of her hold, I gave her a hard look. "Everything."

I'd barely given her my back when she pleaded in a broken voice, "Jared, please."

Instant remorse cut through me when I glanced back and saw the tears she struggled to hold in.

Damn it. I'd never seen Aria Hunter anything but composed, cool, and intimidatingly assertive. Seeing her vulnerable made me feel like an arse.

Cursing under my breath, I faced her. "I can't tell you about Allegra's past. It's up to her who she shares it with."

"She shared it with you, though?" Hurt glimmered in her eyes.

I nodded, my voice a wee bit softer as I replied, "Aye, she's told me everything."

Aria's face crumpled and the tears slipped free.

"Fuck." I moved toward her helplessly. "I'm sorry. I didn't mean to upset you. I just … it makes me angry that you all think Allegra's a fuck-up when she's anything but."

"I don't think she's a fuck-up."

At least that's what I think Aria replied. It was hard to tell because it was garbled by her cries.

Awkward and guilty and utterly powerless before a woman's tears, I lowered the bag of NA wine to the cobbles and put my arms around her. "Hey, it's okay."

To my shock, Aria returned the embrace, her own bag of

wine knocking against my back as she burst into sobs that were wrenched from deep inside her. Concern had me tightening my arms because I could feel the pain emanating from her. And it was *more*. This was more than her relationship with Allegra.

We stood there so long, the arse pocket of my jeans vibrated as my phone rang on silent. It was most likely Allegra checking where I was.

Aria finally got control of herself and she released me. "Oh my God. I'm so sorry." She wiped at the mascara now pooling around her eyes. The sisters looked just similar enough to know they were related. Both were beautiful, even when they sobbed.

Renewed guilt flushed through me because I shouldn't have been such a bastard to her, even if I felt I was in the right. At the end of the day, she was Allegra's sister, and my wife loved her sister so much, she was willing to protect her to the detriment of her own reputation. It was not up to me to interfere with that decision or treat her sister badly for it.

"You've no need. I'm sorry for being a prick."

She shook her head, wiping at her pretty cheeks. "No. It's nice to know someone is looking out for Ally. This wasn't ..." She gestured between us. "I ..." Her eyes filled with water again as her gaze locked with mine. "I just found out I'm not pregnant."

Oh. Shit.

"We've been trying for a year." She sucked in a breath like she might burst into tears again any second.

"I'm sorry." I reached out to squeeze her arm. "Does Allegra know?"

Aria shook her head. "We haven't talked to anyone about it." She shrugged, her smile wobbly with emotion. "I know there're lots of options out there, but I just didn't anticipate that this would be difficult for us, and I'm not handling it too well right now. And Ally and I feel further apart than ever and ... ugh." She waved a hand. "Never mind." Her eyes widened in horror. "Jared, I'm ... I don't know why I just blurted that out to you."

"Because you clearly needed to tell someone." I considered her, seeing her in a totally different light from before. I'd never seen her let her guard down like this. Which meant she needed someone who loved her right now. "Are you in a hurry to get home?"

She shook her head sadly. "No. North is in LA."

"Then come back with me. I have some work to do in my office and you can talk to Allegra."

Aria bit her lip, considering it. Finally, she asked uncertainly, "Are you sure?"

"You need her. And she needs to know that you need her."

Fresh tears brightened her eyes and she laughed unhappily. "I swear, I am not usually this emotional."

"You should cry as much as you want to and never be embarrassed for it," I told her as I lifted the bag of wine off the ground and then took hers too. When I was a boy, growing up where I did, we were made to feel less of a man if we showed emotion. I'd learned from my grandfather, the most masculine man I'd ever known, that crying didn't make you weak. It made you human. "Come on."

Her smile this time was a little warmer, a little less sad. "Okay."

As always, sunlight streamed in through the curtains and woke me before my alarm. As always, since Allegra started sharing my bed, I lingered, waiting for the alarm instead of jumping out of it like I used to. Her soft, warm body tucked against mine made it difficult to get out of bed these days.

Last night was the first night, other than when Allegra had her period, that we didn't have sex. As promised, I'd brought Aria home and then I'd made myself scarce in the office. I'd answered emails from the company building the pods, from produce contacts, from my land agent, catching up on everything that had piled up over the last week. I could hear tears from the living room and, thankfully, I also heard laughter.

Trying not to focus on the sisters meant focusing on work. And focusing on work only reminded me that I'd married Allegra for her money. That had been fine when it was just a business deal. But now that we were together for real, the money element left a bad taste in my mouth. I didn't want her to believe I was with her for her money. I didn't want other people to think that. I certainly didn't want to feel like money sat between us as an inevitable wall. Allegra would always have more money than me. Something that wouldn't bother me so long as I didn't feel like I, or the farm, was beholden to her financially.

Now that was definitely the case.

But if I could get the glamping pods up and running, then perhaps over time I could build enough capital to invest in more holiday lets on the land. Granddad wanted the land to remain a farm, but in this economy it couldn't exist as that. The land needed to bring in profit in other ways, and holiday lets seemed like the thing that made most sense. Perhaps I could even build a holiday park with facilities. It was something to consider. There was enough unused land to do it.

The alarm cut through the bedroom, and I reluctantly eased from my wife's warm body to switch it off.

I felt her sigh as she awoke.

Rolling back into her, I pulled her into my chest. "You okay?" I murmured in her ear.

Last night the sisters had talked for hours. Allegra had asked Aria to stay, but she'd insisted on calling a guard from the estate to pick her up and take her home. As soon as the SUV had driven out of sight, Allegra had hugged me tight.

"Did you tell her ... anything?" I asked.

"No." She raised her head, eyes lit with guilt. "She's hurting enough right now without finding out about our dad. I meant it when I said that she doesn't need to know."

"I'm sorry if I caused trouble."

"You didn't," she assured me. "You actually ... Aria used to believe that something had happened to me to drive me off the rails as a teen. But I think over time, because I didn't confide in her, she started to think I was kind of a natural-born disaster. You reminded her tonight that I'm not. And that's enough for me."

"Is it enough for her?"

Allegra shrugged sadly. "I don't know. But right now she has more on her mind than me." Tears filled her eyes. "I hate seeing her in pain. I mean, I know she and North will figure it out, but I hate that it's going to be a struggle for them to have a baby. And ... oh, Ari is so tough on herself. She feels like she's letting North down, which is ridiculous. I ..." She nibbled on her bottom lip, looking very much like her sister. "I texted North while Ari was in the bathroom. He needs to know how upset she is."

"Will he come home?"

"Already on his way. He literally texted back in two seconds 'on my way.'" Allegra smiled. "Nothing matters more to him than my sister."

The longing in her voice did something to me. I ... I realized that I wanted her to know that's how I felt about her. But I couldn't quite find the words.

Instead, I'd led her upstairs and helped her undress for bed, pulling her into my arms and telling her to sleep because she needed it after the emotional intensity of the evening.

Now, Allegra turned in my arms to face me. She pressed a

soft kiss to my mouth and nuzzled her temple against my beard like a contented cat. "I'm good."

And that's when I finally found the words. "I want you to know that you are what matters most to me now."

She lifted her gaze, those big brown eyes gleaming with wonder. "Really?"

I rested my forehead against hers. "Really."

"I feel the same," she whispered, voice hoarse with emotion. "You matter more than anything."

Too much *feeling* coursed through me, I couldn't speak. How the hell did I get so lucky to have found a wife who was ... my best friend?

"No one makes me feel as safe as you do, Jared. I didn't think I would ever find that." She wrapped her arms around me and buried her face in my neck.

And I vowed then and there that I would always be her safe place, and I'd never let anything harm this woman ever again.

TWENTY-EIGHT
ALLEGRA

T hese last few weeks I'd lived in a strange haze of unbelievable happiness and contentment, tinged with dread and anxiety. Last week, another ewe was found dead. Jared could put security cameras in the dairy to keep his cattle safe, but the sheep were out in the fields and there was no way to look after them twenty-four seven. He'd made the difficult decision to sell the flock again for their own safety. I'd stood holding his hand tight in mine just that morning while the sheep were loaded onto the truck to leave for their new home.

Jared was so despondent, I hadn't wanted to leave him, but I had an appointment with Michelle in Inverness and he insisted I go.

Between this unknown threat hanging over our heads and my worry over Aria (who assured me she was fine, and that she and North were talking about their options), I had a lot of energy and emotion buzzing through me. Since I was a kid, I'd funneled that energy into my art. Back then I'd started sketching. The people and things around me. Then I'd begun sketching from my imagination and that's really when art became a safe place for me and a way to process my feelings. The only time I hadn't spent that energy through my art I'd ended up drinking, doing drugs, having sex with older men, and ending up in rehab.

These days, I stuck to the art.

Throughout the craziness of the last few weeks, I'd started work on a piece that I was especially proud of. And it wasn't glass. It was something entirely different for me. Painting with oils on canvas in a more illustrative style than what people were used to seeing from me, I'd painted a figure that looked a lot like me walking up the driveway toward the farmhouse. The day after Jared told me I mattered more to him than anything else, I'd driven up the driveway of the farmhouse and suddenly felt an overwhelming sense of contentment and safety. I'd wanted to capture that emotion.

Even though I'd yet to spend a winter on the farm, the image came to my mind in the cold season—the farmhouse aglow in the dark snow, me in a hat and coat, the house beckoning me home to warmth and security. And love. Because though that word had not been shared, I was pretty certain Jared was just as in love with me as I was with him.

It might take him a while to get his mind and mouth around *I love you*, but I could wait.

A small smile prodded my lips as I sauntered down Ness Walk and past the buildings that sat along the River Ness that cut through the city. The north end opened out onto the Beauly Firth by the Kessock Bridge, which would take me home to Ardnoch. Following the river south led to Loch Ness.

Michelle's gallery was across the river from Inverness Castle. The rain that had brought much respite to the farm this past week had drifted off to parts unknown. Sun beamed across the water of the Ness, lighting up the building that housed Michelle's gallery. It had to be at least a hundred years old. Inside was a smallish gallery, but she'd created a minimalistic aesthetic broken up into different spaces by walls to separate the genres of art and artists. The walls were either black or white, so that nothing detracted the eye from the artwork.

A bell jingled above the door as I let myself in.

Michelle looked up from behind the counter and greeted me with a triumphant smile.

"Someone in London bought two of your pieces last night. I spent the morning packing them to ship!"

Delight blossomed through me as I reached her. It never ceased to amaze me that people wanted to pay money for my artwork. I hoped that feeling of wonder never went away and returned Michelle's high-five with a laugh.

"That is the kind of news I needed to hear today," I said truthfully.

"I'm glad to be the bearer. Now, what news do you have for me?"

Nervous but excited to show her the painting I was working on, I'd shown her what I could from the photos I'd taken on my phone. The painting was, of course, unfinished and sitting in my rented studio. It wasn't quite the same as seeing it in real life, but I'd taken a video too so she could see the textures and the light, and the glimmers of metallic paint I'd added here and there for interest.

Unfortunately, my nervousness turned to anxiety as Michelle took my phone and looked over the images for a second time. Her lips pursed and she looked up at me regretfully as she handed the phone back. "It's not really what I'm looking for. I already sell an artist that does something similar. I like your glasswork, Allegra. It makes you stand out. You should stay in your lane."

Irritation zinged through me. Utter disappointment too. Because this painting meant a great deal to me. I wanted people to feel that when they looked at it.

If Michelle didn't ...

Stay in my lane?

I guess that's what you told an artist once you started making money from their art.

Stay in your lane.

It fucking hurt. And it chafed.

Giving Michelle a tight smile, I nodded and made conversation about what had sold since the art show, what pieces were still left.

Relief filled me as soon as I could make an excuse to leave. There might as well have been heavy clouds hanging over Inverness for what little good the sunshine did to lift my mood.

Needing a pick-me-up, I walked across the bridge and traversed the streets until I found the coffee place I liked. It was in the opposite direction of where I'd parked my car, but it was worth it for their latte and croissant. I'd thought earlier about doing a little shopping in the city, but now I just wanted to return to Ardnoch.

As I stepped out of the coffee shop, caffeine and carbs in hand, a tingling sensation on my nape caused me to pause. I looked to the left and locked eyes with an unfamiliar man. What was strange and roused my instincts was that he looked away from me as quickly as possible. He scrolled through his phone, casual, as he leaned against the building.

Something about him was too casual.

I tried to place him but couldn't. He was dressed in a long-sleeved dark tee and dark jeans and he really didn't look that threatening. Dark hair, clean cut. But there was tension along the lines of his shoulders that someone who had drawn a shit ton of live-model nudes for four years could easily observe.

My stomach flipped unpleasantly, and I slipped on my sunglasses, trying to shake off the paranoia. For the most part, I could walk around Inverness with anonymity, but occasionally someone recognized me. Trying to remain calm, I strode up the street, past him, heading toward the parking lot where I'd left my Wrangler.

That tingling sensation on my neck returned within seconds. Pretending to stop to fumble through my purse, glancing back as if I'd forgotten something at the coffee place, I caught sight of the man walking behind me. He glanced down at his phone again, slowing to a stop outside a pet store.

My heart beat hard in my chest as I faked finding what I'd been looking for in my bag and walked forward again.

Some people might call it being neurotic, but when your sister and friends had a history of being kidnapped, you kind of jumped to worst-case scenario in situations like this. Fumbling for my phone, I called Jared as I strolled into a clothing boutique. I smiled tightly at the blond woman behind the counter as I pretended to peruse the items, all the while glancing outside.

The man had stopped at the building opposite the clothing boutique and was staring inside at me.

Fuck.

Jared picked up. "Can I call you back?" He practically shouted, the sound of the tractor loud in the background.

I hurried to the back of the store. "Jared, I think I'm being followed."

"What?"

"Jared—"

"Hang on." The noise of the tractor cut off. "What did you say?"

"I think I'm being followed," I hissed impatiently in my freak-out.

"How? What? Where are you?" I heard the panic in his voice and hated it.

"I'm still in Inverness. I noticed this guy watching me and then I turned around and he was following me. Now I've walked into a store, and he's stopped outside the store opposite. It could be paranoia, but my Spidey senses are tingling like crazy."

"Is there a back way out of the store you're in?" His words were calm, but I could hear the sharpness edging them.

"I don't know," I whispered shakily.

"Ask whoever is running the store. Stay on the phone."

Nodding, I ignored the quizzical look another customer threw me and hurried over to the blond behind the counter. Another glance out the window told me the guy hadn't moved and he *was* watching me.

Double fuck.

Smoothing my expression, I asked the woman, "Is there a back door out of here?"

She frowned. "Um ... it's staff only."

"Explain to her who you are and what's happening," Jared commanded sharply in my ear.

I nodded again, even though he couldn't see me. Shifting my sunglasses off my face, I was relieved to see recognition flicker across the blond's expression. That would make things a lot easier. "My name is Allegra Howard McCulloch—"

"I know who you are." She beamed excitedly. "I am such a fan of your father's work. And your sister's husband, oh my God! Congrats on your marriage! Do you—"

"A man is following me," I cut her off, keeping a smile on my face and probably looking deranged.

The woman stiffened.

"Don't react. Don't look. But he's outside and he's following me."

To her credit, she smiled in return, even though it didn't reach her eyes. "Okay. What do you need?"

"Is there a back way out that will let me get to my car on Charles Street?"

She kept smiling as she nodded. "Why don't I show you, madam?"

Relief filled me. "Thank you."

"Thank fuck," Jared murmured in my ear.

I followed her through the store, past changing rooms and into a staff-only area. Out of sight of the man, I dropped the crazy smile. "Thank you for this. What is your name?"

She glanced over her shoulder. "Annie."

"You're a lifesaver, Annie."

"Do you need me to call the police?"

"I'm on the phone with my husband. He'll call if I need him to."

Annie opened a door that led out onto an alley. She gestured to the left where the alley turned into a lane behind the stores. "Stick to the lane until it comes to an end. It'll bring you by Berry's B&B. And from there, you're just a straight shot down to the carpark."

Trembling now, I thanked Annie again and then hurried into the alley.

"I'm out," I told Jared as I jog-walked onto the cobbled lane.

"Run, Allegra."

"What if I'm being paranoid?"

"Then running is just a bit of exercise, but it would make me feel better if you fucking ran!"

"Okay, no need to bite my head off. I'm already freaked out enough."

"Sorry, baby. I just hate being here while you're there."

I murmured my understanding as I regretfully dumped my latte and croissant in the trash. Thankful for the flat pumps I wore, though I felt every little stone under my feet, I ran until I was off the lane and out onto the street surrounded by people and vehicles. If anyone thought I was a crazy lady, I didn't care. I just kept running until my bright yellow Jeep came into view. As soon as traffic cleared, I raced across the street and into the parking lot. Fumbling with my keys and phone, glancing around to make sure the man was nowhere in sight, it took me a tension-building amount of time to get in the car.

I could hear Jared shouting my name from the phone I'd dropped on the passenger seat. But I was in a hurry to switch on the engine and get out of there. I'd never been more annoyed with myself for buying a bright yellow freaking car.

The phone connected to the vehicle as I swung out of the parking lot. "I'm here, I'm here!" I cried in response to Jared's panicked shouts.

"Fuck!" He bit out. "I'm coming to meet you."

"Don't. I'm in my car and I'm on my way."

"If you see anyone following you, call the police."

"You got it."

"In fact, just stay on the phone with me."

"For an hour? Don't you have tractoring to do?" I attempted to tease him to ease the unbearable tension. My gaze kept flicking to my rearview mirror, searching for any signs that I was being followed.

"Not while this is going on. I'll lose my mind with worry if you don't stay on the phone."

Tenderness suffused me. "Okay. I can tell you all about Michelle's shitty response to my painting while we pass the time."

"What?" He sounded annoyed.

"She told me it was similar to stuff one of her other artists is doing and that I should, and I quote, 'Stay in my lane.' Speaking of ..." I glared at a driver who swung last minute into my lane. I had to hit the brakes. "Asshole. Learn to drive! I'm a fucking American and I know how to drive here better than you, pal!"

I heard Jared's huff of laughter. "I can't believe you're yelling at bad drivers after what just happened."

Fear shivered through me. "I don't want to think about

that until I'm home."

He blew out a breath that sounded shaky. Voice gruff, he replied, "Okay. So what does 'stay in your lane' mean?"

"I don't know but ... it made me sad. I love this painting and when I look at it, it makes me ... *feel*."

"Then open your own gallery. You said that was the plan, right?"

My heart raced for an entirely different reason now. That *was* the plan. I'd given myself eighteen months to get it up and running. Now I only had fifteen. Honestly, with everything else going on, I hadn't put as much effort into it as I should have. "Yeah, it's supposed to be the plan."

"Then do it. Allegra, Ardnoch brings in more tourists than any other town in the Highlands. We have no art gallery, which seems like a bit of a failure on Ardnoch's part. You live in the perfect place to open a gallery that showcases anything and everything your imagination can come up with. And the beauty of that is, no one else will control what you sell. No one can tell you to stay in your lane. Especially when they're wrong. Because Michelle *is* wrong. Her opinion is biased because she's making money on your glasswork. That's what she cares about. *I* care about you. And you know deep down Michelle is wrong."

Love. So much love filled me. "Thank you," I whispered hoarsely.

"You don't need to thank me, baby. You just need to get your arse back here so I know you're safe."

"On my way home," I promised.

"I'll be there when you get here."

Tears filled my eyes. It had been a day! And I was emotionally overwhelmed. But in that moment, the tears were happy tears.

I knew what I'd call my painting.

I'll Be There When You Get Here.

TWENTY-NINE
JARED

There was only so much a person could take before they snapped.

Hearing the terror in Allegra's voice when she called to tell me a man was following her in Inverness was my breaking point.

———

Walker Ironside was a former Royal Marines Commando. I had the utmost respect for him because everyone knew it was no ordinary military unit. They were special operations and considered one of the most elite forces in the world. After his time in the military, he'd gone on to join a close protection team in the US, acting as security for high-profile members of the public. From there, he became Brodan Adair's primary bodyguard before returning to Scotland to settle down as head of security at Ardnoch Estate.

The man had contacts and knew how to find people.

He'd found Hamish in just a few hours.

At the sight of Hamish stumbling out of a pub in this

dimly lit area of Newcastle, I quietly got out of the car. Hurrying across the street into the shadows along the buildings, I followed him as he strolled in a slight zigzag toward his flat.

"Whatever you do, make sure there are no cameras around when you do it," Walker had warned me before I'd left Scotland.

So earlier in the evening, I'd waited until someone let me into Hamish's apartment building so I could make sure there were no cameras to witness what I planned to do. There were none. They weren't wanted in places like this by certain people. Graffiti marred every inch of the ground floor of the building's interior. There was a broken, rusted old bike just lying off to the side, rubbish that had been left to rot. The place stunk of urine and rotten food. It would do. I'd departed the apartment building to wait outside the pub Hamish visited every night.

And now there he was.

Blood pumped fast and hot through my body as I followed the bastard, picking up speed without alerting him. A group of lads on the other side of the street appeared, but they were too busy laughing and messing around to take note of me or Hamish.

The apartment blocks came into sight. A group of men were hanging out by a modified GTO and they turned to watch us. I looked away. I wasn't in their business. Hopefully they'd stay out of mine.

Allegra was safe on Ardnoch Estate. Frustrated and concerned that I'd made the decision to go after Hamish alone, but safe and sound. Knowing that allowed me to focus.

Hamish dropped his keys trying to get into the building and almost bollocksed up my plans. But he quickly righted himself and entered the flats.

I picked up speed as he stumbled inside, following him through the door and giving him a shove.

"What the fuck?" He slammed against the stairwell.

As he straightened, his bleary eyes widened. "Jared?"

Loathing almost crippled me. And shame. That I came from such a pathetic waste of space. Grabbing him by the collar, I shoved him along the wall until I had him pinned.

He reeked of whisky.

"Get off!" Hamish struggled, but he was no match for me on a normal day, never mind on a day I still brimmed over with the rage and panic I'd felt listening to Allegra yesterday on the phone as she escaped Inverness.

I never wanted to feel that powerless again.

I slammed Hamish against the wall, his head making a dull thud off the concrete.

As he groaned, his head rolling, I snarled, "You made a big fucking mistake coming after my wife."

The words echoed off the walls and Hamish blinked rapidly. In confusion. "What? What are you talking about?"

"Don't play dumb. I know it was you who killed the sheep, killed the chickens. And I know it was you who had someone following Allegra in Inverness yesterday. That is the last mistake you'll ever make."

Whatever Hamish saw in my face sobered him quickly. "No, no, lad, I didn't come after your missus. No way. I'm not that stupid. I know who she is. Even if I'm not feart o' you, I know who *her* family is."

No.

I ignored what seemed like Hamish's genuine confusion and fear because I knew in my gut he'd been messing with the farm. No matter what he'd told the police.

I slammed him again and pain tightened his features, seconds before he turned chalk. "Oh, I'm gonna be sick."

"You fucked with my farm and came after my wife! Admit it!"

When he said nothing, I pulled the Swiss Army knife I carried with me for work out of my pocket.

Hamish stopped whimpering and locked eyes on it as I brought the blade up to his face. "You wouldnae," he whispered.

"You know what I'm capable of, Hamish. You know who I was before I moved to Ardnoch."

He swallowed hard.

"And I might have stuck to the legal route if you hadn't come after my wife." I pressed the tip of the knife against his throat. Hamish stretched away from it.

And I hoped like hell my bluff would work.

"Fine, fine." Hamish nodded frantically. "It was me. The farm. I killed the first ewe and had someone else do the chickens and the other ewe while I was away. It was me!" Spittle flew out of his mouth. "But I didn't do anything to your missus. I promise! I promise. It wasn't me!"

Fuck. I'd expected to have to hurt him worse than that to get a confession. He really was an utter coward.

Releasing the pressure on the knife, I watched the small prick on his neck open up, blood trickling down. I felt no remorse. Eyes on Hamish, I watched his relief as I pressed the knife back into its slot and slid it into my pocket.

"I believe you."

Hamish watched me retreat in disbelief. "That's it?"

"I got what I came for." Disgust washed through me again as I looked him over. "Genetics are interesting, aren't they?"

"What?" He touched the wound on his neck, his pallor paling further as he saw the blood on his fingers.

"You are nothing like your parents. Either of them. Physically, aye, but personality? It was like you skipped out on all their genes in that respect. You shame the McCulloch name."

Hamish sneered, braver now I no longer had a knife to his throat. "You sound like my fucking father."

"He was a hundred times the man you'll ever be," I reminded him, my tone lethal.

"Aye? What do you think he'd think of this?" Hamish gestured between us. "Maybe you're more like me than you think."

I used to worry that I was. But now, I realized I'd just been playing a part as a boy to survive. That ability had come in useful tonight. I'd shrugged on that part as easily as I had shed it almost a decade ago.

Huffing in amusement, I lifted the hem of my long-sleeved tee, revealing the mic pack Walker had procured for me. "I am nothing like you."

Hamish vomited and I stepped back until I reached the door.

It was barely open when he whined, "Scum! You wee grass. You piece of shite!"

"Nah." I flicked him one last look. "The only shite here is you, Hamish. And you're about to get flushed."

———

Sleep was hard to come by, especially on the hard mattress of the cheap hotel I'd booked a night in. Finally giving up on sleep at three in the morning, I'd gotten in the car. I stopped at the halfway point for breakfast and chatted with Allegra on the phone, explaining what had happened. But I was desperate to see her in person. Because now neither of us knew who had followed her that day.

"I think he probably just recognized me," Allegra had said in my ear as I'd eaten in the roadside café. "Some creeper who didn't think about how intimidating it would be for me. It wouldn't be the first time. Hey, it could even have been paparazzi."

"Do you think?" Some of my tension eased, because that did make sense.

"Yes, I think so. I think we can relax. Especially now that we know for sure Hamish was behind what happened on the farm."

We did know for sure.

That's why I stopped in Inverness before returning home and left the recording of Hamish's confession with Jim Rowley. He'd listened to the recording with a hard look on his face.

"Is it enough?" I asked.

"It's enough to bring him back in for questioning. We'll make him think it's enough and he'll probably confess." Jim had shaken his head. "Hamish always was a thorn in Collum's side. That apple fell very, very far from the tree."

"Aye," I'd agreed gruffly.

"You're more like Collum than Hamish ever was."

Emotion had thickened my throat as Jim studied me.

"You made him very proud, Jared."

The grief of my grandfather's loss still stung, but that day it was fucking overwhelming. Afraid I'd break down in front of the police officer, I offered my thanks and got the hell out of there.

Now as I approached the farmhouse, I could feel that grief building toward the surface. The sight of Allegra hurrying out the front door to greet me caused that burning ache in my chest to rise until my throat constricted. I'd barely jumped out of the Defender when my wife threw her arms around me.

My wife.

I'd never in a million years have guessed how good those words would feel.

Almost as good as how Allegra felt against me.

My grip on her was tight. Too tight. She shook against me, and guilt cut through the grief, because I'd worried her by taking off like that. But as she held on tighter and whispered my name over and over in a soothing tone, I realized she wasn't shaking.

I was.

"He died in my arms," I blurted, the words wrenching out of nowhere.

Allegra jerked back, her gaze wide with anxiety. "Who did?"

"My grandfather."

Understanding softened her expression. "Jared." She reached for me, cupping my face in her palm. I closed my eyes, leaning into her touch. "Tell me."

The memory filled my mind. Still clear as day. Granddad in my arms. That big man, helpless in my fucking arms. My eyes flew open and I felt the wet leak down my face, but I couldn't stop it. I'd never told anyone the details. Just that he'd died in front of me. "I saw him go down. We were looking over a fence that needed reinforced after a gale had knocked the hell out of it. I turned and he was on his knees, clutching his arm. I got to him and he just collapsed onto me.

"I couldn't help him," I gasped. "I called for an ambulance, but I couldn't help him. And he was looking up at me for help. After all he'd done for me ... and I couldn't help him. He was so scared. That big man. That strong man. He was so fucking scared and I couldn't help him."

I was barely aware of falling to my knees or Allegra coming with me. She was like a life raft as I clung onto her and cried like I hadn't cried since the moment my grandfather died in my arms.

THIRTY

JARED

I t wasn't the sunlight pouring beneath the hem of the curtains or my alarm that woke me the next morning.

It was Allegra.

She came bearing breakfast in bed.

I glanced blearily down at the tray she'd put between us as she climbed in beside me. There were eggs and toast and a wee plate of pancakes.

"They're from a batter mix," she admitted sheepishly. "I'm not quite at the pancakes-from-scratch level yet."

Scrubbing a hand over my face, I'd asked, voice hoarse with sleep, "How long have I slept?"

"It's six a.m."

"Christ."

After my emotional breakdown yesterday, Allegra had guided me into the house and into a shower. She'd tenderly washed my hair and body, without intent, other than to comfort. Then we'd gotten into bed, and I'd clearly fallen right to sleep.

It wasn't like me to sleep so long.

It wasn't like me to break down like I had.

As if she could read my mind, Allegra soothed a hand over my shoulder. "It's been an intense few months, Jared. Longer even. You've been worried about the farm, we got freaking married, that turned into something neither of us expected, your asshole father terrorized the farm, and you had to go find him and become someone you don't particularly like to get him to admit what he'd done. That is a shit ton to happen to anyone in a short period. Especially when you've been carrying what happened with your grandfather for the last six years. It's not surprising that seeing your dad brought all the grief for your grandfather up again."

I took her hand between mine and then pressed a tender kiss to her fingers. "You're amazing, you know that?"

Allegra slid her other hand along my cheek, turning my head to her. Her fingers scratched gently over my beard as she whispered, "You're amazing. And you have to know, Jared, that no one could have saved your grandfather. Whatever guilt you're holding on to, you need to let it go. He'd want you to let it go."

Perhaps it was sleep, or perhaps it was finally letting it all out, but I didn't feel that agonizing lump of emotion rise in my chest now. It was a dull throb. Bearable. "I know."

She leaned over to brush her mouth over mine. "Now eat."

My stomach growled in answer. I grinned as Allegra giggled. "You're lucky I'm hungry or I'd be on you like a horny fucking teenager right now."

"Promises, promises." She teased before nudging the tray closer.

We ate as Allegra caught me up on Aria and North's situation. They had decided to try IVF and were cautiously optimistic. Allegra was supposed to stay at the estate until my return but had convinced Walker to drive her back to the farm in time for my arrival.

"Did Georgie keep you updated on things while you were away?" she asked as I finished off the pancakes.

Swallowing, I nodded and reached for my phone on the bedside table. "Did you put it on charge?" I asked, a smile in my voice.

"Yeah." She cocked her head at my expression. "What does that look mean?"

I shrugged, giving her a small smile. "I'm not used to being taken care of like you take care of me."

Allegra released a small, shaky breath. "Do you like it?"

In answer, I bent my head to kiss her, soft, affectionately. "I really like it."

She smiled almost shyly in response, and I resisted the urge to tackle her. Instead, I swiped open my phone. "Georgie said everything was in order yesterday ..." I trailed off at the sight of the missed call from Sorcha and the unread text message.

"What is it?"

Not wanting to fuck things up with Allegra, I answered honestly.

"Oh." She stared at my phone with an unreadable expression. "You should check it out."

I tapped on the text message.

> Was just calling to check in. In a new flat now.
> Doing well. Hope you and Allegra are well. x

I showed Allegra the text message.

Her expression softened. "She seems nice."

"She is." I placed the phone down on the bedside table.

"You're not going to text her back?"

"Would it bother you if I did?"

Allegra shrugged. "No."

Laughing, I gave her a look. "You are shit at lying. No wonder no one believed us about the marriage at first."

She smacked my shoulder. "I'm not lying!"

I gave her a disbelieving smirk.

Rolling her eyes, she huffed. "Okay. I am trying not to be bothered by the idea of Sorcha being your friend. She was in your life, she's your friend. It's just the 'was your lover' part that I am trying to get over. But I am trying. I don't want to be a jealous wife." She made a comical face and shuddered. "Nope, nope, nope. Don't wanna."

Shaking with amusement, I shrugged. "Jealousy is natural. We're territorial beings."

"Have you ever been jealous over a woman?" Allegra challenged.

I studied her, expression serious. "Aye. One."

She waited like she didn't know it was her.

"You, Allegra. I've been jealous over you."

Delight she couldn't quite hide glittered in her dark eyes. "Jealous of who?"

"Any man who's had you like this."

In answer, she reached for the tray and set it off the bed, the cutlery and plates clattering unsteadily as she did. Then she pulled back the covers and straddled me.

Excitement flushed through me in an instant as I gripped her slim hips. She wore a short, strappy silk nightie thing. She probably had one in every color, and I couldn't say I didn't love that part of her wardrobe.

She rested her hands on my shoulders as she kissed me, a barely there touch of her lips to mine. "No man has ever had me like this."

Triumph and possessiveness flooded my blood with scorching heat. My grip on her hips tightened as I pulled her down over my erection.

"No woman has ever had me like this," I promised.

"Not even Sorcha?"

The insecurity in that question killed me. "Not Sorcha. Not anyone. Just you."

"Why?" Allegra cupped my face in her hands. "She seems like a good person. Why couldn't you give her this?"

I wrapped my arms around her, pulling her tight to me as I sat up. I held her gaze, pouring every ounce of sincerity into that look as I said, "Because it's meant for you. All for you. *Only* for you."

Words I hadn't said to anyone but family bubbled on my tongue, threatening to jump loose, but before they could, my wife kissed me. She kissed me with such intensity that all thought but that of being inside her, sinking underneath her skin until I was all she could feel and smell and see, disappeared, consumed by insatiable hunger.

THIRTY-ONE
ALLEGRA

"**W**hoa, Aunt Ally, you look hot!"
Jared chuckled at my side, his palm pressing
deeper into my lower back as we entered Sloane
and Walker's living room.

Callie, who had been sitting on Lewis Adair's knee,
sprung off him to bounce across the room toward me. Her
pretty face was lit with excitement. "You all look like you're
going to the Oscars." She glanced back at Lewis who stood up
to greet us. "Don't they?"

Lewis, at sixteen, was already taller than his dad, Thane
Adair. When relaying every detail about her boyfriend that she
could, Callie had told me Lewis was six two and on his way to
being his Uncle Lachlan's height of six four. He was also broad
of shoulder and had completely skipped that gangly stage most
teens went through. With his messy "I'm in a band" chin-
length dark hair and piercing blue eyes, Lewis Adair was
exactly the kind of boy that teen me would have crushed on.

As he wrapped a casual arm around Callie, pulling her
into his side to press a tender kiss to her temple, I swooned
for her.

Callie didn't stand a chance.

"What?" Callie cocked her head at me.

I realized I was staring. "Nothing."

She narrowed her eyes but when they dropped to my feet, she gaped. "Are those Muaddis?"

"You know your designers." I was impressed. I was, in fact, wearing a pair of Amina Muaddi sandals. They were adorable rose-pink metallic mule heels with an open toe, a funky pedestal heel, and a little embellished bow accent on top. I'd thought them perfect for Ardnoch Estate's end-of-summer party. The D&G black-and-white polka-dot dress I'd paired them with made the shoes pop. It also made me look curvier than I was, designed to accentuate the hips and bust. Jared had almost ripped me out of the dress when he saw me descend the staircase earlier.

"God help us all," Walker muttered in response to the designer shoe conversation as he wandered into the room. He looked almost as delicious as my husband did in his tux.

Speaking of wanting to rip someone's clothes off ... I'd seen Jared in a kilt at Sarah and Theo's wedding. It was a wondrous sight to behold. But for the summer party, both he and Walker had opted for tuxedos.

Jared McCulloch might have been born to wear a kilt ... but in a tux, my husband was freaking hot. Like James Bond hot. But the Daniel Craig rough around the edges kind of hot, not the smooth, clean-cut hot of all the James Bonds who came before him.

"You look good," I told Walker.

He gave me a brief nod of thanks before his gaze zeroed in on Lewis.

Lewis straightened but didn't remove his hand from Callie's waist. "Sir."

"I'll be calling your father to check that you and Callie are at your house, and in separate rooms, by nine o'clock."

"Of course. We'll be there."

Callie grinned. "Aye, that gives us a whole hour to get me pregnant."

While I let my laughter rip, Jared did Walker the courtesy of trying to smother his. Lewis let out a nervous chuckle that quickly disintegrated into panic at the murderous expression on Walker's face. "She's kidding." He nudged Callie. "Tell the ex-Royal Marine that you're kidding, Callie."

"You're a black belt in tae kwon do. You can take 'im." She nudged her boyfriend back.

Lewis stared at her in horror.

Laughing, Callie turned to her stepdad, completely unrepentant. "Don't worry, Dad. Lewis is a perfect gentleman."

Walker did not look like he believed her one bit.

Lewis shot us a panicked look. "Tell my parents that I love them and I'm sorry it ended this way."

Jared and I snort-laughed as Sloane strolled into the room, her dress fluttering around her ankles. "Stop torturing Lewis and your dad, Callie."

Callie shot me a wicked smirk.

That girl.

God, I loved her.

"Mum, you look gorgeous." Callie leaned over to press a kiss to her mom's cheek.

"You do," I agreed. Sloane wore a maxi dress that was high at the neck but backless. The light and airy fabric was a mix of teals and greens with hints of yellow. Perfect for a summer party.

Sloane smiled at me. "As do you. We all scrub up pretty well, huh?"

"Aye, aye, we all look gorgeous," Walker retorted grimfaced, even as he slid his arm around Sloane's waist and pressed a kiss to her lips. "Let's get this over with."

She grinned up at him, her daughter's resemblance to her

uncanny. Then she turned to us. "That's what he said the first time we had sex."

"Mum!" Callie squealed in outrage.

Sloane pointed at her daughter. "You torture your dad, I'm going to torture you right back."

"I think what I actually said was something along the lines of 'Get upstairs and I'm in charge,'" Walker commented like they were talking about the weather.

His wife gaped at him in sincere wonder. "You remember?"

"Ahh!" Callie slapped her hands over her ears. "I didn't hear that! I didn't hear that!" She whimpered comically as she turned to her boyfriend. "I'm scarred for life."

Jared looked down at me, thoroughly amused. "Can we just stay here all night?"

"It is entertaining, isn't it?"

"For you, maybe." Callie grabbed Lewis's hand. "Some of us have just been traumatized." She huffed, cheeks flushed with embarrassment. "Have a nice night!"

"See you." Lewis waved to us before Callie dragged him out of the house.

Sloane and Walker high-fived.

———

Three weeks.

Jared and I had enjoyed three weeks of peace and quiet. Jim had Jared's father interviewed again and he admitted to killing the sheep and chickens. He was arrested and out on bail. The case against him probably wouldn't go to trial, and it was just a waiting game to see how much time he got. It might not be a lot. What really mattered to us was that he was out of our lives. Jared had scared the shit out of Hamish, and apparently, my wealth and family name intimidated the asshole too.

So I was optimistic we wouldn't hear from Hamish McCulloch again anytime soon.

We'd also bought six new chickens and a rooster to get us started on the henhouse, and despite my lingering sadness, I named them all. I'd named the chattiest hen, Cathy, and she, like Ginger, was the first to run to greet me in the mornings.

Our life was bliss.

That sounded overblown and insincere, but for me, it was bliss.

After years of trying to fit into a life that never quite fit, I found Scotland. Then miracle upon miracle, I found Jared. While he split his time between working the farm and managing the ongoing work on the glamping pods, I painted in this new style I'd discovered within myself. I'd also reached out to an estate agent to see if there were any buildings available to rent in Ardnoch for opening my gallery.

At night, I'd cook if Jared was running late, or if he got home early enough, we'd cook together. We'd listen to music on low and chat about our days as we made dinner and ate. Usually, we'd curl up on the couch after and watch some TV. Then, alone in our room, we always seemed to be in absolute sync. The sex was either adventurous and passionate or it was sweet and sexy and slow.

Either way, it was the best sex of my life. More intimate than anything I'd ever experienced.

And as much as I loved our sex life ... I think I might have loved waking up next to Jared even more.

Sometimes I couldn't believe how lucky I'd gotten. How we'd signed up to a fake marriage only for it to turn into a relationship I'd never dreamed I'd one day have. I'd always been envious of Aria and North, of Sloane and Walker. Of Sarah and Theo. Of all the Adairs and their partners. It was incredible to find so many truly happy couples in one place. No way could I be that lucky, right? They'd used it all up.

But they hadn't.

I'd found some luck just for me.

I was thinking all this as Jared and I strolled into Ardnoch Castle with Walker and Sloane. Usually Walker would work at an Ardnoch event, but Aria had wanted him and Sloane to attend as guests, and for once, they'd agreed. Sloane had confessed she hadn't gotten the chance to dress up in a while and fancied getting out of the house. As gruff as Walker was, he'd pretty much do anything to make his wife happy, so he'd agreed to escort her to the party, and Monroe and Brodan, who had decided not to attend, were babysitting Harry.

Feeling Jared stiffen a little beneath my hand, I looked up at him. His face was set in a neutral expression, but there was a hardness along his jaw that suggested more tension.

The great hall was packed with guests in summery cocktail and evening wear. A band was set up on a small stage in the corner, and the pop singer Koda belted out her latest number one single. It didn't surprise me that my sister had managed to snag a megastar to perform at an Ardnoch party. There was a very good reason Lachlan Adair had left the running of the estate to Aria. My sister was excellent at her job.

However, as staff in tailcoats and white gloves moved around the guests, offering glasses of champagne and hors d'oeuvres, I realized how this must all look to Jared.

Like it was another world.

One he didn't feel comfortable in.

The truth was neither did I, but at least I was used to it. "You okay?"

Jared glanced down at me. "Aye, I'm fine."

We weren't just putting in an appearance at the party for Aria's sake. Tonight was the first night Jared would meet my parents in real life. They'd arrived in Scotland yesterday. Together they'd stay at the beach house for a week before Dad flew off to work on whatever film was up next while Mamma stayed on the estate for at least a month. Her time here was spent mostly walking on the beach and luxuriating in the spa, but she loved it. She said it reenergized her for returning to the States. My mother usually spent fall in our family penthouse in Manhattan.

"Allegra?"

The male voice drew our heads to the left. I immediately felt awkward. Pasting on a friendly smile, I turned, not letting go of Jared, to greet the handsome man. "Taka."

If Jared was tense before, he went stiff as a board.

Taka Aikawa. My hookup buddy.

The gorgeous, suave Japanese American actor was killin' it with one hit miniseries after another, so I was surprised he had time to spend at Ardnoch this year. I really hadn't expected to see him or I would have prepared Jared. Taka's dark gaze darted up and down my body with familiarity. "You look great."

"You too. Taka, this is my husband, Jared. Jared, this is an old friend, Taka."

"Husband. Right! I heard about that." Taka reached out a hand to Jared. "Hey, man, congrats. You caught a good one."

I really thought Jared wasn't going to shake his hand, but to my relief he took it firmly (maybe a tad too firmly) in his and gave it a pump.

At his silent greeting, Taka's smile wavered as Jared released him. He stretched out his fingers absentmindedly as he focused on me again. "Do you remember the weekend we met in Santorini? The Greek fisherman Quinn was obsessed with?" He referred to a long weekend I'd spent with him and his best friend Quinn on the Greek island two years ago.

"Yes ..."

"He finally convinced him to move to New York. Took him two years, but perseverance."

I laughed. "Good for Quinn."

"I also saw Rishi Padman at our place in Marbella a few weeks ago." He said it offhand, but I winced a little at him calling the rental where we'd met to hook up last year and the year before as *ours*. "Her parents cut her off. I got her a part in my new show. She's actually good."

"That's great." I glanced at Jared. He wore a flat expression, like he'd disappeared somewhere else, but I knew he was listening to every word. "You know, we'll catch up later, Taka. We have to go say hi to my parents."

"Oh, sure, sure. We'll catch up later." He leaned as if to kiss me and then remembered himself. He gave me a sheepish shrug and then blanched at the scowl on Jared's face.

I attempted to hurry Jared away, but it was like trying to move a brick wall.

"Sorry." I didn't know why I was apologizing. I mean, we both had a past. But I knew how I'd felt at first about Sorcha, so I understood Jared's feelings. To an extent.

"So, that was your fuck buddy," Jared muttered. He tugged at his bow tie as if he wanted to rip it off. He most likely did.

"Jared ..."

"I'm not judging you. I'd be a hypocrite."

"Then what's wrong?"

He shrugged. "He's just ... not what I expected."

"What did you expect?"

Jared met my gaze. "Marbella? Santorini? You flew across the world to hook up with this guy?"

"Every time my visitor's visa here expired." There had been nowhere else I wanted to be but Scotland, so if I couldn't be here, I just went wherever I could.

"Right." Jared blew out a shaky breath. "He and I are very different men, and I don't have to spend a lot of time with him to know that."

"Yeah, you are," I agreed, slipping my fingers through his.

Pressing my breasts into his side, forcing his gaze down to mine, I continued, "That's why he was just a way to pass time and *you* are my husband."

He curled his fingers around mine and squeezed, giving me a nod.

It should have reassured me.

But there was something in his eyes that made a flicker of anxiety flare in my gut. I just hoped that nothing else happened to give me cause to panic.

THIRTY-TWO
JARED

I wasn't able to put my finger on exactly what I was feeling. But after a while, the sinking sensation was suddenly all too familiar. It was a mix of dread and devastating disappointment.

If I was honest with myself, it started with the tux.

I never minded putting on a kilt or socializing with my neighbors at Robert Burns Nights and Christmas ceilidhs at the village hall. I didn't even mind donning my suit for my wedding.

But the tux was ridiculous. I could have handled the jacket, waistcoat, and shirt, but the bow tie was driving me up the fucking wall. Honestly, I thought I hid my discomfort well, but apparently, Allegra could see right through me. About ten minutes after meeting her ex fucking fuck buddy, she'd pulled me into a corner and tugged the bow tie free, stuffing it into the purse thing she called a clutch. She'd unbuttoned the top two buttons on my shirt and I'd instantly felt like I could breathe again.

"Better?" she'd murmured, smoothing a possessive hand over my chest.

I'd bent my head to kiss her in answer.

The best thing about dressing up for these bloody fancy dos was that Allegra looked good enough to eat. She was curvy and sexy in her pinup-style dress. I already planned to fuck her while she wore nothing but those flimsy pink sandals that inexplicably turned me on.

Everything about this woman turned me on.

Which was why as the evening progressed, the biggest black cloud started to gather over my head.

Technically, I knew Allegra had come from this world of wealth, fame, and glamor. Of travel and staff and privilege. It was one of the reasons I'd kept my distance from her in the first place. She and I were from two different planets.

However, I'd allowed myself to forget that while it was just us, living our life on the farm. But seeing Allegra stop to chat with familiar faces I'd seen on the screen and around the village because she actually knew them was an unwelcome reminder that by staying married to me, she would never really be part of this world again. She talked with other guests, and travel came up almost all the time. She'd met them in France. Or the last they'd seen each other was at a bar in Italy. Or a festival in Denmark. A fashion show in Tokyo. I'd never realized how much of the world Allegra had seen, or how much traveling seemed to have been a part of her life.

But Aria had tried to warn me that night at Sloane's. She'd said then that travel was a part of who Allegra was. I'd shrugged it off because Allegra had disagreed.

Yet here we were, faced with the facts.

We'd never be able to just take off to Greece or Spain because we felt like it. The farm was a twenty-four-seven commitment, and I was attempting to grow another business from it. Perhaps I might be able to take Allegra on the odd holiday here and there once the business was up and running and we had folks to look after it in our absence, but traveling all the time was out of the question.

I'd never thought of myself as a broody bastard, but I was brooding. And it only got worse when Allegra led us over to Chiara and Wesley Howard.

I'd seen Chiara's face in magazines, seen her on perfume adverts. On Allegra's phone for that video chat. I knew she and Allegra were alike, but it wasn't until the two women embraced that I saw the resemblance. Chiara either had the skin of a thirty-year-old or she was having something injected into her face to smooth out wrinkles.

Wesley Howard wasn't the best-looking guy in the world, nor the worst, but he had a presence. His green eyes pierced right through me as we shook hands.

Chiara Howard refused to take my hand as Allegra introduced us. She sniffed haughtily, resting stiffly against her husband's side as my wife stepped into mine. As I had when I bumped into Aria, I felt under inspection.

This time, however, I knew I'd been found wanting upon judgment.

Wesley gave Allegra a small, reassuring smile. "Your sister tells us you're very content in marriage."

Surely, he should know that directly from the horse's mouth, but of course, his and Allegra's relationship was secretly strained. Not so secretly, if you asked me. The tension between them was so obvious, it was a wonder Aria hadn't guessed at the partial cause of her sister's issues as a teen.

"We're very happy." Allegra's words were tight. Probably because her mother was eyeing me like I was a criminal who had kidnapped their daughter into marriage.

Fuck that.

"*Tesoro*," Chiara said, smiling sweetly at her daughter, "why don't you go find Aria and North and bring them over so we can talk as a family? We'll keep Jared company."

My wife hesitated, and I wanted her to argue. Instead, she nodded, patted my arm, and murmured, "I'll be right back," and left me with her parents.

Chiara's smile slipped as soon as Allegra was out of earshot. "How much do you want?"

"Chiara," Wesley snapped at her.

My stomach knotted. "Excuse me?"

She waved off her husband's warning. As beautiful as she was, there was a coldness to her that could never make her as appealing as her youngest daughter. Not even her musical accent could soften the harshness of her words. "How much do we have to pay you to annul this outrageous, ridiculous marriage?"

Wesley shook his head. "Unbelievable. I apologize for my wife."

"Do not ever apologize for me," she hissed angrily at him. "Just because you pretend to be 'one with the people'... I know you are not happy that our daughter married a man who cannot give her the life she is used to." Chiara stepped toward me. "I am sorry if I am being rude, but I am doing this for you, too, Jared. Allegra is impulsive, wild, and follows her emotions and artistry wherever the wind blows her. You are just another adventure until she gets bored with playing a farmer's wife, of no doubt pouring all the money my husband and I earned to give her into a thankless business such as farming. She will end up penniless with no backup to protect her. She will miss traveling, parties, seeing the world. She'll be trapped on a farm. With you." She sighed unhappily. "Is that really what you want?"

I glanced at Wesley, but he only glowered at his wife. He did not refute anything she'd said.

After an hour of schmoozing with these people at a party I didn't want to be at, seeing Allegra socialize with them with ease and talk about all the places she'd been ... it allowed Chiara's worries to take root.

Allegra and I were happy now, but what happened if she did grow bored?

I was never going to change.

I was a farmer and I liked my simple life.

"I see you understand."

That dread and disappointment that had been gathering overhead suddenly burst in a thunderous storm of fury. Because I knew Chiara Howard made very valid points.

But she was wrong about one thing. I leaned toward her, my tone hard, "Don't ever try to buy me off. I don't want your fucking money." Every penny of it that Allegra had invested into my farm and business, I was going to pay back. Every damn penny. "Maybe if either of you weren't both so consumed with money and image, you wouldn't have done such a grand job of fucking up Allegra." I stepped toward them both as Wesley's eyes flew to meet mine.

"Allegra isn't impulsive. She was a devastated teen who needed her parents. And instead she found out her father was cheating on her mother and got *slapped*"—I spat the word at Chiara—"for her loyalty, and abandoned for knowing the truth." I shook my head, disgusted by them. "The world may think of you as the perfect parents. Successful. Powerful. Legends. But we both know *I* know differently. Imagine being the partial cause of your kid's pain ... and then gaslighting her, so even her sister thinks *she's* the fuck-up. You should be utterly ashamed. You're not successful. You failed at the thing that mattered most."

I gestured to myself. "You know, in Scotland we call a person a legend if they're a *good*. Not because they're globally successful or historically famous, but a good person who did a good thing for us. My grandfather was a Highland farmer and he was a fucking *legend*. Not a fancy Hollywood director or a world-famous supermodel. And yet as my parent, he was more successful than you two could ever hope to be."

Turning on my heel, I left them behind, satisfied by their stricken expressions.

Maybe it was revenge for Chiara devastating me with the truth, but I liked to think of it more as justice for my wife. And a long time coming.

———

"What did they say to you?" Allegra asked for the hundredth time as she followed me upstairs to our bedroom.

Feeling an intense pressure on my chest, I'd found Allegra just as she'd come across Aria and North, and told her I wasn't feeling great. We'd left the party without returning to her parents and she'd badgered me the whole way home.

"They upset you. I know they did." Hearing the tremor in her voice, I turned as we stepped inside the bedroom and I shrugged out of the jacket.

I didn't want to think.

Thinking made me feel like my chest was caving in.

"They didn't say anything," I lied. "I just couldn't wait any longer to get you alone. Take off the dress. Keep the shoes on."

Allegra's tan cheeks flushed. "Are you serious? You're telling me the truth?"

I nodded, because I couldn't voice another lie. The buttons on my shirt gave as I quickly plucked them open. "Dress off."

She couldn't suppress a shiver. I knew and loved that shiver. My wife was turned on. "Fine. But we will talk about this later, mister." Allegra yanked down the side zipper on her dress a little angrily.

As amusement curled in my gut, overwhelming *feeling* for this woman froze me to the spot for a second. I watched as she shimmied off the tight dress and gracefully stepped out of it. My heart thudded faster as my dick thickened, straining against the suit trousers. She wore a strapless see-through pink bra and matching knickers, the same shade as those fuck-me shoes.

"Jesus," I murmured, hungrily eating up the sight of her.

The thought of never having the privilege of seeing her like this for the rest of my life was so goddamn painful, it left me breathless.

"Get on the bed," I demanded, fighting off the grim thought.

She shot me a sassy look but walked over to the bed and climbed on. Her perfect heart-shaped arse swayed as she crawled up the mattress. I fought the urge to climb up and grab her arse between my hands, rip off her knickers, and just fuck her until we both saw stars.

Clenching my hands into fists, I waited instead for her to turn and lie down on her back. "Hold on to the headboard. Don't let go."

Her breath caught, but she did as I commanded, wrapping her elegant artist hands around two of the metal posts.

I drank her in, my chest heaving with want. Finally, I climbed onto the bed. Allegra's breasts trembled against the flimsy bra, her nipples visibly taut. Dark eyes filled with trust and lust, she waited patiently for me to continue.

Without a word, I curled my fingers around her knickers and slid them down her slender thighs. I peeled them over those ridiculous but sexy shoes that had no place on a farm, and stuffed them into my arse pocket for safekeeping.

"Dirty," Allegra murmured, teasing me. "What do you plan to do with those later?"

I grinned but it was tight with need. "Spread."

She let out a wee whimper of arousal as she widened her thighs. Wrapping my hands around both her slim ankles, I slowly slid them upward, caressing her until her inner thighs trembled and her pussy glistened.

Ready for me.

Always ready for me.

I kneeled between her thighs and gently pushed two fingers inside her. Wet, tight heat made me groan as she arched her back off the bed and moaned. Pumping in and out of her, I watched her strain against her hold on the bed, her heels piercing into the sheets as she met the thrusts of my fingers. I leaned over, pressing my thumb down on her clit as I squeezed her right breast with my free hand.

"Jared!" she gasped. "I'm gonna come."

"Aye, that's it, baby." I rubbed at her clit as my fingers continued driving in and out of her.

Allegra suddenly stiffened and then cried out as her inner muscles clenched around my fingers. Wet flooded them as she shuddered through her orgasm, but I didn't stop. Her clit swelled and I kept toying with her as I finger-fucked her.

"Jared, Jared ..." She reached for me, her cheeks flushed, her chest heaving, her thighs shaking.

"Hands on the bed."

Allegra cursed and returned to holding on to the frame. In less than a minute, I had her climaxing around me again.

"Please, please," she murmured as she shook through my continued torment. "I need you."

Yanking down my zipper, I shoved my trousers and boxers just low enough to free myself. "I want to fuck you bare." We'd both been checked, but we hadn't yet had sex without a condom.

Allegra nodded, her knuckles turning white from straining against the bed frame. "Yes, yes."

One hand gripping her thigh, my other wrapped around my painfully hard cock, I guided myself to her entrance. Heaven met me as I drove inside her. It felt *more*. I couldn't even explain why. Just knowing there was nothing between me and her felt so fucking good, I might die from it.

Grabbing Allegra's other thigh, I spread her, lifting her arse off the bed and I began fucking my wife. Wanting to see all of her, I briefly released one of her legs to reach over to unclip the front clasp on her bra. Shoving the pieces aside, I returned to driving into her. My eyes moved from the pleasure etched on her face to her lush lips parted on gasps, to her breasts trembling with my every thrust.

"God, I want you so much." I pressed her thigh toward her and leaned over, penetrating deeper, my hips slamming against hers. "I can't get enough."

Allegra's cries filled my ears as her inner muscles quickened around me.

"Take me," I growled, fucking her harder, faster. "Take me. Feel me."

My wife screamed with relief as she shattered around me, her climax tight-fisted tugs of her inner muscles that squeezed my dick with such intense pleasure, bright lights sparked behind my eyes.

I fell over her, my head bowed between her neck and shoulder as I filled her with my cum. Some primal, ancient thing left over from a previous time was a powerful possessiveness within me as I sat up to pull out of her and saw the evidence of my release between her thighs.

"Fuck, that's hot," I murmured gruffly.

"Every bit of that was hot," Allegra replied breathlessly. "My God, just when I thought sex with you couldn't get any better."

Staring at her, disheveled, thoroughly screwed, I could feel that edge of panic creeping in again. I didn't want to lose this. Not yet. Instead, I touched her gently, brushing her clit with my thumb.

Her eyes flew wide. "Jared?"

My cock was already twitching, ready for round two. "Again."

"Already?"

"Might as well while you're covered in my cum," I joked as I crawled over her to find her mouth with mine. I kissed her like I intended to take her again and by the time I released her, she was panting and squirming. So I kissed my way down her breasts, taking my time, sucking and biting at her delicious nipples until she was aching and throbbing for me all over again.

If it would hold my dread of tomorrow at bay, I planned to keep my wife coming all bloody night.

THIRTY-THREE
ALLEGRA

B y the end of the next day, the man who had ravished me last night was gone. And yes, I'm using the word *ravished* in the twenty-first century because what my husband did to me the night before was nothing short of a ravishing. I ached deliciously between my thighs. Our bedroom still reeked of sex that morning, and I'd had to open the windows to air it out.

The sheets were covered in us, so I'd ripped those off the bed and put them in the laundry.

I'd done all this humming under my breath, feeling like the luckiest woman in the world, even if I was exhausted from lack of sleep. Little did I know I'd feel so differently just a few short hours later ...

Waking up to Jared would have made it a perfect night, but he was already out of bed and showered by the time I'd woken because he'd switched off the alarm to let me sleep.

There was a missed call from Aria on my phone, which I intended to return as soon as I found my husband. I'd wanted to see him before I headed over to my studio. Mamma and Dad had invited us to dinner tonight, and I wanted to make sure he remembered.

Jared had already fed the chickens, so I said hello and chatted with them a little before jumping into my Wrangler. It took me twenty minutes to find Jared. He was on the field he called Caledonia Sky. Surprise shot through me as I parked behind his Defender, which was parked behind a large truck.

The foundations were being laid for the pods and were almost complete.

As I pushed through the turnstile onto the field, a figure in the distance pointed at me and then the man he was with turned to look. Jared. I waved. He hurried down the field toward me.

The closer he grew, the clearer his expression got, and he did not look happy.

Uh-oh.

"What's wrong?" I asked.

"What are you doing here?" he bit out.

I flinched at his snappy question. "Why?"

He scrubbed a hand over his beard. "There's just a lot of work going on."

"Okay." I didn't understand. "Well, I'm at a safe distance if that's what you mean?"

Jared shook his head impatiently. "What is it you need?"

Shock clamped my lips shut for a moment. After last night, I would have thought Jared would be in a great mood and, actually, kind of all over me. Instead, he could barely look me in the eye, his gaze darting around.

"We have dinner with my parents tonight. I just wanted to remind you."

"I can't go," he answered before I barely finished the sentence.

Irritation zinged through me. "What happened between you three last night?"

"Nothing." He took my elbow and tried to turn me away. "We'll talk later."

I ripped my elbow out of his hold. "Why are you being so weird?"

Jared glowered. "I'm not being weird. We just can't talk here. We'll talk back at the house."

For some reason, panic started to rise. It made me furious. "No, we'll talk now."

"I'll meet you back at the house around four. We'll talk then."

"Talk about what?"

"Allegra," he blew out my name in exasperation.

"Don't Allegra me." Searching his face I saw only impatience. With me. "What happened between the early hours of this morning and now?"

"Nothing," Jared gritted out, anger rising. "I just can't talk right now with men behind me building foundations."

"Well, I'm not waiting an entire day, anxious about your weird fucking mood, until you have *time* to tell me why you're being an asshole to me this morning."

My husband squeezed his eyes closed and sighed. Heavily. When he opened them, remorse glittered in them. But still there was hardness there. A distance. A detachment. "I'm sorry."

"What's going on, Jared?"

"We really can't talk here."

"You're scaring me, so you're going to get in your car and drive back to the house. Now. So we can talk."

He gestured behind him. "I really do have to be here for this. I promise. But I will meet you—"

"When they break for lunch." I gestured up the hill to the men. "You will meet me at the house then."

Jared gave a reluctant nod and I just as reluctantly got back in my Wrangler.

———

Jared never showed at lunchtime.

He didn't answer my calls or texts.

———

There was a part of me deep down that knew. But the hopeful part of me was stronger and kept taking charge. That part kept reminding me that Jared wouldn't have spent all night worshipping my damn body if he intended to end things.

No. My parents had clearly said something to upset him last night and he was just processing. We'd figure it out.

I was pissed at him for not showing when he said he would and for making me spend the whole day at the farmhouse, my stomach churning with anxiety.

When he didn't show at six o' clock, I had to call my parents and apologize for the no-show. My mother was full of annoying questions that I evaded like a champ until I could politely get off the phone.

By the time I heard Jared's Defender come up the drive at seven thirty, I was ready to kill him.

My indignation grew like a ball of fire catching as I heard him come in through the mudroom and take off his boots. The bastard then had the audacity to walk through the kitchen into the living room where I was and say without looking at me, "I'm going to shower."

"Where the fuck have you been?" I snapped, shooting to my feet.

Jared paused, expression annoyingly calm. "Don't start, Allegra."

I guffawed. "You stood me up. Twice! You ignored my calls and texts, and you think that's okay?"

He turned to me, anger quickly blasting that stupid blank look off his face and honestly, it made me feel better. Anything was better than indifference. "I told you when you showed up that I was busy."

"Too busy for me?" I asked, hurt.

"Allegra ... a farm doesn't wait for you. Sometimes it has to come first. You knew that when you married me."

I ignored the pain of realizing that even after our relationship had morphed into something real, I still wasn't his main priority. He'd said I was, but actions spoke louder than words. "So it's okay for you to ignore me? What if there was an emergency? Did you forget all the shit that happened this summer?"

His eyes widened slightly and I realized he had. He'd forgotten. Jared swallowed hard and looked away. "It was my dad. We dealt with that. You're safe here."

What could have Jared so preoccupied that he'd forget that only a few weeks ago he was worried about leaving me alone? "Whatever you're avoiding, please stop. The Jared I know wouldn't treat me like this."

Pain tightened his features. "Treat you like what?"

"Like I don't matter. Like I'm a nuisance you married for money."

At the hurt in my voice, Jared blanched. "I didn't mean to make you feel that way."

"Then please talk to me."

Bracing his hands on the back of the couch, Jared bowed his head. It was the posture of defeat.

Fear cut through me.

No.

No, please.

He looked up, eyes blazing. "I think we should take a break."

The breath knocked out of me, I shook my head, unable to voice the question.

Jared answered, anyway. "I think we've been living in this weird bubble together and not thinking about the reality of a real relationship long term. So maybe we should just take some time to see if this life, here, together, is what we both want."

"What?" The air whooshed out of me and I stumbled back, falling down into the armchair. "I don't under... why?"

"We don't fit."

Rage-filled confusion made me growl, "Bullshit!"

The muscle in Jared's jaw ticked. "I don't mean ... I mean, it's possible that *long term* we don't fit. Look, it became very clear last night that you and I are living in a fucking fantasy right now. We are totally different people and sooner or later, it might dawn on you that you're actually miserable being married to a Highland farmer." He opened his arms wide. "This is my life. I'm not going to jet-set around the world whenever you feel like it. I don't want to."

I was even more confused and pissed off at that stupid explanation. "Who said I did? Did my parents say something to you?"

"Only the truth. And it wasn't just them. Allegra, you fit back into that world with ease because you were born into it. You are used to privilege, and there's nothing wrong with that. It's not about money because I know you have your own. It's about the lifestyle, which I can't give you, and I don't want to be the person who takes you from it. Frankly, I don't want to spend the rest of my life trying to live up to it. Feeling like I'm not good enough. Like the life we have isn't good enough. So I think we both need to take some time to think about if this is what we want."

Flying to my feet again, I rounded the couch to approach him. "Have I ever made you feel like you weren't enough?"

"No." Jared crossed his arms over his chest, his body language screaming back off. "But in time ... it might happen. I might make you feel trapped here. And if that happens, we'll just end up resenting each other."

I couldn't believe he was saying all this.

Only the day before yesterday, we'd been so happy.

Or had we?

Maybe ... it was Jared who needed time to think. He did keep saying "we," even though he only mentioned me. But maybe Jared, the perpetual bachelor, was growing bored. Maybe the party last night was just an excuse ...

"Oh God." I stepped away from him, suddenly needing distance. "Did you ... did you know you felt like this when we came back here last night?" My expression was baleful.

He flinched. "Allegra—"

"Did you know?" I yelled.

Jared looked away. "I didn't want to ... I wasn't sure. That's why I needed today to think it through. And I'm not saying it's over. I'm just saying we should take a minute. A break."

Resentment and bitterness soured my tongue. "But you made sure you thoroughly fucked me in case you decided it was over."

His eyes flashed. "It wasn't like that."

"Like hell it wasn't." My stomach was sick as I retreated. "You ...you knew and you ... you used me."

"Allegra ..." Jared stepped toward me, something like panic in his expression, but I couldn't register it. All I could see was someone I didn't recognize. How could I have thought I loved this man when I didn't recognize him at all?

I felt so cold, I physically trembled as I turned and blindly walked into the hall, looking for my car keys.

"Allegra, it wasn't like that." Jared followed me as I grabbed the keys off the sideboard. He took hold of my arm but the thought of him touching me made me lose it.

"Don't touch me!" I shrieked. The tears that had been locked inside blurred my vision as I wrenched open the door. "You are just like every man I have ever known. Except worse. Because I was stupid enough to think you loved me when all this time I was just a convenient piece of ass. What's worse is you standing there pretending this is all about what I want when clearly, you're the one who wants the break." Shoving out of the door, I stumbled toward the car.

"Allegra!" Jared followed me. "That's not what happened! And you can't drive in this state!"

Yanking open the driver's door, I wiped the tears he didn't deserve off my face and hissed, "Why not? You might get lucky and I crash. Then I'd be dead and you'd inherit all my money. It's all you really wanted from me, anyway, right?"

"Fuck you!" His face suddenly mottled with rage and pain. "Don't ever fucking say that!"

Jared rarely raised his voice, so for a moment, it shocked me into silence. Enough to give me a moment to breathe. To speak without fury inciting my words. "Tell me the truth, then."

Blinking with surprise at my sudden change in tone, Jared straightened. "Truth?"

"My truth is what you've always known. Which makes your suggestion for taking a break completely stupid. I married you because I was desperate to stay here. In this place that I love. This place that nowhere compares to." Fresh tears fell down my face. "So your excuse that we come from different worlds and that I'll maybe get bored, it makes no sense. Right?"

"Fuck." He rubbed a hand over his beard. "I ... I ... I don't know."

A tiny spark of hope lit in my chest. "My parents said something. Didn't they?"

He nodded. "It wasn't just them, though. It was seeing you in that world ..." His expression tightened. "You didn't just live here, Allegra. You were constantly traveling. Finding inspiration in new places. Scotland was just your home base. And what I said still counts. My life is here. The farm is here. I can't up and leave whenever you fancy. You come from a world of parties and travel and art. I come from a world where I had to hold a knife to my dad's fucking throat to get him to admit he was killing animals on my farm."

"Jared—"

"There is a possibility that long term isn't in the cards for us." He shrugged unhappily. "We are so different. Eventually, one of us could remember that. Isn't it better to take some time to really think about it, instead of possibly hurting each other later on?"

That hope didn't just extinguish. It felt like my entire chest caved in on it. "I'm hurt now. Because the idea of taking a break from us kills me. The fact that you would even suggest it tells me we *are* in totally different places." I brushed impatiently at my tears and climbed into my car.

Jared caught the door before I could shut it. His eyes blazed. "What you said ... about last night ... I wasn't using you. I'd never use you."

"Were you thinking of 'taking a break' last night?"

He swallowed hard but nodded.

That knowledge tainted everything about our night. "Then you should never have touched me. What I gave you"—my words shook—"was not yours anymore. And it was wrong that only you knew that."

Pain shone in his eyes. "I don't *want* to let go. I wasn't using you. I'm just trying to be smart here. For us both."

"Do you love me?" I asked bluntly.

Jared glanced away, something indiscernible working behind his eyes. "I'm not saying anything that will manipulate you. Because I need you to really think about this. For both of us," he repeated.

I expected to feel more incredible, unbearable pain at his refusal to admit how he felt. Instead, I just felt numb. I reached out to shut the door but the gold band on my finger caught my attention. Calmly, I removed it and tossed it at his feet. "You want a break? Here it is. I'd rather get kicked out of the country than stay married to you. You'll be hearing from my lawyer." I grabbed the door out of his hand and slammed it shut.

As I spun the car around and wiped at more tears that silently leaked out of my eyes with no sign of stopping, I made the mistake of looking in my rearview.

Jared lowered to his haunches to pick up the ring. He didn't get up. And as I drove out of sight, I'd never felt more confused by anything in my life.

Usually relationships ended with clearly defined reasons.

But I didn't even think Jared knew why he'd suggested we break things off between us. Okay, so he'd suggested a break. But he might as well have dumped me. Suggesting a break was the same fucking thing!

It didn't matter either way.

The end result was the same.

Because if he loved me as much as I loved him, he could never do this to me.

THIRTY-FOUR

JARED

I couldn't stop shaking.

As I strode back into the farmhouse, Allegra's wedding band burning in my palm, it felt like every muscle in my body was tremoring.

The house echoed as I walked aimlessly through it.

All day I'd felt certain about what I needed to do. That I needed to suggest some time apart so we could know for sure that marriage was what we wanted. Fuck, what Allegra wanted. I already knew *I* wanted it.

But I should have known with her history that she'd see it as an excuse for me to end things. And I didn't do a good enough job of explaining because I was afraid she'd just insist she wanted me without thinking it through.

Like I knew her mind better than she did. Fuck. I'd made the decision without actually talking it through with her. No wonder she'd just ended it entirely.

I felt sick.

Because while an hour ago I was so certain suggesting a break was the right thing to do, now I felt like I just self-sabotaged.

Gripping my head, I stumbled into a kitchen chair.

Why couldn't I tell her I loved her?

Because you're a chickenshit. You're terrified.

People you loved either disappointed you or they left you.

"Fuck." I was so fucked in the head.

Allegra's tear-streaked face appeared behind my eyes every time I closed them. I'd hurt her. I'd devastated her. Why hadn't I thought about how this would seem to her? To a woman who had been abandoned and used ... I'd done this all wrong.

Dread swamped me.

My phone blared from the kitchen table, making me jump.

Reluctantly, I pulled it toward me and saw it was Sarah calling. The woman had a sixth sense.

I answered, putting the phone on speaker. "Sarah."

There was a beat of silence, then, "What's wrong?"

"I fucked up." I exhaled shakily. "Sarah, I really fucked up. I'm fucked up, I don't know what I'm doing."

"Talk to me," she said in that calm, gentle voice. "Tell me what's going on."

THIRTY-FIVE

ALLEGRA

By the time I arrived at my parents' beach house, I'd had time to think. Clearly, my parents said something to Jared last night that targeted all his insecurities. Enough so that it had obliterated months of evidence that proved I was all in and not going anywhere.

And then I'd just proven them right by throwing my ring at him and driving off all snotty and butt hurt, my mother's Italian fire flaring to the fore. Instead of thinking rationally and trying to understand why Jared had suggested the break in the first place, I'd done him a disservice by immediately assuming he wanted the break for him, not for me.

A man didn't look at you the way he looked at me if he was faking it.

My husband was in love with me.

I'd never been more certain of anything until today.

Jared was in love with me ... and maybe last night he finally realized that. And it scared the shit out of him and then my parents said something and it just all got twisted up in his head, and he thought he had to offer me a way out?

Jared might come across as this solid, stalwart Scot who

didn't need anything but his farm ... but Jared's heart had been broken before most of us even knew a heart could be broken.

I must scare the absolute shit out of him.

Staring up at my parents' vacation home, the pull to turn around and drive back to my husband was intense. But first I needed all the information. I needed to know what my parents had said to make him think I might not want him for much longer.

The door to the house opened just as I got out of the Wrangler. Aria stood there, arms crossed, as I hurried up the porch steps. "I thought you weren't coming." Her eyes narrowed. "You've been crying."

"I need to talk to Mamma and Dad."

"Okay. What's going on?" Aria pushed open the door, stepping aside to let me in.

Instead of answering, I stormed past her, through the spacious hall and into the open-plan kitchen-living room that faced toward the sea.

My parents were seated at the dining table with North.

Great. I didn't exactly want an audience for this, but I wasn't stopping for pleasantries.

"What did you say to Jared last night?" I demanded.

Dad's expression tightened as he shot a look at Mamma. So she was the culprit, huh? Not surprising. I focused on her. Mamma took a sip of wine with an insouciant European shrug, and I wanted to empty the contents of her glass all over her. "What did you say?" I yelled.

"Allegra." Aria came to stand beside me. "Calm down."

"If Mamma came between you and North, would you calm down?"

My sister shot Mamma a horrified look. "Mamma, you didn't?"

In answer, my mother released her wineglass and stood up, but only to brace her palms on the table. She pinned me with her dark stare. "You are a spoiled child playing house, and that man needed to know who and what you are before you ruined him."

It was even worse than I'd thought.

"Mamma!" Aria snapped. "That's completely unfair!"

Tears burned in my eyes.

"Is it? She put us through hell as a teenager, and she lives a life as a vagabond with no clear focus, from what I can see. Your sister had opportunities others would die for. She could have been a model or an actress. Instead, she marries a man so she can stay in a country just because she is afraid to be far from her big sister."

"Chiara," my dad bit out. "Stop."

"We all know Allegra has been impulsive in the past." Aria's words made me flinch, my gaze zeroing in on my father who appeared suddenly winded by my look of betrayal. "But she is a successful artist now and not flitting around like a vagabond. And I do believe she and Jared are making a real go of their marriage. Even if they aren't, she's an adult, and it's none of our goddamn business. Mamma, you had no right to interfere."

Mamma and Aria argued back and forth, and I barely heard the words because I was watching my father. He wore a strange look as he stared back.

Then abruptly, Dad stood. "I need to tell you something." His voice was loud enough to cut through the arguing. Mamma and Aria instantly shut up.

"Wes?" Mamma frowned.

He shook his head at her. And I suddenly recognized the emotion on his face.

Shame.

"Jared was right last night. We've been gaslighting our own child."

Jared said that? Last night?

She shook her head, rage flashing in her eyes. "Do not do this. Not here. Not now."

Oh my God. Was Dad about to admit the truth?

"Do you want Aria to go on thinking Allegra is some wild child who just put everyone through hell for nothing? Do you want to keep hurting our daughter just so you can keep burying your head in the sand?"

"Do not put this on me!" Mamma suddenly screamed. "This is not my lie!"

"What is going on?" Aria asked, her voice quiet. Afraid.

North heard her anxiety and crossed the room to pull her into his side.

While a slither of envy left a bitter taste on my tongue, I mostly felt gratitude that Aria had a husband who wanted to shelter her from every storm.

Dad moved away from the table, taking a step toward Mamma, but she retreated. She wrapped her arms around herself and looked away, sniffling. And while I resented her for choosing to live in a world of pretend, I was also heartbroken for her. She'd chosen to stay with a man who cheated because she loved him too much to leave.

"I love you, Chiara." Dad turned from Mamma to us, his voice pleading. "I love your mother. Deeply."

"Dad?" Aria gaped at him, as if she knew what was coming.

"But I ... I had a childhood sweetheart who came back into my life about eleven years ago." Tears brightened his eyes. "I ... I couldn't choose."

"What are you saying?" Aria gripped tight to North's hand as she glared at Dad. "Are you saying you've been cheating on Mamma for over a decade? That you have another woman?"

Dad gave a barely there nod as a sob escaped from Mamma.

"And I walked in on them having sex when I was fifteen," I admitted dully.

My sister's head whipped to me, her cheeks paling. "What?"

I tried, but I just couldn't hide the bitterness in my voice. "I walked in on them and when I told Mamma, thinking she needed to know, she slapped me across the face and told me to keep my mouth shut."

Mamma sobbed harder and rushed from the room.

I wiped away a tear that escaped.

It was out there now. I might as well tell the rest. "It messed me up and I started partying. Then partying led me to an older boy. I was just a kid who didn't know how to deal with this secret, and Ashton made me feel seen. It turned out he had some really bad stuff going on at home. He told me about something awful that had happened to him, and when it freaked me out, I cut him out of my life. And he killed himself."

"Fuck." Dad dropped back into his chair and covered his face with his hands.

"That's why I went off the rails a little. Not excusing it. Just explaining that it wasn't because I'm a selfish, spoiled brat."

"Oh, Ally." Aria's face crumpled. "Why didn't you tell me? You should have told me all of this. You told Jared, didn't you? This is what he meant." She looked helplessly at North who rubbed her back in comfort. All the while my brother-in-law stared at me with sympathy and concern.

"I was just trying to protect you." I shrugged, wiping at the tears I couldn't stop. I was a human watering can.

"I'm supposed to protect you!" Aria rushed me, and I stumbled at the sudden movement. But then her arms were around me, and she squeezed tight as she cried.

I buried my head on her shoulder and cried, too, for this shitty, shitty day.

———

My sister was detail oriented. I knew she was deeply hurt by my dad's secret, and that I'd kept it from her too. But for me, I knew she felt mostly remorse that I'd been perceived one way by my family when I wasn't that person at all. It would never excuse my behavior as a kid. However, I could forgive myself for my choices, if not the reasons that pushed me down the path toward them.

For my dad, I saw her anger. Her betrayal. Yet, as always, her need to understand.

North had excused himself once he knew Aria was going to be okay, and we'd sat down at the dining table with Dad.

"What's her name?"

Dad looked exhausted. And maybe a tiny bit relieved. "Maggie."

Aria nodded expressionlessly. "And you love her?"

"Yes."

"But you love Mamma too?"

"Yes." His voice cracked.

"Is she married?"

"No. She lost her husband. That's how we got back in touch. I heard and reached out to give her my sympathies."

"And you started an affair? A long-running affair that Mamma pretends not to know about but clearly does."

Dad sighed heavily. "Your mamma isn't faithful either."

Wow.

Aria raised an eyebrow. "Did she start cheating before or after she found out you were?"

He gave us a sad smile. "After."

"Why don't you just leave each other?" my sister hissed angrily.

"Because we love each other."

"Well, I'm sorry, but if North told me he was in love with another woman, that would destroy me and I would leave him." Aria shoved away from the table. "You don't ... you can't ... it would be different if this was a life you and Mamma had chosen together. To be in an open marriage. But you forced this on her because you don't have the balls to choose!" Her eyes flew to me. "And then you put a fifteen-year-old kid in the middle of your bullshit and you left her to deal with it because you were both too fucking cowardly to face your own fucking mess!"

I'd never heard my sister say the f-word that many times. Life with a Scottish husband was rubbing off on her. It was easier for me to laugh internally at this thought than process all the anger she was feeling. I knew that anger. I'd had ten years to process mine, though.

"I know." Dad's voice was rough with emotion as his eyes met mine. "Ally, I am so sorry. I didn't ... Jared made me face up to some harsh truths last night. I've been a shitty father. This"—he gestured around the beach house—"what the fuck does any of this matter when my kid feels abandoned by her parents?"

"I can't believe you all hid this from me for so long." Aria looked between us, her hurt shining bright. "I just ... I need some time." She strode away without another word, her heels clicking on the hardwood floor.

At the sound of the front door opening and closing, I looked at Dad. "Is Jared the reason you decided to tell the truth?"

"It's been building for a long time. The lie. Jared just opened my eyes to things I've been denying about myself, and about you." He blanched. "I didn't know your mother hit you when you went to her with the truth. Jared bluntly relayed that information last night."

Wow. Jared pulled no punches with my parents. Because he cared about me.

"Mamma just gave me the slap she probably wanted to give you."

"Don't." Dad shook his head. "Don't shrug it off like it's not a big deal. It's a big deal that you walked in on me with another woman when you were just a kid and a big deal that your mother hit you because of it. Has she hit you since or before?"

"No," I promised him vehemently.

He visibly deflated with relief. "I can't imagine Chiara lifting her hands to anyone."

"Her actions are her own, and I'm not putting the slap on you. But she was in pain. A lot of pain when she hit me, and she wasn't herself." Lots of therapy had helped me get to a forgiving, compassionate place about that traumatizing moment between my mother and me.

"My selfishness has caused all my family pain. And Maggie. Jared was right." Dad scrubbed a hand over his face. "The whole world can think I'm a legend, but I know the truth. The people who matter most know that the truth is unbearably disappointing."

It was strange seeing my dad so down on himself. The man exuded confidence and self-assurance. This version of him was unrecognizable. But then hadn't I always known that I didn't really know my parents? They didn't really know me.

"What is it about Maggie?" I asked out of morbid curiosity. "What makes it so hard to choose?"

Dad's expression fell. "It's difficult to explain. I just ... with your mother, it's always been exciting and passionate and adventurous. She challenges and excites me. But with Maggie, it's more emotional. We connect on a soul level that I can't explain. It's quiet and simple and I feel at peace when I'm with her."

Just like that, I experienced crystal clear clarity. What Dad had with two women, I was lucky to find with Jared.

I couldn't let my husband go. Not without a fight.

"It's not that I don't have that with your mother. Your mother and I are a team, and we can talk about mostly anything. Maybe ..." Dad shrugged, despondent. "Maybe with Maggie I could hold on to the guy I was before I became *Wesley Howard*."

Truthfully, I'd never considered the pressures my dad must be under to live up to himself. Probably because he never gave the impression that he felt any pressure. But, of course, he did. He was only human. The thing about being a human, though, was that it wasn't perfect. It was messy. It was ugly and painful. And you couldn't always have what you wanted. Choices had to be made.

"I think you have to choose, Dad. Ari's right. It would be different if you and Mamma were on the same page. That you both wanted an open marriage. But she loves you and just you. Burying your heads in the sand and pretending there are no affairs ... it was always going to end badly."

"I know." He gave me a tremulous sigh. "I'm really sorry, kid."

"I know you're not a bad guy, Dad," I whispered tearfully. "You're just human. And we're complicated."

"Do ... do you think we'll ever be able to start over? You and me?"

I nodded, my tears slipping freely now. "I think so." Getting up from the table, I crossed the room and Dad stood to enfold me in his arms. It was the first time in ten years I'd hugged him for real and not for show in front of cameras or Aria. "Thank you for telling the truth."

He squeezed me hard. "You don't need to thank me for that."

After what felt like a long time, Dad reluctantly released me. He captured my face between his palms and said, "I'm sorry if what your mother said to Jared messed things up. But the man who confronted me last night didn't give a shit about who I was. All he cared about was you. Jared isn't that angry at me over someone he doesn't care about."

Determination fired my blood. "I'm going to fight for what I want. You should go figure out what it is you want."

"I'm proud of you, kid."

Those words hurt, but in a good way this time. Neither of my parents had said those words to me in forever. I needed to hear them. Not just because I wanted that from my dad, but because it made me realize something that fixed a little broken piece of me. "I'm proud of me too."

Thirty-Six
Allegra

I tried to check on Mamma before I left the house, but she wouldn't open her bedroom door. Life was too short to hang on to resentment, and I didn't want to feel that way toward her anymore. Yes, I was pissed that she'd come between me and Jared. But we'd let her. Jared and I were as much to blame.

Right now I only had room in my heart for compassion for Mamma. I whispered through the door that I loved her and I was there for her if she needed me. As I walked out of the beach house and got into my Wrangler, I hoped Mamma finally decided to do what was best for her. I'd told Dad he needed to choose, but he wasn't the only one. Mamma had to choose him back, and I'd support her, no matter her decision.

It was unfair of me to judge her for staying in the relationship. Love was messy. People were all over social media screaming their relationship opinions at each other as if emotions were capable of sticking within the strict lines of moral black-and-white zones. In reality, all the gray space in the middle was a pool of emotions sinking and swimming, sinking and swimming, never really quite making it out of

there. When would people realize that humans are too complicated to be forced to feel anything but the way we felt?

We didn't have to like those feelings, but we should try to
understand. As I stared up at my parents' beach house, that's
what I tried to do. I tried to see past my own hurt and understand Mamma and Dad. And hope for the best for them.

As I drove away, I hit Jared's number on my phone. My
heart pounded. Because I'd already seen past my hurt with my
husband, and I think I understood.

We were just two scared people who didn't mean to fall in
love.

But we had.

Relief flooded me as he answered in three rings. "Allegra?"
He exhaled my name, sounding unbearably relieved.

"I'm coming back."

Another heavy sigh of relief. "Aye. Good. I'm ... I fucked
up. *I* don't want this to end," he confessed hoarsely. "I just ... I
was trying to protect myself from getting hurt down the line
and I fucked up. I'm sorry."

Tenderness was a sharp ache in my chest. "So what? We're
all a little fucked-up, Jared."

"Aye?" he asked hopefully.

"We'll talk when I get home."

He hesitated. "Home?"

I smiled at the security guards as they let me out of the
estate. "I don't want a break. I think my butt-hurt reaction to
the suggestion probably clued you into that. So yeah, I'm
coming home."

"Good," my husband said, so gruff it made me smile
harder. "I'll see you when you get home."

"Be there in five."

Honestly, I was exhausted and would probably sleep for
hours. But not until Jared and I had hashed it all out. This
couldn't happen again. Sure, we'd argue. However, not like

that. Not the ignoring me and then assuming the worst about each other. That was way too freaking painful to deal with on the regular.

With summer on its way out, the sun set earlier. My headlights lit up the dark country roads as I drove toward the farm. In the morning, once Jared and I knew where we stood, I'd visit Ari and make sure she and I were good. I knew all the revelations tonight had hurt her, but I needed her to know I'd only ever wanted to protect her.

At least she had North.

Like hopefully I would have Jared.

"What a day," I muttered to myself. I couldn't remember the last time I'd been on such a roller coaster of emotions.

Antsy to get home, I picked up the pace a little, but had to slow almost immediately when a car came around a bend on the opposite side. They had their headlights on full beam, blinding me. I hit the brakes, flashing my lights to let them know. Suddenly, I felt the Wrangler slam sideways. The world whooshed past me in a blur of night and headlights and crunching metal. Everything was so loud and confusing, I didn't know what was happening.

When everything finally stopped moving, all I could hear was the rushing of blood in my ears.

Something warm and wet trickled down my temple, and I lifted a trembling hand to it. My fingers blurred in front of me and as much as I strained, I couldn't get my eyes to focus. Yet I knew it was blood on my fingertips.

How did I hit my head?

Something like a car door slamming filtered through my brain.

Someone was here.

Everything was going to be okay.

But then I heard the sound of wheels against tarmac and an engine fading off in the distance. That's when I realized the whooshing in my ears wasn't blood. Turning my head, I looked out the window and my breath caught as panic suffused my body.

In the moonlight, I saw the waves crashing against the hillside. Yards from me.

"Oh God." I whimpered as my vision cleared. The headlights of the car beamed across the grass-covered rocks.

My Wrangler had rolled down the hill and was on its side. By some miracle it hadn't toppled into the sea—

Metal squeaked, and the SUV shifted. Sucking in a scream, I held still as it settled again. Fear shuddered through me and every inch, every muscle, every nerve in my body trembled with it. I could barely catch a full breath, and I knew if I didn't calm down, I would hyperventilate.

Taking in slow, deep breaths, I tried to stay calm, but the wind caught the Wrangler and it swayed again. My fingernails dug into the seat in terror. The thought of crashing into the water, of the car filling with sea, made me sob.

My cell phone suddenly blasted and I let out a startled cry. By some miracle, the engine was still running. The phone was still connected to the car. With a violently shaking arm, I reached out and tapped the vehicle home screen, trying not to move too much, despite my tremors.

"Allegra?" Jared's voice cut through the car.

I whimpered. "Jared."

"Allegra?" He was alert now. "What's wrong?"

"I-I-I ..." I sucked in a sob. "M-my c-c-car r-r-rolled. I'm ... I'm ... it's on its side. On the hillside. I-I ... Jared ... I think it's going t-to roll into the ... the water." I sobbed.

"Allegra. Allegra." My husband's rough voice cut through my cries. "I need you to stay as calm as possible. I'm coming for you. Okay? Nothing is going to happen. How far from the house are you?"

I tried to think. Think past the headlights. The car. "There was someone ... I was about two minutes away. There was someone, though."

"Okay. I'm coming. Do not move. Stay perfectly still. I will be right there. Nothing is going to happen to you."

Just then wind caught the SUV again and it shuddered, metal creaking. "Jared!"

"It's okay, baby, it's okay." He sounded breathless now and I thought I heard his car engine in the background.

"I love you," I blurted out.

"No, no. You are not saying that to me now," he bit out harshly. "Not now. You'll tell me later. Okay? You'll tell me later."

"Jared."

"No. I'm coming for you."

"Okay." I sucked back a whimper, trying to focus past the terror.

"I have to call the emergency services. But I will phone you right back."

Rationally, I knew Jared needed to do that. Even if the thought of letting go of his voice right now made me crumple inside. "Okay."

"I'll call you right back."

When his voice disappeared, there was nothing but the wind whistling through the car, the gentle creak of it as it balanced precariously against what I could only assume was a rock jutting out of the hill. And the sea below might have been crashing gently against the hillside, but it would also gently kill me if the car fell in. I'd drown. A slow, tormenting way to go.

Panic tightened my chest and I forced my head away from the water. My door was obviously caught against the rock and if I tried to climb out of the window, the Wrangler would tip and take me with it. Turning to look out the opposite window, I saw the shadowy ascent of the hillside toward the road. My headlights cast a little glow at this angle, and I could see that it was a steep climb up. But maybe if I was fast enough, I could climb over the middle console and passenger seat and get out of the passenger side door before the Wrangler toppled?

It was too risky, wasn't it?

But if I didn't do something, if I just sat there, maybe that was riskier than anything.

THIRTY-SEVEN
JARED

I knew I would never forget the sound of terror in my wife's voice. The threat of powerlessness nearly took me out at the knees. Was I really back here again? With the life of someone I loved hanging in the balance and me powerless to stop it?

But you're not powerless, I snarled at myself as I gazed down at the Wrangler.

I'd just hung up on the emergency services after giving them the location.

My heart raced. I couldn't wait.

Even in the dim moonlight, I could see how precarious Allegra's position was. I fumbled with my phone.

Ironside picked up on the third ring. "Walker," he clipped.

As quickly and concisely as I could, I explained the situation. "I've got rope and I'm going to tie it to the Defender and climb down there myself. I need you to get here as soon as possible ... just in case something happens to me."

"You should wait for help."

"Would you? If it were Sloane?" I was already unraveling

the rope that was attached to a hook with a locking mechanism I could snap onto a tow loop beneath the tailgate.

"Point taken. Send me your location." He hung up.

I quickly shot him a text. Once the rope was locked to the SUV, I tied it around my waist. I grabbed the headlamp from my glove compartment. It lit up my path as I made my first steps down the steep hillside. Even my sturdy work boots skidded on rocks as I tried to ground myself. If Allegra knew I was there because of the light, I couldn't tell. I couldn't hear anything but the sea below and the pounding of my fucking heart.

I couldn't think about her fear or how close I was to losing her.

I forced myself to focus on getting to my wife because it was the only thing stopping me from losing my fucking mind.

Halfway down the hillside, sweat lashed my back and my palms burned from the rope, but I could see her. The light from my headlamp washed over the Wrangler with my movements, and I caught glimpses of Allegra's terrified expression.

It only made me more focused.

After what felt like forever, I slowed upon approach of the SUV. I didn't want my movements to cause it to slide and I could see that it was wavering with every slight push of the wind.

I ducked, looking under, and surmised it was caught on a large boulder. The good thing was it wasn't quite at a ninety-degree angle, and the wheels were only lifting slightly off the ground with the movement.

"Jared!"

Straightening, I closed in on the passenger side, not touching the car, but peering in so she could see me.

"Jared." Her face crumpled, but she sucked in a breath. "Tell me what to do. What should I do?"

I was afraid if we waited too much longer for help, the car

would go over. But if I opened the passenger door to pull her out, that might *cause* it to go over. "We can wait," I called to her, "or we can risk it and try to pull you out now."

"E-either w-way, it's a r-risk, right?" she stuttered.

Fear that she was going into shock made me realize I hadn't even asked if she was injured. I did so now.

"M-my head hurts and it's bleeding. But I think I'm okay. Maybe some bumps and bruises."

What if she was injured but just couldn't feel it because of the adrenaline? I couldn't think about that too hard. "Do you want to wait?"

"N-No. I can't ... I can't stay like this another m-minute."

Untying the rope from my waist, I took a deep breath and grasped the handle of the passenger side. It was awkward to pull it at this angle, especially when I was trying to do it slowly. Gritting my teeth, I hauled it gradually open against gravity, my breath catching as the Wrangler shuddered precariously. Once the door was open, a gust of wind caught it and the hood of the SUV started to tip south.

Allegra's scream filled my ears as I grabbed for purchase on the roof until the gust passed. My muscles strained as I gritted my teeth and held on for dear life.

Metal creaked as the Jeep lowered again and my heart stopped throbbing sickeningly in my throat.

"Here." I threw the rope to Allegra. "Unclip yourself and tie that around you. I'm holding on to the car. You've got this."

Her face was pale beneath my torchlight and I saw the blood streaked down her temple as she very slowly and shakily undid her seat belt. Her breath caught as the car creaked with her movements.

"You've got this, baby," I prompted her. "You're so brave. You've got this."

My words seemed to steady her and she gave me a tight nod before she quickly wrapped the rope around her waist.

"Tie that knot as tight as you can."

"Okay. Done."

"Now ..." I braced my legs, one hand holding open the door, the other gripping the underside of the roof. "You're going to climb over the center console toward me."

Her eyes held mine, the fear in them breaking my fucking heart. But Allegra nodded determinedly and pushed herself slowly up. She reached for the passenger seat to pull herself along and the SUV started to tilt.

What happened next was so fast. Her eyes widened and she just threw her whole body toward the passenger side. I let go of the car and gripped onto the rope tied around her waist as the nose of the vehicle started to slide south again.

Allegra scrambled over the passenger side, her shins clipping the doorway as I hauled her out just in time. My back hit the hillside, pain shooting down my legs as I made contact with rock.

Nothing mattered but Allegra, who lay sobbing against my chest, holding on to me for dear life. My headlamp lit up the Jeep as it crashed into the sea below us.

I tightened my arms around my wife as she shuddered against me.

"I love you," Allegra sobbed, her whole body shaking violently.

I squeezed her closer, trying to soothe her shock.

"Jared, Allegra!" a deep voice cut through the dark and cold.

"Who's that?"

I tilted my head back, looking north toward the road. "We're here!"

"Can we pull you up?"

"Is that Walker?" Allegra sniffled.

"Aye." I rubbed a hand down her back. "Do you think you can stand? I have the rope tied to my Defender. Walker can pull you up."

"Not without you." Her hands fumbled between us and I realized what she was doing.

"Stop. Keep that tied on."

"Not without you," she insisted stubbornly.

With a sigh, I nodded, even though she probably couldn't see it. Then I quickly untied the rope and retied it around us both. "Ready?"

"Yes."

Slowly, very slowly, I helped her to her feet. "We're coming up!"

"We've got you!" Walker yelled back.

Standing over the Wrangler while Allegra was inside it was the longest moment of my life, but trying to get her trembling body safely up that hillside was a close second. I was drenched in sweat by the time Walker and North pulled us to safety. Head-lights from several cars lit the country road, which was now blocked off by an ambulance, a fire engine, and a police car.

Walker and North weren't alone. Sloane and Aria were there. Wesley and Chiara.

I gave Walker and North a nod of thanks but immediately turned my attention to Allegra.

"You're safe."

She looked up at me, eyes round, pupils dilated. "Thank you. I ..." She bent over suddenly, pain flashing across her pale face.

"Allegra?"

My wife's expression slackened as her eyes rolled and her knees gave out.

"Allegra!" I lunged, catching her before she hit the ground.

The next few moments were a panicked, confused blur as

paramedics shoved me out of the way. I just kept asking them what was happening, renewed terror flooding me as they lifted my wife's prone body onto a stretcher.

"What's wrong with her?" Aria cried, tears streaming down her face.

"Where are you taking her?" Wesley demanded.

I didn't hear the answers. I just followed.

"Family only." One of the paramedics tried to bar me from the ambulance.

"She's my wife," I answered as Aria snapped, "He's her husband! I'm her sister!"

"Just one," the paramedic said.

"Go, Jared." Aria pushed me toward the vehicle. "We'll follow."

I stumbled up into the ambulance, sitting across from Allegra as the paramedics worked over her.

"What's happening?" I repeated, feeling as if I was watching that Jeep fall again with my wife barely out of it.

"It might just be a concussion, but we'll need to check for internal injuries."

Internal injuries.

"Can I take her hand?"

The other paramedic gave me a sympathetic look. "Of course."

I reached for Allegra. Her left hand was missing her wedding ring. I rubbed my thumb over the empty spot on her slender, small finger. She'd told me she loved me and I hadn't said it back because I didn't want to say it like that. I didn't want to believe that it would be the last thing we ever said to each other.

But I should have told her.

If she didn't wake up ...

I took her hand in both of mine and bent over to press a

kiss to her knuckles. Wet splashed her skin and I realized it was my tears.

I didn't care.

Looking at her, I squeezed her hand and whispered, "You promised to come home. Please ..." I bowed my head. *Please come home.*

THIRTY-EIGHT
ALLEGRA

The beeping woke me up.

My eyes felt heavy and gritty as the irritating sound pulled me out of unconsciousness. The brightness of the room hurt and I blinked rapidly, trying to focus.

The first people I saw were Aria and North, talking quietly as North held my sister and stroked her cheek. They were whispering too low to hear what they were saying.

I almost opened my mouth to ask them what the hell they were doing in our bedroom, when movement to the left brought my gaze swinging around. Dad? Mamma?

They were huddled on a tiny sofa, my mother asleep while my dad scrubbed tiredly at his face.

Where the hell—

The crash over the hillside came rushing back.

"Allegra?"

I followed the voice, and found Jared reaching for me. He was pale with dark circles under his eyes, but I'd never seen him look so openly happy. Before I could speak, he was kissing me. Short, quick, hard kisses, first on my dry lips and then my cheeks and temple.

"Thank fuck," he breathed, leaning his forehead against mine. "Thank fuck."

"What happened?" I asked, my voice croaky and dry. The last thing I remembered was Walker and North helping Jared and me off that hillside.

I looked past my husband as the rest of my family crowded around my bed, touching my legs, my arms. Mamma pushed past everyone to scatter tear-soaked kisses across my cheek.

"Internal bleeding." North seemed to be the only one composed enough to explain. Even so, I saw he was as pale-faced and exhausted as Aria. "You needed surgery."

"I'll get the doctor." Aria squeezed my leg with a teary smile and then hurried from the room.

"I'm okay, though." I looked at Jared. My beautiful husband. "You're okay, right?"

"He's got a few bruises, but he's all right," North assured me.

Jared nodded. "I'm okay now. You scared the hell out of me."

"All of us!" Mamma threw up her hands. "You scared all of us. These roads here. So dangerous! No more driving them at night. No, no!"

"Oh my God," I gasped, her words reminding me. "I wasn't ... it wasn't my fault." I reached for Jared, grabbing his hand, the movement making me wince. Okay. Body hurting. No more sudden movements.

"What do you mean?" Jared sounded impressively menacing.

"Someone ran me off the road. Their headlights were too bright and I braked, but I think they swerved into me. I remember hearing them stop up on the road once I went over. Then they drove off."

Fury tightened my husband's expression and his grip on me almost hurt.

"You're sure?" North asked.

I nodded. "Yeah. It was probably an accident, but they didn't try to help. They just took off."

"Coward." My dad cursed under his breath. "If I find out who it was, they're dead."

"It doesn't matter," I said wearily. "All that matters is that I made it. Because you saved me." I gave my husband an exhausted smile as something prodded at my memory. "When can we go home?"

A suspicious sheen covered Jared's beautiful eyes and he had to clear his throat, the words husky as he replied, "As soon as you're ready."

THIRTY-NINE

ALLEGRA

I t was an understatement to say that I did not like playing the patient. After staying in the hospital for a week after surgery, I was ready to get home and back to life. However, neither my husband nor my family would let me. Since I determinedly did not want to remain in bed, Jared insisted I plant my butt on the couch. Two days I'd been home and I was ready to lose it.

The only thing that passed the time was the visitors. Sloane, Walker, and Callie had shown up almost every day at the hospital and again when I returned home. I think Sloane and Callie might have experienced flashbacks to their own trauma years ago, and they just needed to reassure themselves that I was okay. That *they* were okay.

They weren't alone in visiting. The entire Adair family showed up. Not all at once (thankfully, because who had room for a clan their size?), but over the course of the next few days, they popped by with gifts and to check in. And, of course, Sarah and Theo had driven from Gairloch to stay for a while. Since they were both members at Ardnoch, they were living on the estate but spending most of their time here at the farmhouse. I knew Sarah was worried about how Jared was handling it all.

Jared was a champ.

He'd saved me.

Something I'd never forget.

But I also hadn't forgotten that I'd twice told him I loved him and so far he hadn't said it back.

Perhaps it was because I'd been on my way home to hash out our relationship. Maybe he wanted to wait to talk about it all when I was better. From the way he hovered over me, I couldn't believe that he didn't return my feelings. I remembered his emotional response when I woke up in that hospital bed.

So what was holding him back?

It was a thought for another time because today Mamma and Aria were visiting. Jared had gone to check on the farm, which he'd left in Georgie's capable hands, and Sarah and Theo had made an excuse to leave so I could be alone with my mother and sister.

"Where's Dad?" I asked as Mamma sat next to me on the sofa and took my hand in hers. She'd been clingy lately. And very affectionate.

Aria and Mamma exchanged a look before Mamma sighed. "I need some time, so I moved into Aria and North's while your father is still here. He is going to visit you later today, alone."

I covered Mamma's hand. "I get it. I'm glad you're taking the time you need."

"You know ..." She held my gaze and I saw shame in it. "I was so angry at you before the accident. It was easier to be angry at you than at your papà. Then when North told us your car had gone over the hillside ..." Mamma sucked in a shaky breath, tears sliding down her beautiful face. "I was so scared."

"I'm here, Mamma."

"I know." She cupped my cheek. "But you could have died and it would have been with a mother who put her needs before her child." Mamma turned to look at Aria, heartbreak on her face. "I am so sorry that it has taken almost losing both my daughters to be a good mother."

"Mamma." Aria got up from the armchair and crossed the room to sit down on our mother's other side.

"Maybe it is punishment for not being better."

"What's punishment?"

"What has happened to you both."

Aria sighed, rubbing Mamma's back. "Everyone has ups and downs, Mamma. Money doesn't protect people from pain. But look at where we ended up. Both Allegra and I have found what we love and need here. Now it's time for you to figure out what you need."

Mamma nodded, grabbing our hands. "I have two very kind daughters who inspire me to be kinder."

Tears burned in my eyes at her words, and she turned to look at me. Her face crumpled. "I am so sorry I ever raised a hand to you. Or that I was so blinded by my own hurt that I could not see how much this mess between me and your father hurt you."

"I forgive you," I promised.

She squeezed my hand tighter. "I never wanted to be a woman who ever touched her child in anger. My mother often would slap me when we were alone and pinch me in hidden places when others were around, and I vowed never to cause that hurt to my daughters. It is my greatest shame that I did."

I was shocked at this revelation about Nonna. We didn't see our Italian grandparents a lot, but the few times we had, Nonna was a jolly, affectionate lady. Though in hindsight, she did criticize Mamma a lot. I just thought it was their dynamic. Now, as Aria and I shared a look, I had to wonder if it was more than just distance and time that kept our visits with Nonna and Nonno few and far between. Once again, I was met with the sad realization that we didn't really know our parents all that well.

I wanted that to change. I didn't want to hold on to resentment or see only the bad in our relationship. Yes, my parents had always been a little distant, a little too busy, but before that day I walked in on my father with another woman, I'd been a kid who knew she was loved by her parents. There were plenty of happy memories together as a family. I wanted to hold on to those memories. I wanted to forgive. For me and Aria more than anyone.

"You never did hurt me before then or since." I leaned into Mamma. "People make mistakes. What matters is learning from them. Right? I forgive you."

Mamma nodded, eyes bright with heartbreak. "You are an angel, tesoro. I cannot believe I almost lost you."

"I'm right here."

"So what now?" Aria patted Mamma's leg.

She knew what my sister was asking. Letting out a shuddering breath, she replied, "I do not know. For now, I just want to be with my children."

Resting my head on Mamma's shoulder, I whispered, "We can do that."

———

Though they protested, I insisted on walking Mamma and Aria out to their car a few hours later.

"Jeez, the doctor says I've got to exercise, okay! You all are coddling me way too much."

Mamma harrumphed but hugged me and got into the SUV.

Aria searched my face and body for signs of fatigue and

pain. But I was feeling much better and ready to get back to life.

I gripped my sister's biceps and gave her a wee shake. "I'm good. Are *we* good?"

"I can't believe you were hiding this from me the whole time—I know you were just protecting me. I get it. But I hate that you went through this. And when you're better, if you're up to it, I want to hear more about the boy who died."

"Ashton." His name was hoarse on my lips and always accompanied by a guilt that no amount of therapy could assuage.

"Ashton," Aria repeated sadly. "When you feel up to it, will you tell me about him?"

"Yeah. Of course."

"Okay." She pulled me into her arms and kissed the side of my head. "I love you, Ally."

I smiled. "I love you too."

———

A few days later, I'd finally convinced everyone to let me get back to life as I knew it. Dad had postponed the start of his new movie, and it was costing the studio thousands of dollars a day, so I'd insisted he leave. Before he did, however, he told me that he'd ended it with Maggie. Although he loved her (and I could see that he was cut up about his choice), she belonged to a past life. Dad had been clinging to nostalgia. In the end, he'd decided he didn't want to lose Mamma.

Unfortunately, Mamma wasn't sure she didn't want to lose him. I think Dad was ready to fight for her, though. It was up to my mother if he was too late. I'd stand by her, no matter what. And I'd stand by Dad too. They'd both made mistakes. I'd like to think that there were people who would love me through the worst things I'd ever do, and I wanted to be a person who loved the people I loved, even when they did something that wasn't very lovable.

As always, Jared and I were up early. We'd eaten breakfast and Jared had gone into the living room to switch on the news for the weather for the week. My gold wedding band glinted on my finger as I washed our dishes. While I was recovering, there had been no sex, but Jared held me every night before we went to sleep and I always woke up in his arms.

There was no discussion about the fight we'd had the night of the accident. I think we both felt that words were kind of unnecessary. Well ... most words.

I was still waiting on three particular words from my husband.

As I put away the dishes, the news presenter caught my attention as she announced breaking news from the US. I wandered into the sitting room, my heart jumping at the announcement on the news ticker below her on the screen.

BREAKING NEWS: California Attorney General Andrew Gray Arrested in FBI Raid.

"Oh my God, turn it up."

Jared flicked me a look but did as I asked.

"Last night, California Attorney General Andrew Gray was arrested on suspicion of international child sex trafficking. Sources reveal Gray has been under investigation for more than two years while the FBI gathered evidence against him. His home in the Hollywood Hills and his offices in Los Angeles were raided simultaneously last night. Gray has served as attorney general for three years and was public in his aspirations to advance to the Senate. The US president has yet to make a statement ... In other news ..."

"Fuck."

Jared frowned. "Am I missing something?"

Heart racing, I grimaced sadly. "Andrew Gray was Ashton's stepdad."

Understanding dawned and Jared crossed the room to pull me into his arms. "I'm sorry."

I clung to Jared. "It's okay. This is good. This means Ashton's finally getting the justice he deserves." I trembled thinking about all the kids Gray had most likely hurt over the years. "I hope he rots in jail for the rest of his life."

Jared rested his cheek on my head and just held me. We stood there for a while, and I knew he would stand there holding me for as long as I needed. But I also knew he had work to do.

Reluctantly, I released him and gave him a reassuring smile.

My husband cupped my face in his hands. "Why don't you spend the day with me?"

"I don't want to get in the way."

"I want you there." He brushed a thumb over my cheek. "I'll just worry about you otherwise. That"—he gestured to the TV—"is a lot to take in."

Actually, the thought of some physical work keeping me distracted and busy sounded like exactly what I needed. "Okay. But no coddling me."

"I'll coddle you just enough," he promised. Then he smacked my ass playfully, making the hem of my short dress flutter. "Let's feed the chickens first."

"Hey, no touching my ass if you don't intend to follow through," I grumbled as he led us out of the house to the chickens.

Jared shot me a wicked smirk and I decided right there and then that tonight I was going to torment the hell out of him until he broke and made love to me.

Realizing he'd already distracted me from the news about Ashton's stepdad, my annoyed glare turned to a tender smile. It was a beautiful day, the breeze a little cooler now that summer was on its way out, and on this farm with this man (who was good down to his soul), I was as far from the darkness of my past as I could get. The news about Andrew's arrest didn't change that.

This here was my future, and it was everything pure and real and true.

Jared glanced back at me from the henhouse and paused at whatever he saw on my face. He swallowed hard and took a shuddering breath. Then he strode to me. When he reached me, he took my face in his hands. Leaning his forehead against mine, his breath puffed against my lips.

Then he whispered raggedly, "I love you so fucking much. You have no idea. I'm sorry it took me so long to say, but those words just didn't seem big enough for what I feel for you."

And just like that, somehow, miraculously, my life got even better.

I leaned back to meet his gaze. "I love you too."

His lips crashed over mine, his kiss hungry and desperate and filled with all that love he'd just confessed. I stumbled back as he moved us toward the house without breaking the kiss. My back met the brick wall near the mudroom door as Jared's hands coasted frantically over my body, like he needed to touch me everywhere and all at once.

I wanted him to.

I never wanted him to stop.

The need to connect was so intense that we didn't make it past the wall or out of our clothes. On that cool morning with late-summer sun cast out by the shade of the building, my husband and I had hot, frantic sex against our farmhouse.

It was perfect.

I whispered as much as Jared bowed his head in the crook of my neck and shuddered through the aftermath of his orgasm.

He groaned and lifted his head. "I love you," he repeated.

Stroking the nape of his neck, my right leg still wrapped around his hip, I replied, "I love you more."

Jared grinned, that wicked sexy grin that made my heart beat fast. "Not possible."

"You saved me, Jared." Tears of happiness burned my eyes. "In more ways than one."

Suddenly, his smile dropped, his expression fierce. "You saved me right back. No man has ever been prouder to call a woman his wife. And I have felt that way long before you were ever in my bed."

Joy and thrill suffused me. "Really?"

"Aye, really."

"You should know I knew I had feelings for you when we got married," I confessed.

"You should know I also had feelings for you when we got married, but I was a clueless stubborn bastard too stupid to realize it."

I laughed and Jared grinned, pulling me into his embrace. He buried his face in my neck and groaned, squeezing me tight.

"I love you," I repeated because I just couldn't get enough of saying it now that I was allowed to.

Jared lifted his head to whisper in my ear, "*Tha gaol agom ort.*"

I pulled away in surprise. "What was that?"

"Gaelic." His stunning gaze roamed between my eyes and my mouth. "Granddad taught me."

"What does it mean?"

"I love you. But a better translation is 'my love is upon you.'"

Emotion thickened my throat. "That's so beautiful."

"Not as beautiful as you," he whispered hoarsely.

"Say it again."

"Tha gaol agom ort."

"Ha g-eul ..."

"Agom ort."

"Ah-kum orsht?"

Jared nodded as I repeated it correctly.

I bit my lip against a cheesy grin. "Your granddad was kind of a secret romantic."

My husband brushed his thumb over my lower lip. "He loved my grandmother until the day he died. He never touched another woman after her death. Couldn't even contemplate loving another woman." Jared swallowed hard, and I realized it was against emotion. "I never truly understood that ... until you."

Oh wow.

"You better call Georgie." I curled my fingers into his shirt, almost ripping the buttons. "Because you're going to be late this morning. Very, very late."

Jared grinned wolfishly and then picked me up like I weighed nothing to haul me into the house.

We didn't even make it past the kitchen before he was on me. Inside me.

And I made him speak those Gaelic words over and over again as we made love on the kitchen floor.

EPILOGUE

JARED

September was a busy month for the farm. Georgie and I had to cultivate the fields, so they were ready for barley. On top of that, the glamping pods were constructed, but we had a ton of interior design decisions to make. Allegra had already created a social media presence and website for the business, and we had followers watching the progress of the build. She was doing all this on top of her plans to open an art gallery in the village. There was an empty building up for sale just off Castle Street. She'd already ordered signage and was creating social media for that too. She was calling the gallery Skies Over Caledonia in ode to the farm and our field, Caledonia Sky.

Between all of that and the farm, we grabbed what time we could together in the late evenings. Hopefully things would quieten down a bit for us, but I realized that we'd also just have to bloody make time.

And I had grand plans to make time for my wife.

The last thing, however, I ever wanted to hear again was Allegra upset on the phone. But that morning as I drove my tractor and combine through the fields, my phone rang.

"There are police officers here," Allegra had told me as I stopped the growl of the tractor to answer her call. Usually my phone was switched off when I was at work, but ever since the accident, I'd attached my phone to a holder on the cab so I could see it if it rang.

At her frantic tone, I'd left the tractor in the middle of the field and ran to the Defender.

By the time I pulled up to the farmhouse, I was out of breath and my gut knotted.

The car parked next to my wife's new Wrangler was unmarked.

I marched into the farmhouse, coming to an abrupt stop at the sight of the two individuals who rose from the couch. Allegra stood up from the armchair and immediately crossed the room to press her body into my side. Seeking comfort.

"These officers are from the NCA. The National Crime Agency." Allegra looked up at me, dark eyes filled with concern. "I wanted to wait for you before they told me why they're here."

Nodding grimly, I reached out to shake the officers' hands. "Jared McCulloch, Allegra's husband."

"I'm Banes. This is my partner, Dobbs." The female officer gestured to the tall male at her side.

"How can we help you?"

Banes turned her attention to Allegra. "Are you aware of the arrest of an American attorney general, Andrew Gray? He's a US politician."

My wife stiffened against me, and I slid my arm around her waist.

"I heard."

"Do you know Andrew Gray?"

"What is this about?"

Dobbs spoke now. "We're working in conjunction with

the FBI and Europol in the child sex trafficking case against Gray."

"Okay ..."

"We believe you were in a car accident a few weeks ago, Mrs. McCulloch."

What the fuck? "What does that have to do with anything?"

"In the raid against Gray, we found correspondence and transactions to a contact that was involved in the trafficking ring. Gray paid this man to kill you." Banes pulled out her phone and held up the screen. "Do you recognize this man?"

Allegra turned chalk white. "That's the guy who followed me in Inverness."

Shit. My blood turned cold.

"You were followed?" The officer frowned.

"We thought it was just paparazzi at the time."

"No. This is Simon Sutcliffe. A known London-based criminal and contact of Gray's."

At my wife's shudder, I tightened my embrace. The thought of someone targeting her like this ... Why?

I must have said the word out loud because Banes continued, "We discovered a laptop in the floorboards of one of Gray's bedrooms. It belonged to Gray's deceased stepson Ashton. On that laptop were saved emails between you and Ashton, where Ashton confided that Gray was sexually abusing him."

Fuck, fuck, fuck. Fury and concern and more fury coursed through me as I pressed a hard kiss to Allegra's temple.

"Yes, Ashton confided that to me when we were kids." Tears brightened Allegra's eyes. "Are you saying that Andrew Gray discovered this recently and tried to kill me?"

"The circumstances of Gray discovering this is supposition without a confession from Gray. We do know his home was under renovation this year, and it could be he discovered the laptop during the reno. But we have solid evidence that he put a hit out on you, yes. There's correspondence and transactions between him and Sutcliffe regarding the contract. His last correspondence was regarding the car accident you were in. Sutcliffe was behind it, had realized you were still alive, and was asking Gray for more money to try again. It seemed they were being cautious about making sure your death looked like an accident."

Was this even real bloody life? My heart thudded in fear. "Is my wife safe now?"

Banes nodded. "Allegra is safe. However, we would like you to make an official statement in the case we're gathering against Gray."

"Not if it's dangerous." No fucking way would I let her be put in danger again.

Allegra placed a placating hand on my chest, and my worry heightened. Christ, she was going to do this. My stomach dropped. I didn't know if I could handle her swinging her arse out there like that. This trafficking ring was serious shit with serious people who had probably murdered many innocents to keep it going and hidden.

My wife looked at the officers. "Do you think Gray is going away for a long time, no matter what?"

Banes and Dobbs shared a look. "We have a good case against him."

"Then you don't need me."

Banes frowned. "This man tried to have you killed."

"Yes, he did. But he's going to prison for a long time for causing a hell of a lot more terror and pain than what I felt when I went over that hillside. I'm not being a coward or taking the easy way out." Allegra slipped her fingers through mine. "But my family has been through so much in the last ten years, and if I put my name on that witness list, we'll be splashed across the world news again. I'm sure you realize who my father is and that the media has a special interest in my family. If my name gets out there, then Ashton's story will be splashed across the news on a much bigger scale than it might otherwise. He didn't ask for that. Without his permission to do that, I don't think I can."

Allegra swiped at the tears gliding down her cheeks and I kissed her temple again, letting her know I supported her, no matter what. "He will get justice without my statement. Gray will never see the outside of a cell without my statement. And my family can finally try to move on from all the shit that's been thrown at them for the last few years. It's not the noble choice, but it's the one I'm willing to make for them."

The male officer scowled in irritation, but Banes sighed heavily in acceptance. She plucked a card from her jacket pocket and held it out to Allegra. "If you change your mind, call me."

"Thank you. And thank you for letting us know about the crash."

"Will he be arrested?" I growled, thinking of the scum who pushed my wife off a fucking cliff and had planned to come for her again.

Banes responded emotionlessly, "Sutcliffe was killed in a police raid four days ago."

Good.

"And you're sure she's safe?"

"We're positive no one else was involved."

I nodded, satisfied as much as I could be by that news.

As soon as the officers got in their car and drove off, I pulled Allegra into my arms and held her so tight, I was probably crushing her.

"This fucking world," I muttered against her ear.

She ran a soothing hand down my back. "But we're here and we're alive. That world isn't our world."

I nodded and brushed my lips over hers. "Are you okay?"

"Surprisingly, yes. I don't think I'll ever stop feeling guilty about Ashton, but I feel more at peace knowing that the man who hurt him can't hurt anybody else. I mean"—she shook her head in amazement—"I can't believe Gray tried to have me killed. Wait until I tell Sloane she's not a special unicorn anymore. We've both had hits put out on us."

"It's not funny."

Allegra offered a sympathetic smile, amazing me with how well she was taking this. "I'm sorry. I just ... I need to joke about it or I might crumple up into a ball."

My hands tightened on her arms.

"I'll be okay. *We'll* be okay," she reassured me. "This is good. We know now for sure what happened, and we know the people responsible can never hurt me again."

I blew out a shaky breath. "I know ... I just ... nothing can happen to you, Allegra. It would fucking end me."

She caressed my cheek, her fingers scratching over my short beard. "I'm not going anywhere. I'm your wife for life, Jared McCulloch. Not just for eighteen months."

At her teasing, I swung her up into my arms, making her squeal with laughter. The sound warmed me to my very bones. It pleased me beyond measure that I could make her happy after something as fucked up as the NCA visit.

"What are you doing?" she cried, giggling as I carried her upstairs.

"Being a very, very bad farmer." I pushed into the bedroom. "I have a tractor sitting in the middle of a field waiting for me ... but first I need to—"

"Plough your wife!" Allegra cut me off, shaking in my arms with amusement at her own joke.

I gave a bark of laughter as I fell onto the bed with her, careful to keep my weight from crushing her. She spread her legs for me, wrapping them around my back as I grinned down at her. "How long have you been waiting to say that?"

"I've been waiting for months to use that line!"

We kissed through our laughter until need overtook everything.

Months ago, the thought of abandoning duties on the farm, even temporarily, filled me with a fear of failure. Now, as important as this place was to me, I knew taking time for my wife when she needed me wasn't going to cause a disaster for the farm.

I could be both.

I could be what the land needed me to be.

And I could be what Allegra needed me to be.

I also knew if it came down to a choice, I would choose the woman in my arms a million fucking times over. And I knew my granddad would understand. Once upon a time, he'd loved a woman as much as I loved mine.

————

ALLEGRA

"Jared, we have a gazillion decisions to make," I grumbled as I followed him through the woods. "We don't have time for this."

My husband reached back for me, and I held his hand as we descended. It was a little slippery and muddy from last night's rain. Now, however, the sunshine beamed through the trees.

"This might be the last time the loch looks this good this year. Autumn is almost here."

I frowned. "And it'll look beautiful in autumn too. We could look at it then when we've decided on kitchen cabinets and countertops and flooring and furniture and a million other things we need to decide if we want these pods up and running by New Year's Eve."

"Will you just hush, woman, and follow me?"

I made a sound of indignation. "Hush? I'll hush you, Jared McCulloch. Hushing me ..." I muttered under my breath.

Jared's shoulders shook with laughter, but he didn't stop dragging me down toward the inland loch behind Caledonia Sky.

Then, as we reached the flat, I glanced up and saw the building poised over the loch that hadn't been there the last time I was here.

"What the—ah!" I tripped over a rock, but Jared turned at my cry, catching me before I face-planted. "Shit. Thanks." He helped me straighten, searching my face, a gleam of mischief in his eyes. "What is that?" I pointed past him.

Jared grinned and stepped away to let me have a good look.

A modern, small building similar to the pods (except rectangular, not arched), sat on a new deck that had been built out onto the loch. Two walls of the building that met at a corner were made entirely of glass facing out over the water.

"You built another rental? Why didn't you tell me?" I smacked his arm with a playful huff.

Instead of answering, Jared took my hand. "Come with me."

Curious as to why he was being so mysterious, I let him lead me around the loch and to the back of the building. There was a small window on this side and an entrance door. Jared smiled before he led me inside.

My breath caught as I looked up at the light spilling through the huge skylight above. There was nothing in the rectangular open room, but a door that was slightly ajar. I could see the glimpse of a small restroom behind it. Otherwise, it was just one big room with so much light and that view out over the loch. It felt like we were floating. One of the walls was actually a sliding door that led onto a side deck.

Then I realized it wasn't an empty room.

An easel and stool were set up near the glass wall.

Oh my God.

Jared squeezed my hand. "I had the guys build you a studio. You said it was the perfect place for one, right?"

Disbelief and gratitude and love—immense love—filled me as I gazed up at my husband in wonder. "You remembered that?"

"Couldn't get it out of my head as soon as you said it. Knew this was meant to be for you." He grinned at the marvel on my face and tugged my hand. "Come on." Staring around at the beautiful space, already imagining it filled with all the materials I needed to make my art, I followed him out through the sliding door to stand on the deck. Sunlight spilled over the green loch, and birds sang in the trees.

It was perfect.

A slice of utter heaven.

Yesterday, my visa was granted. I was now officially a resident of the United Kingdom. I thought that my week couldn't possibly get any better.

And despite all the shit that had happened in the last few months, I honestly couldn't believe how perfect my life felt right now.

I said as much.

"Good." Jared shrugged. "You deserve perfect."

"I do?" I grinned.

He didn't smile, though. In fact, he took a shuddering breath before speaking again. "That's why I want a do-over."

Confused, my brows drew together. "A do-over? For what?"

Jared pulled something out of his pocket and lowered to one knee.

My breath whooshed right out of me. "Oh my God."

He snapped open a blue velvet ring box and revealed the most perfect engagement ring. The band was gold but matte instead of shiny, and it looked handcrafted. In the center of the band was a cluster of pearls in differing sizes and small diamonds encrusted in the gold beads that separated them.

"Jared ..." I gaped at the ring.

"Every time I think about that wedding ceremony, I can't stand it," Jared admitted. "I can't stand that's the way you and I got married. Because we deserve so much more than that."

I nodded, understanding.

"This time I want to marry you and have you know that you are marrying a man who will love you for the rest of his life."

Tears slipped free as I kept nodding in agreement.

"Allegra Emma Howard McCulloch, will you marry me again?"

"Yes," I sobbed happily. "Yes, of course, yes!" I lowered myself so I could kiss the living daylights out of him. "Why are you so perfect?" I laughed through my tears and his kisses. "You're making it really hard to live up to."

Jared chuckled against my lips. "You've got it twisted, baby. I'm just trying to live up to you."

"And he says more perfect things." I pushed him playfully, my gaze dropping to the ring. "It's so beautiful, Jared."

"I had an artist make it for you. I sent her pictures of the kind of jewelry you wear and she came up with this."

I cupped his handsome face in my hands. "See? Perfect."

"Let's see it on, then."

Grinning tearfully, I bobbed my hand in excitement so much, Jared had to hold it still so he could slide the ring down beside my wedding band. It looked beautiful. So beautiful I immediately jumped him.

Jared made a sound of surprise against my lips seconds before his back hit the deck. His laughter rose up over the loch as I peppered his face with kisses before swallowing the sound against my lips.

Straddling him, I kissed him hungrily as I reached between us for the zipper on his jeans. Jared grunted against my mouth as I slipped my hand inside his boxers to grasp him.

"Fuck, here?" His cheeks were flushed with excitement.

I nodded, suddenly desperate to have him inside me. "I want to christen my deck with your dick."

He laughed, grabbing my ass. "Fuck, I love you."

"I love you more."

"Not possible." Jared pulled my hand up and rubbed his thumb over my engagement ring. "Tha gaol agom ort, Allegra McCulloch."

"Tha gaol agom ort." I brushed my lips over his and pressed our hands down on the deck beside his head. "Let me show you just how much."

And so there on the loch behind Caledonia Sky, we undressed to the witnesses of nature and made love on the land that had given us both so much. It was our home, yes. But a home we'd found in each other.

Looking back, I don't think I was desperate to stay in Scotland just for Scotland. I think somehow my soul knew that the missing piece of me was here. In Jared. So I'd done whatever it took to stay. To find it. To find him.

I'd do it again. I'd climb any mountain, travel any road, cross any ocean, and bend any law to stay by Jared McCulloch's side for the rest of my life.

After all, it was where I belonged.

Milton Keynes UK
Ingram Content Group UK Ltd.
UKHW040642050524
442173UK00004B/57